The Adventures of
Miss Boston
The First Female Detective

also translated and introduced by Nina Cooper:

Emile Gaboriau: *Monsieur Lecoq*

The Adventures of Miss Boston
The First Female Detective

by
Antonin Reschal

Illustrated by
André Galland

Translated and introduced by
Nina Cooper

A Black Coat Press Book

Edited by
Paul WESSELS

With the generous contribution of
Daniel AULIAC

Visit our website at www.blackcoatpress.com

ISBN 978-1-61227-113-2. First Printing. August 2012. Published by Black Coat Press, an imprint of Hollywood Comics.com, LLC, P.O. Box 17270, Encino, CA 91416. All rights reserved. Except for review purposes, no part of this book may be reproduced or transmitted in any form or by any means, electronic or mechanical, including photocopying, recording, or by any information storage and retrieval system, without permission in writing from the publisher. The stories and characters depicted in this novel are entirely fictional. Printed in the United States of America.

TABLE OF CONTENTS

Miss BOSTON

La Seule détective-femme du Monde entier.

Prix **0,25**

N° 6. Le roi des faussaires

Les papiers s'éparpillèrent : et Miss Boston, révolver au poing, apparut.

Introduction

Long before *Charlie's Angels* (1979 original series), before Miss Marple, before Jessica Fletcher and the host of contemporary female detectives in American literature and in television series, and shortly after Violet Strange, Araminta (Amelia) Butterworth, Dorcas Dene, Mrs. Paschal, Mrs. Gladden, Miss Lois Cayley, Dora Myrl, Judith Lee [1] and others, there was Ethel Boston "the only female detective in the whole world." She was also the final product of the New Woman, the term used at the end of the 19th century to denote the independent woman, the woman who believed and fought for sexual and legal equality with men. Such a woman had a job, was educated, was athletic and vigorous, and sometimes avoided marriage as interfering with her self-fulfillment and independence. Miss Boston carried all these attributes to the extreme. She not only achieved equality, she surpassed it. No male in any of her stories even approaches her abilities as a detective.

She was created by Charles Marius Eugène Antonin Arnaud (1874-1935) (better known as Antonin Reschal) in 1908 for pulp-like French magazine serialization dubbed "*fascicules.*" Her adventures, with her companion and foil, Chief Inspector Sokes, ran through 20 installments of 32 pages each during the years 1908-1909, published in Paris by Albin Michel.

Until recently, much of Reschal's literary work was lost or attributed to others. Reschal has been resurrected by Daniel Auliac's research at the Bibliothèque Nationale in Paris.[2] While doing research on a painter, Léo Fontan, Auliac discovered a wooden cabinet holding biographical information about Reschal. Intrigued, he continued his research but found that the

---

[1] See The Complete Adventures of Judith lee by Richard Marsh, Black Coat Press, ISBN 978-1-61227-071-5.
[2] Daniel Auliac. *Le Roman de Reschal*, Paris: Publibook, 2010.

available archives that gave useful information were "patchy" and "difficult to find." His research led him to Reschal's publisher, Albin Michel, where the publisher's archives added information about Reschal's work and life. In addition to novels of fiction, books on cuisine, and lithographs of political caricatures, Reschal published journals such as *Le Sourire*, and worked with well-known illustrator André Galland and lithographer Auguste Jean-Baptiste Roubille amongst others. He published works in various genres: books on gardening, books on gastronomy, and even postcards of nudes along with some mildly erotic works, daring by 19th century standards. Only two of his several novels are currently easily available from contemporary booksellers. These two are part of his work in *petit érotisme*, although some of the other novels can be found at rare book dealers. These two erotic works are *Vénus Damnée : Documents Curieux et Rares sur la Galanterie Secrète du XVIIIème Siècle* [*Venus Damned: Curious & Rare Documents on the Secret Gallantry of the 18th Century*] and *La Névrose Galante au XVIIIème Siècle: Aventures et Portraits d'Amoureuses* [*Love Neuroses in the 18th Century: Adventures & Portraits of Famous Lovers*].

Since the "roman judiciaire," the detective story, began in France with Paul Féval's notorious *Habits Noirs* series, followed by Emile Gaboriau's five novels featuring M. Lecoq,[3] it would be logical to assume the same evolution would continue in French as it did in English-speaking countries which produced the first female detectives listed above and many following them. The earliest authors in English-speaking countries using a female sleuth were William Stephens Hayward (1835?-1870?), James Redding Ware (1832-1909), and Anna Katherine Green (1845-1935). Hayward's Mrs. Paschal, Ware's Mrs. Gladden and Green's two female sleuths, Araminta (Amelia) Butterworth and Violet Strange date from the 1860s into the beginning of the 20th century. Daring as the concept of a female sleuth was, these authors did not, with their creations, break the mold of the typical 19th century female, detective or not. Hayward's Mrs. Paschal and Ware's Mrs. Gladden are women of their time, respectable, widowed ladies forced to earn a living anyway they can; circumstances have decreed they become detectives. A younger woman detective, Dorcas Dene, must work to support her mother and blind husband. Amelia Butterworth is a comfortably situated, inquisitive spinster. Violet Strange is a young socialite who likes money and luxury and will only be satisfied with a superabundance of both.

It was not until Charles Grant Blairfindie Allen (1848-1899) created Miss Lois Cayley (1899) and McDonnell Bodkin (1850-1933) created Dora Myrl (1900) that a character resembling Miss Boston appeared. Both Lois Cayley and

---

[3] Féval's *Black Coats* series is available from Black Coat Press in seven volumes translated by Brian Stableford; Gaboriau's *Monsieur Lecoq* is also available from Black Coat Press, translated by Nina Cooper.

Dora Myrl are professional women. Cayley has just taken a university degree when her adventures begin; she refuses to settle for the few occupational choices available to a woman. Dora Myrl has taken both a university and a medical degree but has no patients because she is a woman. Both are young, attractive, energetic, and intelligent women with a sense of adventure and knowledge of their own worth. They are "New Women."

With his Miss Boston, Reschal contributes additional character traits to the evolution of the strong, professional female sleuth. Miss Boston differs from the early American or British female detectives in that she has not come to the profession of detective out of need, boredom or chance. She has chosen the profession out of supreme confidence that she is the best in the world at the job. Reschal leaves no doubt as to her pre-eminence. She is the "illustrious detective," the "famous female detective," the "courageous young woman," and she never sells herself short. Although she wears modest ankle-length dresses, she doesn't hesitate to chase malefactors across the fields, follow them into dangerous tunnels and barns, climb up shaky ladders and pursue them at night through New York slums and even across the deserts of Arizona. She carries two revolvers, her "bulldogs," and is a crack shot. Her automobile chase in *The Grosvenor Place Murder* must be a first in car chase history. Even though a woman in a role usually reserved for men, she is still essentially feminine, dresses elegantly (Reschal insists on this), fits into New York high society and likes presents of emeralds and diamonds. When Reschal has Miss Boston answer offers of professional fees with "We'll talk about that later," he doesn't mean she has refused, only that her fee will perhaps depend on the extent and danger of the job. She is not only well paid for her work, but sometimes earns posted rewards of thousands of dollars.

In one sense, Reschal's Miss Boston is a transitional figure. She continues the role begun by Mrs. Paschal and Mrs. Gladden in the 1860s and expanded by Miss Cayley and Dorcas Dene at the end of the century. Like them, she is unmarried, although Dora Myrl does marry another detective ultimately and have a son who continues the profession, and Miss Cayley finally marries her long suffering suitor. The male in Miss Boston's life is Chief Inspector Sokes, who is described as thirtyish, handsome, and conservatively but well dressed. He primarily serves, however, to represent the judicial system and never upstages Miss Boston. He is a useful foil as well as a faithful friend. Miss Boston also differs from almost all previous female sleuths in that she is familiar with and uses some of the technology modern at the time and some not yet perfected in her professional lifetime. Everyday use of electricity was uncommon in 1908, but she carries an electric flashlight. As Chief Inspector of the New York Police Bureau, Sokes has access to a soundproof electric vehicle, almost more advanced than those of the 21st century. Miss Boston carries a lead-covered apparatus, the Y ray, which can penetrate wood and show the interior of what is beyond. She also carries a very small apparatus, a microphone, which can hear sounds from the other side of doors, trunks, etc. Small microphones were not in use until 1964, and innovations in their use and size continue to the present day.

The New York subway, which Miss Boston and Sokes frequently ride, was in operation in 1898, but the first official system opened only in 1904, some four years before Reschal published *Miss Boston*. The electric car had only been in operation by the Electric Carriage Company since 1897. The electric automobile co-existed with the hansom cab, as is clear from Miss Boston's frequent trips in both. Miss Boston takes a hansom cab if she has time to spare, but she takes an automobile if the case is urgent.

Readers in the 21st century will have to willingly suspend disbelief as to place names and United States geography, which Reschal reorganizes and shuffles around with wonderful imagination. They must always keep in mind that Reschal is not writing history or geography, but fantasy. Savannah City, where Miss Boston lives, is not in Georgia, but is an upper middle-class suburb of New York. Galveston, actually on the Texas Gulf Coast, is near Chicago. Illinois is a city, and Chicago is in Michigan. The Seine is a street. Arizona is close enough to New York to transport wounded men there by train in less than a day. Well-known English place names also occur in Reschal's New York from time to time; Holyrood is not in Scotland, but New York.

Miss Boston was not the "only female detective in the whole world" in 1908-1909 as Reschal maintains. There were many female sleuths in American and English literature, and at least one in Australia. But she was the only female detective in French popular literature of any note until 1914, the year in which Miss Edith King, the female Nick Carter, was created by Jean Petithuguenin, a university professor and translator of Norwegian and English. Miss Boston's creator, Antonin Reschal, was not, unlike Petithuguenin, from the academic world. He was in many ways, a man before his time, and literature was only one of his many sidelines.

Reschal's style of composition for *Miss Boston* was anything but refined or academic, and he has been harshly, and perhaps unduly, criticized for this. The entire series of 20 installments which went on to sell approximately 50,000 copies was produced, seemingly without revision, in under three months, that is, between August 25 and October 28, 1908.[4]

An interesting though vague opinion that the French critic H. Y. Mermet adds to his criticism of Reschal's style of expression as "incorrect" even "barbaric,"[5] is that the scenes he evokes are rarely pleasant. But rather than being an indication of failure on the part of Reschal, this should be a prescient observation on the critic's behalf, as Reschal seemingly anticipates the "mean streets of crime noir" in the 20th century one century earlier:

---

[4] Daniel Auliac. *Le Roman de Reschal*, Paris: Publibook, 2010. P. 144.
[5] Michel Lebrun. *L'Année du Polar*, Paris: Ramsey, 1986. pp. 294-297.

After dark the cities of Los Angeles, Chicago and New York seem to be made of a menacing black and white, Harsh lights, dark shadows, black clothes, pale skins and violence constantly threaten to erupt. The same can be said of London and Paris, which explains why it was only a matter of time before hard-boiled fiction crossed the Atlantic. And in the wake of the stories of Hammet, Chandler, Cain and Burnett, writers in Europe made their own contribution to the history of crime fiction: "crime noir," a term invented by the French to describe the phenomenon.[6]

Mermet's criticisms could be amplified many times to describe the style of Frédéric Dard (writing under the pseudonym of "San Antonio"). While Reschal produced only 20 installments of *Miss Boston*, the hundreds of San Antonio stories made Dard famous and rich in the 20th century.

There are today many references to *Miss Boston* in French, but the fascicules themselves, either separate or bound, are both out of print and hard to find. A few can be found in rare book shops and even fewer have wound up in the hands of critics. Both information and misinformation are passed from critic, to blogger, to other internet sources. What must perhaps be remembered about the author of *Miss Boston*, is the fact that he was one of the first writers of popular French literature in the 19th century to create a strong, independent female detective, a "New Woman."

Nina Cooper

---

[6] Peter Haining. "The Mean Streets of Crime Noir" in *The Classic Era of Crime Fiction*, Chicago Review Press: Chicago, Illinois, 2002, p. 158.

Bibliography of Miss Boston

Periodicals illustrated by André Galland published by Albin Michel in 1908 and 1909:
1. L'Assassinat du Plus Célèbre Détective [The Murder of the World's Most Famous Detective] *
2. La Bande des Évadés [The Gang of the Escapees]
3. Les Cadavres aux Masques de Cire [The Corpses with Wax Masks]
4. L'Aéroplane Mystérieux [The Mysterious Airplane]
5. Le Ressuscité du Cimetière de Cleveland [The Resurrected Corpse of the Cleveland Cemetery]
6. Le Roi des Faussaires [The King of the Forgers]
7. Les Secrets de l'Hypnotisme [The Secrets of Hypnotism]
8. 25.000 Cadavres [25,000 Corpses]
9. Le Drame de l'Express de Chicago[The Tragedy of the Chicago Express]
10. Les Souterrains Maudits de Clifford; ou La Revanche de la Détective [The Accursed Tunnels of Clifford; or The Detective's Revenge]
11. L'Homme Invisible; ou Le Gang aux Mille Bras [The Invisible Man; or The One HundredThousand Arms Gang] *
12. La Poignée de Main Fatale; ou La Rentrée en scène de Teddy [The Fatal Handshake; or Teddy's Return] *
13. La Femme aux Yeux Verts [The Woman with Green Eyes] *
14. L'Élixir Magique [The Magic Elixir] *
15. Haine de Femme; ou La Capture de l'Homme Invisible [Woman's Hatred; or The Capture of the Invisible Man] *
16. Le Meurtre de Grosvenor Place [The Grosvenor Place Murder] *
17. La Main Coupée [The Severed Hand] *
18. Le Rapide de l'Arizona; ou Les Cow-Boys Rouges [The Arizona Rapid Train; or The Red Cow-Boys] *
19. Les Embaumés de Chicago [The Chicago Embalmed Heads] *
20. L'Association des Riffleurs; ou La Mort de Sokes [The Association of Riflers; or Sokes' Death] *

*: included in this volume.

Notes: Miss Boston was trained by William Hopkins, the rival of Sherlock Holmes created by Hector Fleischmann. A letter from her to the French publisher dated 3 September 1908 authorizing him to publish her adventures was included in the first issue.

THE MURDER OF THE WORLD'S MOST FAMOUS DE-
TECTIVE

I. A Sensational Crime

It was 7 p.m. in Brooklyn, New York. There was an avalanche of newspaper boys along the street; newspaper sellers shouted at the top of their lungs, hawking the latest edition of *The Daily Mail*. Brooklyn is to New York what the Grand Boulevards and the Avenue de l'Opéra are to Paris. Everywhere in the street there was an enormous brouhaha of repeated shouts which rose above the crowd: DEATH OF SHERLOCK HOLMES! MURDER OF THE WORLD'S MOST FAMOUS DETECTIVE! A MYSTERIOUS TRAGEDY ON THE RALEIGH EXPRESS!!!

Just as one of the news boys turned into Osborn Street, a young woman, slim, elegant, who seemed to be enjoying casual window shopping along the couturier and jewelry stores, stopped the seller, gave him a penny and took a newspaper. The young woman took several steps away from the crowd and by a bar's flashing lights unfolded the newspaper just to see the article which announced in huge letters the death of the most famous detective who ever lived, the illustrious and famous Sherlock Holmes. Just as she was about to fold up her newspaper, someone greeted her and said:

"Newspapers at this hour in the street, Miss Boston?"

"Ah! It's you, Mr. Clampton! How are you?"

"Marvelous! What do you think of this business?"

"Nothing."

"How's that?"

"But I really think it could be something."

"Something?"

"Or everything. But at your office, Clampton, what do they say about it?

"At our office, Miss Boston, we're up to our eyeballs in work, that's all."

"Who's handling the case? Is it Toby, Sanfield, or Sokes?"

"None of the three. It's Morton."

"He's the one, really?"

"Yes, him, really."

While talking, the two had continued down Osborn Street. Around them shocked people were unfolding newspapers, excitedly discussing the extraordinary event. The man who had greeted Miss Boston was one of the ablest policemen of the New York Police Administration, Harris Clampton. He had known Miss Boston from the time when she was the aide of William Hopkins, the most famous amateur detective in the United States. But what was not known about her was that Miss Boston, all by herself, solved most of the terrible and tragic problems that had been submitted to him. At the death of William Hopkins, felled by the Green Tie Gang, she said to herself:

"Why not work alone? Why not, in my turn, become famous? Should Hopkins be the only one to achieve celebrity?"

These were her thoughts when Clampton met Miss Boston in Brooklyn Street. The police's point of view about the murder of Sherlock Holmes could be seen from their conversation.

"Then," said Clampton, "does the case interest you?"

"How could I not be interested in it? Wasn't Sherlock Holmes the master of all of us? For William Hopkins as well as for Nick Carter?"

"That's true."

"So there's a double reason for a detective to be interested in this shady business."

"And what's that, Miss Boston?"

"Wasn't Sherlock Holmes the most subtle, the strongest among us, and if he was brought down, it was because he was dealing with terrible criminals, stronger then he was, stronger than we are. Now what's more glorious than, in this case, catching Sherlock Holmes' killer?"

"You're smiling, Clampton. I'm a woman, that's true, but I have courage. Do you remember the case of Prick Salmon? I held my own against three men."

"And the three men were caught."

"That's right. Then you see I can go after Sherlock Holmes' murderers."

"Really. And that's what's called telling it like it is. And when do you begin, Miss Boston?"

"I've begun."

"You have?"

"Yes."

"Decidedly you're better than our detectives."

"Let's understand each other, Harris. I've begun because I know which of the Central Bureau detectives has charge of the case, because I know how they feel about the case, and because I know they have no suspects."

"Who told you that?"

"You did."

"Me? Really, Miss Boston! You're mistaken. It seems to me I didn't say anything of the sort."

"You think so?"

"I'm certain of it."

"Because you didn't tell me anyone was suspected; therefore you have no suspects. Right?"

Clampton gave Miss Boston a sincerely astonished look, where there was at the same time mute admiration as well as bewilderment.

When they came to the corner of Osborn Street and 138th Avenue, Miss Boston said:

"Clampton, I really must leave you. I'll see you later."

"Until then, and good luck."

"Thank you. And by the way, do you know if Dr. Watson is in New York?"

"Yes, since this morning."

"He wasn't here at all yesterday?"

"No, he was in Raleigh."

"Ah! Good. Goodbye, Clampton."

And the two separated. Clampton, walking slowly, went back up 138th Avenue toward Circus Place, and Miss Boston went back down Osborn Street. When she got there, about the middle of the street, she hailed a cab which was driving about aimlessly looking for fares. She gave her address: 38 Savannah City, and told him to hurry.

II. Miss Boston Picks Up the Trail

While letting herself be lulled by the fast pace of the horse, what was Miss Boston thinking about if not the big question of that evening, the affair of the murder of Sherlock Holmes? The details in *The Daily Mail*, which might be exciting for the public at large, was hardly that for the detective accustomed to never looking for dramatic and exciting stories but for facts in their tragic and simple truths. Now these facts, how could they be learned?

That was the object of Miss Boston's thoughts, while the cab carried her across the dark East Side streets toward Savannah City. The carriage soon stopped. Miss Boston was home. The house where she had chosen to live looked both peaceful and middle-class. Like most New York apartment buildings it had 10 floors. The apartment the detective occupied on the ninth of these floors was simple and comfortable, furnished without luxury but with convenience. Doors to a little sitting room and dining room opened off a spacious and bright entry hall. Beyond was situated the detective's bedroom, adjoining her study. This study was carefully organized, holding thousands of cards about most of the New York criminals in neatly arranged files. That was the room the detective entered as soon as she reached her apartment. One file gave her a small notebook that she consulted, address by address.

"In 1902," she said softly, "Sherlock Holmes stayed at the American Hotel. In 1904, at the Continental; in 1904, on his second trip; in 1905, this time he must have stayed at the Circus. There was certainly order in his choice of residences." And after having returned the notebook to its usual place, she added:

"And now, what case was he working on."

Another notebook was taken from the files and leafed through rapidly. But after some moments the female detective, leaning back in her chair, began to reflect.

"It's one of two things: either Sherlock Holmes was looking for London criminals in America, and if so, the case had its origins in England, or he was called to New York by a case which originated in New York itself. There was no middle ground. Therefore, if that's so, let's see the important cases worth the trouble that can be found in this situation."

Each leaf of the notebook Miss Boston had consulted carried at the top the name of a criminal case, of whatever seriousness. It was like a directory of all the crimes of New York, of all of America. It was a sinister list where robberies, murders, swindles, assassinations, offered a terrible field from which to observe human perversity.

"The case of 12th Avenue...No, it can't be that, "murmured the young woman while looking through the file; the case of staked plain, of Nebraska, no, not that; the theft of the Princess d'Oldenbourg's diamonds, no; the disappearance of Miss Stanton...Ah! Ah! Could that be it? Let's see."

She immediately took a file bearing in big letters *STANTON CASE* from the same drawer and consulted the leaves pinned together in a huge packet. While she was searching, a smile of satisfaction played over her face and she exclaimed:

"That's the case! I'm on the trail!"

She put her hat back on in haste, picked up her coat and went downstairs. The escalator deposited her in a few seconds in the vestibule, from where she rapidly reached the street. She had to go back up as far as Coal Street to find a cab which carried her at a gallop to the Continental Hotel.

"Is Doctor Watson in?" she asked the porter standing at the entry.

"I don't know," the man said, "but the clerks at the office can tell you."

"Very well."

Miss Boston went to the glassed-in office where the clerks seemed to be excitedly talking to each other. She even heard the name Sherlock Holmes pronounced, which led her to believe that all the hotel employees were already talking about the assassination of the famous detective. At some distance from the office, hardly a few meters, a gentleman smoking his cigar was reading his newspaper, standing near the light from the vestibule. Miss Boston noticed him, as she noticed everything by habitual professional caution. But nothing about the facial appearance or the general aspect of the reader struck her.

"Is Dr. Watson in his apartment?" she asked one of the clerks.

"Quite so, Miss. He just returned a few minutes ago."

"The number and the floor?"

"Apartment 138, on the fifth floor. It's the eighth door to the left."

"Good."

And Miss Boston walked toward the elevator which would quickly let her off on the fifth floor of the Continental Hotel. At that moment, the reader standing near the office threw away his cigar and like a man in no particular hurry, walked toward the hotel exit, as if going for a walk. But if Miss Boston had followed him, she would have been surprised to see that man, who had seemed to have time to waste, get in a hurry as soon as he had left the Continental. He then ran to find a cab, threw an address at the coachman and added:

"A dollar for the ride." The driver, happy for the tip, whipped up his horse, and the cab went down Central Avenue at full speed toward Brooklyn Bridge.

During this time, Miss Boston reached Dr. Watson's apartment and after announcing her name, entered. She found herself in the presence of a man about 50-years-old, dressed very formally in a black frockcoat. His swollen eyes testified that he must have wept a long time. He rose at the entry of his visitor. His silence, preceded by a formal greeting, clearly indicated that he was waiting for Miss Boston to explain her unexpected visit.

"Dr. Watson, I believe."

"Himself, actually, Miss."

"Sherlock Holmes' friend?"

"Alas!"

Dr. Watson fell back into the chair from which he had just risen.

"Forgive me, Miss, but the burden of my sorrow is really too great. For 20 years I was the friend of that illustrious man, the only friend I might say; 20 years in which I shared his dangers, his troubles, his successes and his triumphs. And now he is dead, dead in a terrible way, puzzling and atrocious. Ah, and really, why did we leave London to get involved in that damned case!"

"The Stanton case?"

"What! You know about it, Miss?"

"Yes."

"But...who...are you then?"

"I'm the former colleague of Mr. William Hopkins."

"The famous detective, my friend Sherlock Holmes' rival?"

"Yes."

"Ah! Miss, you're welcome. How can I be of service to you?"

"To arrest the murderers of your friend, in one word, to avenge Sherlock Holmes!"

"Oh! That with all my heart! I'll help you in that task with all my strength. And how is that to be done?"

"First of all, sir, answer the questions I'm going to ask you about your friend and his last investigations."

"Go ahead. I'm ready to give you precise answers, Miss Boston."

"It really was the Miss Stanton case that Sherlock Holmes was working on?"

"Yes. Two months ago, in London, he received a letter from Mr. Stanton, the father of the young girl, telling him of her disappearance."

"And that letter asked Sherlock Holmes to come to New York?"

"It even begged him to take the first transatlantic ship departing."

"When he arrived in New York, what did he do, Mr. Watson?"

"As soon as he got off the boat, he took the case actively in hand."

"Did he go to see Mr. Stanton?"

"Immediately."

"What was the result of that visit?"

"My poor friend was given every latitude to work as he saw fit in that sad and mysterious business."

"Good. And to your knowledge, had he achieved any result?"

"I don't know, unfortunately, and Mr. Stanton, whom I saw this morning, doesn't know either. He saw Sherlock Holmes the evening before his departure..."

III. The Prologue to the Crime

Come to that point in her interrogation, Miss Boston took a moment to collect her thoughts. Dr. Watson's precise answers were going to place her definitely in the presence of the mysterious preparations for the drama in which Sherlock Holmes had so tragically lost his life. She then asked the dead man's friend:

"So he left?"

"Yes. Last Monday for Raleigh, in North Carolina."

"On what train?"

"On the 7:08."

"Good. Please continue your explanations, Doctor."

"Sherlock Holmes saw Mr. Stanton the day before his departure and here's what he said: 'Sir, I'm on the trail. In three days you'll see your daughter again.'"

"And that's all?"

"Yes, that's all. Going to catch the train at Presidio Bridge, he scarcely told me more. All I can deduce from these few words was that the denouement of this mystery was to take place near Raleigh, or in Raleigh itself. Alas! My unfortunate friend was murdered on the trip. On the eve of a new triumph!"

"Forgive me for stirring up your sad memories, Doctor, but please tell me if you noticed anything unusual when you took your friend to the Presidio Bridge station?"

Dr. Watson seemed to think deeply for several minutes, then, having collected his thoughts, he answered:

"Yes, now that I think about it, there were certain details that particularly struck me in that departure."

"What were they?"

"I don't know how to explain it, but I'm going to tell you, Miss Boston, exactly how things happened. You understand that there isn't always a big crowd at Presidio Bridge, from which the lines for Iowa, Pennsylvania, Kentucky, Illinois, Virginia, and North Carolina depart. We arrived at exactly 7 o'clock. Sherlock Holmes was carrying a little traveling valise. He bought his ticket with paper money and slipped the ticket into the palm of his hand through the opening of his leather glove. At loading platform number 12 he went to find his compartment in the Express train."

"What time was it then?"

"7:03."

"Good. Please go on."

"On the loading platform there was a bad-looking fellow seated on the corner of a trunk he seemed to be guarding. The man was looking in front of him at nothing in particular. Sherlock Holmes had been seated for several moments. I was with him, chatting about things in London, when he suddenly said to me:

'Watson, look there at the porter...'

"Where's that?" I asked.

"'There on the loading platform,' he told me."

"I looked and I saw the porter counting on his fingers in a low voice: 'one...two...three...four...five...six...'"

"Just then a man wearing a green four-collared frock coat, who seemed to be looking for a compartment, got into the compartment next to the one in which Sherlock Holmes was sitting. Holmes rubbed his hands together.

"Why do you seem pleased?" I asked him.

"I am, in fact. The fellow I was looking for is there, right next to me."

"The fellow in the frock coat?"

"Yes, Parker."

Here Miss Boston interrupted Dr. Watson's story.

"Parker, did you say?"

"Yes, that was the name of the man in the frock coat. I'll continue. Sherlock Holmes was smiling.

'This Parker,' he said 'is an unmitigated scoundrel. I know he's capable of every ruse and every daring. A man who's forewarned is a match for the one he's warned against. I'll know how to deal with him.'

"Sherlock Holmes had taken from his pockets a pair of good quality bull dogs, continuing:

'If Parker is on the train, it's because he has some bad design against me. In that case, he'll know what's speaking.'

"Having just then heard the departure whistle, I left my friend, advising him to be careful. Alas! My advice that day wasn't worth anything!"

"And then?"

"And then the porter, as soon as the train began its departure, left, his hands in his pockets, leaving the trunk there. I then saw he was not at all charged with guarding it and that time, saying that he was being followed, Sherlock Holmes had again spoken accurately."

"I have only a few more questions to ask you, Doctor. The newspapers said that on arrival in Raleigh, Sherlock Holmes was found dead in his compartment. His two bull dogs were beside him, still loaded. He seemed to be asleep. No trace of violence was found on him. It was believed to be a natural death."

"That was exactly it. Since they found my name and the address of the hotel on him, they telegraphed me. I left immediately and I only this morning returned from that sad trip."

"And what did you find out?"

"That Sherlock Homes did not die a natural death, but that he was murdered."

"By Parker?"

"Yes, and I told the police so, but they said Parker had been in Sing Sing prison for two years and that in no way could it be a question of him."

"And in your opinion, how was Sherlock Holmes murdered?"

"He was chloroformed!"

"That seems most impossible."

"It's certain, Miss Boston. I smelled the odor. That explains the absence of any trace of violence on him."

"Then this famous detective let himself be approached by Parker, by that Parker he knew to be his enemy?"

"I don't know. I limit myself just to reporting, and I say that my friend most assuredly was killed with chloroform."

"There's the mystery," Miss Boston said. "That's what has to be explained. And I give you my word, Doctor, that I'll explain it to you. And now I'm going to sum up the situation in a few words. Criminals kidnapped Miss Stanton, hoping to get her father to pay a large ransom. Sherlock Homes came, picked up the trail of the criminals, who, feeling they were about to be caught, murdered him. How? That's what has to be discovered, and where my role begins. Is that correct?"

"That's exactly it, Miss Boston."

"Doctor, you've brought a valuable element to my investigation. I appreciate it. I will likely bring you good news this evening. Good-bye."

"Miss Boston," said the Doctor, "if Sherlock Holmes' murderers must be caught at the cost of my fortune, well, I'm ready to give it!"

"Oh! I don't ask so much," the young woman said, smiling.

Having thus taken leave of Sherlock Holmes' friend, Miss Boston went down to the hotel lobby. Just at that moment, a man with a blond mustache, speaking to the clerk's office, asked casually:

"Have you a free apartment?"

"On what floor, sir?"

"On the fifth."

"Yes, certainly. We have apartments 132, 134, 136. Apartment 138 is occupied. 140 will be free this evening."

"Comfortable?"

"Oh! We have only very comfortable apartments here, sir."

"In that case, give me 136."

The number 136, adjacent to 138 occupied by Dr. Watson, caught Miss Boston's attention. She had a sudden movement of astonishment and excitement; the man asking for the room next to that of Dr. Watson was wearing a green four-collared frock coat! The man, however, preceded by the bellboy, was in the elevator going up to the fifth floor. The proximity of that strange coincidence of Parker in a green four-collared frock coat accompanying Sherlock Holmes in the Raleigh Express, and the traveler in the green four-collared frock coat asking for the apartment next to that of the friend of the dead man, strangely impressed her.

She asked the clerk, "Could you please tell me the name of Dr. Watson's new neighbor?"

"I don't think I have the right, Miss, and I don't know if..."

But Miss Boston had taken out of her handbag the little silver badge that the American police administration gives to agents or to others like the amateur detectives who are capable of rendering them significant services. The sight of the badge overcame the employee's hesitation.

"Oh! In that case, Miss, I'm at your service."

"Not a word of this, right?"

"I guarantee my silence, Miss."

"Good. What's the man's name?"

The clerk looked at the sign-in register and said:

"His name if Rekrap."

"Rekrap"

"Yes."

"Thank you, and I'll see you later."

Miss Boston left and, walking slowly, thought about the sequence of events. Rekrap, the name didn't tell her anything, and it was certainly a borrowed name, an assumed name. What if the man who gave it had something to hide? What should be done? Alert Watson? That would perhaps be wise. She decided to do that and returned to the Continental Hotel. There was a man ahead of her who was asking the office for Mr. Rekrap's room. Miss Boston recognized that man as the one who, on her arrival at the Continental, was smoking a cigar, standing under the light reading his newspaper. Then that was for her an awakening (enlightenment). Wasn't that the porter who had been on the lookout for Sherlock Holmes on the loading platform at the Presidio Bridge station? And

Rekrap, wasn't that Parker himself? And the name Rekrap...but that was it, it was the name Parker simply turned around. So marvelous chance was helping her. She had luck with her against the murderers of Sherlock Holmes, because it was certain that Parker was the guilty one. But how had he carried it out? That was, and she had already said so to Dr. Watson, the obscure point that remained to be cleared up in this agonizing mystery. Why had Parker and his accomplice come to check in at the Continental if not to do away with Dr. Watson himself? They knew he was Sherlock Holmes' confident, that he had seen Parker get on the train and that he was as a consequence a formidable and dangerous witness. Now it was Watson who was in danger and the criminals' plan was simple. Should they be arrested on the spot? Miss Boston considered this idea. But then wouldn't the chances of finding Miss Stanton at the place where the criminals had hidden her be lost? Therefore, it was first of all urgent to save Watson. After that she would see.

Miss Boston asked to see Mr. John Johnston, the owner of the Continental. After having spent an hour in consultation with him, she left and went up to Dr. Watson's apartment.

"Already, Miss Boston," he asked in a tone both trusting and sad.

But Miss Boston, with a rapid gesture, made him understand the danger he ran by speaking aloud in the room.

"Where is the valise with the wigs and the false beards that Sherlock Holmes had with him?" she asked briskly.

"There it is," Watson said.

"Let me get to work, Doctor," the young woman said.

She picked up a beard and a wig, fitting it to him perfectly. In five minutes Dr. Watson was marvelously disguised so that he resembled a modest employee. Only his friend Sherlock Holmes would have been able to recognize him in the transformation so quickly executed. That operation was hardly finished when Miss Boston raised her voice and said:

"It's agreed, my dear Dr. Watson. I'll take charge of that business of murder. I'll leave tomorrow evening for Raleigh, by the same 7:08 train. It's not necessary to go with me. I'll know how to handle the affair by myself."

Dr. Watson, not understanding anything about his sudden disguise and this unexpected statement, was startled.

"I'm going downstairs," Miss Boston said in a low voice. "You'll follow me in five minutes and go sit down at one of the clerk desks. That's been agreed to by the director of the Continental. You'll call the least possible attention to yourself. And when your neighbors come down, you'll look at them. I'm certain you'll recognize them immediately. I'll ask you by telephone the result of your observation. As for me, I'm going to leave and I won't come back now that you're out of danger. I'm going to enter the game in my turn, because I'll be followed until tomorrow."

"You want to go to Raleigh?"

"Yes, because during the trip I'm persuaded I can learn the way in which Sherlock Holmes was murdered. I'll go into Raleigh, because isn't it there that your friend said the denouement of the Stanton affair must take place?"

"Certainly, yes."

"In that case, do as I ask you, Doctor. I'm leaving. Don't follow me until after five minutes."

That said, Miss Boston took a pince-nez out of her handbag. This pince-nez itself was certainly nothing remarkable, but it was a marvelous piece of ingenuity. The glasses were just pieces of mirror. Thanks to this pince-nez, placed in a certain way, you could see, above the glasses, what was happening in front of you, and in the glasses what was happening behind you. Having put them on, Miss Boston left Dr. Watson's room and went down the fifth floor corridor. She had scarcely passed the door of room 136 than she saw it open silently and the traveler with the blonde mustache, wearing the green frock coat, looked out the opening. The man's eyes followed the woman detective, and when she was in the elevator, he softly closed the door and said in a low voice to the one who had joined him at the same time Miss Boston arrived at the Continental Hotel:

"Joe, I know her! She's the colleague of that devil William Hopkins, who chased us for such a long time. It's the woman detective."

And Joe's voice answered:

"Then we know what we have to do."

The door closed. A few instants later, Dr. Watson silently left his room and went down to the hotel office where the clerks gave him a seat at one of the desks. From there the fake employee could easily, and without being recognized, observe the faces of those who came to the office either for information about registering or anything else. He had been there about an hour when the two travelers from room 136 passed calmly in front of the office. Dr. Watson suddenly started, but hid his excitement, leaning over the open books in front of him on the clerks' desks. Shortly thereafter, the telephone rang and he was called to answer it. A rapid conversation at both ends of the line began.

"Hello! Hello! Is that you, Doctor?"

"Yes,"

"Well?"

"They were the ones."

"You recognized them?"

"Wonderfully."

"Was that Parker?"

"Yes, and his friend."

"The porter at the Presidio Bridge station?"

"He's the same."

"No doubt about that?"

"None, Miss Boston."

"Good. Tomorrow evening Sherlock Holmes will be avenged. Goodbye, Doctor."

"Goodbye, Miss Boston," and the communication was cut off.

IV. The Two Murderers against the Detective

The two men from room 136 walked rapidly down Central Avenue without saying a word. When they came to Brooklyn Bridge, the one who had registered at the Continental under the name of Rekrap, whom we now know to be the Parker Dr. Watson saw on the Raleigh Express, hailed a cab and shouted to the driver:

"To Town Square."

The carriage immediately started at a trot and Parker's companion said:

"Why do you want to go at this hour to Town Square, Parker?"

"Because I'm sure we can talk there and throw off those trailing us."

"Then you think, Parker, that we're being followed?"

"No, but it's better to foresee everything."

"At least that damned Miss Boston isn't on our heels."

"I don't believe so, because if she suspected us, we would already be under surveillance. You didn't notice anything unusual in leaving the Continental?"

"No. And you?"

"Neither did I, fortunately! But I think we're here."

The two men got out of the cab and went into the walks of the Square, deserted at that time of night. A pale December moon turned the dark leafless branches of the big trees to silver. Joe turned up the collar of his overcoat because his teeth were chattering and remarked:

"This is a little drawing room conversation that seems a little cold to me."

"We won't be too bad here," Parker said.

And while talking in a low tone, the two men began a slow walk around the frost-bitten lawns.

"You see," Parker was saying, "since our adventure in Philadelphia, where we made plans in our room and where the walls had ears, I don't trust talks that invisible ears can pick up. Here there's no such thing. We have a drawing room, in the open air, without walls, to talk in."

"I'm cold," Joe retorted.

"You'll get warm tonight," Parker laughed derisively. But picking up his serious tone immediately, he added: "We have no time to lose."

"I'm listening, Parker."

"Here it is, Joe. The situation is simple. Sherlock Holmes is out of the game. We still have Miss Stanton, but there's a new danger."

"Miss Boston."

"Herself. It's certain she won't be slow to find out what case Sherlock Holmes was working on. We must be on our guard. That damned detective was on our trail, because leaving for Raleigh, he was going where he hoped to find the young girl."

"Are you forgetting, Parker, that Miss Boston spoke to Dr. Watson about going to Raleigh?"

"I haven't forgotten it, Joe, but what I fear isn't so much that she's going to Raleigh."

"Why then?"

"Because she may be searching for clues about Sherlock Holmes' death."

"Oh! Then..." and Joe burst out laughing.

"If she's counting on finding it out, that's wasted effort. That's a little trick we'll take charge of explaining to her in person, one of these coming days."

"You want to use the famous Express treatment during the trip, Parker?"

"I could, since she told that imbecile Watson that she was leaving tomorrow for Raleigh. But I won't do it, because what worked the first time must not necessarily succeed the second. The Express treatment has dangers."

"For her..."

"For me also. We have to work rapidly, and here's what I've decided. Tonight we're going to get rid of Miss Boston. She told Watson her address, so we won't have the trouble of looking for her. Me, I'll take care of Watson. I'll make that my business. He has to go join Sherlock Holmes. How do we know Miss Boston hasn't already informed the Doctor and that he hasn't already warned the police about us?"

"That's true."

"Therefore, here's the job. You'll go to Savannah City. I'll go to the Continental. I'll wait for you there. Watson's death won't be noticed until tomorrow evening at the earliest. We have time to make a get-away from that direction, but we'll be free to wind up the Stanton business."

"If I had known..."

"What, you're complaining, Joe?"

"Yes, this affair will have cost us three cadavers: Sherlock Holmes, Watson, and Miss Boston, and nothing says that Father Stanton will give enough to pay for all this extra work."

"We have the daughter. We'll have the money. I'll see to that."

He took out his watch:

"11:15, Joe."

"Already? Time goes quickly."

"Then let's get on the road. Take a cab. I'll wait for you at the Continental. Good luck!"

"Dirty job!" Joe grumbled.

The two men left Town Square. At the corner of Central Avenue and Brooklyn they separated, respectively going about their sinister and shady tasks.

Let's let Parker return to the Continental and not find Dr. Watson in his room, and let's follow Joe making his way toward Savannah City. He arrived there about midnight and easily got into the house. He found in the entry, following the American custom, a list of the names of the occupants, showing their floors. He climbed the steps softly and without incident reached the apartment of the woman detective. In front of the door, he opened a type of long and flat billfold, which was nothing but an admirably complete kit of the most modern burglar tools. Using a jimmy, he tried the lock and found the door was locked with a key and the key was on the inside. That was only child's play for Joe. The teeth of the jimmy took hold of the key and turned it in the lock. But it was bolted on the inside and held solid. Joe didn't seem unusually thwarted by that surprise. He took a steel blade from the kit and with it he tested the sides of the door. At 30 centimeters above the lock he felt some resistance. That was where the bolt was. The kit furnished a little thin short saw which was pushed into the wood and silently cut out in a few minutes a square piece in which the bolt could be seen. Joe placed it beside him on the corridor floor, closed his kit and took out of his pocket a kind of flexible blade 50 centimeters long. It was a piece of hollow rubber filled with sand as reinforcement, making a terrible weapon for silently striking someone dead. He held it in one hand and with the other he held a little electric torch the size of a box of matches. The door was open. Joe entered.

He was in a dark entry hall from which there were two doors. Joe pushed the first at random. From the light of the torch he made out that he was in a little sitting room. He took several steps forward, but at the same moment he felt something cold on his neck, while an ironic voice was saying to him:

"So what are you looking for here at this hour, sir?"

He jumped forward, and turning around saw in front of him, a revolver in each hand, Miss Boston herself in a dressing gown. He let out a terrible oath, but the young woman said to him, always with the same irony:

"Shame on you! Shame on you! To swear in front of a woman! How impolite of you, sir!"

But Joe had summed up the situation at a rapid glance. Miss Boston, standing in front of the entry door cut off all exit. The window blinds were closed. It would take two minutes to open them, two minutes in which to turn away from the woman detective's two revolvers. But Miss Boston, seeing Joe looking around, understood what he was thinking about.

"Sir, would you please place your little playthings over there."

"Where?" said Joe in a dull voice.

"In the armoire to your right."

"And if I won't?"

"Then we'll let these little birds here sing out, sir."

And she raised the two revolvers.

"Done!"

But at the same time he turned off his torch and the sitting room was plunged into darkness. He let out a howl of joy and lifting his piece of rubber, brought it down in front of him in the direction of the woman detective. But she had foreseen the maneuver and had jumped to one side. Joe had struck only the void. But immediately, as fast as lightning, he had rushed toward the door and grabbed the door knob. A thousand sparkles, blue, green, red, one after the other, lit up the room with flashes of light, and Joe cried out in pain.

"You should be careful about electric appliances used by burglars," joked the detective.

However, Joe had immediately recovered. The light had allowed him see the place where Miss Boston was at that moment. He lifted his terrible club a second time and rushed toward the young woman.

"Stop!" the voice of Miss Boston commanded. "Let's not play this game, my friend, or we're going to get angry and ask our little steel birds to sing a little song.

"Damnation!" screamed Joe.

"Put your hands up, sir. Take four steps backward...Have you done that?...Yes?...Turn around and to your right you'll find the electric light switch. Are you there?...Yes?...Turn it on!"

Joe had automatically obeyed and switched on the lights which brilliantly lit up the little sitting room. He then saw Miss Boston, still standing, holding her two revolvers.

"And now?" he grumbled. "I'm caught. What are you going to do?"

"We're going to have a little chat."

"I have nothing to talk about."

"That's what we'll see. But, please open the armoire to the right."

He opened the armoire. On the little shelves were lined up weapons: knives, brass-knuckles, complete burglar implements.

"Those are my collections," Miss Boston said, laughing.

"What am I supposed to do?"

"Except for the papers, put what you have in your pockets there."

Joe obeyed the order, still threatened by the revolvers. He threw into the armoire his kit, his weapons, his rubber stick. When he had put it all in, he turned toward Miss Boston and said:

"I don't have anything else. That's all."

"Really?"

"Honestly, yes."

"Turn your pockets inside out, please."

He turned them inside out. They were empty.

"And no papers? No billfold?" the woman detective asked.

It was Joe's turn to laugh.

"I'm not stupid enough to carry them with me."

"That's not important." Miss Boston said quietly. "We'll get them this evening or tomorrow at Parker's."

At that name, Joe turned frightfully pale.

"What! What!...You!...know!...then!..." he stammered.

But without answering him, the young woman said in a perfectly natural voice:

"Lock the armoire, please!...two turns, if you will, sir, and bring me the key."

Joe did as he was ordered and gave up the key without resistance.

"And now, let's chat," said Miss Boston.

Joe collapsed rather than sat down in one of the armchairs which were there, and full of both amazement and anger listened to the young woman, who was still calm and mistress of herself.

"You're Joe Starling," she told him. "In 1898 you were condemned to six years hard labor; you escaped June 1, 1899. Unfortunately I can't tell you where you hid out until October 21, 1901, at which time you took part in the robbery of the American Bank of St. Louis. From 1901 until 1906 you were in complicity with Nat Parker, Sanfield, and Tom Clarkson, robbing and murdering in several localities. I have the list. December 3rd last year you were on the loading platform of the Presidio Bridge, disguised as a porter. You signaled Parker which compartment Sherlock Holmes had entered. On the Express, Parker murdered the detective. How?"

"I don't know."

"I'll find out tomorrow evening."

"You won't find out!"

"And why not, please, sir?"

"Because you'll be dead."

"Oh! Oh! You exaggerate. On the contrary, I'm the one who'll see your friend Parker walk to the electric chair. And you too, maybe."

"Me, I haven't murdered. I've only robbed. You don't get the death penalty for that."

"And in that New Jersey business. Did you really do nothing but rob there?"

At these words which recalled to him a horrible tragedy of some months before in which he had played a bloody role, Joe began to tremble all over and remained silent.

"Well, Joe Starling, that's a little something I won't talk about when I'm testifying at your trial."

"You'd do that?"

"Certainly."

"There's a condition."

"Naturally, sir."

"What is it?"

"You'll tell me where Mr. Stanton's daughter is hidden."

"But that would be betraying Parker!" Joe shouted.

"Would you prefer the electric chair?"

"All right. Miss Stanton is hidden at Raleigh, in an abandoned house on the east side of the city, in a suburb called Galveston."

"You're not lying?"

"No, I swear to it."

"Well, Joe Starling, I'll keep my promise if you've kept yours. Testifying before the High Court, I'll forget the New Jersey business, if, after tomorrow I deliver Miss Stanton back to her father."

"After tomorrow. What do you mean?"

"I'm leaving tomorrow evening for Raleigh on the 7:08 train."

"The train where Sherlock Holmes was murdered! But you..."

"I will not be murdered, sir. I'll reach Raleigh; I'll release Miss Stanton; and day after tomorrow, I'll be back in New York with her; that's what I want to do."

"And me?"

"You, you're going to stay here until I return. You'll patiently wait for me and be kind enough to let yourself be handcuffed. That's what I've decided."

"And after that?"

"After that, I'll take you to the Police Administration where you'll rejoin you friend Parker."

"But I'll be arrested!"

"Did you expect to remain free? Bah! You'll finish your years at hard labor and the ones added and 15 years from now you'll again be free to risk the electric chair. That's all."

"That's something we'll really have to see!" Joe grunted hatefully.

"Now be quiet. I'm going to handcuff you and put a little security chain on your feet. You'll be free to walk about tomorrow in my apartment, without touching anything, naturally, and if, when I return I have found Miss Stanton, I'll do as I said."

"If not?"

"If not, I'll remember you took a part in the New Jersey affair."

"All right, then. I'm quiet. You'll find Miss Stanton in the Galveston suburb of Raleigh"

"So much the better for you. Will you please hold out your hands, sir?"

Docilely, seeing there was no way to resist, Joe let himself be handcuffed and the chains put around his feet. In that way he would take a few steps, but it was impossible for him to use his hands for anything. Miss Boston had taken her precautions. He was a total prisoner, without being able to think of escape. When this was done, Miss Boston told him:

"You're free now to take a little nap, if you'd like to, sir."

"I wouldn't like to," the criminal answered furiously.

"Too bad! Good evening. And in the future, beware of the silent electric buzzers which communicate from all the doors of my apartment to an apparatus at the head of my bed."

"If I had known!..."

"There you are! You didn't know! Good evening, sir!"

She turned off the light, locked the door to the sitting room and left the robber alone and a prisoner.

V. Parker's Night

Parker arrived at the Continental Hotel without having noticed anything suspicious. He was now certain that the police hadn't been alerted as to him and that there were no suspicions directed toward him. He wasn't eager to prolong his stay at the Continental because of the presence of Watson, who would necessarily be mixed up in the research into Sherlock Holmes's death. That was why he had decided to make the first move, to do away with Miss Boston and the Doctor at the same time. The way thus cleared, he would be free to bring off the

Stanton affair. It isn't useless to give some explanation of that business that the reader has seen come up several times in this story.

Mr. Stanton was the steel king. Widowed for 15 years, he had lavished all his tenderness on Miss May Stanton, 14 years old. One day, during a walk with her governess, she had disappeared. How? They were not able to find out, despite all the police investigations. After a week, desperate, Stanton had telegraphed Sherlock Holmes, offering him a fortune to undertake the matter. It wasn't for the formidable sum offered but for the mystery of the affair that the celebrated detective had accepted. He arrived in New York with Dr. Holmes and just at the moment when his investigations were going to be crowned with success, the criminals he was tracking had thrown him off their trail by killing him. At that moment, Mr. Stanton's sadness and despair had been terrible and thereafter he had given up hope of ever seeing Miss Stanton again. What was the goal of those who had abducted her? Right up to that moment, nothing could be foreseen, but it was nevertheless certain that they hoped to get a huge ransom for their prisoner. All were astonished though to see them keep silent in that regard, right up to the present.

But Miss Boston had guessed the secret.

The young girl's abductors hadn't wanted to compromise themselves by a risky step or with a letter. They knew very well that the police would have found thereby the fatal clue, the trail which would have led to the discovery of those guilty and the place where the kidnapped girl was hidden. So, up until now, they hadn't tried anything, biding their time and waiting for the proper moment.

And, in fact, that was Parker's innermost thought. He alone was the major guilty party in that dark machination; he was the one who came up with the plan; from him came the major part of its execution so daringly carried out.

When he arrived at the Continental Hotel office, there remained only some few night clerks who had replaced the day clerks. Among the first there was the modest old employee, reserved and silent, still at his post.

Parker rapidly climbed up the four floors and got settled in his room. He also, like Joe, possessed a kit marvelously filled with tools, but his need was more delicate. The door of room 138 communicating with room 136 was bolted on both sides. Since it was important not to leave any traces of a break-in, Parker found himself for a moment somewhat perplexed.

What was to be done? In front of that door he was wondering how he could get to the doctor. It was easy, certainly, to break it in, but criminal caution at the same time forbade that course of action.

Suddenly he laughed, and this derisive laugh in the silence of the empty room was truly sinister. He left the door and went to a valise placed on a chair. He opened it rapidly and took out make-up and brush. In front of the mirror he made himself up to have a face distorted by sorrow, ravaged by suffering. When he was satisfied with that transformation, he rumpled the bed, crushed down the pillows, as if a sick person had rolled about there in terrible pain. Then, partially undressing, he opened the door of the room and went to that of the doctor.

He knocked as if he had no strength, and in a feeble voice the criminal moaned:

"Doctor...Doctor...help...come...I'm dying."

But nothing answered his appeal. He repeated it as if to convince himself of the Doctor's absence. And realizing that the silence in room 138 was justified, he opened the door with the help of a minute jimmy, the same kind that Joe had used to get into Miss Boston's apartment.

The room was dark. Parker carefully closed the door behind him and used his electric torch. Only then did he see that the bedroom no longer contained either valises or trunks. He told himself that Dr. Watson had apparently left the Continental Hotel during the evening. That made him both perplexed and happy. What hid this sudden departure? Did they suspect something? Had the alarm been raised?

There remained nothing more for him to do but go back to his room and wait for Joe to return. It was then a little after midnight. Parker got dressed again, inspected his tools to pass the time and smoked several cigars. At 3 a.m. he began to be somewhat worried and walked up and down the room asking himself what could be keeping Joe. At that time he still had no doubt that Miss Boston's murder was something taken care of and accomplished. At 5 a.m. he began to doubt the success of the affair.

"Could that imbecile by some chance have gotten himself picked up?" he murmured, somewhat perplexed. He began pacing the bedroom floor like a wild beast in a cage. Suddenly he stopped, thinking:

"If Joe is picked up, he might talk?"

And after another minute:

"Well, too bad. I think it's more prudent to make a break for it."

In order not to give the alarm, he waited for another hour. He filled his pockets with small objects from his valise which he had decided to leave behind so as not to be uselessly encumbered. He exchanged his felt hat for a traveling cap, made himself up cleverly and turned the cloth of his frock coat inside out. Instead of being lined with silk, that frock coat was lined with cloth. That meant that, by turning it inside out, it became a piece of clothing with the same shape but with a totally different color. Disguised in that way, Parker was certainly completely unrecognizable even by the eyes of watchful and experienced detectives. Toward 7 a.m. he found the preparations were finally complete. And Joe still had not returned!

This time Parker no longer had any hope. For him there was no longer a doubt that his companion's attempt had not succeeded. He might even be under arrest. Prudence demanded that he skip out as fast as possible. Parker went downstairs, left the stairway, and watched the hotel elevator. Nothing seemed suspicious to him. In the hotel hallway, with domestics walking about, no one paid attention to his early morning departure. Parker took a deep breath and rapidly walked away.

VI. A Mysterious Counter

Parker then felt himself in danger, so he walked faster. He took Trow Street and went down as far as the bank of the Hudson, where he took one of the little boats that are for rent along the river. He followed the current as far as the Knewsee Station, which is one of the areas with the worst reputation in all of lower New York. The dirty, narrow streets of this suburb seemed familiar to him because he walked through them like a man certain of the path he was following. He walked this way for almost a quarter of an hour, then suddenly he turned around and retraced his steps. That tactic was designed to surprise the police who might be shadowing him. It was useless at this time, because Parker quickly convinced himself that he wasn't at all being followed.

Through little streets down which walked individuals with sinister faces, shady appearances, he reached a bar already filled at that early morning hour. The owner, standing behind the big counter, greeted him cordially.

"You're keeping early morning hours today, Parker. Is there something new?"

"I have reasons for that, Man! Is Clarkson in the workroom?"

"Yes. Don't you want to have a drink of good warm gin before going down, Parker?"

"No, but when I come back up, I'll gladly take a glass. Is the passage open?"

"For you, always."

"Good."

Parker went behind the counter and bent over as if to pick up a fallen object. He disappeared.

The counter was a marvelous fake. Pressing on one of the panels revealed an opening large enough to allow one tall man to pass through. Parker had quickly slid through it. He was now in a narrow spiral stairway which sank into the earth in the darkness. Parker went down carefully, counting the number of steps. At step 18 he stopped. He now found himself in a narrow corridor several meters long and closed off by a door from which no light filtered. Parker knocked at that door in a certain way. He struck his fist at the top of the door on the right, twice at the top of the door on the left, three times at the bottom on the right, and four times at the bottom on the left. The door immediately opened quietly and a man in a dressing gown appeared, holding a lighted lamp in his hand.

"Is that you, Parker?"

"Yes, Clarkson, it's me, really."

"You're here. Good morning."

"It ought to be."

"What news?"

"Bad."

"Can you say why?"

"Joe's been caught."

"Oh! That damned boy!"

Clarkson had closed the door of the mysterious hideout. It was a rather long but narrow room holding two iron beds, one of which Clarkson had certainly used that night, because it was unmade. The other was ready for the one whose rank made him welcome in that den of crime.

In fact, there was no doubt possible about that. The most diverse, cast-off clothing was hung on the walls. On a wooden table were the usual instruments of counterfeiters, the inks, the chemical products which admirably betrayed the illegal industry which had its refuge here. Clarkson, a fellow about 40 years old, with a shaggy beard, his clothes in disarray, contrasted strangely with Parker's elegance and neatness. The latter was seated on a bad chair with a straw seat while Clarkson, holding his lamp, was looking at him wanting to know the circumstances which had led to the arrest of Joe, one of the members of that formidable gang, some of whose crimes Miss Boston had earlier reminded her prisoner of.

"So then," Clarkson said, "here he's arrested, this Joe who was still acting the devil yesterday?"

Then Parker told him what our readers already know, right up to the time the robbers separated at Town Square.

"We were supposed to meet at 2 or 3 a.m. at the latest," said Parker. "At 7 a.m. Joe hadn't returned. From that I concluded..."

"That he was arrested."

"That's exactly it. You've guessed very well."

"What are you going to do, Parker?"

"I thought about that while coming here. Here, then, is what has to be done. You're going to go to Savannah City."

"To Miss Boston's?"

"Yes."

"To get myself caught in my turn?"

"No. Listen to me. A tailor lives in the same house. You'll carry a package of clothes to him, but you'll make a mistake."

"How's that?"

"Clarkson, you're picking up very fast this morning. You'll take this package first to Miss Boston. You'll try to find out if she's there. According to what you find out, we'll see what's to be done. Have you understood this time? Afterward, you'll take the package to the tailor. You'll go in dressed like a delivery boy, Sanfield's, by the Mandson Street door. You will leave by the Plain Street door in the costume of a coachman. From there you'll come here. That's the job.

It's really simple, Clarkson, but I really think that you can't not understand the absolutely capital importance of it."

"Provided that damned woman doesn't smell the ruse," Clarkson said, while making a package of clothes he was hastily and haphazardly taking down from the wall.

"It's up to you to avoid it, if you're smart," Parker retorted in a tone which admitted no reply from Clarkson.

A few minutes later Clarkson was ready. He took leave of Parker and went back up to Man's bar by the little staircase. The owner gave him a slight nod, signaling that nothing dangerous was on the horizon. Clarkson reached the street and went down toward the Hudson boat dock, his package under his arm. He went back up the river as far as Hudson Station and took the electric tramway as far as 39th Avenue. There he was in the vicinity of Savannah City. Some minutes later, he rang at Miss Boston's door. It was the woman detective herself who came to open the door to Clarkson.

"I have this packet of clothing to be mended," said the fake delivery boy.

"But I wasn't expecting any clothes," answered the astonished young woman.

"Isn't this the tailor's? I was told it was on this floor."

"No, friend, you're just simply here at Miss Boston's."

"Then a thousand pardons, Miss," said the man, raising his hat. And he added:

"I certainly made a mistake."

"I believe so," said the detective. "The tailor is on the floor below."

"Then I'll just have to go back down," said Clarkson.

And he left quietly.

When the door closed, Miss Boston burst out in silent laughter.

"If he believes I was deceived!" she said. "The fellow wanted to know if his colleague had succeeded. However, it seems to me that wasn't Parker. Who was it then? I must find out."

VII. Where One Sees the Pursued Roll the Pursuer

She quickly put on her hat and took the elevator to the fifth floor. She saw the delivery boy go rapidly down the last of the steps, and she turned away so as not to be seen. But Clarkson had guessed that, and with a very natural and innocent air, he reached the street, deliberately not looking at a cab which had drawn up alongside the curb. The cab began to follow the man who, his hands in his pockets, was whistling a lively tune and walking as if not in a hurry.

"Ah! Ah!" Clarkson was thinking. "You think you're going to trick me, my little lady. You want to know who I am and where I come from? You'll find out only where I'm going."

He went along in that way, following Parker's instructions, right up to Mandson Street and entered a house which appeared calm and respectable. The cab was some meters from him. Once inside, Clarkson hurried. At the back of the courtyard he entered a wardrobe shop where a man seemed to be diligently sorting through some old shoes.

"Hello, Sanfield. I need costume No.12 quick. Somewhere around here there're cops in the street."

"Come down, Clarkson. It's the big safe on the left; you'll see. What's the matter?"

"Parker sent me. It seems some things are turning out bad in the business of our friend Sherlock Holmes."

"Parker hasn't been arrested?"

"No, thank God! But Joe has. Besides, this evening at Man's you'll get whatever information you want. I'm going down."

A trap door opened behind a mass of old clothes. Clarkson slid through it. He arrived in a cave that he must have known marvelously well because having lit a match, he went directly to an obscure place where there was a lamp. When it was lit, he took a coachman's uniform, a coat and a hat from one of the trunks stocked in that room. He threw the clothes he had just taken off into the trunk and went toward the door. He found the key hanging on the wall. That door opened onto a dark corridor at the end of which could be seen a faint light. Clarkson soon reached it and opened a new door which opened into a kitchen. He went through two rooms filled with old, unused boxes and finally exited through a door opening into Plain Street. It was deserted and the fake coachman went down the street quickly. He reached the Park Avenue electric tramway, which carried him to the Hudson River boat dock. He went back the same path already traveled that had led him to Miss Boston. Less than an hour later, a coachman, after having drunk a class of gin at Man's bar, disappeared into the mysterious bar counter.

Parker was waiting for Clarkson with impatience that had become feverish.

"Well!" he exclaimed to Clarkson, as soon as he had entered the hideout after having knocked on the door ten times as Parker himself had done when arriving.

"Were you successful? Was she there?"

"Well, she's alive, in flesh and blood, like you and me."

"Then Joe failed in his night attempt, the imbecile."

"That's possible."

"Come on, Clarkson. You can now openly say that it's absolutely certain."

"In any case, the cops are devilishly on their guard."

"Did she recognize you?"

"No, but she shadowed me."

"Did you go by Sanfield's shop?"

"Yes, and that's what left her at the door, empty-handed, still searching."

"Are you certain?"

"As certain as I am that I drank my glass of gin upstairs with Man."

Parker remained silent a few minutes and seemed to be thinking deeply about what his envoy had just told him.

"What do you intend to do now, Parker?" Clarkson asked.

"What I had at first decided," answered the criminal.

"And that is?"

"Get rid of her."

"The Devil! How are you going to do that?"

"I'm going to do it as it has to be done?"

"It's your business, after all. You know your projects. And you have a plan?"

"Yes, that damned detective is taking the 7:08 Express for Raleigh this evening. I'll be on it and I..."

"You're going to use the same thing with Miss Boston as what brought down Sherlock Holmes?"

"Yes."

"Parker, you're a man of genius."

"I know that," the robber said, smiling. "But my genius isn't exactly of the same quality as that of Sherlock Holmes and of that which soon will be the late Miss Boston. Aside from that, we're evenly matched."

VIII. Drama No.2

Miss Boston hadn't seen the suspicious delivery boy, the package of clothes in hand, escape her without being annoyed. If she had been certain that this was Parker, she would never have forgiven herself. But that person probably had only an obscure and vague walk-on part in the drama. This was only half-bad. After having waited for an hour in Mandson Street, she understood she'd been played by the delivery boy and that the house had two exits. She immediately decided to examine the thing, and having gone into the house, she began her investigation. Everything seemed normal to her except the armoire shop. Why had this businessman set up shop in a courtyard and not on the street? Who were his clients and his visitors? These questions were unanswered and merited being elucidated. But that couldn't be thought about today when time was pressing. She had to catch Parker in the net she had prepared. Her only worry was seeing him not show up for her. But she thought that surely Joe's disappearance would make the movement speed up, accelerate the carrying out of the criminal's plan. She must not be mistaken.

At 7 p.m. Miss Boston arrived on the loading platform at Presidio Bridge for the Raleigh Express. She came from the Continental Hotel where they had informed her of Parker's sudden departure. She had been extremely annoyed, thinking that Sherlock Holmes' murderer had definitely taken to his heels and given up pursuing her. But whatever the cost, she would carry out her plan right to the end. She asked Dr. Watson not to accompany her to Presidio Bridge but to wait calmly in New York.

But what she hadn't at all told him was that in the afternoon she had gotten permission to visit and carefully examine the car in the train where the detective had been found dead. This car, sealed by the judicial investigation, had furnished her, through a meticulous investigation, valuable clues. Coming back from that visit, she had met the Police Inspector, Clampton, with Morton, officially in charge of that case. The latter seemed extremely nervous.

"Well, Miss Boston," Clampton had said, "have you pinched Sherlock Holmes' murderers?"

"Not yet," the detective had answered, smiling, "but I think that will be a done deal tomorrow at the latest."

"What! You're on the trail of the murderers!" Morton exclaimed. "And me, I haven't found anything yet. What have you done, Miss, to arrive at this truly miraculous result?"

"I searched," she said.

Morton bit his lips.

"And you know who did the job? You know the fellows?"

"Yes."

"Is it really that Parker Dr. Watson talked about?"

"That's a little secret I'll let you in on tomorrow, Mr. Morton."

"Then you want to be the only one to have the fame of the capture?"

"Is it too much to ask, sir, that everyone has his share?"

"But Miss Boston, you may perhaps be in danger..."

"Then I didn't work with Hopkins."

"No question...but..."

"But what? What do you mean, Morton?"

"A man would perhaps be very helpful to you, Miss, in case of danger..."

"Sir," Miss Boston said drily, "since the master of us all, the famous detective Hopkins is dead, I work alone."

With these words, she had taken sudden leave of the two policemen to return to her apartment to make her last preparations for departure. So, then, Miss Boston arrived on the departure platform of the Raleigh Express, and on arrival had a smile of success. A porter was calmly sitting on a trunk in the middle of the station platform.

"Ah! Ah!" she said, "There's my delivery boy from this morning. I recognize him marvelously."

Despite his make-up, his new clothes, his wig and his false beard, she had recognized Clarkson perfectly. She immediately drew a breath of relief. If Clarkson was there, Parker wasn't far away and Parker would take the same train as she. Therefore her plan could be carried out as hoped. They were going to put in place for her the same machinations that had caused Sherlock Holmes to perish. In fact, hardly had she taken her seat in the seventh car on the train when the porter on the platform began counting on his fingers: one...two...three...four...five...six...seven...

Just at that moment, a man with a brown beard, and wearing a black frock coat arrived on the platform and took a seat in the compartment next to that occupied by the woman detective.

"Marvelous," said Miss Boston. "The bird is finally in the nest. I've got him."

It was Parker who had come to take a seat in the train for Raleigh. The whistle of departure soon blew. Miss Boston saw the porter put the trunk on his shoulders and leave. Two minutes later the Express went across the Albany Iron Bridge and left New York at full steam.

"Now, my friend Parker," Miss Boston murmured, "we're going to see you at work. At least I still hope so!"

Let's see now what was happening in the compartment where Parker had taken a seat.

The criminal had taken the hourly train schedule out of his pocket, and in a low voice had read: "Harrison, 10:20 p.m.; Philadelphia, 12:02 a.m.; Dover, 1 a.m.; Delaw, 3:04 a.m.; That's it. I have two hours...just as for Sherlock Holmes."

He leafed through several more pages and continued: "Delaw, 5:08 p.m. for New Haven; I'll be in time to dine in New York at the latest. Good. It's going well."

He took out a cigar and lit it leisurely, like a man who wants to make the pleasure last as long as possible. After the last puff, he looked at his watch and said:

"I still have time."

According to the time table of the West End Railway Company, limited, the train went through Harrison at 10:20 p.m. It went through the enormous Philadelphia station at 12:02 a.m. At 1 a.m. it passed Dover. As that last town was passed, Parker came out of his immobility. He took off his coat and began an unusual task. He carefully tapped the right hand partition of the compartment with his hand. It didn't have little windows as did European cars. Here in America we, with reason, judge it indecent to let curious eyes look in on us. You are at home in American compartments. Young ladies and respectable people must be sheltered from the uncomfortable attentions of people who worry very little about their reputation.

Parker's examination didn't take long. He noticed that the partition was covered with a thin sheet of rubber. Wood must be under the rubber. He immediately began to work very rapidly. His pockets seemed deep, because he took an assortment of instruments out of them: small, elegant, truly toys and gems at the same time. First of all he used a long and flexible steel shaft, flat and pointed. With that he cut out a disk the size of an ear in the rubber. He began to eavesdrop through the hole thus formed. At first he didn't hear anything, then a slight rubbing as if a shoulder had brushed against the back of the next door compartment's seat.

"Very good," Parker murmured. "That's what I thought. She's in the left-hand corner."

He took a brush, dipped it in a flask and again glued the rubber disk into the hole in the partition. It was done so delicately that it was impossible, even to an experienced eye to perceive the operation that had just been completed. It had probably taken Parker some time, because having looked at his watch, he grumbled:

"Already! I have to hurry"

At once, with activity that, although hasty, was not feverish, proving his cold-bloodedness, he again picked up the steel shaft and this time cut, ten centimeters lower, a long rectangle in the rubber covering. The piece that was thus detached, he put carefully aside. He had reached the wood of the compartment's partition. Grabbing a little crankshaft of shiny steel from his equipment, he perforated the wood with ten little, almost imperceptible, holes. Nevertheless, Parker was able to distinguish in the wood ten little bluish lights. It was light from the neighboring compartment where Miss Boston had drawn the blue cloth screen.

Parker seemed delighted. While he was working cautiously, a satisfied smile puckered the corner of his lips under his beautiful black mustache. He was then certain of the perfect success of his project. It was now the turn of a new instrument to join the game. This time it was a kind of vaporizer, but a vaporizer of an unusual sort, to which had just been added a rubber tube that terminated in a set of ten minute lancets. The man fixed the ten lancets into the ten holes of the partition. Before beginning the operation, he protected himself from them in a way that amply proved he wanted to be sure he wasn't the first victim. He covered his nose with two levels of padding, and put another piece of padding between his teeth. Only then did he slowly, gently, carefully press on the elastic bulb of the vaporizer. A clinging, insipid pharmaceutical smell spread out into the compartment during that operation. It was the odor of chloroform. For several minutes Parker pressed on the rubber bulb of the vaporizer and when he felt the liquid spit out its last little drops, he laughed derisively.

"I believe that damned detective has now got what was coming to her."

"Do you really think so, Mr. Parker?" a voice beside him asked.

The criminal's vaporizer suddenly fell from his hands. Miss Boston was in the compartment beside him.

"My compliments, sir," she said to him. "You murdered Sherlock Holmes in a truly remarkable way. You see me admiring your way of working..."

"You won't do that for very long," Parker shouted.

He grabbed the revolver in his pocket, but at the same instant Miss Boston lifted hers and fired. The bullet hit Parker in the arm. The criminal collapsed on the compartment bench, howling with pain.

"Please believe me that I acted this way with regret, sir. I could have just killed you."

"You would certainly have done better than doing it this way."

"Pardon! You're forgetting that I must reserve you for the New York High Court. It's not on the Express and from a bullet in your arm that you're supposed to die, but in the electric chair."

"Oh! Why aren't we at this moment on different ground," screamed the exasperated bandit, filled with anger and pain.

"On different ground," Miss Boston said calmly, "I would have broken your leg, that's all, really, sir."

Grimly mute, Parker stopped talking. He felt himself irrevocably lost.

"So then," Miss Boston said, "that's how you murdered Sherlock Holmes. By your little ingenious system, you first put him to sleep and death by chloroform followed sleep. I understand now why he was found without any wounds. Sir, you are a great criminal, truly!"

"Yes, even greater than Sherlock Holmes himself!"

"That wasn't exactly in the same style," Miss Boston said.

Still rumbling, the train rolled on through the countryside plunged in darkness.

The two characters in this drama remained silent, one thinking of his irremediable defeat, the other of her definite victory.

Miss Boston, as soon as they had left New York, had left her compartment and gone to observe Parker's actions and gestures in his compartment. Standing on the outside rail, whipped by the wind and snow, she waited with super-human courage, the moment when the criminal would have begun the slow and silent piercing of the partition. When she saw the chloroform vaporizer, she immediately understood by what hellish ruse Sherlock Holmes had been sur-prised. At that moment she had softly opened the compartment door and, re-volver in hand, had answered Parker's cry of joy.

"You're going to turn me over to the Raleigh Police, aren't you?" asked the criminal, stretched out on the bench with his broken arm.

"Yes, first, then I'm going to release Miss Stanton."

"You won't find her! I defy you to!" Parker laughed derisively.

"Do you believe that?"

"No! No! You won't. You won't find her! Even on the seat of the electric chair I won't tell where I've hidden her! I'll admit nothing! Nothing! Nothing!"

"To find her I don't need your confession, sir!"

"You won't find her. I tell you so, on the word of Parker!"

Parker stared at the detective with amazement so profound and prolonged, that she couldn't keep from smiling.

"What if I found her in the abandoned house in Galveston!"

"You know everything!" he exclaimed.

"Almost!" was the response. "You have friends with loose tongues, sir!"

"Joe talked! Joe betrayed us! Ah! The damned rascal!"

That was his last shout. Right up to the arrival in Raleigh he didn't open his mouth and it was without a word that he let himself be arrested by the police requested by Miss Boston. While waiting for his transfer to New York, Parker was guarded in one of the rooms at the train stations reserved for the police.

IX. The Forgotten Well in the Old Abandoned House

However, Miss Boston's job wasn't yet finished. She still had to find and set free the daughter of the steel king. As soon as the formalities of the arrest were over, she started to work. Before noon she had found the abandoned house at Galveston. It was, as Joe had said, situated to the east of Galveston, almost at the end of the suburb, in the middle of empty fields and ruined houses. The window panes were broken, everything was deserted.

Miss Boston's heart tightened at the thought of the life the poor young girl prisoner must have endured in that hovel. Going across the garden where there was a crumbling cabin and an old well, she entered the abandoned house. But the house was empty! No furniture, nothing else, not the least trace of Miss Stanton.

"Joe must have deceived me," Miss Boston thought. "Alas! I only half suc-ceeded!"

She tested the walls, the floors, but all her search was in vain. There wasn't the slightest trace of the prisoner there. Thinking, Miss Boston remained a moment in the garden. Suddenly, and she didn't know why, she was drawn toward the well. She looked down the top casing of the well and having thrown a stone into the deep, black hole, confirmed that the well didn't have any water in it. Then she remembered that in the cellar of the abandoned house she had seen a long ladder. She went immediately to get it and let it slide into the well. Something told her she was approaching the solution to the mystery. When she had gone down five meters into the well, she encountered an opening in the wall. She stepped into it and with all her strength shouted:

"Miss Stanton!...Miss Stanton...Answer me!...Are you there?"

A weak and far away voice answered her.

"This way!...This way! Down here!"

Miss Boston walked quickly in the direction of the voice. The excavation formed a corridor where you could only walk bent over. At the end of several meters, she encountered a strong wooden door that with the help of a master key she had no trouble opening. At first she could scarcely see the place where she found herself, but little by little, her eyes became accustomed to the darkness. She saw a not very long cubbyhole with a low ceiling. It was there the daughter of the millionaire had been held prisoner. The poor child was frightfully pale and could hardly stand, since for three days her tormentors had not visited her. Our readers know the reason for that temporary abandonment. The unfortunate young girl had also been without nourishment.

"Oh!" she cried out on seeing the detective, "have you come to deliver me, Miss?"

"Yes, I've come to set you free and return you to your father."

"Poor Papa," May sighed.

And she broke out in convulsive sobs that made her delicate and frail breast heave. The detective did her best to console the poor child.

"You must be courageous and strong," she told her, "if you want to get back to New York to see your father."

"Oh! I will be," the young girl promised.

Before finding out how the miserable kidnappers had accomplished the abduction of the millionaires' daughter, Miss Boston decided to get her out of the dark and unhealthy cubby hole that without Joe's confession and the successful searches of the detective, would have been forever the tomb of Mr. Stanton's daughter.

Excited and happy, Miss Boston held the unfortunate girl tight in her arms, and with a thousand precautions, began the ascent which led to the exit of the fatal well. When she came to the last step of the ladder, she breathed a deep sigh of satisfaction. Her job, finally, was finished. She had twice succeeded: first of all, in rescuing the daughter of the millionaire, in completing, in realizing, rather the work begun by Sherlock Holmes, and so tragically interrupted, and finally in avenging the death of Sherlock Holmes by the arrest of his murderers.

When she reached the top of the well, bringing Miss May into the light, the detective got busy restoring her strength. With the rescued young girl, she made her way to a humble little restaurant for workers at the entrance of the Galveston suburb. She ordered some strengthening food that helped Miss May return completely to her senses. When her hunger was satisfied, Miss Boston could finally question her on the details of her kidnapping that had taken place during a walk.

"So, then, Miss Stanton, "you were abducted from Mildley Park?"

"Yes, Miss Boston."

"How did that happen?"

"I don't understand that too much, myself...I don't remember very well."

"Try to remember well. I'll help your memory."

"I'm going to try, Miss Boston."

"Just answer me as you remember all the details. What time did you go out with your governess?"

"About noon."

"Exactly?"

"Oh! It could very well have been 2:30 p.m. I don't remember exactly."

"You didn't notice someone following you?"

"No, not at all, because I would probably have pointed that out to my governess. But there was something else!"

"What else then?"

"Ah! I'm beginning to remember now. It was in the park. I was playing on the lawn, when suddenly..."

Miss Stanton began trembling as if the baneful vision of her kidnapping suddenly rose before her eyes.

The detective was anxiously following that reaction in the young girl, because the method of kidnapping used by Parker and Joe appeared ingenious to her. It merited her knowing it so as in the future she could avoid being caught in the trap of that diabolical ruse. She was watching carefully the words on Miss Stanton's lips.

"So, what did you see?" she asked her.

"I saw...I saw...my father..."

"Mr. Stanton?"

"Yes! Himself!"

"You're not making a mistake?"

"Oh! No, I recognized him very well!"

"And then?"

"He was walking in a pathway adjoining the lawn where I was playing. I remember perfectly that he was holding a rose."

"And you went toward him?"

"Yes, right then. Can you imagine, Miss Boston, how surprised I was to meet papa, who never leaves his office, at Mildley Park?"

"And where was your governess at this time?"

"She was seated in front of the lawn, reading a book."

"And she didn't see you go meet...your...the man who looked like your father?"

"No, she was too engrossed in her reading to do that."

"Good. And after that, what did you do?"

"I ran down the pathway...and papa was smiling when he saw me coming. Then he let me smell the beautiful rose he was holding."

"You smelled the flower?"

"Yes, but after that I don't know what happened. I woke up in the dark, humid room in the well where you came to get me. And that's all. When I was tired I went to sleep. When I awoke I found food in a terracotta plate next to me."

"You never saw the man who brought the food?"

"Yes, I did, once. I wasn't asleep. Someone opened the door; he came in with a lantern..."

"If I showed you that man, would you recognize him?"

Oh, yes. He frightened me so much!"

"Well, we're going to go see him."

A terrible tremor shook the young daughter of the millionaire from head to foot.

"He's not going to take me away again?"

"No, don't be afraid of anything from him as long as I'm there."

And the detective started back to Raleigh with the daughter of the steel king. On the way, a slight smile lit up her face, which was beaming with joy. She now understood perfectly the cunning trick used by Parker or his accomplices to bring off the kidnapping of Miss Stanton. She was definitely beating the feared criminal all along the line of his daring criminal operations.

Less than an hour after the miraculous deliverance from the well of the abandoned house, Miss Boston and the young girl arrived at the station where, as we have already said, Parker was held prisoner. With Miss Stanton, she immediately confronted the prisoner. Seeing them, Parker turned pale. He understood that for him the game was irremediably lost. But in the debacle of his sinister and dark projects, there remained a last hope, one that Miss Boston wouldn't know about and couldn't testify against him at the High Court of New York, which would judge the crime. Vain hope! A last illusion that Miss Boston, her again, would make it her business to take from him.

"Miss Stanton," she said on entering, "look at that man over there and say if that's the man who brought you food in the well of the old abandoned house in the Galveston suburb."

"Yes...that's him...I recognize him very well," the young daughter of the millionaire answered in a voice trembling with terror.

Parker laughed derisively and only shrugged disdainfully.

"You understand, sir," said Miss Boston, "that young girl is accusing you. What do you have to answer?"

"Nothing."

"Really! You have nothing to answer, nothing to say?"

"I'm saying that she doesn't at all know what she's talking about. That's all."

"Oh, yes, I do! Yes, I do recognize you!" Miss Stanton cried out.

"Agreed," Miss Boston interrupted, "She knows very well that you were carrying a rose in the pathway of the Mildley Park the day of her kidnapping."

"A rose? Me? But that's a joke, my God!"

"For you, maybe, Parker, but not for her. She also knows that you were marvelously made up to look like Mr. Stanton. She also knows that you had her smell her rose..."

"And then, so what?" the daring criminal mocked.

"So, she doesn't know anything else," the detective continued, with a disconcerting calmness." She no longer knows anything more because she is really too young, but me, I know more."

"Ah! Ah! Really? I'd be very curious to learn what you know, Miss Boston."

"I'm going to tell you, sir. The rose was soaked with chloroform."

"What...you..."

"By having Miss May Stanton smell it, you put her to sleep, paralyzed her movements, and committed a new crime for which you'll have to answer to justice."

Completely unmasked this time, Parker leaned back in his chair and didn't budge again right up to the time the train that, with the detective and Miss May Stanton, was to take him back to New York...toward punishment.

As soon as she had left the Presidio Bridge Station, Miss Boston took a cab to the sumptuous dwelling of the millionaire. However, she earnestly asked, and she had her reasons, Miss May Stanton not to enter her father's house immediately with her. She had her calling card sent, by one of the numerous servants in livery in the entry hall, to the steel king, who received her at once. When he saw the detective enter alone, despair was painted on his features.

"Alas!" he said. "I understand now, Miss Boston, that I must give up the idea of ever seeing my daughter again."

"But, sir…"

"Oh! It's useless to try to console me…What do you expect me to do now with my life, alone, without my daughter…my only family…Ah! I would have gladly given up, abandoned all my millions, to see her again…"

Smiling, the famous woman detective said simply: "Here she is."

And she opened the door to the drawing room where she had just been received by Mr. Stanton.

Miss May Stanton, with a cry of joy, threw herself into the arms of her weeping father.

X. The Final Menace of the Condemned Man

Upon leaving the millionaire's town house, Miss Boston's first concern was to go to the Continental to tell Dr. Watson about the fortunate success of her expedition to Raleigh. A cab on lower 28th Avenue took her there rapidly at full speed. In the clerks' office of the Continental, the modest little employee was still seated behind his desk, watching with a suspicious eye the comings and goings of the travelers. Miss Boston entered the room, and deliberately in a loud voice said:

"Sir, you can without fear again become Dr. Watson!"

The man she spoke to suddenly jumped up.

"What…what…they were…" he stammered, and it was understandable that joy made his altered voice tremble.

"Sherlock Holmes' murderers have been arrested," Miss Boston answered, "and our illustrious master has been avenged, finally."

"Thank you! Thank you!" Dr. Watson exclaimed with extreme gratitude. And at once becoming himself again, he added:

"Miss Boston, you are the Sherlock Holmes of the United States."

In the mouth of the faithful companion, of the greatest detective's best friend, wasn't that the most beautiful and the most magnificent praise that could recompense the daring courage of the only female detective?

Dr. Watson was given all the minute details of Parker's arrest in the Raleigh Express. But suddenly Miss Boston stopped.

"The Devil!" she said. "I forgot!"

Worried, Dr. Watson asked: "What more is there?"

"Joe! There's still Joe!"

"Parker's companion, the porter on the Presidio Bridge platform?"

"Himself. Do you know, Doctor, where this same Joe is at this moment?"

"In the police station?"

"No, better than that!"

"I don't see…"

"Well, Joe is at my apartment!"

"At your apartment? That's not possible!"

"That's how it is, sir."

And the detective brought Dr. Watson up to date about the criminal attempt at which the night before she had almost been the victim on the part of Joe.

"And now," she said, "I absolutely must leave you, and immediately, to go deliver my prisoner."

"Deliver, Miss Boston? What do you mean?"

"Deliver him into other hands, Doctor. I think he'll be better off in the Central Police Bureau than in my hands."

"That's my opinion also."

"Until later, then. We will see each other again at the interrogation of these fellows."

"That's right! Good luck, Miss Boston!"

"Could I get any better than I've just had?"

At this, she took leave of Dr. Watson to go to her apartment in Savannah City. Less than a half hour later she arrived there.

"That scum must be getting hungry, I think," the detective told herself.

She opened the door to the sitting room which was plunged in darkness.

"Well. Mr. Joe," she asked in a joking tone, "how have we passed the time?" but she got no answer.

"I see you hold it against me," the detective said. "You're wrong, very wrong, sir."

Saying this, she pushed the electric light switch and the brilliant light bulb sudden lit up the room. It was empty! Nobody! Nothing! Joe had disappeared! The detective let out a cry of amazement mingled with anger.

She examined the windows carefully, but the windows were locked on the inside, and as a result, he couldn't have escaped that way. She looked at the door but the door bore no trace of forced entry. How had the criminal disappeared? It would have seemed he truly flew away. But that was supernatural, and inherent to the nature of detectives is never to believe in the supernatural. Therefore a practical explanation had to be found. Miss Boston looked for that explanation everywhere and in everything in every room, but in vain. She could only give in to the evidence and state that thing precisely and clearly: Joe had escaped. It was simple and very clear; that's all there was to it.

On a cold November morning in the year 1906, a cortege composed of four gentlemen in black frock coats, entered the cell of the man in Sing Sing Prison in New York condemned to death. The one of those four gentlemen who seemed to be the leader tapped on the shoulder of the condemned man who, lying on a steel cot seemed to be sleeping deeply.

"Parker," he said, "it's time."

At these words the condemned man sat up, a little pale, and looked at the four men.

"You...you...you're coming for the thing?" he asked.

"Yes, today's the day that you must pay your debt to society."

"All right," Parker said. "I'm ready."

He got up, dressed quickly, and let himself be handcuffed.

The previous month, on October 18, the High Court of New York had condemned him to death, guilty of the murder of Sherlock Holmes. The time had come to make atonement. A few minutes later, crossing the dark corridors of Sing Sing Prison, surrounded by four men, the condemned man reached the waiting room of the electric chair. Two people were standing beside the instrument of death. The first was the man who carried out the capital punishment executions for the State of New York, the second was Miss Boston. She had promised to lead Parker to the electric chair herself. She had kept her promise.

When he saw her, Sherlock Holmes' murderer shook with anger. He felt the rage of having been beaten mount to his heart, him, the daring criminal, him, a man, not a woman. He stared at the detective and said:

"I'd rather be in my place than in yours. My friends will avenge me!"

And he sat in the chair. They attached the electrical wires to his feet and his wrists. Just as they were going to put on the helmet which activated the electricity to the head, he said again:

"I will my vengeance to the Green Tie Gang!"

Those were his last words. The executioner quickly pressed a switch. The criminal's body was shaken by a powerful current which shook him for some minutes. Then the electric shocks were reduced. The body stayed immobile. It was no longer anything but a cadaver. The electric punishment had done its work!

THE ONE HUNDRED THOUSAND ARMS GANG

I. Three Millions' Worth of Gems

It was 5 p.m. when Mr. Flippers, the great Broadway jeweler, went downstairs to his vast showrooms where all the New York millionaires shopped, to cast his proprietary glance, as he did every day, over the counter exhibits where his select as well as elegant clientele was crowded. A gentleman, suitably dressed, but with an exotic appearance, a Mexican, it seemed, entered the store at that moment.

A little doorkeeper went to meet him and asked:

"Which jewelry counter would you like, sir?"

"Pearls," answered the Mexican.

The usher immediately took him to the pearl counter where a salesman had already opened in front of a client a great number of jewelry cases containing some of the most beautiful, and of a considerable price, Oriental pearls. Another employee hurried to take orders for the Mexican's purchases. He stood some steps from the first client.

This first man was a tall blond fellow, expensively dressed, with the look of one of those fashionable people you meet with a cane in their hand, a Havana cigar in their mouth, strolling casually down Broadway or down St. James Road, the usual promenade for the elegant of New York. At that moment, the fashionable fellow was selecting from the necklaces which were spread out in front of him.

Mr. Flippers, coming down from his own offices on the second floor, took in the scene in his boutique with a glance. Here and there, at the various counters, elegant buyers had stopped in front of the glistening of the stones, the brilliance of the diamonds, the splendor of the gems.

This store was majestic and luxurious, one of the most beautiful in New York. It started on Broadway with three grand show case windows displaying the most beautiful jewels of the House of Flippers. Currently, the manager had put on display there the marriage presents of the charming Miss Aymes, daughter of the steel king. She was to marry Mac Gins, the nephew of the petroleum king, some days later. This jewelry was appraised at three million dollars. It had been presented to the fiancée by her father's millionaire friends. Mr. Flipper had been charged with filling the orders. However, he had wanted to display the gems to public curiosity before delivering them. Naturally, a feeling of pride and vanity had caused Mr. Flippers to make that display. He wanted to show all the

New York Broadway curious what masterpieces came from his stores, who his clientele was, and the value of royal jewelry of this kind. Wasn't this his best advertising?

Nevertheless, that display wasn't without danger. These jewels, protected just by fragile glass, must certainly excite the covetousness of the daring robbers who infest New York. So Mr. Flippers had taken his precautions and had contacted a private detective agency which supplied him with five of its staff. Two, dressed like doormen, were watching the window from inside the store. Disguised in various ways, the other three were standing in the street in front of the show case window. These were watching the curious in front of the store. They would have taken down those who might have tried to break the glass to grab the gems. In addition, the window was closed on the inside by security locks to which only Mr. Flippers had the key. Each evening he himself opened the display window and had the gems put in the jewel cases in his presence. Then they put them in a safe in front of which the three private detectives mounted guard all night. Every precaution had been taken, it would seem. The future was to show Mr. Flippers that the thieves he was so justly afraid of were still more ingenious than he.

He had hardly been a few minutes in his store when the noise of voices rose above the counter where the fashionable man and the Mexican man were choosing pearls. Mr. Flippers approached them. An altercation had suddenly broken out between the two buyers.

"Sir," the Mexican was saying, "you have just insulted me."

The fashionable man turned his head disdainfully and asked in a disinterested tone:

"What does this badly-washed fellow want?"

At these words, the Mexican, who had a bronzed complexion, jumped forward. "You will give me satisfaction! Immediately!"

"I'll give you a cane whipping!" was all the fashionable man answered.

"We'll see about that!"

The Mexican was about to spring, when Mr. Flippers intervened in the discussion.

"Gentlemen," he said, "this isn't the place to settle your quarrels!"

"What does that man want?" roared the furious Mexican.

"Please, calm down!" continued Mr. Flippers. "This store isn't used to such shouting."

"Then you have only polite clients!" the Mexican retorted.

"And they throw out the poorly washed ones!" laughed the fashionable man.

The clients had gradually gathered around the noisy group and were watching the two antagonists curiously, one of whom seemed as cold and disdainful as the other appeared excited and violent.

But Mr. Flippers was not at all eager to see his elegant and plush store transformed into a battlefield, so he continued:

"I don't know which one of you is in the wrong, gentlemen, but I simply ask you to go settle your quarrel somewhere other than here."

"All right!" said the Mexican, "let's go; we'll settle this with revolvers in the street!"

"Brute!" said the fashionable man. But turning toward the owner, he said:

"You are perfectly right, sir, and I apologize in the name of this coarse person who ignores the rules of politeness. It's in some other location, on another field, that this must be settled."

He took out his billfold, removed a card from it, and held it out to the Mexican, who snatched it from his hands.

"Here is my address," he said. "I will expect your witnesses."

He turned his back on his antagonist and returned to selecting from among the pearls spread out in front of him.

The Mexican, grumbling, left the store and at the door shouted:

"I'll get my revenge!"

The undercover detectives inside the store hadn't missed any of that scene. Knowing all about the tricks of big American thieves, they had been afraid that the Mexican and the fashionable man were accomplices and that a third thief had taken advantage of the situation to steal pearls. But their fears hadn't been realized. Not one pearl had disappeared from the counter. They let the Mexican leave, therefore, while the fashionable man, as if nothing had happened, continued making his choices. That lasted a few minutes more, when suddenly the front door of Mr. Flippers' store opened violently, letting enter one of the detectives entrusted with the surveillance on Broadway.

"The show window! The show case!" shouted that man.

One of the inside detectives asked him:

"What is it? Which window?"

"There, there..."

The detective stammered in amazement.

"And so, the show case, what's wrong with it?"

"It's disappeared!"

There was immediately an enormous uproar in the whole store. Everyone, Mr. Flippers ahead of everyone, rushed toward the show window containing the three million dollars' worth of jewelry. The detective had told the truth. The whole inside of the show window had disappeared.

II. The Mystery of the Locked Show Window

There had been a crowd on Broadway in front of the jewelry show window composed of every kind of individual, of all classes and of all professions. They were admiring Miss Aymes' marriage present jewelry, exchanging opinions among themselves. The three detectives, disguised as ordinary bystanders, were joking among themselves while closely watching those who were in the first row of the curious. At this time the window was brilliantly lit by 100 electric light bulbs. The vivid and glaring illumination had been well designed to show off the price and the splendor of the jewelry.

These gems were on a large table covered with red velvet. The remainder of the show window was hung with the same material, which completely prevented seeing what was happening inside Mr. Flippers' store. The role of the detectives on the inside was limited to watching the approach to that show window. A minute before the Mexican's exit, something, strange and curious, happened inside the show window. All the electric light bulbs went out.

With the same movement, the three detectives had placed themselves against the show window so as to prevent by their presence the thieves from making a move and taking advantage of the darkness to break the window and grab the jewels. On this point their fears had been badly founded. No attempt of this kind had occurred. Besides, the obscurity in the show window had lasted only a minute. Suddenly the lights went back on. The three detectives, with a certainly very understandable amazement, saw that the table in the show window on which the jewelry had been placed had disappeared. At that spot there was no longer anything but a black, deep hole. The table seemed to have sunk into the ground. It was at that moment that one of the three detectives on duty, distraught, had burst into Mr. Flippers' story to announce the strange event.

As we said, clients, employees, doormen, everyone dashed toward the window that the store director feverishly opened with the key that only he possessed. He pushed aside the red velvet hanging and let out a moan of despair. Of the three million dollars' worth of gems, diamonds, sapphires, emeralds, pearls, nothing remained. Everything had disappeared.

But one of the private detectives came forward, examined the hole through which the table had disappeared, and, having summed up the situation, didn't lose his head.

"The table is in the cellar," he said.

"How's that?"

"I don't know. But we have to go to the cellar!"

"I'm going there!" said a calm voice. Everybody turned around. A slim and elegant blonde young woman, dressed in exquisite taste, had just come into the store. She had by accident stopped in front of the jeweler's show window, had witnessed the disappearance of the gems, and had judged it fitting to intervene. It was Miss Boston, the only female detective in the whole world.

"Who are you?" demanded Mr. Flippers, suspicious on thus seeing an unknown woman take a role in the mysterious and troubling affair of this daring robbery.

"I'm Miss Boston," answered the detective.

At these words a ray of joy and of hope came into the great jeweler's eyes.

"Oh! Miss Boston," he exclaimed, "find the gems, I beg you!...Miss Aymes can't wear them for her wedding!...I'll be disgraced!...I beg you, Miss Boston, do the impossible...My fortune is yours!"

"We'll talk of all this later, sir," she said, "but now there're more pressing things to do."

The private detective, jealous at seeing Miss Boston take a hand in the affair, said in an impertinent tone:

"But it seems to me the thing is clear, and there's no need..."

Without answering, Miss Boston asked Mr. Flippers:

"Where is your cellar, sir? Go ahead of me, please."

The jeweler, followed by the detective and the two others in charge of the inside surveillance moved rapidly toward the back of the establishment. Opening a door, they went into a dark corridor leading into the back of a courtyard. The door to the cellar opened in the middle of this corridor. Miss Boston, with the group accompanying her, went down. Thanks to her electric torch, she lit the stairs ahead of her, looking carefully, as if to see the possible traces of the thieves. Several small vaults made up the cellar. They were absolutely empty except for two among them where they stored old boxes, debris of all kinds.

"Which one is the vault directly under the show case of the vanished gems?" the detective asked the jeweler.

Mr. Flippers immediately pointed it out. The door to it was open. She had scarcely entered than Miss Boston saw clearly how the thieves had operated. The gem table was upside down in the middle of the vault, but without the least jewel. Everything had disappeared.

Then the detective began the investigation with a minute inspection of the premises. Broadway Street buildings are very old, since they date from the founding of New York. That fact explains why the houses haven't all been constructed following the rules of modern architecture. Mr. Flippers' had the floor boards directly above the vault, supported by steel beams. The thieves had sawed through the beams at the spot supporting the table from the show case window. That allowed them to let the table fall into the vault in one piece. The traces of their work could be seen. The thieves had left a valise there which, when opened, was found to be empty.

The detective concluded that the jewels must have been thrown rapidly into the other bags. Judged superfluous, that one had been abandoned as an encumbrance. Miss Boston suddenly stooped down. The light from the torch had just shown her a little square of cardboard abandoned in the dirt of the vault. She picked it up, examined it, and slid it into her small bag. It was a subway ticket stamped at Greenpont Station. She then investigated how the thieves had been able to break into the cellar and how they had left. It didn't take long for the celebrated detective to find this out. The wall of the neighboring house had been broken through to a height of about 40 meters. The hole must have been covered up for several days with the help of some old sacks, since a pile of this rubbish extended almost the length of the opening. Miss Boston slid through the opening and found herself in the basement of the neighboring house. The door to it was open. The thieves had certainly escaped that way. She was easily convinced of it because the dirt floor of the cellar still carried the obvious and very fresh traces of footprints. Examining them closely, Miss Boston concluded that there must have been two of the thieves. That clue led her toward the cellar stairs, and when she had opened its door she found herself in the house next door to the jeweler. She at once questioned the concierge.

"Did two men with a valise just pass by here?" she asked the astonished woman

"Yes," said the concierge, "they were two of my lodgers, Fred and Connor. They told me they were going to Washington for three days. They were carrying a valise."

"Your lodgers, you say. What floor did they live on?"

"On the ninth. Oh! They have a little bachelor apartment, $30 a year."

"Do you have the keys?"

"No...But you won't go into their place while they're gone without them, will you?"

"That's where you're mistaken. We'll go in whether or not you have the keys."

"But who are you then?"

"Me, I'm a detective, and your tenants are thieves."

"Them!...Great gods!"

Miss Boston left the concierge with her astonishment and climbed rapidly to the ninth-floor apartment of the daring, departed thieves who had had ample time to escape.

III. From Broadway to Greenpont Station

Miss Boston knew by experience that it is useless to chase criminals that fear of being caught makes nimble. What she also knew was that thieves always make a mistake which follows on their heels and finally trips them up. While climbing the stairs she mentally organized her first steps. At the ninth floor she stopped in front of the apartment of the men called Fred and Connor. Since the concierge didn't have the keys, Miss Boston used the steel jimmy which would open any lock. She entered and saw that she hadn't been mistaken in her expectations. The apartment was very small and scantily furnished with a small table, two chairs and two iron beds. On the table were lock jimmies and hammers wrapped with cloth, showing clearly how the thieves had been able to operate in silence. What remained in the apartment proved very clearly that it had been rented solely for the purpose of robbing Mr. Flipper's jewelry store. Of what was left, no paper, no document could give a certain clue about the thieves. The jeweler, present at the search, who could see the few results obtained by the detective, never stopped moaning and complaining.

"I'm dishonored if the gems aren't found!...What will those gentlemen say when they learn what has been stolen! ...I will lose my reputation! What a misfortune! ...What a terrible misfortune!"

Miss Boston interrupted him:

"So when is Miss Aymes getting married?"

"The 28th of this month."

"That is to say, nine days from now."

"Yes, exactly, Miss Boston."

"Then everything is all right. Miss Aymes will have her marriage presents and will be able to wear them the day of her marriage."

"God grant it would be possible!"

"It will be, sir, if luck is with me."

"Oh! Miss Boston, if what you're saying could be true! I don't know what I would give to believe you!"

"Don't give anything, Mr. Flippers, and believe me."

With these words, Miss Boston went downstairs. She questioned the concierge about Fred and Connor but got no exact information. They had rented the apartment a week before and during all that time had received neither a letter nor a visitor. They went out during the day, never having said where they were going. Obviously they weren't going to admit to the concierge that they were just in the cellar. And that was all. Miss Boston concluded that the thieves must be from New York, that they had operated on Broadway, while at the same time having another place to meet and another domicile. Where? There was the problem and the difficulty. She then took leave of Mr. Flippers in order to return to her home in Savannah-City, where she had an evening appointment with Inspector Sokes of the Central Police Bureau.

Miss Boston had just finished her frugal dinner when Sokes entered the apartment.

The two detectives, frequent companions in so many dangerous and difficult expeditions, shook hands cordially.

"Have you heard the news, Miss Boston?" asked Sokes.

"But the big news, the…"

"The Broadway robbery? Yes, Sokes, I know about it."

"Already?"

"I even know how many robbers there were and how they operated."

"Not possible!"

"That's the situation, Sokes. I was by chance on Broadway when the thing took place. I took the business in hand at once…"

"And you found?"

"Nothing. Oh, but, yes, I did find something, however."

"What was that?"

"A subway ticket from the Greenpont station."

"That's not much!"

"That's what I told myself also, Sokes, but after all, and you know it as well as I do, nothing must be overlooked."

"Then you're taking charge of the investigation."

"Yes, since I promised Flippers to recover the gems."

"It seems he's in despair."

"I can understand it: three million dollars' worth of gems! Now that's something!"

"Really! But, say, Miss Boston, if you need me, you know I'll always be available."

"I know it, Sokes, so I won't hesitate to call for your help if the situation arises."

"So much the better, Miss Boston. That's not only an honor, it's more a real pleasure to work with a detective like you!"

Sokes stayed another hour at Savannah-City, had a cup of tea, and didn't leave until 11 p.m. After his departure, Miss Boston set down in writing the evidence from the day. She went to bed promising herself to be at Greenpont Station in the morning the next day, the first reference point she had in that affair.

At 7 a.m. she arrived at the New York subway station situated in the Greenpont suburb. That part of the great city is mainly made up of houses surrounded by gardens; the distance from Greenpont to the center of the City is rather considerable. That agglomeration is formed of somewhat irregular streets, of little squares, and makes up what could be called a small town.

On the way, Miss Boston made a discovery she hadn't noticed on the first superficial examination of the ticket. The ticket had not been punched. In addition, the edge was jagged, indicating it had been torn from a book of tickets. Therefore this ticket, issued to the subscribers of the Metropolitan subway, at the station of their usual departure, proved that the man who had lost the ticket customarily took the subway at Greenpont Station. In addition, it had yet another importance for Miss Boston. For her it was now certain the robbers must live in the Greenpont-Station neighborhood. Now, this point established, it was easy for her to narrow her center of operations. She had laid out her hunting area; the only thing left for her to do was to find the game.

IV. The Man with the Tell-Tale Knee

To tell the truth, Miss Boston was primarily making Greenpont Station this step in her investigation to clean up loose ends. But now with the ticket, she thought she held the clue which would put her on the right track. She therefore entered the loading platform of the station, walking about like an ordinary commuter waiting for the arrival of the first cars going toward New York. She had been there for several minutes, when there arrived on the platform an individual who didn't particularly call her attention, but at whom she nevertheless glanced rapidly, just as she did every person near her, for whatever reason.

This man was dressed rather neatly, but a bizarre thing struck Miss Boston immediately. His right knee had dirt stains, as if he had been kneeling. The soil stains were less apparent on the left knee. It looked as if it had been brushed by the back of a hand. A chain of events immediately ran through Miss Boston's head. In the Broadway cellar the thieves had escaped through a hole in the wall, forcing them to crawl on the ground. In the same cellar she had found a Greenpont Station ticket. Now at Greenpont Station she encountered a man having dirt stains on his knees as if he had been crawling. Wasn't this factual, logical, reasoning striking? Was this step a trail to follow? But Miss Boston, who had that rapidity of decision which made her such an adversary to be feared by criminals, hardly asked herself the question. She immediately approached the ticket agent.

"The gentleman over there," she said, pointing out the man with the tell-tale knee, "did he give you a ticket from a book of tickets?"

"Right," said the ticket agent.

"Do you know him?"

"No. But I see him take the subway here rather often."

That was the first point gained. At the same instant the train pulled into the station and the man took a seat. Miss Boston followed him there and before taking a seat went up to the conductor of the compartment and said some words to one side rapidly in his ear.

The man at first looked at the detective with a certain hesitation, but at the sight of the little silver badge of the Central Police, his one look meant:

"Understood, Miss. You'll get what you ask."

He consequently began stamping the tickets and three minutes later punched that of Miss Boston. But at the same time, he said in a low voice:

"CB01894."

"Thanks!" whispered the detective.

She at once took out from her small purse the ticket found in the Broadway cellar and consulted the number. It carried this: CB01892.

The detective smiled.

"Luck is with me," she murmured.

In fact, the number the conductor had slipped to her was that of the ticket of the man who had boarded at Greenpont Station. Between this number and that of the Broadway cellar there was only a difference of one cipher. The number CB01892 had been lost; the number CB01893 had been used on the return trip after the robbery; the number CB01894 was that being used at this moment. Therefore the man who was in the compartment using a book of tickets with numbers following consecutively had something to do with the daring Broadway robbery.

Miss Boston wanted to proceed knowing exactly what she was doing. She wanted to catch the accomplices at the same time as the main perpetrator. In arresting the man with the tell-tale knee on the spot, she would cut off the trail of the other thieves, and who knows but what that trail didn't hold some surprises. In fact, Miss Boston, taught by experience, knew that on this terrain you had to be ready for everything. Consequently, she would follow the man, note down the places he went, and pick him up at the right moment. Besides, decisions had to be made on the spot. The subway had just stopped at Falls Station and the man Miss Boston was tracking got off rapidly. The detective followed on his heels. The thief was unaware he was being followed. He was walking quickly in the direction of Hudson Ban saloon and, about the middle of the avenue, disappeared into it. The detective had no time to lose. If she wanted to find out who the man was going to meet in this saloon, she must enter quickly. But it seemed to her that it would have to be stupidity to enter there in her usual dress. She might be recognized by some of the saloon clients and an alarm given would lose her the trail.

The detective signaled to a cab driver who had just pulled his vehicle up to the curb. Miss Boston gave him 50 cents with the order to drive a few meters. At the end of some meters, she jumped lightly from the cab. She was unrecognizable, marvelously disguised. This way, without fear of being recognized, she could penetrate the Hudson Ban saloon. But just as she was approaching, the man with the tell-tale knee came walking out of the saloon accompanied by another individual.

Smiling, the detective observed: "They're multiplying."

And suddenly she thought:

"Aren't those the two lodgers in the house next to Mr. Flippers on Broadway?" Glancing around them, the two men started walking rapidly toward Falls Station. Miss Boston followed, immediately convinced that they were going toward the subway entrance to Greenpont Station. Both were returning where the first had come from. The detective immediately went back up the avenue, again got into the cab waiting for her, and had herself driven quickly to Greenpont. Once again she took advantage of the trip to disguise herself. On the loading platform, dressed as a newspaper seller, she awaited the arrival of the train from Falls Station.

She didn't wait very long. Scarcely two minutes later, it stopped at the platform. With a smile of unspeakable satisfaction she saw the men she was looking for get off. She saw them throw away their tickets as they went toward the exit. Miss Boston picked them up and slid them into the secret pocket of her dress. That done, she continued shadowing the two men who had left the station. They went across Greenpont Square and took Hux Street, going up to the last house. There they suddenly turned the corner of the street. When Miss Boston got there, two seconds later, they had disappeared as if vanished into thin air.

V. The Electrified House

Miss Boston found herself in an unusually deserted place. There were houses here and there in the middle of gardens enclosed by walls or thick hedges. How had those two men been able to vanish in that place? Where had they disappeared to? The detective quickly examined the spot. The last house on Hux Street turned at a right angle into Koch Street. However, an alley opened in Koch Street at that angle. It was probably through there that the two thieves had made off. Was that their usual domicile? If it was, the detective could congratulate herself on being lucky. She would throw her net over the Broadway thieves with one fell swoop.

"I absolutely have to see what's at the end of this alley," she said to herself.

She went in cautiously, her revolvers in her hands. The alley was long and narrow, turning at sudden angles. The detective noticed that the wall had various marks at certain places, the meaning of which wasn't clear. But she thought these were signs left by the thieves in case of situations she would later clear up. Nevertheless, these marks showed her clearly that she had not been mistaken when picking up the lost trail of the two vanished men in this alleyway. An unusual thing Miss Boston immediately noticed in the alley was some narrow plates about three meters apart sealed in the ground. Each time she had stepped on one, it seemed to her that the steel plate moved under her foot, but without breaking, however. Suddenly, at the fourth plate, Miss Boston got a surprise. She had hardly placed her foot when electric sparks lit up under her.

She realized that electricity so suddenly released corresponded to a secret signal and once again she was convinced she was on the right track. Therefore it was important to advance with extreme caution. At the end of the alley she saw a garden, and at the end of the garden a little house which appeared uninhabited. But Miss Boston was not duped by that apparent abandon. So she decided to approach the house. The important thing was to approach it without being seen, without raising the alarm, unless the electric flashes from the steel barrier hadn't already done so.

In the garden the holly and other bushes hid the walls. And while watching the walls, the detective slid skillfully behind these bushes and continued to advance. Nothing seemed suspicious; everything seemed actually abandoned. Nevertheless, Miss Boston remained cautious. In a 15 minute walk she reached the back of the house. She realized that nothing would be easier for her than to enter a little, low door. The lock was very simple. When she had checked to see that nothing was suspicious, with a silent snap of the jimmy, she opened it. She found herself inside a little room having only one door opening onto another room. No furniture, nothing.

While listening for noises, the detective went into the second room. She heard nothing. She advanced. That second room had three doors; two were closed. The only one open, the third, Miss Boston, went through. Of the two doors there, only one was open. The detective then entered the fourth room where there was no door but the one she had just entered. She saw the flooring was made of steel plates like those she had already seen in the alleyway. A harsh, violent noise made her turn around. What was happening? The door of the room had just closed. Miss Boston went to it quickly and tried to open it. Useless! The bolt wouldn't give. Suddenly a green and blue light filled the whole room while thousands of sparks crackled in flashing bouquets exactly like fire crackers. Electricity exploded from all parts of the flooring. Miss Boston knew she had fallen into a trap. But it was too late! Whatever the cost, she had to find a way to escape if there was still time! Alas! It seemed this time the detective was lost. She wanted to throw herself against the door, but that door was reinforced with steel. It resisted all the detective's desperate efforts. The electricity surrounded her with its magnetic current. She felt her strength leave her; she grew weak, closed her eyes and fainted among the showers of little blue and green crackling flames that licked at her.

Miss Boston was right to be wary in the alleyway when the steel plates had released sprays of electricity. That crackling had warned the thieves who lived in the seemingly abandoned house. Their diabolical ingenuity had thus rigged the house and warned about the detective's search. From room to room, the courageous young woman had walked toward the trap. Despite her intelligence and genius she had fallen into the ambush so cleverly prepared. As soon as she fainted, the electric crackling stopped. The door immediately opened and the two men that Miss Boston had trailed from Falls Station entered.

"There she is, that damned detective," said the one whose dirty knee Miss Boston had noticed.

"Not possible. Was she already on our trail?" asked the other one.

"You can very well see, Mors, since there she is."

"That's true, Teddy, but what're we going to do about it?"

"You know the chief's orders?"

"The same death as for Patson, the detective from last month."

"Exactly, since that worked so well, we have no reason not to do the same thing."

"Then, this evening we'll throw the detective on the subway tracks?"

"Yes. In the meantime we're going to leave her here and get the chief's orders about the jewelry."

"Say, Teddy, I have an idea."

"What?"

"The Broadway jewelry, everything considered, we're the ones who took them without anyone's help."

"Oh, no, with the chief's help."

"What do you mean, the chief? He didn't come; he never comes; he's never seen anywhere."

"That's possible, but he prepares the operations. He's the one who set up the Broadway job and the way to carry it out."

"That's possible, but…"

"But what? What's your idea?"

"To skip out on the first transatlantic about to sail. We'll split two ways, Teddy."

"If I tell the chief about your idea, you're done for. But since you're a nice guy, I won't say anything. I'll keep what you've said to myself. As for your idea, it won't work."

"Why?"

"Because the jewels are hot, well known. It would be impossible for us to get rid of them. No fence in Europe or America would agree to take them and we would run the risk of dying of hunger with three million dollars' worth of gems in our pocket."

"But the chief himself will easily get rid of them. So how does he do it?"

"That's his secret, Mors. I don't know it. That's why he's the chief. He knows how."

"So?"

"So, we're going to ask for his orders about the gems. He'll tell us what has to be done. While we're waiting they'll stay in the cellar hiding place. At the same time we'll ask him his orders about that damned detective."

"There's a terrible breeze through here, Teddy. Close the door."

"No use. We're leaving."

"Are we leaving Miss Boston there?"

"With the door closed and fainted as she is, there's nothing to fear. There's no remedy for electricity in the way it's been applied here."

"The chief will be happy when he learns about our prize!"

"I'll say. With good reason, and I bet, Mors, that we'll earn some extra dough for our information."

"So much the better, Teddy. We need it."

The two robbers went out, leaving Miss Boston still unconscious in the mysterious room where electricity, their accomplice, had carried out their hideous crime against the brave young woman.

VI. On the Metropolitan Railroad Tracks

Night falls quickly in autumn. Dusk that day was about 5 p.m., immersing and hiding all that far off quarter in twilight. Already deserted during daylight, this neighborhood became frightening solitude at the approach of night. You could wander through it for hours in every direction without meeting a living soul. That's why, at about 8 p.m., two men, carrying a rather heavy bundle under their arms, came out of the alleyway of the electric house. It was Mors and Teddy carrying the still unconscious detective. Teddy glanced rapidly around, and having made sure everything was deserted as usual, said to Mors, who was waiting, holding the detective's body:

"We can leave."

"Nothing around?"

"Nothing."

"Lift up the detective. I'll take the arms."

"All right. I'll take the legs."

Then the men went rapidly across Koch Street into a narrow little lane formed by hedges enclosing gardens. At the end of that lane was a fence made of boards that the carpenter had sharpened to a point at the top. Teddy and Mors followed that cloister for about 20 feet, then suddenly stopped. They dropped the detective on the ground carelessly, not noticing where. It fell in a puddle of water which splashed over Miss Boston and spurted in wet showers over the two robbers. Mors complained a little, but didn't lose any time in vain swear words. With Teddy, he took off three boards from the fence. Each of the three boards was marked with a white cross and an arrow. It was apparently not the first time they had been taken off because they came away easily. A passage large enough for a man to get through was opened in the board fence. Teddy and Mors slid through the fence, still carrying the detective completely soaked by the fall into the puddle of water. They were now at the top of a grassy bank overlooking the Metropolitan subway tracks. The lights of the station could be seen in the distance, while the red signal lights alternately flashed and dimmed some distance from there. To descend the slope, a stairway reinforced by pieces of wood had been cut into the bank. Teddy and Mors descended very slowly and with the greatest difficulty, because the weight of the detective's body halted them every few moments. Finally, they reached the Metropolitan subway tracks.

"Here?" asked Mors.

"Yes, here," answered Teddy laconically.

The detective was placed on the tracks, her head on one rail, her legs over the other. The passing train would crush her completely. It was a hellish plan. Who would think anything but that Miss Boston had been the victim of a horrible accident? Just as she had been thrown down there, the whistle of a train was heard in the distance. In the obscurity its red lights could be seen approaching and its whistle was getting closer.

"Quick! Quick!" said Mors. "Let's go back up."

And with Teddy, he scrambled rapidly up the stairway of the slope. The locomotive was approaching.

Back at the board fence, Teddy said to Mors: "We'll let the train go by and then we'll go down and see if the detective has been smashed as she was supposed to be. If something went wrong, we'll be there to finish her off."

"Oh! Don't worry about that!" said Mors. "When you've had a train run over your body, there isn't much more to say and even less to do."

"I know that, but those are the chief's orders."

"In that case..."

In the obscurity the two thieves tried to locate the position of Miss Boston's body, but the night was already so dark it was impossible for them to distinguish one thing from another. Suddenly the locomotive appeared with its puffing smoke stack, its clacking pistons, its roaring boilers, the red flame of its furnace, and the sharp strident screech of its whistle which hooted in the night to announce the arrival in the Greenpont station. It was no more than 10 or 20 meters from Miss Boston's corpse. Those 20 meters would be passed over in a lightning flash. Leaning over the shadow of the rails, their hearts beating, the two robbers were waiting, watching... Suddenly the train slowed down. It had come to a rather sharp curve, forcing it to decrease its speed, especially since it was approaching the station. Mors punched Teddy's shoulder.

"It's slowing down...Maybe it's failed..."

"No it hasn't...It's the curve...You know the same thing happened the last time..."

"The train always slows down?"

"Yes, always. It's the curve, I tell you."

As these rapid words were exchanged in a low voice on the top of the embankment, the train passed by. The curve passed, it little by little picked up
speed. The two thieves saw the illuminated windows of the compartments pass
by. That took hardly a minute. Soon the train was lost in the distance, in the
direction of the Greenpont Station.

"Let's go see what's left of the great and famous detective," Teddy laughed
satanically.

They went down the embankment stairs to the tracks, Teddy going ahead.
They went immediately to the spot where they had placed Miss Boston.

"It's amazing how dark it is," he complained. And speaking to Mors he
said: "Hand me the electric torch."

Mors took the flashlight used by American burglars out of his pocket and
turned it on. Shining that light on the rails, Teddy searched.

"Oh! Now that's extraordinary." Teddy grumbled.

"What's that, Teddy?"

"She's not there anymore!"

Mors explored the rails with the help of the flashlight and like Teddy he
verified that there was not the slightest trace of the detective.

"Oh! Oh!" he exclaimed, "What could that mean exactly?"

Teddy thought.

"She might have been dragged a little further on by the locomotive."

"Let's check that out," said Mors.

The two explored the rails carefully, one on each side. Their search turned
up empty. Nothing remained of the famous detective!

"Listen Mors," said Teddy. "There's something funny in this. The detective couldn't disappear like this without a reason. The smart thing to do is to get out of here, go back to the house, and send the package of jewels to the boss. After that, we'll go to the hideout."

"You're right, Teddy. Now that Miss Boston has stuck her nose in, who knows what she has in store for us, if by some miracle she's escaped being crushed by the subway?"

"Huh! Huh! This begins to stink to me, Mors. Let's get out, but first to the jewels. Let's not let the three million dollars' worth of gems fall into the detective's paws. That's something that would have a great effect on the boss!"

VII. The Two Faces of the Mystery

The two thieves left the subway tracks and went back up the embankment stairs. At the top they replaced the three detached planks carefully and, hurrying, regained Koch Street. Teddy scrutinized the neighboring streets, and having seen everything was quiet, he and Mors crossed the alley quickly and went through a little door into the house where Miss Boston had been ambushed.

"I need a drink of whiskey to settle my nerves," Mors said.

"Coward!" Teddy jeered.

"Oh! I'm not afraid," the thief defended himself. "But I'm not used to it yet."

"Ah! It's easy to see that you're still a beginner on the job. So, go on then, drink some whiskey and then we'll go down to pick up the package."

From a little cabinet set in the wall, Teddy took out a dusty decanter from which he poured a drink into a glass. Mors drank with evident satisfaction.

"That hits the spot," he said. "That warms me up."

"Let's go. Get up some courage. It's going to take some tonight if we have the cops on our backs. Are you all right?"

"Yes," said Mors. "I'm ready to go."

"All right. Let's go down."

Teddy lit a lamp and they went down to the cellars of the electric house by a little spiral stairway usually hidden in the thickness of the walls. That staircase had 62 steps and ended in a little cold, humid room littered with old upright barrels the length of the walls. Teddy went to one of the barrels with its iron bands painted in red and made it pivot. It immediately revealed a little low door closed by a sheet of steel, exactly like a safe. That door was closed by a complicated set of letters. Teddy opened it in an instant and, crawling, slid through it. Mors followed him and thus entered an underground room furnished with an iron bed, a mattress, and steel boxes containing provisions. This refuge served as a secret hideout for the robbers and let the police search the entire house without discovering them.

The police, if they did discover the hiding place, could only enter one by one. The thieves would cut them down as they slid through the little low, narrow door. It was obvious the thing had been put together ingeniously. However, Teddy didn't stop in that room. He went directly to the wall at the back and pushed with all his strength. That wall was also false. It slanted back slowly and thus formed the floor for a new room. It contained only seven planks of wood fixed to the wall. On these shelves were boxes, chests, and little packages, the hauls from various thefts of jewelry, securities, or precious objects awaiting the order of the chief to send them to him. In addition that room had a telephone, by which the invisible chief gave instructions. Teddy went to the third shelf and searched among the packages. Mors saw him suddenly become terribly pale.

"What's wrong, Teddy?" he asked.

"The chest..." stammered the robber.

"What...What..."

Mors in his turn began to tremble.

"The...chest...isn't there anymore."

"Search again...maybe you put it on another shelf."

"No...no...I'm certain I put it on the third shelf, and it's not there anymore! Somebody's been here, Mors!"

A frightening silence followed his words. Mors, terrified, trembled all over.

"What should we do?" What should we do?" he stammered.

Teddy himself, so decided, so daring, had lost all his assurance. The discovery he'd just made had literally torn him to pieces. He couldn't believe his eyes. Finally, he said:

"Ah! I knew the detective's disappearance had something of..."

But he didn't have time to finish. A strange noise at the steel door of the hideout stopped the words on his lips.

"Silence! There's somebody there!"

"Who's there?"

"Me! Miss Boston!" A voice cried out, and that voice was that of the courageous detective. The thieves staggered back, wild-eyed. Miss Boston, because it was she, very much alive, in flesh and blood, was leaning through the low door of the hideout and saw the thieves who were carefully loading their revolvers ready to defend their lives.

"No use to fire," she shouted to them.

"Damn!" swore Teddy.

"I give you two minutes to throw your guns out the door!" shouted Miss Boston." I know there are no other revolvers in the cellar. Throw out those you have and then you'll come out separately. It's useless to resist! You're caught!"

"Not yet!" screamed Teddy.

"Give up!"

"Never!"

At the same time a prolonged crackling was heard and the celebrated detective distinctly saw that Teddy and Mors had just pulled down in front of them the false wall of the second cellar.

She knew perfectly well that second cellar had no way out and that in closing the wall, the two robbers had sealed themselves in. She then decided to go into the first cellar. The two thieves were sealed in with their thefts.

Raising her voice, she yelled:

"Teddy and Mors, I'm here. The police will be here in five minutes. Tear down the wall and I'll arrest you. You'll have harmed your case by resisting arrest. For that violation the High Court will add ten years at hard labor to those you'll get for the Broadway theft. These ten years, I give you two minutes to avoid them. You'd be smart to give yourselves up because the game's up for you. You have two minutes. I repeat. I'm taking out my watch."

On the face of her watch the detective followed the slow movement of the hand and at the end of a lapse of silence she said:

"One more minute, Teddy and Mors."

But from behind the wall she heard a derisive laugh. She looked at her watch one last time.

"Two minutes!" she said. "Now it's too late." And she sat down on a chair, her revolver in her hand. At the same instant a voice coming from the ground floor shouted to her:

"Where are you, Miss Boston?"

"Down here!" she answered. "Is that you, Sokes?"

"Yes, Miss Boston!"

The detective shouted the way to follow to the Inspector and a minute later Sokes entered the hideout with a squad of policemen. When he saw the detective alone, he seemed to be disappointed.

"The birds are flown?" he asked.

"No, in the cage," answered Miss Boston.

"Where's that?"

"There, behind the wall."

"But there's no door!"

"Yes, there is. The wall is fake."

"What do you suggest?"

"Have your men break down the wall; it's made of wood."

"Get to it!" Sokes commanded the police.

The six men worked together as flying buttresses against the partition and with a strong and vigorous movement made it give way.

The partition fell into the second cellar and a cry of anger and astonishment broke from Miss Boston.

The cellar was empty.

VIII. The Telephone Passageway

Miss Boston explained her close call to Sokes.

She said that when Teddy and Mors had dropped her in the puddle of water, the sudden coolness and freshness of the puddle had soaked through and brought her out of her faint.

Little by little, she had come to life and by the time the thieves had placed her on the tracks she had completely recovered. She was careful not to show that she had returned to consciousness. Stretched out on the rails, she knew what the robbers had in mind. She thanked Heaven and her lucky stars that she hadn't been bound. In that case, her situation would have been a thousand times more serious and more dangerous. She knew the criminals wanted her death to look like a simple accident.

She waited until they had gone back up the stairs to the embankment and only then did she get up, throwing herself to one side of the roaring locomotive. Miss Boston knew she had fallen into the hands of the Broadway robbers. She remembered Teddy's words about the case containing the three million dollars' worth of gems hidden in the cellar. Her triumph over the thieves depended solely on her speed.

All these thoughts had gone through Miss Boston's mind like a bolt of lightning. The train having slowed down for the curve, came abreast of her. When it passed, Miss Boston, with a bound as brave as daring, jumped on the footboard of a compartment, and, clinging to the emergency bar running the length of the cars, she arrived at Greenpont Station.

Without losing time with explanations to the controller she ran to the station master's telephone, demanded to be connected to the Central Police Administration, informed Sokes of the state of things, and asked him to come with six policemen to the house on Koch Street.

Then without stopping she had run from Greenpont Station to the electric house, and had courageously entered, her two revolvers drawn.

She had carefully avoided the two rooms where the ambush had taken place that morning. A few minutes searching had led her to the cellar staircase. One of the barrels lined up against the wall must cover a hiding place.

At the sixth one she moved, she found the little steel door that she opened with her jimmy. From there she entered the hideout. Tapping the walls to see if a cabinet hadn't been hidden there, she found that the one at the back sounded hollow. In tapping the wall she had accidently pushed on the secret button that made it slide back.

She soon found the seven shelves with the stolen gems. She took the case containing Miss Aymes' marriage presents, raised the fake wall again, left the hideout, closed the steel door firmly, rolled the barrel back in front of it, and reached the garden of the house just as Teddy and Mors came back from the

Metropolitan subway tracks. For the reasons Sokes now knew, they had not found the cadaver of the famous detective.

Miss Boston, seeing the two criminals emerge from the alley, threw herself into the bushes along the wall of the enclosure among the shrubs. She put the precious case there, covered it with a bed of dead leaves, and picking up her revolvers again, went for the third time into the house where the two bandits had disappeared. The open door of the cellar clearly pointed out that Teddy and Mors had gone down to their secret hide out. She followed them there; just at the moment they verified the disappearance of the gems, she called out to them to surrender. A little later, Sokes and the six policemen arrived.

When the wall was reversed, the cellar was empty. Miss Boston's cry of astonishment was answered by the roar of fury of the policemen who thus saw the criminals escape under their noses. Miss Boston recovered quickly. How had the criminals escaped? Looking around for a minute, she understood. The telephone she had noticed at her first visit lay broken on the floor. It had been snatched from the wall and in its place was a round hole, a sort of hallway wide enough for a man. The two robbers had slipped through this passage.

"Sokes, follow me," commanded Miss Boston. "We have a chance of catching these fellows."

And still holding her revolvers, she slid into the telephone corridor. Walking there was exceedingly difficult because they had to bend almost in double so as not to knock against the stone wall that jutted out over their heads. It took the two detectives almost a quarter of an hour to reach the end of the passage. There it was ended by old shafts in the walls which were sealed up with little iron bars permitting access to the outside world. Miss Boston and Sokes soon climbed them and came out in a wasteland. It seemed to be in the middle of a field. At that moment the Moon appeared from behind a cloud. Its pale rays lit up the landscape.

"We're on the Ascott Road," Sokes said as he got his bearings.

Preoccupied with looking for the two fugitives, Miss Boston didn't say anything. She was keenly searching the horizon, when suddenly she seized the Inspector's arm.

"Look," she said

"Where's that, Miss Boston?"

"Down there! On the road."

"But, by God! I really think those are our crooks!"

In fact, the two running shadows couldn't be other than those of Teddy and Mors.

"All right, Sokes, keep your revolvers ready. We're going to go after them."

And the two detectives, after having checked their arms, jumped into the ditch which bordered the road. The grass in the ditch muffled the sound of their steps and allowed them to lie flat on their stomach if Teddy and Mors turned around. A minute later the chase began.

IX. Manhunt in the Woolwich Suburb

Clearly the two thieves were hurrying toward the Woolwich suburb. This area was more deserted than Chelsea, but even though deserted it nonetheless had a bad reputation. Miss Boston had to prevent the two criminals from reaching this suburb, because there they could slip into a saloon or into a familiar house. Under these conditions their capture, if not impossible, would be at least extremely difficult. The brave young woman slipped into the ditch, gaining ground on the thieves with each step. Once Mors made a movement as if to turn around. At the same instant Miss Boston fell flat on the grass. Sokes, who had not seen the robber's movement, was forced to jump over her. Fortunately it was only a false alarm. But that put Sokes in front, ahead of Miss Boston. Almost at the same time, Sokes let out a muffled cry. He had just sunk right up to his waist into a section of the ditch full of mud. He got out of it, fuming, but the detective had already jumped up to the road, pursuing the thieves. Despite the speed of these movements, one of the two bandits, Teddy, had escaped and disappeared. Miss Boston didn't lose any precious time trying to find which way he had fled. She rushed on the heels of Mors, who had just reached the first houses of Bander Road, where the Woolwich suburb began. The robber's agility was great. That of the celebrated detective wasn't less so. She was gaining on Mors with each step. She was about to reach him when suddenly he dashed into an evil-looking house on Bander Road. Miss Boston followed him. Mors climbed the steps four at a time, and when he came to the last floor of the house, broke in a door with a vigorous blow of his shoulder. The door was in splinters and he disappeared into the room. Two seconds later, the detective went in too. The room was empty. The skylight to the roof was open. Mors had disappeared through it. With an agile, rapid movement Miss Boston hoisted herself through the skylight and reached the roof. She soon saw Mors, who was slipping from chimney to chimney, holding on with difficulty, because the night mist had made the slope of the roofs excessively wet and dangerous. But that wasn't something to hold back the detective. She hurled herself in pursuit of the criminal, who, in that dangerous game played his last and supreme card.

Miss Boston, before using extreme measures, thought it right to warn him.

"Mors," she yelled at him, "stop or I fire!"

But the criminal didn't answer and continued his doomed flight. Miss Boston decided to act. She lifted her revolver, took aim, and fired. But the shot certainly missed its target, because the detective saw the criminal make a prodigious leap into the void. A moment later, she found Mors had reached a roof facing the street. There was only emptiness in front of him. Between the roof where he was and that of the neighboring house facing the street, there was a distance of at least six meters. Pressed by danger, having the detective on his heels, he didn't hesitate to make the jump. Fatal movement! He had in his jump reached the rainspout of the house across the street. Under the shock and the weight of his body, the rainspout had bent and had sent him bounding into the street. Miss Boston saw him lying unconscious on the pavement. She used a quick and simple method to get down to the street. She grabbed the drain pipe and slid down to the sidewalk.

But at the same time three individuals came into the street and surrounded Mors' body. They took out their revolvers when they saw the detective approach.

"Leave!" commanded the detective,

"What do you want here?" asked one of the men.

"It's not up to me to answer you," retorted the detective.

"Clear out!" said one of the men. "Or else our guns will sing you a pretty tune."

And they pointed their weapons toward the brave young woman in a menacing way. Just then someone came to stand beside her. It was Sokes come to the end of the race.

"Here I am, Miss Boston, and not too late, I think, to be able to help you."

"No, Sokes, you arrive just in time."

"All right! Faster than that; beat it!" those surrounding Mors, still stretched out unmoving on the pavement, again shouted.

As the only response, Sokes and Miss Boston raised their revolvers, and the detective shouted:

"I give you, gentlemen, one minute to clear out. That's all I can allow you."

A volley of profanity answered her and immediately the men fired three shots.

The detectives immediately shot back, and their shots must have hit their target because the three individuals didn't repeat their orders and, screaming with pain, made off. They disappeared in the darkness at the end of the street, abandoning Mors' body. Miss Boston then approached the body.

"Is he dead?" asked Sokes.

"I don't think so."

"That would be too bad."

Miss Boston felt the thief's body.

"He's still warm. Nevertheless his heart beat is weak."

"Where is he wounded, Miss Boston?" Sokes asked.

"I think he has a broken leg, Mr. Sokes," the detective answered after examining the unconscious man.

"Then you didn't shoot him?"

"No, Sokes."

"Nevertheless, I heard a shot go off."

"Yes, I shot, but I missed."

"You missed him, Miss Boston? Impossible, with the accuracy of your shooting."

"Perfectly. I missed him because he jumped. Something I wasn't expecting."

"Then you chased him over the roof?"

"Yes. And his broken leg is due to his fall."

"But the other one. What's happened to him?"

"Right now I don't know. But we'll catch him. We're going to take this fellow to a pharmacy before we wrap him up for the Central Bureau."

Sokes and the detective picked up the wounded man with a thousand precautions and went down toward Bander Road. There they were lucky to find a little pharmacy still open. They gave Mors basic medical attention after having brought him to with strong spirits. During this time Sokes had gone looking for a cab that he brought five minutes later. Mors was put inside where he howled as much with pain as with rage.

"Take this fellow to the infirmary of the Central Bureau, Sokes," said the detective.

"What, Miss Boston? You're not coming with me?"

"No, because I have a little package to pick up at Greenpont."

"And without being indiscrete, may I ask you what package, Miss Boston?"

"Oh! There's no indiscretion in that, Sokes. That's just the stolen jewelry from Mr. Flipper's."

"The three million dollars' worth of Miss Aymes' jewelry?"

"Precisely."

"You recovered them?"

"No problem."

Miss Boston cut short Sokes's praise and arranged to meet him at the Central Police Bureau that evening.

The cab with the wounded robber left at a trot in the direction of central New York. Miss Boston started toward the electric house in Greenpont. She arrived there a half-hour later and as she expected found it completely empty. She made a routine investigation. She found nothing except the stolen jewels on the seven shelves of the second cellar. She put them in a valise she found, not to her surprise, exactly like the one abandoned by the Broadway thieves in the sub-basement of Mr. Flippers' great store. She added these jewels to the case hidden in the garden bushes and satisfied with her busy work day, carrying the valise, she left to take the Greenpont subway.

The travelers in the compartment where she took a seat didn't at all suspect that that pretty and elegant young woman, her clothes a little in disarray from all the events of the day, carried with her, in that little valise, the three million dollars' worth of jewelry, wedding presents of Miss Aymes, the fiancée of Mac Gins, the nephew of the petroleum king.

X. The Mystery of the Invisible Man

It was almost 11 p.m. then Miss Boston walked into the Central Police Bureau. She met the Head of the Detectives Administrative Division. He had come, as every day before going home, to glance over the reports of the day's events.

"Good evening, Miss Boston," he said, shaking her hand. "What happy circumstance brings you to our neighborhood this evening?" Noticing the valise the detective was carrying, he added:

"Are you coming back from a trip?"

"Oh! From not very far away," answered the famous young woman, smiling.

"You seem to be watching over your valise!" said the Chief of Police, laughing. "You'd think it contained the royal crown jewels."

"Almost, sir," Miss Boston replied.

"What do you mean, almost?"

"The valise in fact holds the jewels of a princess."

"What joke is that, Miss Boston?"

"It's not a joke at all; it's the truth."

"I don't understand."

"In America we have only kings of industry don't we? The steel king, the railway king, the transatlantic steamer king, the petroleum king, the gold king."

"Yes, and so?"

"These are the jewels of the steel queen that I have in my valise."

"You've recovered the jewelry stolen from Flippers on Broadway and you have them there? That's fantastic, Miss Boston."

"I have something even better, sir."

"What's that?"

"I have one of the thieves."

"Arrested?"

"He's here!"

The Chief of Police's astonishment and admiration were translated into the most eloquent of silences. Miss Boston preceded him into his office. Inspector Sokes came to join them some minutes later. Without saying a word, Miss Boston opened the valise brought from Greenpont and spread the magnificent wedding present jewelry of Miss Aymes on the Chief of Police's desk. There were streams of pearls, piles of diamonds, riots of emeralds, in essence all the splendors that the formidable sum of three millions represented.

Sokes alerted Mr. Flippers by telephone to come identify the stolen jewelry. Mors was brought into the Chief's office on a stretcher and in handcuffs. Having handled the affair from the beginning, only Miss Boston was capable of asking meaningful questions. However, before beginning, Miss Boston reviewed Mors' prior arrest sheet. She told the criminal, on his stretcher, trembling in every limb, that she knew his name was James, but was known under the name Mors, that he had done four years at hard labor in the Chicago work house for theft by forced entry of the East State Bank, and that she also knew he had, as Connor, lived on Broadway in a bedroom next to Mr. Flippers' jewelry store, a room shared with a man named Teddy, who called himself Fred.

"Then you know everything?"

"I know also that you broke through the cellar into the basement of Mr. Flippers' store; that you sawed the iron crossbeams to cause the table in the window to fall, and that you hid the gems in the house at Greenpont. I know too that I was the victim of an ambush and attempted murder by you. You wanted to have me crushed by the Metropolitan subway."

"It wasn't me...It wasn't me, Miss! It was Teddy!" The robber protested.

"You were his accomplice, that's enough," declared Miss Boston. "The high court gives the same punishment to accomplices."

"This will be the electric chair for me," trembled Mors?

"Yes, if you refuse to answer what I'm going to ask you."

"And if I don't?"

"I will forget what relates to me, that is the attempted murder and you will have to answer only for the theft. Instead of the electric chair, it will only be the iron cage at Sing Sing."

"I prefer Sing Sing, Miss."

"I can understand that. Are you ready now to answer my questions?"

"I'll tell everything I know, Miss."

"Good. On whose orders and for whose benefit did you execute the theft at Broadway? Even if I humiliate you bitterly, I must say that I don't consider you intelligent enough to have brought off such a daring job alone."

"That's true, Miss. I didn't do it alone."

"I know that. You were going along with Teddy, who seems more set in criminality than you."

"He was the one who pushed me into it. He led me into that job."

"That's up to the High Court, but I want to know who was the mastermind for whom Teddy pulled off the job."

"It was the Chief."

"What Chief?"

"I don't know, Miss."

"Do you mean to say you don't know?"

"Yes, I've never seen him. I swear to you, I'm telling the truth."

"You've never seen the Chief of your gang?"

"Never! Teddy himself has never seen him."

"Then how does he work for him?"

"The Chief only gives orders over the telephone or by letter. Those letters always come from a different place, from Cleveland, from Boston, from Chicago, from Saint-Louis, from New York, from Philadelphia, from Washington. All the jobs to pull are set up by the Chief. He's the one who puts them together, prepares them. He gives orders and advice for carrying them out. That's all."

"What do you call him?"

"The Chief."

"Chief Who, what name?"

"Chief, that's all. He's not called by any other name. But I believe Teddy knows his name. The Chief has a secret house somewhere. By telephone he commands the One Hundred Thousand Arms Gang in the four quarters of the world."

"Why the One Hundred Thousand Arms Gang?"

"Because there are so many of us we don't know each other. We work only in small groups, two, three, four or more. A mechanized, fake hideout is given to each of these groups. Ours was at Greenpont, there where you were caught."

"Where are the other hideouts?"

"I don't know, Miss, since the groups don't know each other. Only the Chief knows it."

It was beyond doubt that Mors was telling the truth and that he didn't know anything more than what he had just said. The detective found herself facing a formidable organization put together by a diabolical genius capable of holding at bay the police of the whole United States. The one who directed it understood that the real head of a gang had to remain unknown and invisible to his accomplices. Thus it was impossible for them to divulge his identity. The case of Mors was an example. Nevertheless the capture of the thief wasn't without importance because thanks to him Miss Boston learned about the organization of that gang. This might have remained enigmatic and mysterious for a very long time. In this situation the interrogation couldn't clear up anything more. In addition Mors' suffering didn't allow him to give any further useful answers. She ordered him carried back to the Central Bureau infirmary.

Just then, Mr. Flippers, the great Broadway jeweler arrived. He was brought in and shown the stolen jewels. It's useless to try to describe the joy of that honorable merchant.

"You have saved my honor," he told the brave detective.

He verified that all the jewelry was there, and after having signed a receipt, he carried them away in the valise in which Miss Boston had put them at Greenpont.

"I will keep the valise to remember this adventure by."

"Don't let it get taken from you on the way!" Miss Boston observed, smiling.

"Oh! No danger of that, this time!" the jeweler swore.

After a last "thank you" he left with the reassurance that the very next day he would deliver them to Miss Aymes. As for Miss Boston, she stayed another hour chatting with the Chief about that adventure, showing herself only halfway satisfied with the results obtained, since Teddy was still free.

"Console yourself, Miss Boston," said the chief. "You'll get lucky, you'll collar the fellow."

"I hope so," answered the detective, taking leave of the Chief and Sokes to go to Savannah City to enjoy a well-earned rest after the many dangers of that adventurous day.

The next day, toward noon, the detective received a letter and a small package. The letter contained this:

Miss Gracie Aymes begs Miss Ethel Boston for the honor of her presence at her marriage ceremony which will take place the 18th of October of this year at Chilburn Church.

As for the package, it was a jewel case containing a magnificent two tier pearl necklace—truly splendid. This present was accompanied by a visiting card:

P. C. Flippers
Jeweler
with his warmest thanks.

Miss Boston smiled at the present and murmured:

"This compensates *that* very well." *That* was the dangers run the evening before in the terrible chase of the robbers. The detective worked carefully that same day to pick up Teddy's traces. She followed his trail to the bar where she had seen him come out with Mors. The whole day was spent in fruitless investigations. The electric house at Greenpont gave up no more clues. The Central Police Bureau took away the things found there and dismantled the electrification which had almost been fatal to Miss Boston. They blocked the telephone corridor. In a word the house was put out of commission from the criminal point of view. At the end of a week's search, Miss Boston was absolutely convinced that it would be impossible for her to lay her hands on Teddy. And she left it to chance to find the one guilty of the daring robbery on Broadway.

The marriage of Miss Aymes, the daughter of the steel king with Mac Gins, the nephew of the petroleum king was celebrated at Chilburn Church the 18th of October. All New York was present at that ceremony where all the millionaires were assembled. Among those, most elegantly attired, was Miss Boston, the famous, only female detective in the whole world, accompanied by Sokes, the courageous Inspector of the Central Police Bureau. The dramatic story of the stolen jewels was known by all of New York and had made Miss Boston the heroine of the day. At the reception after the ceremony everyone greeted and congratulated the new Mrs. Mac Gins. When it came Miss Boston's turn, the young bride stepped out of the receiving line and, in a charming voice, she said simply:

"Thank you, Miss Boston," and took from her finger a magnificent ring set with enormous emeralds, surrounded by brilliants. She slid that ring on the detective's finger, saying:

"It is I, Miss Boston, who remains indebted to you."

That evening the groom sent Sokes a beautiful tie pin. Leaving Chilburn Church with Miss Boston, he remarked that the detective looked worried.

"You don't seem happy, Miss Boston," he remarked.

"I'm not, really, Sokes."

"And why is that?"

"Because I'm asking myself a question with no solution."

"Can I know what?"

"Yes, I wonder who can be the invisible Chief of the One Hundred Thousand Arms Gang?"

THE FATAL HANDSHAKE

I. A Mysterious Present

"What a pretty ring you have there, Mr. Sokes," Miss Boston, the famous woman detective said to the Central Bureau Chief Inspector, smiling.

It was one of those old rings that are found at antique jewelry stores. It had a big gemstone setting encircled by a gold enamel serpent, the tail of which formed the back of the ring inside the palm. Sokes handed the ring to Miss Boston who examined it curiously.

She asked:

"When you got this present, Sokes, were you told what this ring was?"

"No, I wasn't told for the simple reason that I don't know who gave me this ring."

Sokes explained that the ring was delivered to his office at 10 a.m. the day before when he wasn't there. The ring box had a letter in it from Mr. Flippers.

"He sent me this ring with his thanks for our capture of the thieves who stole the three million dollars' worth of jewelry."

He said he went to Mr. Flippers' store to thank him, but Mr. Flippers denied he had sent the ring.

"I apologized To Mr. Flippers for having bothered him. I went back down Broadway. Then suddenly I remembered the letter that came with the jewelry box. I took it out of my pocket; I read it. It had a letter head like this:

JAMES FLIPPERS
CENTRAL JEWELRY
BROADWAY

"I resolved to clarify this last point immediately and I went back to Mr. Flippers to whom I showed the letter. It was his turn to be extremely astonished. He was both astonished and angry about the forgery. I spent the rest of the day looking for the motive for this mysterious present."

"And you didn't find it, Sokes?" asked the famous detective.

"No, Miss Boston, because after all, that didn't seem to me terribly important."

"It seems to me, Sokes, that the present was rather unusual."

"Without a doubt, without a doubt, Miss Boston, but it could be sent by some unknown person obligated to me. But you? What's your opinion?"

"You really want to know?"

"Certainly, Miss."

"You are the victim of a plot."

"Me!"

"You, quite plainly, sir."

"And what is your basis for saying that? Miss Boston?"

"First of all by the time you were sent the package."

"But that time had nothing out of the ordinary."

"On the contrary, it was completely unusual. Everybody at the Central Bureau, agents as well as criminals, knows that at 10 a.m. you are in conference with the Chief, that in that meeting assignments, procedures, and arrests for the day are decided, and that as a consequence you are away from your office until at least 11 a.m."

"No doubt, but what can that prove?"

"That proves that the man who brought you the package was absolutely certain not to encounter you, consequently, not be obliged to explain anything about his message. He would risk even more."

"What's that?"

"Being arrested in case you noticed the forgery of Flippers' letter."

"That's true, but it seems to me that this logical argument errs most of all by the inexplicable circumstances surrounding it."

"They are less inexplicable than you think, Sokes."

"How's that?"

"You remember my first question about that ring? When making that gift, Sokes, did they tell you what that ring was?"

"Does it have something unusual about it?"

"Yes, sir, it certainly has something unusual about it."

"What's that, pray tell?"

"It's poisoned!"

II. Motives for the Gift are Vaguely Guessed

The police inspector was startled at these words.

"Poisoned!" he exclaimed. "You say the ring is poisoned, Miss Boston?"

"I say so, sir, and I'll prove it."

The detective took the ring; she pressed lightly on the ring's setting and a little drop of liquid, almost imperceptible, glistened on the serpent's tail.

Sokes cried out in astonishment.

"What does that mean, Miss Boston?"

"That means, Sokes, that the cavity inside the artificial setting contains drops of poison. Applying pressure on it, shaking hands, for example, the little pointed tail of the serpent breaks the skin of the palm. The drop of poison flows into that imperceptible scratch."

"But that's diabolical!"

"Oh! It's ingenious and made simply to deceive those who don't get to the bottom of things."

"Then you believe…"

"That the gift was made with a predetermined purpose."

"And that end?"

"It was to get rid of me."

Sokes' astonishment was so great he was silent. Nevertheless, the detective, following her logical and inflexible reasoning, continued her explanation.

"It's known that we're close, that we make the most difficult and dangerous searches and investigations together. Now, Sokes, we've just attacked a dreaded group, the One Hundred Thousand Arms Gang commanded by the Invisible Man. What is the result of our investigation to date? We've captured only one accomplice, and what a poor and mediocre accomplice he is! And we've discovered a single hideout, which will be useful for nothing in the future because it's been torn down."

"Those are some accomplishments, Miss Boston!"

"Of course, but clearly diminished by our bad luck in letting escape the main guilty one who had pulled off the daring Broadway robbery, the one named Teddy. This Teddy was apparently one of the Invisible Man's lieutenants and was in on a lot of secrets. His escape alerted the whole gang. But anyway, we have to take the good with the bad. If Teddy escaped, it was a miracle, that's all."

"And what to you make of all this, Miss?"

"My conclusion, sir, is that the Invisible Man gave Teddy orders to do away with me and you were chosen as the intermediary. In that way suspicion was diverted from those really guilty."

"That wasn't a bad idea."

"You must admit, Sokes, that outwitting it wasn't bad either."

"Oh! Miss Boston, for you!"

"This isn't the time for compliments, sir. I want to give you yet another proof to show you evidence that the gift of the ring came exclusively from the One Hundred Thousand Arms Gang."

"And what is that?"

"You'll see, Sokes, if, however, I'm accurate in what I expect. Let's go to the Central Bureau."

From Savannah City, where the famous detective lived, she took a cab, which went down 9th Avenue at a fast trot toward the center of New York to the offices of the Central Police Administration. On the way, she said to Sokes:

"If I remember correctly, sir, you've never seen Teddy."

"No, since when I arrived at the time of his attempted arrest, he had already gotten away. I only caught sight of his heels."

"That's really not enough as a description," Miss Boston joked.

"That's a fact!"

"Then since you can't recognize him, I'm going to describe him to you. Actually, it's rather simple. Teddy is of medium height, clean-shaven when he needs to be, has blue eyes, a scar on the right side of his nose. And that's description enough; I don't need to talk about his clothes, because the fellow changes disguises..."

"Just like a detective!"

Miss Boston smiled.

"That's the only ground," she said, "where detectives and lawbreakers are sometimes equal."

They had arrived at the Central Bureau.

"Where are we going, Miss," Sokes asked. "To the Chief?"

"No, to the desk clerks of your office."

"Ah! You want to interview them about the man who brought the package."

"Exactly. Go ahead of me, Sokes."

Sokes, followed by Miss Boston, in the very busy hallways of the Central Administration, greeted by everyone they met, reached the clerks' antechamber. Everyone rose when they entered because their respect was mingled with a kind of admiration for the exploits of the courageous young woman, the terror of the United States' criminals. Miss Boston behaved toward them in a friendly and open way, without familiarity. Those were the reasons she was adored at the Central Bureau.

"My friends," she said on entering the clerks' offices, which one of you yesterday morning, at 10 a.m., received the little package for Mr. Sokes?"

One of the clerks came forward.

"I did, Miss Boston," he said.

"Ah! It was you, Humphrey, my friend. Good. You'll probably be able to furnish me details about the man who brought the package."

"Possibly, Miss."

With some small amount of prompting Humphrey remembered that the deliveryman was of medium height, had dark hair, was clean-shaven, and had only one identifying mark, a scar on the right side of his nose.

"Marvelous, Humphrey. We've got it now." And the detective looked triumphantly at Sokes, who stood amazed.

"Did you understand, sir?" she asked.

"If I understand correctly, Miss Boston," the Inspector answered, "that's point by point the description of Teddy that Humphrey's just given."

And smiling, the detective retorted:

"That's all I wanted to show you, Sokes."

"Then this is becoming serious."

"I've never doubted it, sir, particularly if Teddy has returned to the scene."

"Yes, he's a bold fellow."

"There's the focus of the job."

"I'm afraid so."

Sokes went into his office to look over the reports which had come in during his absence. He hadn't been there five minutes when the clerk Miss Boston questioned entered.

"What is it Humphrey," asked the Inspector.

"The Chief wants you, sir."

"Immediately?"

"Yes, right now."

"What's happened?"

"A crime at Hyde Park, it seems."

III. The Mysterious Hyde Park Cadaver

Three minutes later the two detectives entered the office of the Chief of Police of the Central Bureau.

"You're arriving just in time, Miss Boston," said the chief, on seeing the brave young woman enter.

"What's the matter, sir?"

"A crime in Hyde Park, Miss Boston."

"What are the circumstances?"

"I still don't know at the present time. The police station at Grammercy Avenue has just phoned me the information with few details. The thing took place at Park Hotel. Unfortunately, I can't go there right now. I have important depositions to take. I'm going to ask Inspector Sokes to take charge of initial investigation."

"If you don't see any objections, sir," Miss Boston said, "I would ask you to authorize me to accompany Mr. Sokes."

"I was going to ask you to do so," the Inspector put in.

"Gladly," the Chief said and he added:

"I won't leave my office before 6 a.m. If you have any news for me, you'll find me here until then."

"Right, Chief!"

Miss Boston and Inspector Sokes left his office to go directly to Hyde Park. From the Central Administration to Hyde Park is a relatively long way, almost an hour, and so the detectives took an automobile to cover the distance.

Park Hotel, as its name implies, is a great restaurant hotel situated in Hyde Park, one of the elegant sections of New York. This restaurant, well known by all the "gentry," is usually frequented by a clientele as choice as it is elegant, composed of stock brokers, bankers, directors of industrial companies, or financiers. They come there to negotiate or conclude business over excellent lunches or dinners. The manager of Hyde Park Hotel is Mr. Joe Holborn. He met Miss Boston and Sokes in his office on their arrival. Two gentlemen who appeared to be doctors were standing over a couch in that office. The body of a person elegantly dressed, rather large, red haired, solid, lay stretched out there.

"Is that the victim?" asked Miss Boston as soon as she was introduced to Mr. Joe Holborn.

"Yes, Miss, but victim is perhaps an exaggeration."

"How's that sir? Didn't someone telephone the Central Bureau that it was a matter of a crime?"

"I don't know, Miss, but the two doctors over there don't believe that it's a question of murder. Besides, in my business, a very respectable business…"

Never wasting her time, always efficient in work, the detective turned toward the two doctors and said to them:

"I'm Miss Boston. The gentleman accompanying me is Mr. Sokes, the Inspector from the Central Bureau; we are charged with the preliminary investigations. What did the man whose body you've just examined die from, gentlemen?"

"I know nothing about that," said the first doctor.

"But the cause of death?"

"The autopsy will determine that, Miss. That person may have succumbed to a heart attack, to heart trouble. We wouldn't be telling you anything by saying what is only guess work."

"Then that's the present case?"

"Oh! Exactly!"

"Then it wasn't worth the trouble to bring us out for so little if it was only a matter here of an accidental death," said Sokes, in a tone of obvious bad humor.

However, Miss Boston's principle of acting only with absolute facts and logic caused her to question Mr. Joe Holborn about the circumstances surrounding the deceased.

"This gentleman," he answered, "dined here with one of his friends. It was scarcely 20 minutes ago that they shook hands and parted company. The dead man here, having forgotten his coat, returned to look for it. He hadn't taken ten steps than he fell down dead."

The fact of that handshake struck the detective. Mr. Joe Holborn had scarcely pronounced these words than the detective walked toward the couch where the body was stretched out and took his hand. She quickly turned it palm side up. Sokes immediately heard her murmur:

"So there's the explanation."

The people who had witnessed that scene had drawn near Miss Boston.

"What's there?" the doctors asked.

"This," the detective answered concisely.

They all leaned over the hand of the dead man. A little drop of blood glistened in the up-turned palm.

"But that's only a drop of blood," exclaimed Mr. Joe Holborn.

"No, it's more and it's better," retorted the famous detective in dry and firm tone.

"Then what is it?"

"The proof of the crime."

The doctors let out a cry of amazement. "What?" they exclaimed.

"That man was murdered," Miss Boston responded forcefully.

One of the doctors, faced with such a categorical affirmation, shrugged.

"I would be very curious to learn how it was done!" he sneered, his scientist's ego wounded by the cold and determined assurance of the young woman.

She in her turn was no less wounded by the doctor's ironic question. She walked over to Sokes and took off from his finger the ring so mysteriously sent by Teddy; that was no longer in doubt. The ring in her hand, she went over to the doctor, placed it under his nose and scornfully said:

"Here's the instrument of the crime."

"That ring?"

"Yes, gentlemen, just that ring."

"Oh! Oh! And how did that happen?"

"Like this."

The detective pressed on the setting and the little drop of poison again glistened on the sharp tail of the golden serpent.

"What is that?"

"That's poison."

"And the dead man there was poisoned in that manner?"

"The autopsy will show it with no doubt, sir."

Silence fell in the office. The manager and the doctors began to doubt. That attitude did not surprise the detective. She was used to seeing the most hesitant lose their assurance confronted by the logical assertions that she put forward only with exact knowledge.

"I know," she said, "how the victim was struck down, but I also know who the murderer was."

"What…you?..." stammered Mr. Joe Holborn.

"Yes, answered the detective, "and I'm going to prove it to you right now. Didn't you tell me the victim had dined with a friend and that friend had shaken hands with him? Well, without having seeing him, I'm going to describe that friend to you."

"Then he was the murderer?"

"Yes, and I know his name."

"What's that?"

"He's a man named Teddy. But before going any further, Mr. Holborn would you please call the headwaiter who served lunch to those two gentlemen?"

Through an intercom installed on his desk, Joe Holborn ordered the hotel office to send up the headwaiter Miss Boston asked for. A few minutes later someone knocked on the office door.

"Come in!" shouted the manager,

The head waiter entered.

IV. The Circle of Destruction Closes Around Teddy

The headwaiter looked like people of his class who work in great establishments. He was serious and solemn.

"Tom," said Mr. Holborn, we have a few questions for you. Please answer those the lady here is going to ask you."

"Yes, sir," the head waiter answered.

With one look, Miss Boston summed up the man. He seemed to her insignificant, nothing remarkable.

"Waiter," she said to him.

But the man interrupted her sharply with a totally comic gravity.

"I'm not a waiter," he said. "I'm a maître d'hôtel."

The detective smiled at that claim.

She continued: "Maître d'hôtel, then, please tell me if you served at table today at lunch the person lying on that couch."

"Exactly, Miss. I also believe that is the same person who suddenly fainted under the hotel's canopy."

"You're not completely mistaken. It is the same person in fact, but he wasn't alone at the table..."

"That's right."

"The gentleman having lunch with that person was of medium height, wasn't he?"

"Yes."

"With dark hair?"

"Exactly."

"With a scar on the right side of his nose?"

"In fact, that's what I noticed."

"Was he clean-shaven?"

"That's right, too."

"Then you have seen this person?" asked Joe Holborn, addressing Miss Boston.

She, remembering her dangerous and tragic encounter with Teddy in the electrified house at Greenpont limited herself to answering, smiling, only:

"That's right. I have seen him before...but in different circumstances."

Then, continuing to question the maître d'hôtel:

"You didn't notice anything during the course of the meal?"

"Nothing, no, Miss, except that at coffee the victim signed a check that he gave to the brunet man."

"And that's all."

"Yes, that's really all."

"Very good. That's all I have to ask you."

The maître d'hôtel again bowed formally and left.

"Well?" Miss Boston asked. "Was I wrong?"

"Everybody knows you're never wrong," Joe Holborn slipped in with flattery. "But, Miss, what do you intend to do now? A scandal like this, such a crime, would be very unfortunate for a reputable well-known establishment like mine. Wouldn't you have some way to arrange this deplorable business?"

"You're talking like a businessman worried about his interests, sir," answered the detective, "but as for me, I have to think about the interest of justice. However, I'll try to reconcile these two opposed sentiments. For the moment, we'll avoid newspaper publicity about the affair. Besides we don't want to warn the murderer. On the contrary, it's important to let him believe that nothing of his criminal act has been discovered. I'll make it my business to set him straight by collaring him."

"Marvelous! Marvelous!" exclaimed Joe Holborn, rubbing his hands together.

"But entrusted by the Central Bureau with the preliminary evidence," continued Miss Boston, "there remains one other formality for me to carry out."

"What's that," asked the manager.

"The examination of the dead man's pockets. I assume no one up to now has touched anything in them?"

"No one, Miss."

"That's marvelous."

Miss Boston, aided by Sokes, emptied the inside and outside pockets' contents of the cadaver's clothes and spread them on the manager's desk. There was a superb gold timepiece, ten dollars, some small objects, a billfold and a book of checks. Miss Boston quickly leafed through the checks to verify the name written on the check the maître d'hôtel had seen signed at the end of the meal. She was disillusioned. The check, for the sum of $5000, had no name stated, but had been simply written to the bearer, on his signature at the Preston Bank in Baker Street. Miss Boston then examined the signature and saw it was that of Mr. Preston, the Bank's director. Thus the dead man's identity was perfectly established. As for the billfold, it offered Miss Boston a revelation. It contained an unsigned letter, type-written, but the text left no doubt that it had been sent by Teddy:

> Today is the fixed date. The papers have arrived from Phila-
> delphia. I have orders to finish it tomorrow. We demand $5,000
> dollars net by check made out to bearer, or cash. If you warn
> anyone at the Central Bureau, the business will be automatical-
> ly cancelled and more papers will come from Philadelphia. On
> the other hand, the papers against the check will be left at the
> Park Hotel. Answer by means of The Sun.

As soon as she read that letter, Miss Boston was sure. Preston had simply been the victim of blackmail with compromising papers, and the blackmail having succeeded, to make the traces of it disappear, they had done away with the victim. In addition, the billfold contained the proof of it. There was a bundle of love letters signed by Mr. Preston to his mistress. They had probably threatened to give them to Mrs. Preston in case he didn't buy them back at the price fixed by the thieves. Having opened *The Sun* newspaper found on the manager's desk, Miss Boston quickly found the banker's response. It was on page 18, among the miscellaneous notices:

> *For the man from Philadelphia. Agreed. At 5,000 for all the*
> *pieces. Park Hotel lunch today. Nothing to the Bureau C. —P*

This time Teddy was again in the affair, but the detective knew very well that everything was set in operation by the invisible chief of the One Hundred Thousand Arms Gang, that he was the head and Teddy only the arm. Now that the celebrated and only female detective had the trail, she swore to follow it to the end.

"Would you, please, draw up a report about all this with these gentlemen?" she asked Sokes. "You can take it to the Chief. As for me, I'm leaving. I have something urgent to do. At 6 p.m. a rendezvous at the Central Bureau, Sokes."

With these words, she took leave of the doctors and the manager of the Park Hotel and went down as far as Master Road, where she picked up a cab-man, to whom she handed the address of the Preston bank in Baker Street. The cab started off at full speed, while in a corner of the vehicle the detective was sunk in deep thought.

V. The Cashed Check

It was exactly 3 p.m. when Miss Boston walked into the Preston Bank, across the larger glassed hall onto which all the teller windows opened. She walked rapidly toward the main teller window, reserved for the cashing of checks. The teller, a middle-aged man, greeted Miss Boston with the utmost courtesy as soon as she had given him her identification.

"Hasn't someone presented a check for $5,000 signed by Mr. Preston?" she asked him.

The head cashier answered that someone did only ten minutes before. Given Teddy's description, he declared that it wasn't Teddy, but a woman with green eyes who presented the check.

Miss Boston regretted having arrived a few minutes too late to put her hands on the bearer of the check. However, the cashier's information was important; a new accomplice, a woman with green eyes, had become mixed up in the affair. That strangely complicated things. Instead of one trail to follow step by step, the detective found herself faced with two. That meant a double expenditure of daring, intelligence, and genius. But that wasn't something to frighten her. As for the rest of it, she now found herself faced with the clearest of situations.

1. Preston had obviously been murdered by Teddy by means of the poisoned ring.

2. Teddy had picked up the $5,000 check paid by Preston. The head waiter's testimony had confirmed that.

3. The check had been cashed by a woman with green eyes, unknown to the detective at the present.

And finally:

4. The plot was certainly the work of the One Hundred Thousand Arms Gang.

Such was the problem. How to solve it? That was the question Miss Boston was asking herself. She had just been cruelly and strangely disappointed.

When the testimony relative to the cadaver at the Park Hotel was drawn up, Sokes had returned to the Central Bureau and reported to the Chief. With great impatience and curiosity he awaited the arrival of the detective, completely ignorant of the motive for her absence.

The young woman didn't arrive at the Central Bureau until 6 p.m. The Chief pressed her with questions, which she answered setting out a detailed expose of the facts.

"What a shame those ten minutes' delay were," said the Chief. "You would have caught the woman with green eyes in the act."

"What do you expect, sir," the detective responded. "You can't always be lucky. Luck sometimes runs out, turns against detectives, but that's the nature of the job. However, right now I don't have too much to complain about."

"It certainly seems to me, Miss Boston, that in escaping you that way, the woman with green eyes, didn't do anything to make you happy."

"Maybe, Chief, but I haven't told you everything yet."

"Ah! What else?"

"I've found where the woman with green eyes lives."

"That's not possible!"

"That's the truth, however."

"But, then we've got Teddy."

"Not yet! You're rushing the job a little. Teddy's a cunning fellow. He's strong enough to fight."

"You know him better than I do, Miss, but it seems to me that to find a house, knowing what we do now…"

"…is a big problem. Yes, Chief, I grant you that. But that's not everything."

"Naturally, since everything hinges on Teddy's capture."

"That's what I'm going to try to do this evening."

"Already?"

"Am I in the habit of wasting my time, sir?" asked Miss Boston, with a slight hint of irony in her words.

"That's true, Miss Boston," the Chief confessed. "Supposing you could ever be reproached for anything, that would be last, at least."

The detective bowed, smiling.

"We're talking a lot, but it's better to act," she said. "Here, then, is what I've decided. Thanks to an investigation of the cab numbers in the Preston Bank vicinity. I've found the house of the green-eyes lady, whose name, whether true or false, I don't yet know, is Nelly Corms. Sokes and I are going to Delaware Street, where she lives. There is no possible doubt that Teddy won't return to this nest."

"And if he comes back, we'll be there!" Sokes said in a firm and positive voice.

"Let's hope so!" Miss Boston added.

With a cordial handshake to the Chief, Miss Boston and Sokes left the Central Bureau. A half hour afterward they came to Delaware Street and walked up as far as No.108. She said:

"Here it is."

The Inspector looked at the house. It looked comfortable, even luxurious.

"So much the better," he thought aloud.

"Why?" asked Miss Boston, surprised by that comment.

"Because that house must have a servant's stairway entrance. That's often better than a main stairway entrance."

"Sokes, you guessed all my thoughts."

"Then you had already thought about that?"

"To the point that all my plan is based on the existence of that stairway."

A minute later the two detectives entered the house. At the end of a large entry hallway they found the service stairs. They rapidly conferred. Sokes was to remain at the bottom of the stairs, ready to climb to the fourth floor where Miss Corms lived at the least signal from the detective. As for Miss Boston, she would enter the apartment alone. How! The idea had come to her suddenly.

"Sokes," she said, "you'll go up to the fourth floor and ring at Miss Nelly Corms' door."

"All right. And what am I to say?"

"That you've made a mistake and you're going back down."

"And you, Miss Boston?"

"Me, I'll go in."

"How so?"

"I'll enter the apartment by the service entrance while the servant is opening the door to you."

"Ingenious plan."

"Let's put it in effect."

Sokes rang; the woman servant came to the door; he asked for the solicitor Jefferson. He was told he had made a mistake; he made a thousand excuses and went calmly down to hide on the first floor.

During this time, Miss Boston, with the help of her jimmy, opened the door to the service stairs, slipped into the kitchen, reached a dark corner of a bedroom, the first one she came to. When, the servant came back to the kitchen, grumbling, the detective was in place.

VI. The Y Rays

At the end of several minutes of perfect immobility in complete darkness, clothes and the smell of a woman's perfume told her she was in Miss Nelly Corms' closet. In addition, her electric torch confirmed that and showed her a closed door. With a thousand precautions, she placed her microphone against the wooden panel.[7] That admirable, precise, little instrument allowed her to hear the slightest noise in a neighboring room. Applying her ear to the door, the detective heard nothing. Then she gently tried the door knob and Miss Boston found herself in a new room into which filtered a soft light coming from under the door at the back of the bedroom. The microphone placed on the door told the detective the neighboring room was occupied. She distinctly heard the sound of leaves of paper moved about and the sharp little screech of a pen forcibly applied by someone writing rapidly. But listening certainly wasn't enough for Miss Boston. She wanted to see, whatever the cost. Unfortunately, the key hole was completely plugged by the key in the lock of the room next door. No use to think of seeing anything through the key hole.

---

[7] Emile Berliner (1851-1929) improved the Bell telephone and developed the microphone in 1876. The microphone was still new in 1908-1909 when Reschal gave a very improved, fantastic version to Miss Boston. The small microphone was not in use until 1967, and is still being perfected in the 21st century. (*Note from the translator.*)

"Too bad," grumbled Miss Boston, "let's risk it anyway. We'll see what will happen."

That decision taken, her lips pinched, her chin lifted, she took a diminutive apparatus from her handbag. On top of that little apparatus was a lead cover. The detective lifted that cover, pushed a button fixed to the underside of the cylinder and immediately a strange light illuminated the room. However, that light, unlike other lights, didn't spread out. It went straight as an arrow to where it was pointed. Miss Boston directed it toward the panel of the door and immediately something extraordinary happened. The door became as transparent as glass! In this situation Miss Boston had simply used Y rays, recently discovered in Chicago by the honorable Professor David Williamson of the University of that city.[8] And if Sokes had been there she would have said to him: "Fortunately!"

Indeed! Miss Boston saw a woman seated at a little table, her back to the door, in an elegantly furnished sitting room. She couldn't see the sudden unusual transparency of the wooden door. Miss Boston recognized that woman on the spot. It was Miss Nelly Corms. She had just finished writing something. She put down her pen; blotted her paper and rose. The detective immediately replaced the lead cover over the Y ray cylinder. Darkness returned. No longer being able to see, Miss Boston listened more closely. She heard Miss Corms shout: "An-

---

[8] The x-ray and the microphone were among the inventions and scientific discoveries which rapidly expanded in the late 19th century and early 20th century. The x-ray was discovered in 1895 by Wilhelm Conrad Roentgen (1845-1923), just 13 years before the first *Miss Boston* installment. Here, Reschal imagines his own ray, the Y ray. (*Note from the translator.*)

na!" That was probably the servant's name. A moment of silence. The servant didn't answer. Miss Nelly Corms shouted a second time, stronger:

"Anna! I'm waiting for you."

The servant apparently was hard of hearing, because that time again Miss Corm's shout was in vain. Miss Boston heard her grumble:

"I really have to act like Anna's servant!" And she left the little sitting room.

The detective immediately knew she was going to the kitchen to give the servant a piece of her mind. Miss Boston quickly entered the room, picked up the blotter which had remained on the table and placed it in front of the mirror over the fireplace mantel. The mirror then revealed very readable writing. Here's what the detective read:

Steamer Transatlantic "Gibraltar"

Dock 116, Port of New York,

Mr. Terry Hupsey, passenger

Everything quiet. I will inform chief with excuses and explanations. I will take the mail boat 18. Await telegram promised from London.

Nelly

Then the detective put the blotter back in place, went back to the bedroom, crossed to the closet, and reached the kitchen as fast as she could, and thanks to her microphone, she easily heard the conversation going on at that moment. Miss Corms was saying:

"Anna this is totally unendurable. I have called you twice."

"I didn't hear you, ma'am."

"Really, that happens much too often. Stop your work a moment."

"Is there an errand to run, ma'am?"

"Yes, go to the telegraph office on 12th Avenue. Send this telegram. Here's a dollar. Don't waste any time."

"I'll go there right now, ma'am."

Various noises indicated that the servant had left the kitchen and that Miss Corms had returned to her sitting room. The situation was both simple and complicated. Considering the text of Miss Corms' telegram, the detective was beginning to understand. Teddy, under the name of Teddy Hupsey, had taken passage aboard the transatlantic steamer, the Gibraltar, leaving New York that same night destined for London and Southampton. Whether he judged it expedient to disappear from America, or had taken flight, cheating the invisible chief of the One Hundred Thousand Arms Gang of the $5,000 extorted from the banker Preston, or for some other reason, Teddy had gone free. Nelly Corms was to explain his disappearance to the Chief; therefore she knew the chief. When she had set the chief's mind at ease, she would join Teddy in London and they would both go live safe from the punishment they merited. It was a lovely plan, beautifully constructed, but to carry it out, the two crafty devils hadn't counted on the famous woman detective. She was there! And she knew their plan! From now on the game would be decisive.

Miss Boston's course was decided immediately. Promising herself to get her hands on Miss Corms after having gotten them on Teddy, she hurried to follow the maid. She signaled to Sokes as she passed his hiding place and with him followed on the heels of the servant walking very rapidly toward 12th Avenue, the telegraph in her hand.

"Where are we going?" Sokes asked as they walked.

"To the telegraph office on 12th Avenue."

"And after that?"

"Maybe to London."

"All right," said Sokes, who was no longer amazed at anything.

"Do you have your pen?" asked the detective.

"Here it is," said Sokes, passing it to her.

"Thanks. Watch the servant for me. I need to write a note."

The detective stopped and on a piece of paper torn from her notebook rapidly wrote a few lines. This done, she walked a little faster and caught up with the servant, who had gotten a little ahead during those two or three minutes.

"All right, Sokes," she said. "We have to be a little brazen."

Miss Boston then walked toward the servant and, as if by accident, bumped into her. In this movement she snatched the telegram from the woman's hands.

"Pardon, me," said Miss Boston.

"Oh! Miss Corms' telegram!" the servant exclaimed.

"Here it is; you dropped it," the detective said. And she gave the servant the telegram she had just drafted two minutes before. The servant thanked the detective for her courtesy and a few minutes later entered the telegraph office on 12th Avenue. She sent off a telegraph to this effect:

Steamer transatlantic Gibraltar
Dock 116, Port of New York
Mr. Teddy Hupsey, passenger.

Everything quiet. I will inform chief with excuses and explanation. I will take the mail boat of 18. Send trunk with contents. Open in London. Await telegram promised.

Nelly

Through the office windows she saw the servant send the telegram, not suspecting the substitution just taken place. When the detective was sure the telegram had left for its destination, she said to Sokes:

"And now, sir, there's not a minute to lose. To work!"

VII. The Telegram Trick and what Followed

In a few words, Miss Boston brought the Inspector up on the various events and important facts just discovered in Miss Corms' Delaware Street apartment. At the same time, the detective explained to her companion the underhanded act, or rather the reasons for jostling the servant on 12th Avenue.

"So we have Teddy," he concluded joyously. "That's the main thing. After Teddy I think we'll go pick Miss Corms out of the nest. She seems to me to play a rather active role in the Invisible Man's affairs."

"That's my opinion also," answered the detective, "but first, before anything else, to Teddy!"

"We're going to the port, to the steamer?"

"Yes. But first we're going by the Osborn Street Bazaar. What time does the Gibraltar leave, Sokes?"

"At 10:05 p.m. That's the time printed on the Red Star Line timetable."

"Good. Then we have two hours ahead of us."

"To do what?"

"To prepare the snare for Teddy."

"Hum! Don't you want just simply to collar him?"

"No, Sokes, so long as this fellow isn't in the middle of the ocean, he won't think he's safe. He'll be on his guard so long as there isn't enough water between him and America for him to avoid detectives. I don't want to go on board the Gibraltar as I am now. That's why you're going to disguise yourself quickly into a stoker. At the Osborn Street flea market we're going to buy a trunk big enough to hold me. Teddy's waiting for that trunk because Nelly Corms' fake telegram told him about it. I'll be taken to his cabin and there I'll wait. You, Sokes, I've just told you, are going to disguise yourself as a stoker, or as a mechanic, it doesn't matter which. You're going to find the transatlantic captain and explain to him confidentially what it's all about. He'll find some way to take you on board. There, you won't let Teddy out of your sight. As for me, I'll come in at the psychological moment."

"Understood. It'll be done."

At the big flea market on Osborn Street, they went in and Miss Boston chose a trunk big enough for her to fit in without being too uncomfortable. She had it put inside an automobile and on the way, Miss Boston slipped into the trunk, made several holes in the sides and fixed a padlock on the inside. It was unlikely Teddy would open the trunk—in case he was curious—before being in the middle of the ocean, that is, at the end of at least a day. That delay was sufficient for Miss Boston to pull off her project.

She made sure her detective's kit was complete. Everything was there: knife, steel pliers, electric torch, the Y ray cylinder, special glasses, without forgetting handcuffs and steel chains. Before having herself hoisted aboard the Gibraltar Miss Boston wanted to show Sokes the astonishing spectacle of the trunk's transparency. She lifted the lead cover off the little Y ray cylinder and pointed the ray in front of her. She saw Sokes lean over her, astonished, and heard him let out a cry of amazement. The Inspector congratulated her warmly for having thus contributed the recent inventions of modern science to judicial inquiries. The lead cover put back on the cylinder made the trunk opaque. Just at this moment the automobile driver shouted:

"Here we are!"

"Get me aboard," Miss Boston told Sokes, "and don't waste any time to disguise yourself."

Sokes jumped out of the automobile and walked toward the dock where there was total uproar. The majestic mass of the great transatlantic steamer, the Gibraltar, could be seen under the formidable bright electric lights of the port. It was one of those beautiful, enormous ships which leave with thousands of passengers, most of them rich or well off, at each departure for continental Europe. In fact, a veritable floating town. They were hauling aboard the last baggage; the passengers were exchanging good-byes with relatives on the dock; sailors were clambering up the ropes; and, standing on the bridge of the vessel, the captain was shouting orders through a megaphone to the crew.

Sokes walked up the gangplank to the ship. He asked for the steward.

"I have a trunk to be taken to a passenger, sir," said the Inspector.

"What is the name of the passenger?"

"Mr. Teddy Hupsey."

"What class? What cabin?"

"I don't know it, sir. I only know the person who sent it, and they neglected to give me these details."

The steward leafed through the registry of those on board and after a few minutes he found the information.

"Teddy Hupsey, 2nd class, between decks, cabin 902. Bring it aboard, sir. I'll inform the passenger."

Two workmen hauled the trunk up the gangplank of the Gibraltar, where it was rather roughly thrown on the deck.

"Be careful," Sokes said to the men. "There is something fragile in the trunk."

However, nothing, no cry out, no sound, no movement had betrayed the detective's presence. Teddy, who had been told, soon came to sign the receipt for the trunk.

"Oh! Yes," he said. "I was expecting it. I forgot it in the haste of departure."

"Should that be put in the baggage section?" the steward asked.

"Oh! No," Teddy answered. "The trunk has personal things in it. I want it in my cabin."

"Pick it up!" the steward curtly ordered the men who, seizing the trunk by the handles, carried it to cabin 902.

VIII. The Action of the Wireless Telegraph

Miss Boson was in place; she was in the middle of the operation, on the ground of the investigation. Here the drama would play out and end that frantic chase that had begun the day after the Broadway robbery. Since she was accustomed to the most difficult, the most dangerous, the most perilous situations, she did not think herself too badly situated in the confined space. She felt herself at first roughly thrown down on the deck of the Gibraltar. She heard the conversation between the steward and Teddy; then again lifted up, she knew they were carrying the trunk down to a lower deck. At the end of some yards, she heard a voice, and that voice was that of Teddy, say:

"It's here."

A door opened; the trunk was pushed across the floor, then Teddy added to the men:

"That's good. Leave it there where it is. Here's five cents to drink my health with."

The men thanked him and left.

Teddy remained alone in the cabin and grumbled some indistinct words between his teeth. He then crumpled up some papers and a few minutes later left, locking the door. This was the moment Miss Boston was waiting for. It was extremely important for her to understand the layout of the place where she had to operate. If Teddy should open the trunk unexpectedly, she wanted at least to know where the fight would take place and what resources the cabin offered. The Y rays were going to tell her. Without leaving the trunk, the detective began to examine the cabin. The lead cover off the cylinder, the stream of light pierced the holes in the trunk and illuminated the cabin. The cabin was furnished with a narrow, small couch, a wash basin, a table and two chairs. It was painted white and its general aspect was bright, clean, and luxurious. It had a thick carpet which muffled the sound of footsteps. The corridor door opened across from the little couch. The cabin was lit by a porthole, a small round window, big enough, however, to let in abundant light and air. Through it could be seen the immense, greenish-blue ocean washed by high, frothy waves.

Her plan was simple. She would get out of the trunk at the proper moment to arrest Teddy and keep him from avoiding the vengeance of the law by suicide. She had to choose night when the criminal was sleeping. But Miss Boston wanted to see if it was possible, before that, to get some details about the invisible head of the One Hundred Thousand Arms Gang. In case she found nothing, she would just arrest Teddy. She was completely convinced she would then deliver a telling blow to the terrible gang of which Teddy seemed to be a primary lieutenant. The detective listened attentively. The ring of the departure bell on the ship's deck came through the holes, as did the grating of the cables and the screeches of the chains holding it to the dock. The boatswain's pipes hooted lugubriously. Then suddenly the waves beat with greater force against the ship's sides; an enormous backwash seemed to set the Hudson waves in motion. It was clear the Gibraltar was weighing anchor, setting its course toward the high seas. It was 10:05 p.m. She would arrest Teddy toward morning. At that time the transatlantic wouldn't be too far from the coast. Executing the arrest warrant she carried, she could require the ship to dock long enough to disembark the criminal. Sokes, on his side had orders. From now on Teddy, caught between two fires, couldn't escape his fate. When the detective had played her last card he would be lost.

However, Teddy was still absent. Miss Boston wasn't worried about it for the moment. She knew it was cocktail time for the passengers. In addition, Teddy might be in the smoking lounge or the reading room and Sokes was on his heels. While Miss Boston was reasoning this way, the door suddenly opened and Teddy entered.

"Yes!" exclaimed the robber, letting out a sigh of relief. "We're off! I am at last finished with those detectives! It's good to breathe the open air!"

And believing himself definitely forever out of danger, he joyfully rubbed his hands together, walking up and down the narrow cabin. He spoke a monologue softly with a happy voice which underlined his words.

"You're going to see some country, Teddy, my boy. You'll wind up in the skin of a fine gentleman, honored and respected, thanks to his income! That'll change that good Nelly. She's really a fine girl, very devoted, alert, who knows how to pull it off like the best lieutenant of the chief...even better than the chief's wife. Actually, the chief's going to be furious when he finds out I've disappeared from circulation with the $5,000 of that imbecile Preston. But so what? Everybody has to have his share...I think I've worked enough risking my skin for the Sing Sing electric chair...Nelly's going to join me...But what has she put in that trunk to make it so heavy?...Well, I'll see."

Miss Boston heard the murderer take a bunch of keys from his pocket. The moment was critical! If Teddy opened the trunk, what would happen? A fearful moment that Miss Boston, nevertheless, envisioned coldly, calmly. Teddy approached the trunk, chose a key and slid it into the lock. Suddenly he stood up. Someone had just knocked on the cabin door.

There was a moment of silence; then the criminal raised his voice and asked:

"Who is it?"

Miss Boston heard the hammer of his revolver click. Teddy held himself on the defensive. On the other side of the door a voice answered:

"Telegraph service aboard ship, sir."

"Ah! Good!" Teddy answered and went to open the door.

The voice that had just spoken was not unknown to Miss Boston. She knew it perfectly. It was Sokes' voice. Miss Boston immediately knew something had happened. If Sokes was intervening, for whatever reason, it was because events were speeding up. She redoubled her attention.

"Ah! Telegraph service. Very good," said Teddy. "Ah! From New York?"

"Yes. Here it is. Please sign a receipt for me."

The detective heard the pen scratching on the paper.

"But tell me," Teddy continued, "how is it that this telegram is just now reaching me?"

"Because it was sent from New York when the ship was already under way."

"But how did it get aboard the Gibraltar?"

"It was sent by wireless telegraph."

"Marvelous. Thank you, my friend."

"At your service, sir."

The door slammed. Teddy was alone in the cabin.

IX. The Key to the Telegram

The telegram's arrival had made Teddy completely forget about opening the trunk. Miss Boston heard him murmur:

"A telegram in code. Oh! Oh! What's happened?"

A minute of silence followed.

"Let's see the key," said Teddy.

Reading the coded telegram took Teddy some minutes.

"Hell and damnation!" he swore.

And crushing in the same enraged movement the key and the telegram, he threw them on the cabin floor.

"What's to be done?" he exclaimed in a dull voice. "Followed me even here!"

And he began to rummage in all the corners of the cabin, lifting the mattresses from the little couch, pushing back the trunk. In his fever and hurry, he didn't try to open it. Miss Boston heard him open a valise, rummage through some papers, then leave the cabin, slamming the door.

She knew she had to move quickly. Opening the trunk lid, she got out and the first thing she saw was the telegram with the key rolled in a crumpled ball on the carpet. She picked it up and fearing she would be surprised by Teddy's sudden and unexpected return, she left the cabin. The central corridor was deserted. She walked rapidly to its end and reached the stairs leading to the bridge. Two small sharp, clear whistles made her lift her head.

"This way, Miss Boston," a voice whispered.

It was Sokes. The detective slipped behind the Inspector and guided by him reached the poop deck and entered a cabin. Sokes carefully closed the door behind him.

"Well, sir, what's happened?" asked Miss Boston.

"Everything went as hoped. I let the Captain know about our mission. With the most perfect courtesy and grace he put this cabin at our disposal. Disguised as a stoker I inspected the ship and took up Teddy's trail. He was in the smoking lounge. I couldn't go in dressed as I was. I went back five minutes later dressed as a regular ship employee. Teddy was reading all the evening papers carefully and slipped *The American Messenger* into his pocket. The details of the Park Hotel crime were covered extensively. Smoking a cigar, he took a walk on the bridge. I noticed that the Gibraltar had a wireless telegraph station. I went there out of simple curiosity, I asked if aerial transmission telegraphs in the middle of the ocean were relatively numerous. Less numerous, I was assured, than I might think. Just then, the Hertzian waves put the apparatus in motion. The New York station was transmitting a message to the transatlantic post. I saw that the telegraph was addressed to Teddy Hupsey. Thanks to the Captain, I was able to carry it to its destination myself. I saw only then that the message was in code, unreadable for us."

"I saw it," said Miss Boston.

"What! You were able to see the telegram."

"Here it is."

"What a pity it was in code," he said.

"That's not important, sir."

"How's that?"

"Because I also have the key."

"I should have known so," he said. "With you, criminals never have the last word."

But Miss Boston had already unfolded the telegram and the key on the table. Leaning over the crumpled up pages she examined them carefully.

Here's what the telegram contained:

409 37489214914390822

7 294108092

49991X2X3X 904 72898 427381

This hieroglyphic problem, which would have required several days study, with the alphabet key she had, was only a game for Miss Boston. In a minute she passed Sokes a piece of paper on which she had written six words.

"Here is the first line of the telegram, sir."

Sokes read:

My first telegram was changed.

A second later the detective added: "And here's the second."

Miss Boston is on the boat.

"Damnation!" Sokes exclaimed. "We're done for!"

"Not yet!" retorted the detective, "but this brings the end closer!"

"Then who could have sent this telegram?"

"Miss Nelly Corms, obviously."

"But how can she know?"

"Oh! That's not difficult, sir. She knew the dangers threatening him. She dreaded me as much as Teddy feared me. The servant probably told her about being jostled, and she would immediately have understood what happened. She saw that I knew the name of the ship Teddy boarded. That's the whole secret of the telegram. It's simple, but it's nonetheless true and the warning given, Teddy is certainly on his guard."

"He left the cabin?"

"Yes, after having ransacked it every which way, but uselessly. I heard him load his revolvers. Right now he must certainly be looking for me on the ship."

"So much the better. You can meet him face to face."

"I doubt it, sir. It's not usual for these criminals to meet someone face to face, even if this someone is a woman."

"What do you intend to do?"

"To go looking for Teddy."

"Might he be in his cabin?"

"Not very likely, but in any case, we'll start our search there. Have your guns ready."

"They're here."

"Good. I have mine and the handcuffs also."

"Good. Then I'll follow you."

The night was dark and humid. The starless sky stretched its heavy, gloomy veil over the sea. From the waves came the roar of the great surges beating the powerful sides of the Gibraltar. There was a strong wind and from time to time sea foam washed over the deck. All the sailors on duty were at their posts and, vaguely outlined by the red lanterns on the poop deck, the second lieutenant was standing near the copper megaphone used to transmit his orders to the mechanics and stokers. The deck was almost deserted. The passengers had gathered, some to the bar, others to the gambling room and still others to the smoking or reading room. The sound of their laughter and chatting reached the lower decks. Miss Boston and Sokes crossed the deck and descended toward the corridor of the interior cabins. A thick waterproof padded carpet muffled the sound of their footsteps. Without hindrance of any sort, the two detectives came to the closed door of cabin No.902.

X. Man Hunt on the High Seas

Then, to be absolutely sure, Miss Boston quietly opened the door and found the criminal was still absent.

"The bird isn't in the nest," whispered the Inspector.

"Let's go find the one he's chosen," Miss Boston answered in the same tone.

The two detectives retraced their steps and headed toward the end of the corridor.

"Sokes, let's divide the work. You go search the reading room and the smoking room. Me, I'll go look at the bar and the gambling room. If you find your man, don't wait!"

"Collar him immediately?"

"Exactly! If not, make your little steel bird sing out."

"There're six little tunes in its throat," joked the Inspector.

"Then good luck, Sokes, And if our man can't be found, let's meet in an hour on deck. We'll work out a new plan."

"Agreed."

"All right, let's go!"

Sokes visited the reading room first. Old gentlemen, ladies and some girls were seated around tables where all the major newspapers were spread out, not only American, but even European. Conversations were rather subdued. There was more reading than talking. Sokes, not seeing Teddy among those readers, passed on to the smoking room. There were only gentlemen there, leaning back in big leather chairs, laughing, joking, chatting to each other. But there too, no Teddy.

"Too bad," Sokes said to himself. "It's up to Miss Boston."

Miss Boston, however, hadn't found the criminal in the luxurious, elegant bar where, in evening dress, the rich passengers were having drinks. The gaiety there was noisy. They seemed the fortunate of the world trying to spend time in the most agreeable way possible. Miss Boston then passed on into the gambling room. Exquisite pictures were painted on the ceiling. A dozen beautiful crystal electric lights attached to the ceiling were lowered to illuminate a huge table covered with green baize. Around this table were seated gentlemen whose silence contrasted unusually with the noisy gaiety of those in the bar. Piles of gold pieces, bundles of bank notes, stacks of dollars were spread out on the green baize. With a curt and cutting voice the croupiers, holding ivory rakes to pull over money lost, were announcing the cards turned up. The game had reached its height. The fever of winning shone on every face. Miss Boston searched for Teddy among the players. Suddenly she stiffened. She had just seen him, eyes shining, hands trembling, in front of a stack of gold at the end of the table. The criminal was gambling to forget as others drink to forget.

Slowly, Miss Boston circled the table. She had her revolver in one hand and held the handcuffs in the other. She came up behind Teddy's chair. There was profound silence in the gambling room. The voice of the croupier was heard to announce: "King of clubs! Place your bets!"

Suddenly a strong voice said: "Teddy, in the name of the law, I'm arresting you."

Miss Boston had just put her hand on the criminal's shoulder. The whole room was shocked. With one bound, Teddy stood up. He was as pale as death.

"The detective!" he screamed.

The muzzle of Miss Boston's revolver faced him.

With a sudden, violent movement, Teddy took hold of the gaming table. There was a dull crack. The whole table tilted, knocking over the players and scattering all the gold and dollars across the room. A cry of rage and anger arose from every direction. Teddy took advantage of it. While the jostled or thrown backward players righted themselves, while the croupiers hurried to the gold pieces and picked up the bank notes, the author of all that disaster had disappeared, thanks to the tumult, the crowd, and the disorder. From everywhere there arose furious exclamations, cries of anger. Finally, a person who seemed particularly furious came toward Miss Boston.

"Miss, what's your name," he asked. "Will you explain what this means?"

The detective pushed the exasperated players aside with a definite, firm gesture. In a strong voice dominating the tumult in the game room she shouted:

"I am Miss Boston and the man who has just escaped is the murderer of the banker Preston who was killed this afternoon in New York."

Silence followed these words. You could see the scene had suddenly changed. Everyone moved aside in front of the detective who, revolver in her hand, dashed ahead on the trail of Teddy. On the deck, Sokes ran to meet her.

"Quick, sir," shouted the detective. "The fellow's escaped!"

"Where are you going?"

"To cabin 902."

"I'll follow you."

The two detectives, followed by a crowd of passengers, arrived in the corridor in front of the cabin Teddy occupied. That door was locked. Sokes came to the detective's aide and with a solid blow of his shoulder, broke in the door. It flew apart in splinters. Immediately a wave of smoke invaded the corridor while big flames licked at the walls. Suffocating, the two detectives retreated. The cabin was on fire!

"The fire extinguishers! Quickly!" cried Miss Boston.

That cry, repeated, reached the bridge to the sailors on duty. The Captain's lieutenant immediately took command and less than two minutes later, the fire extinguishers arrived in the corridor and four powerful jets of water inundated the burning cabin. The fire was soon put out. In the middle of a pool of floating debris, Miss Boston entered and carefully explored. She believed Teddy had not chosen this kind of suicide. The fire had only been a ruse. She acquired proof almost immediately. The cabin was empty! Teddy had disappeared! How?

The detective raised her eyes toward the porthole looking out over the ocean. The porthole was open. That was the way Teddy had fled. Had he really jumped into the sea?

XI. The Gibraltar Passengers' Justice

"Too late!" cried Sokes. "Alas, Miss Boston, we're here too late!"

The detective didn't answer. She remained thoughtful in the middle of the cabin in ruins.

"Is the Captain here?" she asked the sailors working the fire extinguishers.

"He's on the deck, Miss," they answered.

"Come, Sokes. The last word hasn't been said yet."

She asked the Captain:

"Sir, do you have on board some electric search lights powerful enough to reach 30 to 40 meters?"

"Absolutely, Miss."

"Can you turn them on right now?"

"If it's useful, yes."

"It's useful. These search lights, are they fixed or mobile?"

"Mobile."

"In that case, will you bring one down to the right side of the ship."

"I'll give the order, Miss."

A powerful arc light was lowered over the ship's rail on the right side. The waves were brightly lit and let the detective clearly distinguish Teddy hanging on to an iron ring above the waves. He was suspended on the ship between heaven and the ocean, probably waiting for the opportunity to get back into the transatlantic.

"There he is," shouted the detective.

The criminal screamed with rage, but didn't let go of the iron ring. Suspended there by one hand, with the energy of despair, he took out his revolver and pointed it toward Miss Boston.

"Give up! Teddy," the detective shouted.

"I'd rather die!" he answered in a furious voice mingled with the whistling of the wind and the angry roaring of the huge waves. And he fired. The bullet passed by Miss Boston, who had leapt back rapidly. The passengers had come running. Several of them had their guns drawn. A concert of curses, shouts, and insults arose loudly.

Several gun shots exploded in the direction of Teddy. Miss Boston tried to intervene.

"Gentlemen," she shouted to the menacing passengers, "that man is under arrest! You don't have the right to kill him!"

"We're taking that right," was the retort.

New shots broke out. Miss Boston leaned over above the foaming ocean. She saw that a shot had hit the criminal. He put his free hand on his heart, closed his eyes, and let go of the iron ring. He disappeared into the water. The drama had taken only an instant. Miss Boston saw it wasn't a ruse this time. The murderer had fallen helpless, irremediably and forever lost. The ocean waves had closed over him. The passengers' justice had done its work.

At dawn the next day the transatlantic made a short port call allowing Miss Boston and Sokes to disembark on the American coast, near Halifax. They hurried to reach New York, where their first duty was to report to the Chief. Miss Boston was enthusiastically congratulated. The Chief expressed only one regret; that was not to see the famous and brave detective conduct Teddy Hupsey to the electric chair at Sing Sing. Miss Boston explained that she still had one criminal to find, the Invisible Man, but she must first lock up Teddy's accomplice, Nelly Corms, the woman with green eyes.

An hour later, Miss Boston arrived in front of Miss Corms' house. This time she wanted to go straight to the job. She intended to go to the woman with green eyes' apartment, ring the bell, enter, her revolver drawn, and say:

"Ma'am, I have an arrest warrant for you."

The first part of this plan came off without a hitch. Miss Boston rang at the apartment of Teddy's accomplice, but no one answered. Seeing that there was no answer, the detective opened the door with her jimmy and went carefully into the apartment. Everything was in order. The furniture was there, but passing by the clothes closet where several days before she had hidden, she saw all the clothes had disappeared. She inquired of the building's concierge and the mystery was explained.

"Miss Nelly Corms has gone away?"

"Exactly, Miss, and for a long time."

"She's away on a trip?"

"No, she's moved."

That answer surprised Miss Boston. No furniture had been moved.

"Moved? How's that?"

"Yes, Miss Corms' apartment was furnished."

"And do you know where she lives now?"

"I don't know anything at all. She left without leaving an address."

Miss Boston thanked her and left.

THE WOMAN WITH GREEN EYES

I. Chloroform

For at least an hour that morning the clerks of the Director of the Jarvis Bank's waiting room had been trying to calm the impatience of the clients waiting to see the Director.

"Mr. Jarvis is busy…You'll have to wait…He can't see you right now."

"We can't go in unless he calls."

"I've been waiting more than an hour!"

"Have a little more patience, sir!"

Suddenly that door was opened violently and roughly.

Haggard, his hair tousled, his clothes rumpled, a man burst into the waiting room, shouting in a broken voice:

"Arrest her! Arrest her! The bank notes!...the billfold!..."

The clerks rushed forward, astonished, and in that over-excited man recognized the Honorable Jeff Jarvis himself, the Bank Director. People rushed forward from everywhere. There was an indescribable jostling while Mr. Jarvis continued shouting:

"Arrest her! The woman with the green eyes."

Finally, exhausted, supported by two clerks, he collapsed in an arm chair, murmuring in a weak and dead voice:

"Call the police…the Central Bureau." And he fainted.

News of this unusual incident spread quickly through the bank. Employee exclamations crossed from counter to counter asking what had happened. They saw the head cashier, like a madman, burst from his office, tearing his hair in despair, crying out:

"$12,000! $12,000! I paid out $12,000!" and he ran to Mr. Jarvis' outer office. Mr. Jeff Jarvis, who had come around, was telling those around him about the daring criminal who had just victimized him. When he saw the cashier come running, he seemed suddenly to remember a forgotten fact, and breaking through his listeners, he ran toward his employee and in a gasping voice cried out:

"Toby…Toby…Did you cash the check?"

"Yes, Mr. Jarvis…"

"Alas! $1,200 lost," groaned the banker.

"What do you mean, $1,200?" asked Toby, stupefied. "It wasn't $1,200 Mr. Jarvis!"

"What are you talking about, Toby?"

"Twelve..."

"What? $12,000?"

"Yes...I...I...paid $12,000."

Mr. Jarvis turned pale and fainted, groaning: "It's lost...I'm ruined...ruined..."

While these events were taking place at the Strand Road bank, the head of the Solicitor's fraud division had telephoned the Central Police Bureau. So, fewer than five minutes after the event, the judicial administration knew what had happened. While a doctor was hastily called for Mr. Jarvis, an automobile arrived at the bank. A young blonde woman, very elegant, but whose calm and business-like beauty was united with strong will, got out, followed by a handsome, clean-shaven 30 or 35 year-old square-shouldered man with intelligent eyes.

It was Miss Boston, the famous woman detective and her friend, her usual companion on cases, Mr. Sokes, Chief Inspector of the Central Office. Mr. Jarvis was again conscious and lamenting the loss of his $12,000.

Miss Boston saw it was impossible to do anything in the midst of that confusion. She introduced herself to the bank Director and asked him to grant her a few minutes' interview in his office. Jarvis, very happy to see the police, above all Miss Boston, take charge so quickly, gave the cashiers some brief orders. These immediately cleared out the waiting room, sending the employees to their various stations.

The detective whispered a word in Sokes' ear. He nodded and went rapidly to the bank's entry door. Miss Boston took this elementary precaution even before knowing about the affair. She then said to Mr. Jeff Jarvis:

"Sir, I am at your service."

The bank Director replied: "Please come into my office, Miss Boston."

The room was sumptuously furnished with as much originality as good taste. Bookshelves full of books lined the left and right walls. A large table desk loaded with papers filled the center of the room. The rug covering the floor was magnificent.

Miss Boston stopped at the threshold of the door as if to admire it. In reality, she was sniffing the air.

"Sir," she said, "you were robbed, weren't you?"

"Yes, Miss, exactly."

"Without knowing the details and circumstances, I can tell you how it happened. It was simply by chloroform."

II. A Dead Man's Accomplice Reappears

"In fact, Miss Boston," Mr. Jarvis answered. "It seems to me it was chloroform. I verified its importance an hour later. You must know, Miss..."

The detective stopped the Honorable Jeff Jarvis in his explanations with a firm gesture.

"Sir," she said, "as a business man you must like order. It's the same with me as a detective. So, please, we're going to proceed with order and method and as fast as possible."

She ascertained that the Director had arrived at his office as usual at 10 a.m., that he had attended to mail and current business, had then received visitors waiting their turn in the outer office.

"Perfect," said Miss Boston. "It was very likely one of those responsible for the chloroform."

"Yes, and here's what happened. After two or three various applicants, I was visited by a very elegant young woman with green eyes..."

"Green eyes, you say, Mr. Jarvis?"

"Yes, do you by chance know her?"

"I'm beginning to fear so. But continue your story, sir."

"Well, that young woman came to ask advice about selling some Dakota Railways' stock. I looked at the titles and advised her to sell them. She asked me to take them, alleging a pressing need for $1000. You understand, Miss, it's difficult to refuse anything to a pretty woman. I agreed to buy them, although that wasn't usual for my bank. I signed a withdrawal slip for $1,200 for the seven bonds of the green-eyed lady. While I was writing, I was blinded by some drops of a liquid thrown in my face. I tried to rise, but a handkerchief was placed over my face. I fell. I don't know what happened after that. An hour later I regained consciousness. I saw the lady had disappeared with the Dakota Railway stock and the $1,200 withdrawal voucher. I called out, but too late, naturally."

"The lady with green eyes had adequate time to disappear. Did she cash the withdrawal slip?"

"Yes, and that's the most astonishing thing in the whole affair. I signed a voucher for $1,200 and the cashier paid $12,000."

Mr. Jarvis called Toby, the cashier, who brought the voucher with him. Miss Boston examined it and saw the amount was $12,000. She took a very powerful magnifying glass out of her purse and looked carefully at the last zero. She smiled.

"There's nothing false on the voucher except the last zero, which has incontestably been added."

"That's the only way that could have happened," Toby said. "I examined the voucher carefully. Nothing seemed suspicious to me. I paid it."

"And you made me lose $12,000," Mr. Jarvis shouted, furious.

The cashier lowered his head at that unmerited reproach. Miss Boston politely interrupted to get back quickly to the point. She concluded by saying:

"Besides, the woman in question has swindled people even stronger than you."

"Then you are acquainted with her Miss?"

"Almost, sir. That woman, Nelly Corms, from Delaware Street, disappeared a few days ago. She's under an arrest warrant for theft at the Preston Bank, an accomplice of the man named Teddy Hupsey."

"The one who was killed aboard the transatlantic?"

"The same. I followed Teddy, but he slipped through my hands. I found his trail aboard the transatlantic to Europe, but the angry passengers shot and killed him. His accomplice was the woman who chloroformed you."

"But you're going to arrest her, I hope!" Jeff Jarvis exclaimed impulsively.

"I'll do my best," the detective answered.

"But do I have some chance of recovering my $12,000?"

"You have a one in a hundred chance, sir," the detective answered seriously. "Thanks to you I know where to begin my investigation. I have nothing to do here. I'll keep you informed of the result. Good-bye."

Miss Boston quickly rejoined Inspector Sokes at the main entrance. For the first time Miss Boston was faced with a criminal as much to be feared as she was feared as a detective. Which of the two would carry the day: Miss Nelly Corms or Miss Boston? Crime or the law? Daring or genius? A terrible duel was beginning.

"Where are we going?" Sokes asked.

The detective replied frankly: "I don't really know."

Miss Boston had never found herself in that situation. This time she was dealing with a gang that slipped away, vanished, disappeared, flew away. What trail to follow?

She raised her eyes involuntarily and recoiled, suddenly a little pale! The woman with green eyes was ten steps from her.

III. Miss Boston Loses the First Match

"Look, Sokes," she whispered.

"What is it?"

"Her!"

Luck had entered the game. Going toward Newgate, was the woman with green eyes, Miss Corms. They began shadowing her immediately. She was wearing a suit which fitted her marvelously, hugging her charming figure, making her truly elegant, and carrying a little Russian leather purse. Certainly no one would have guessed that pretty woman was a dangerous criminal, wanted as an accomplice, and the author of two daring thefts.

Their shadowing began well.

Nevertheless, Miss Boston wondered if the woman with green eyes hadn't gotten wind of it, as they say in police slang. That was what had to be feared most of all. If Miss Corms wasn't on the alert, everything was for the best and the shadowing could put them on the certain trail of that Invisible Chief of the uncatchable gang, the One Hundred Thousand Arms Gang. If, on the contrary, she smelled something, she would be quick to get to safety, mix up the clues, and take advantage of the disorder to escape. That had to be avoided at all costs. Miss Boston was infinitely more concerned with capturing the Invisible Man than the small fry, even if dangerous.

Miss Corms was still walking toward Newgate, never turning around. She stopped at a jeweler's window and then continued walking.

"Hum! Hum!" Miss Boston said. "That doesn't tell me anything helpful."

She also stopped at the window. "That's what I thought. Look at the mirrors," she murmured to Sokes.

In fact, the mirrors clearly reflected the high end of the street, where Miss Corms could see the detective and the Inspector following her if she had looked. But did she? Only what happened would solve that problem. And while waiting, the shadowing continued.

In the middle of Newgate, Miss Corms suddenly turned left. She continued her steady, fast pace. Turning toward Boffers Gad, she went into No.18.

"Now I'm certain, Sokes. She knows we're following her,"

Miss Boston ran to the end of Boffers Gad and dashed into a little narrow street just as Miss Corms was coming out of a small, low door. And the chase began again, more heated, more obstinate, but made infinitely more difficult because the detective was convinced the criminal was on to them. Miss Corms took advantage of the least encumbrances in the street, slipping in between small groups and disappearing into crowds. She was obviously trying to throw Miss Boston and Sokes off the track. On 7th Avenue, she jumped into a hansom cab which left at a trot toward Brighton City. Miss Boston took another cab, decided to finish it, since she had nothing to safeguard, now certain Miss Corms wouldn't put her on the trail to the Invisible Man.

Encouraged by a five dollar tip, Miss Boston's cabman whipped his horses to a fast trot. Suddenly she said to Sokes:

"Quick, Sokes! Something new!"

She jumped quickly out of the cab and walked with Sokes toward the Broad Street subway station. She gave her name to the ticket agent and jumped into the train starting off. There was no trace of Miss Corms. At every stop the detective and Miss Boston looked carefully at all departing passengers right up to Canon Station. There Teddy's accomplice was rapidly climbing the stairs to the subway exit. As Miss Boston exited on Canon Place, she saw Miss Corms jump into a hansom cab. The chase began anew. It lasted almost a half-hour. Suddenly, in that mad race, the cab horse of Miss Boston's cab slipped on the carriage way and fell. Miss Boston, without worrying about the horse or cabman, immediately jumped onto the sidewalk with Sokes and took an automobile toward Liverpool Church. All that lasted hardly two minutes, but Miss Corms' cab had profited by them to get ahead. It turned obliquely into Circus Road. Miss Boston's vehicle caught up with their cab there, sputtering, rumbling, drawn along by strong momentum.

"Stop! Stop!" Miss Boston yelled at the cabman, but he continued to whip his horse as hard as he could. She renewed her command, adding: "In the name of the law!" Only then did the cabman rein in his horse. She opened the cab door shouting:

"Miss Nelly Corms, I have a warrant for your arrest! Don't resist!"

But the cab was empty. The coachman got down, somewhat stunned, not understanding anything about that hellish ride, that chase, and finally about that order to stop in the name of the law.

"Where is the person you picked up at Canon Place?" the detective asked curtly.

"But...But...She's inside the cab!"

"There's no one in the cab!"

"That's not possible!"

"Look for yourself!"

"But who's going to pay the fare?"

"Likely not me," answered the detective, "unless you tell me about that lady."

"But I don't know her, Miss. I've never seen her before."

"Where did she tell you to take her?"

"She told me to drive straight down Drury Lane."

Miss Boston thought it useless to question the cabman further. During the trip, Teddy's accomplice had jumped from the cab when Miss Boston's cabman's horse slipped and fell. The woman with green eyes had muddled the trail and Miss Boston had lost the first match.

IV. A Telephone Call Made By Mistake

To Inspector Sokes she said: "What do you expect, Sokes; luck's against us. Those things happen sometimes. We'll just have to wait until it turns against the woman with green eyes, that's all."

The two detectives had reached Liverpool Church, next to the electric tramway which goes down toward the Central Police Bureau. Miss Boston separated from Sokes, who went to report to his superior officer the results of the morning's operations. On arriving at her apartment in Savannah City for lunch, she found a telegram just arrived which set her to laughing, accustomed as she was in her profession to threats and blusters from criminals she mercilessly tracked in the jungle of the great American city.

The telegram said:

I took you for a ride this morning, Miss, to prove to you that I am as clever as they say you are. Don't meddle in my business or I'll meddle in yours, and then we'll be forced to settle the account of poor Teddy's death. So, everyone for himself. Make everybody your business, except me.

The woman with green eyes

The detective threw the threat disdainfully into the waste paper basket. However, the audacity of that woman astonished her. It was rather common for men to risk their life and their skin in a crime with great returns, but for a woman used to elegance, to ease, to the comforts of existence, that was in reality somewhat rare. She thought about that during lunch and about 2 p.m. was about to call Sokes to see if he had any new information. She asked for the Central Bureau, but by accident was connected to a line where there was already conversation. With natural, instinctive discretion, she was about to hang up and report the error to the telephone operator, when a word of one of the speakers caused her to listen to the end of the conversation.

"Really," said one of the voices, "that Jarvis is so stupid!"

Jarvis was the banker from whom the woman with green eyes had so ingeniously and so daringly extorted $12,000 that morning.

"Naturally the Central Bureau was alerted?"

"Yes, and it was Miss Boston who came!"

"Damnation!"

"What do you expect, Chief. So long as you don't put someone seriously on her heels to get rid of her, she'll always be there!"

"Is she following you, Nelly?"

"Yes, she shadowed me for an hour this morning."

"And you shook her off?"

"Yes, but that could start again tomorrow."

"I'll think about it. And the $12,000?"

"Ready for you, Chief, where and when you like."

There was a moment's silence before the answer. Then the voice Miss Corms called Chief said:

"Bring the money this evening to Grant."

"Why Grant?"

"I've chosen him to replace Teddy. And, speaking of Teddy, I still don't know what he was doing aboard the Gibraltar where he was killed."

"You didn't get his letter?"

"No."

"He told me he had written you."

"I received nothing. That's a great misfortune for you, Nelly. But what is, is. So, see Grant this evening. Go in through Maël Street. They'll be on the lookout."

"All right. I'll be there about 9 p.m."

"Until one of these evenings, Nelly."

"Right. Give my regards to Mary."

"I certainly will. Good-bye."

And they hung up.

Miss Boston was suddenly enlightened. Without wasting time, she called the telephone operator and asked her the number of the subscriber whose call she had just overheard. At first the telephone operator refused, citing regulations. When Miss Boston gave her name, there was no further difficulty. The young detective learned the call had been placed at public telephone 3834, Liverpool Church section and subscriber no. 829AM48. That was all telephone operator could say, but that was more than enough for the detective.

She immediately picked up the New York telephone directory. She learned that 829AM48 was listed for a Mr. Holland, profession pawnbroker in Buffers Ban, which was situated at the intersection of Maël Street and Osborn Lane. There was incontestably no doubt the person speaking to Nelly Corms was the Invisible Man, the feared, all powerful head of the Hundred Thousand Arms gang. This chief was telephoning from Ruffers Ban where his telephone number corresponded to that of Mr. Holland. But was this Mr. Holland himself? This was a point needing clarification.

Teddy had been replaced by someone named Grant. But as for Mary, who could that be? A woman, naturally, but what role did she play in the association? A role similar to that of Nelly Corms, maybe? In any case, this was new information about the terrible gang.

She resolved to go that evening to Ruffers Ban at the hour the woman with green eyes was told to arrive there. There must be an unknown or hidden entrance at Mäel Street. The detective contacted Inspector Sokes, informed him of the good news and told him to meet her that evening at 8 p.m. at the corner of Ruffers Ban and Mäel Street. She asked him to place ten uniformed policemen in Osborne Lane. She said:

"We'll need them. It never hurts to have a lot of solid fists."

V. *The Ruffers Ban Shop*

Ruffers Ban, located in a somewhat remote section of New York, is not exactly a slum, but despite the certain decorum it retains, it has nevertheless something shady and no one goes there after dark with a light heart. The police sometimes check there, but less often than elsewhere. There's a single row of houses on the right side of Ruffers Ban; the left side has vacant land behind a flimsy fence. The houses are old but well kept. Mr. Holland's pawnbroker shop was located between the offices of two small manufacturers: a sawmill and Connecticut Papers. Miss Boston had doubts as to the legality of its business. The shop was narrow and dark, cheaply lit by a petrol lamp on the counter. A bald fellow with glasses on his nose, and adorned with a long beard was sitting behind the counter. He resembled an old bird of prey. Holding his pen delicately, he was leaning over his books; packages wrapped in gray wrapping paper were organized in white wooden bins around him. At the end of the shop there was certainly a door, but hidden by an old cheap red cotton drape.

"That smells of disguise to me," she said when she saw the old man with his long patriarchal beard.

"Sokes," she said, "turn up your overcoat collar and turn down your hat brim and go see if this Holland isn't a fence. See if his beard isn't a fake."

The Inspector did so and his person was totally transformed and unrecognizable. Stooped, with a shuffling walk, his hat turned toward his nose, he perfectly resembled some shady individual from Chelsea or Woolwich. So, while Miss Boston went to reconnoiter the secret entrance to Maël Street, Sokes went cautiously toward the shop of the so-called pawnbroker. Some feet from the entrance, he let out a short, shrill whistle. A similar whistle responded from far off. Sokes knew the ten policemen were at their post. He daringly went into the shop. The old man with a long white beard lifted his head when Sokes entered.

"What do you want?" he asked in a not very friendly tone.

"Are you the owner?"

"Yes, do you have a word?"

Sokes knew the old man expected a password agreed on by those who frequented the shop.

"I don't have a password," he said.

"I only lend with security."

Sokes took his detective's kit out of his pocket. It was exactly like that used by burglars. He put it on the counter in front of the old man.

"Do you lend anything on toys like that?"

"Oh! Where did you steal that kit, pard?"[9]

"I took it from a gentleman of the Central Bureau, but I don't intend to sell it."

"You're talking in riddles, Pard. Tell me in two words what you want."

"Money to pull off a nice job with these little instruments here."

"Where?"

"If I told you, you'd go in my place."

"You're distrustful, Pard."

"Professional habit. You see my tools are of good quality. Look at these steel pliers, these little cold chisels…"

The old man leaned over and while he was examining them, Sokes accidentally tugged at his beard. The old man didn't react, seeming not to notice. Sokes then knew the beard was fake. He excused himself for clumsiness and looked around the shop, noting there was no telephone. However, he continued to show the old man his little tools. He said:

---

[9] *Pard* is a slang word used between burglars meaning friend.

"Look at these pincers and this steel screw driver."

Suddenly, a voice behind him said: "Holland, did the Inspector also show you his detective's badge?"

At the same moment, something soft and hard hit Sokes' head. The old man, suddenly vigorous, hit him full in the face and he fell on the counter. Grant, hidden behind the red curtain hiding the little exit door, had appeared. He said:

"Blow out the lamp, Holland. You can see from the outside and I think there are cops in the vicinity."

"You are certain, Grant, that he's a detective?"

"I'd bet on it, Holland, because I saw his face."

They decided to carry him upstairs and advise the Chief, who would come later that night. Carrying their victim, the two scoundrels took the little back door. A long, narrow corridor led to a stairway. On the fourth floor they entered an empty apartment. Crossing it, they entered a room filled with packages and boxes where they threw down the detective. Holland wanted to leave, but Grant insisted on tying up their victim. They did so, but it was a superfluous precaution. Sokes was at that moment completely unconscious.

VI. An Unusual Young Man

On leaving Sokes, Miss Boston had walked up to the Mäel Street intersection, where she hoped to discover the secret entrance. She had counted the houses of Ruffers Ban. There were 31; Holland's house was the 18th on Mäel Street which also had 31 houses. Therefore the entry must be in the 18th house. She looked at the time on her little watch, so small she wore it on her finger as a ring shaped like a kitten. That watch showed exactly 8:35 p.m.

Sokes' absence for such a long time seemed unusual to her. She went back to Holland's shop on Buffers Ban. The shop was plunged in darkness and locked.

"What did that mean?" she wondered. The detective had to choose between two courses of action: the first was to enter the shop, whatever the cost, open the door with a jimmy, explore the interior to find traces of Sokes. But that demanded time and patience. Miss Boston had no time to lose and the second alternative depended on timing. Miss Nelly Corms had said she'd arrive in Mäel Street at 9 p.m. Her trail led to the Invisible Man. Therefore that came before Sokes, momentarily. With that decision, she gave a sharp whistle. Another whistle answered. The detective whistled again; shadows slid into Mäel Street.

"Any special orders, Miss?" whispered the head of the squad.

"Oh, yes. Break into the house I enter at the first gun shot."

"That's all?"

"Yes, and be careful."

Miss Boston had taken a position some feet from the supposed entrance to the house with two entrances. She could closely watch the entire street. Only two street lamps lit the street and cast a dim and blinking light. The area seemed entirely deserted. In the distance, 9 p.m. struck. Nothing yet moved and she was beginning to fear some surprise. At 9:05 there was a brief alert. A drunk came up Mäel Street singing at the top of his lungs. He zigzagged across the street, but after several seconds went down Osborne Lane. He could be heard shouting in the distance. Then once again there was silence.

Suddenly the detective heard a step resound on the pavement. She looked at the shadow and hesitated. What she saw in the distance was the elegant silhouette of a young man dressed in a large Inverness cape and wearing a large-brimmed felt hat. He was smoking a cigarette, casually twirling a cane and whistling a very popular American tune. The young man passed Miss Boston in the shadows without seeing her, startling the detective. She smelled the odor of the elegant young man's cigarette.

"That's not a man's tobacco," she said to herself. She examined the young man's walk and added: "That's not the walk of a man. That's just what I thought. That's Nelly Corms disguised as a man. That's not stupid."

Just then, Nelly Corms quickly entered the 18th house on Mäel Street.

"There's the bird in the next," she said, and she began to run. Passing the head of the police squad, she threw out: "Be alert! We're moving!"

"Following you?"

"Yes, but don't go upstairs. Stay in the courtyard that's probably at the end of the corridor. The orders are the same. Break when you hear the first shot. Another thing: don't let anyone leave the house and send five men to guard the pawnbroker's shop in Ruffers Ban. That's the second exit of the house."

The chief sent five men to the shop and leading the other five, he entered the house where Miss Boston had preceded them.

VII. The Broken Armoire Dodge

At the end of the stairs, the detective took out her gun, her bulldog. Quickly and silently she went up the stairs. At the second floor landing there were two doors. Which to take? She decided to take a chance on the one to her right. It was open, completely dark and seemed uninhabited. Investigating, she found the other rooms empty, long deserted. Thick dust covered the floors; the ceilings were literally covered with spider webs and in several rooms wind whistled through broken tiles and windows. Miss Boston decided to explore the apartment on the left. Time was pressing and Sokes could be in real danger.

That apartment was exactly like the first. She mounted to the third floor. The apartment on the right was like those below. However, in one of the rooms on the left there was an old forgotten armoire with a mirror. But the mirror was cracked; one of the panels was off and the shelves inside were broken. This debris evidently abandoned, Miss Boston had to go up to the fourth floor. The same abandon there, and on the fifth floor, the last in the building, everything was empty! What did that mean? She was sure Nelly Corms, disguised as a young man, had entered the house. There must be a particularly well concealed hiding place. But where? Then she remembered the dilapidated armoire. Why had she not thought to examine it further? In a second she was on the third floor in front of the armoire. She tapped on the wall behind it. Nothing. Then she pulled the armoire away from the wall and with an ease only partly surprising her, she made it pivot on one of its feet. Behind the wall was a low door closed with a security lock. Using her microphone, she heard a confused murmur of half stifled voices. But that faint sound was dominated by another, closer sound, not like a voice, but like someone crawling to stifle the sound of his movements.

Suddenly, the sliding became more distinct, coming from just behind the door where Miss Boston was listening. She slid the armoire back in front of the opening and waited in a dark corner. She heard the security bolt slide back, the door open silently and the armoire cracked under the weight of someone stubbornly and silently pushing it.

Then she understood the mysterious sliding sound. It was a bound man who had crawled into the empty room. To do so he had certainly used a super-human courage, incontestable will power. He stretched out, exhausted, on the floor, whispering:

"Finally!...Free!..."

That voice! It was Sokes! The detective approached him.

"Cut the cords," the Inspector asked. That done, he stood up with difficulty and whispered to Miss Boston: "You've saved my life."

Knowing how weak he was, she held out to him the flask of brandy from her purse before asking him for explanations. Sokes drank a swallow avidly and declared:

"That's better. I feel ready now to attack those bandits."

"They're in there?"

"Yes, three of them. The old man from the pawnshop, the one called Holland; another named Grant; and a young man I saw pass by rapidly, but I don't know him."

"Well! I know him. That young man, sir, is Nelly Corms disguised."

"We're going to trap the three birds!"

"Where are they now?"

"In the room at the back. Grant's sudden attack surprised me in the pawnshop; I was knocked unconscious. I came to in a quarter hour, tied up, bloody, thrown in a corner with sacks and packages. Crawling silently, I came to this door without knowing where it led. Luck miraculously saved me. You were here. I'm ready now to attack with you."

"Do you have your gun, Sokes?"

"My guns and detective's kit are in the hands of these lowlifes."

"Here's one of my bulldogs. It shoots a half-dozen bullets."

Miss Boston pivoted the armoire, found the door, opened it and slid into the darkness, where Sokes joined her.

VIII. The Moveable Staircase

A long, narrow, dark corridor turned suddenly with a sharp angle to the left. The policemen's rubber-soled shoes made no sound. They came in absolute silence to the room where, less than an hour before, the robbers had thrown Inspector Sokes. Just as they were going further, the sound of steps behind, they threw themselves behind a pile of boxes. The half-light let them see the new arrival was Holland, carrying a little white wooden box. Visibly preoccupied, he didn't notice Sokes was not tied up there. Holland went into the second room where the detectives distinctly heard him mount a wooden stairway which creaked under his feet.

"That ladder will be hard for us to climb," Sokes said.

Just at that moment a voice, Grant's, shouted:

"Holland! Pull up the stairs!"

"All right," Holland said, "but it's not necessary. The gentleman's in no state to fly away."

"Pull it up anyway."

A prolonged creaking began and with the grinding of the pulleys the pieces of wood groaned. There was not a trace of the stairs. However a circular hole cut in the ceiling showed the last steps of a suspended stair. The criminals' refuge was above and by lifting the stairs they cut off communication with possible assailants. And who knows, upstairs they possibly had a secret exit allowing them to escape at the least alert from the room below.

"What's to be done?" Sokes murmured. "That lowlife could shoot at us from above."

"I'm thinking about it right now," the detective said.

While talking, she was looking attentively at the circular hole in the ceiling. She was trying to determine two things: how far the robbers were from that upper room and how to reach the circular hole in the ceiling. She guessed the bandits were at least one room from there and not in the one suspending the stairs.

"Look there!" she said to Sokes.

She pointed to a spot in the ceiling adjacent to the circular hole. It was a decorative plaster rose from which objects were suspended from the ceiling with a strong steel ring. She went back to the first room and returned with the rope

she had seen when she entered. She also carried a tall box that she placed immediately under the plaster rose.

"Climb up on the box," she told the Inspector, "and tie the rope through the ring."

She then tied big knots in the cord, making a ladder. She hoisted herself up and reached the first steps of the hanging stairs. However, Miss Boston was bitterly disillusioned. The raised stair steps almost filled the circular hole, block-ing all passage. Finding it impractical, she went down again to Sokes, who asked:

"No way in?"

"Oh, yes, if you were a snake."

"Since we aren't, we have to stay here."

The detective's forehead clouded. Her voice had somewhat lost its strength. She was trembling slightly.

"Oh, yes, there would be one way, only one way," she finally said. "It's dangerous and we'd be risking our lives."

"Nothing risked, nothing gained," Sokes said.

"I know that, Sokes. So we're going to try that method."

"And that is?"

"To bring the stairs back down."

"The devil!" said Sokes.

"Get your gun ready. As soon as the stairs touch the ground, jump on it."

The detective climbed back up the knotted rope, reached the circular hole, and grabbed a steel chain wound around a pulley. She pulled with all her strength. At first there was a prolonged creaking, then suddenly the chain began to unwind. The movable stairs fell on the floor with an enormous crash.

IX. Gun Shots in the Shadows

The two detectives climbed the length of the stairs, their guns drawn. They came into a dark room opening into a small corridor. Miss Boston went in cautiously. However the loud noise of the stairs falling had alerted the robbers.

"What's that?" Holland shouted.

But Grant's voice answered harshly:

"This way, idiot!"

Miss Nelly Corms added:

"I'll bet it's that damned detective on our heels!"

Miss Boston saw the door to the room occupied by the criminals suddenly shut. Without wasting time, she turned toward Sokes:

"Break it down, sir!"

And Sokes broke down the door. With a vigorous blow to the middle panel, he shattered it and broke away the pieces blocking the detectives' entry. She jumped into the room. The window was open. The three criminals had disappeared. Suddenly the current of air created by the open window and the shattered door blew out the petrol lamp on the table in the middle of the room. Darkness! But Miss Boston ran to the window in time to see Grant slide down the drain pipe. Her pistol shot certainly hit him because he howled in pain and fell into the street, the one where Miss Boston had placed five men in front of Holland's shop. Hearing the shot, the squad arrived just in time. The Invisible Man's lieutenant was shot in the shoulder as Miss Boston had intended. The wound was more painful than dangerous.

Seeing the policemen take charge of the criminal, she shouted to them to fasten the handcuffs solidly. Just then pistol shots in Miss Boston's direction rang out from the vacant land to the left of Ruffers Ban. The bullets only broke some windows beside the detective.

"Quick, Sokes!" she shouted. "The vacant land! The woman with green eyes and Holland must be there!"

She ran to the door, but as soon as she crossed the threshold rapid firing broke out behind her in the apartment's shadows. She drew back to avoid the avalanche of bullets she heard sink in the walls and woodwork beside her. At that moment the policemen on guard in the courtyard came running. The detective heard the policemen's heavy, hurried climb to the moveable stairs. Continuing to shoot, she called out:

"Guns out, gentlemen!"

Everybody was shooting in the darkness at an invisible target. Windows broke noisily; woodwork cracked; bullets hit the wall with a dull thud. Suddenly a cry resounded; likely one of the invisible shooters who was hit. Strange thing! Now only the policemen were firing. They had heard the dull thud of a body on the floor, then a table turned over, and firing from the criminals' direction had completely stopped. Taking out her flashlight, Miss Boston surveyed the battlefield. She exclaimed in astonishment! Instead of several criminals, she was fighting against just one! It was Holland, who, a pistol in each hand, had alternately fired at Miss Boston and the detectives. He had taken shelter behind the table and among all the countless bullets fired by the policeman, only a stray bullet had hit him in the middle of the forehead. He had keeled over in a mass, bringing down the table with him.

Miss Boston touched the cadaver of the fake old man. His heart had stopped. A thin stream of purple blood ran out of a little circular hole. He had died instantly. They relighted the petrol lamp, placed Holland on the table and covered him with an abandoned small coat. Miss Boston sent Sokes and the policemen to search the vacant land, rejecting Sokes' offer to leave policemen for her protection. The detective then began an investigation of the empty apartment. In the next room she found various stolen objects, notably pieces of silk of considerable value, all carefully stacked on shelves. In a safe she found several silver ingots made from melted jewelry or silver pieces. All this spoil took up four rooms. While investigating, Miss Boston thought about how Miss Nelly Corms had been able to escape. In catching her she was almost certain to reach the Invisible Man. Suddenly she heard a movement and, moving pieces of silk, a gaping hole appeared in the wall. A small, spiral staircase led to the ground. This secret passage must have been used by Miss Nelly Corms for her escape.

X. First Invisible Man Encounter in the Secret Tunnel

The descending stairs were narrow and rough, requiring a thousand precautions to avoid a fall. At the end of some time, Miss Boston calculated she had gone down two floors. Her calculations were correct because the stairs then ended, becoming a tunnel with a slight incline. The ground was hard dirt, somewhat humid, showing it was underground. The walls were worn; here and there pieces of wood held up the arch of the ceiling. The tunnel was recently constructed and its opening dated to only a few months back. Miss Boston still advanced, more and more curious to see where this tunnel led.

Suddenly, having passed pieces of wood holding up a particularly weak section of the ceiling arch, she stumbled. She had just been hit a violent blow on the right temple. She saw standing before her a man with a sly, beardless face, wearing a traveling cap. He hit her head again with the butt of his revolver and she lost consciousness. The man then grabbed with both hands the pieces of wood holding up the tunnel arch and shook them. They fell, bring down a part of the ceiling, burying the detective under the debris. The man then dashed back the way the detective had come. He stopped in one of the rooms above in front of the chest of silver ingots, putting as many of them as possible in his pockets and left the apartment by way of the moveable stairs. Whistling a happy little tune, he went to Liverpool Ban, called a cab and was taken to the center or New York.

After having left Miss Boston, Inspector Sokes went down Mäel Street to Ruffers Ban where two men were holding Grant, handcuffed. There, removing some palings, they searched the vacant land behind the fence. This land was absolutely abandoned, littered with construction rubbish, and tall, overgrown weeds. Here and there stones from ruined hovels littered the broken, encumbered ground. Working in a straight line, the policemen methodically explored the ground step by step. After several minutes, one of the men stumbled on a pile of stones, fell, and disappeared. The policeman was lying at the bottom of a hole five or six meters deep, accessed by stairs. In his fall he had fractured his leg. Sokes immediately went down to where he was moaning at the bottom of the ditch. In bringing him back to the surface for medical attention, he was astounded to see an underground passage. He ordered the men to make a torch of wood debris and follow him into the tunnel. It was narrow, dark, and wet. Steps sank in the soft ground as if in slimy clay. Sokes suddenly stopped. Impossible to go further! The passage in front of him was totally closed. There must have been a cave in, because pieces of the ceiling arch were on the ground, pieces of rock were broken, broken beams crisscrossed each other, pieces of wood mixed with bits of earth.

"The devil!" Sokes exclaimed.

Precious time would be wasted clearing the rubble. Suddenly one of the men saw boot heels and exclaimed:

"There's someone underneath there!"

"A cadaver maybe!"

"Certainly a victim of the cave in!"

In fact, under the pieces of wood, two narrow and elegant feet in fine boots appeared.

Suddenly worried, Sokes exclaimed:

"Could that be Miss Boston? Then quick, get to work! Clear out the rubble!"

"She's perhaps dead…"

"Quickly! Quickly!"

The squad set to work, but it took them almost a quarter of an hour to uncover the body buried under the debris. Finally it appeared. It was Miss Boston! She still had her handbag around her shoulder. Sokes took out the flask of brandy and poured a few drops on the pale, discolored lips of the unconscious detective. At the same time, he ordered the men to go for water and a doctor. Examining the detective, he found a rather deep gash on her temple. Then the victim regained consciousness.

"Thank God I came in time," Sokes exclaimed. "Do you feel better?"

"Yes…a little…" Miss Boston smiled feebly.

She was still weak but her vigorous strength and robust constitution soon returned. And she said: "I'm all right, Sokes."

"How did you come to be here?"

"That's a long story…but our fellows?"

"We got only Grant."

"And the woman with green eyes?"

"Disappeared!…Flown away!…"

"That's too bad. We'll have to start over." With a charming smile the detective added:

"Sokes, you saved my life."

"Didn't I say I'd return the favor?"

"Thank you," she said. "You're a sure and good friend and I know you always keep your promises."

XI. The Invisible Man Strikes Again

In the cab carrying the handcuffed Grant to the Central Bureau, she told Sokes about the attempted murder, the secret tunnel, and how she had miraculously escaped.

"But that man," Sokes asked, "did you know him?"

"It's strange," the detective answered. "It seems to me I've seen that face before, but right now I can't put a name to the face or recall under what circumstance I saw it."

"You have no doubt it was he you saw?"

"Absolutely none, Sokes. That was certainly the Invisible Man."

"Grant's interrogation may enlighten us."

"I really don't think so."

"Why's that?"

"He won't talk any more than the others."

"It's true they have their mouths sewn shut."

Miss Boston was right. At his interrogation Grant refused to give the least information. To each question he answered only:

"I have nothing to say."

Finally, asked the name of the Chief, he sneered and said: "Look for it!"

The detective looked him straight in the eyes and said:

"I did, and I found it."

"What…you…the chief…" the robber stammered. But he quickly mastered his emotion and insolently answered:

"Since you've found it, I've nothing more to tell you."

That same evening Grant was locked up in the Tombs prison.

Miss Boston's investigation had resulted in dismantling part of the operations of the One Hundred Thousand Arms Gang and removing Grant and Holland from the game. Every day Grant was taken from prison and brought to the Central Bureau where the Investigating Magistrate conducted interrogations and listened to witnesses. With the massive dossier of proofs the magistrate had accumulated against him, Grant was sure to be sent by a jury to the New York electric chair.

Monday, October 18th, was the ninth day of Grant's interrogation. As usual he was taken at 10 a.m. by a prison vehicle to the Central Bureau. The magistrate was ready to see him at 11:15. However, the clerk sent to bring him into the magistrate's office returned out of breath stammering:

"Sir…Sir…"

But when the impatient magistrate said severely:

"Enough. I don't like jokes. Have Grant brought in." The clerk answered:

"He isn't there, sir."

"What do you mean, he isn't there? Is the prison vehicle still not here?"

"Oh, yes…the vehicle is here…but Grant isn't here. The prisoner has disappeared."

"You mean to say Grant has escaped?"

"I'm afraid so, sir."

"Is the driver of the prison vehicle here?"

"Yes, he's searched the vehicle thoroughly and is tearing at his hair in despair"

"Have him come up!"

When the frightened driver appeared, the magistrate demanded:

"What's all this about?"

"It means the accused man Grant has gotten away."

"Under your nose, without a doubt?"

"Yes, sir, and I don't understand it."

"How did that happen?"

"I picked up the prisoner at the Tombs this morning and I myself locked compartment No.3. Arriving here, I found compartment No.3 locked as it was at the departure, but it was empty. The prisoner had disappeared."

Miss Boston was told of Grant's mysterious, unknown departure during the day. Understandably, she was in a bad humor, saying:

"It's not worth the trouble to risk the lives of so many brave men for this sad and pitiful result."

"What do you expect, Miss Boston," the Chief answered. "Our trouble and effort are daily at the mercy of the least negligence. The wise thing is to do your share and try to repair the damage."

This was the only reproach uttered by Miss Boston. She examined the prison vehicle and quickly discovered the ingenious method of Grant's escape. The floor of vehicle No.3 had been sawed through and, taking advantage of a traffic jam, Grant had slipped through into the crowd and disappeared.

Miss Boston knew The Invisible Man was the author of the escape. She told Sokes:

"He has won once again, but I swear I'll win the last match."

THE MAGIC ELIXIR

I. The Carnival Night Drama

That evening of the 1898 carnival, New York was in full uproar, total madness. Along Broadway there was nothing but joyous crowds, masked revelers shouting, laughing, calling to one another, some in cars, and others on the sidewalks. There were avalanches of confetti and streams of paper falling down on balconies full of spectators, and floating through the warm, perfumed air. Little by little toward the dinner hour Broadway emptied but by 9 p.m. it was animated again, even more so, especially around the Empire Theater. The famous carnival, so long anticipated by the elegant of New York as well as revelers, would take place that night. Lines of hansom cabs and automobiles crowded the area, letting out charming and expensively costumed party goers. There were harlequins in black, red, gray, and white silk; there were sumptuous disguises: rajahs from India, Roman emperors, Constantinople princes in fur cloaks, great lords with gigantic plumes. There was everything from New York costume shops that was sumptuous, rare, and elaborate. This description is less than the reality. It was only when the first dancers came out that the main characters of this new adventure emerged.

At about 3 a.m. in the morning a red harlequin and a black harlequin came down the great Empire Theatre stairs and halted under the monumental canopy. They sent a doorman to find a cab and the black harlequin gave the address of "Peters," the famous night club. The black harlequin said to the red:

"So you don't want to tell me your name?"

"If you absolutely insist, yes. I'll take off my mask at supper."

"Thank you, dear heart. Do you know your personality has intrigued me to the point that I love you?"

"Don't joke!"

"I'm not joking. I'm serious."

"Well, we'll see later."

The black harlequin helped the red harlequin out of the cab in front of the brilliantly lighted Peters Restaurant on Seine Road. A maître d'hôtel in livery came solemnly to greet them and asked:

"Where would you like to sit, sir?"

"A private room," the black harlequin ordered curtly.

And the maître d'hôtel took them up the stairs to the luxurious private rooms. These rooms opened onto a corridor with a thick carpet and as brilliantly lighted as the rest of the restaurant. They entered room No.8.

"You'll be comfortable here, sir," he said, and bowed.

This private room was a delight. Great mirrors, hung over sumptuous couches, ornamented the walls. A chandelier with 20 globes lit the room. The table, waiting only for the diners, was already set up and decorated with flowers and crystal.

The black harlequin and the red harlequin both took off their masks. They were an elegant couple. The man, about 40 or 45 years old, was in evening dress. His fortune must have been great because his shirt front buttons were diamonds of great price. As for the woman, she was supremely elegant, very pretty, with extraordinarily limpid green eyes.

At table, the woman with green eyes was seated facing the door, whereas the gentleman had his shoulders turned to the door. They were joking and flirting and it was easy to see the man was wealthy and had met his companion at the Empire Theatre ball. At a certain point during the meal, the woman shivered.

"What's wrong, dear?" the gentleman asked. "Is there a draft? Perhaps the door is ajar." He got up to go see.

He quickly returned, but he was absent long enough to allow the woman to slip a little white ball about the size of a pearl into her companion's glass. It dissolved immediately in the champagne. Two minutes later, when the man drank his champagne, he rose as if dizzy.

"What's wrong with you, sir," the young woman asked with admirably pretended concern. The man was stuttering and gasping, his breathing suddenly irregular.

"I don't know…I'm choking…I…I…"

And he fell in a heap on the couch behind him.

The woman with green eyes seemed to expect this denouement. A smile of satisfaction played furtively over her beautiful lips.

"The job succeeded," she said, "provided the chief doesn't make me wait too long."

She returned tranquilly to sit at the table and finished her meal, while glancing rapidly from time to time at the unconscious body of the gentleman stretched out on the couch.

Suddenly there were some light, brief, spaced taps on the door. The woman with the green eyes said: "Come in!"

The door opened and a man with an unusually strong face entered.

"I'm on time," he said.

"Yes," the woman answered, and you see on my side everything went off well."

"That's the one?"

The man leaned over the gentleman's body, felt the pulse, sounded his chest, and nodded.

"Perfect," he said. "Let's finish it."

From a billfold in the inside pocket of his suit, he took out a small flat flask containing a colorless liquid. Forcing the gentleman's lips open, he slowly poured some of the liquid into his mouth. As he was pouring, he counted: "one…two…three…four…five…six…seven…eight…That's the dosage. He's good until day after tomorrow."

The gentleman's face became livid, pale as death. His chest stopped moving and he became almost as rigid as a corpse. The man with the flask slid a letter into the gentleman's pocket, took out his wallet and poured its contents on the table. The stack of bank notes there he pushed over to the woman with the green eyes, saying:

"That will be enough to pay for the supper."

Then he proceeded to take off the jewelry, the diamond buttons on the front of the shirt, the rings off the fingers. All that was done in absolute silence and great rapidity. The man ended by writing some words on a scrap of paper which he pinned to the body of the unconscious man.

"Let's go," he said to the woman with green eyes.

They put on the harlequin costumes and masks, the man taking those of the gentleman, paid the bill at the cashier and disappeared in the Seine Road.

II. The Body in Private Room No.8

At about 5 a.m. the last diners had left Peters Restaurant. This was the time the waiters began to put to rights the private rooms on the second floor for the next day. Room No.8 held a surprise. Thinking the man was asleep, the maître d'hôtel called the waiters who cleared tables. They leaned over the body which had a note pinned to it. The maître d'hôtel read aloud the three lines written in a large, strong hand:

My name is Harry Times;
I live at 147 East Avenue
Please take me home.

The maître d'hôtel and the employees burst out laughing. Finally, one of them said: "We have to wake the gentleman."

The maître d'hôtel agreed, saying: "That way he can go home by himself." He shook him vigorously. "Hey! Sir! It's 5 a.m.! The restaurant's closed! Wake up!"

The sleeper seemed perfectly indifferent to these appeals.

"He's a heavy sleeper, that gentleman," said the maître d'hôtel.

He began again to shake the sleeper even harder. Suddenly he stopped:

"He seems to be cold!" he exclaimed.

A waiter touched the body. "That's true! He's dead!"

There was a moment of panic in the private room. Everyone gave his opinion, advising this or that, and finally they decided to tell the hotel director, Mr. Peters. They telephoned him and five minutes later he was there. In his turn he recognized to his profound amazement that Harry Times was dead. He told his employees not to touch anything and to telephone Central Police Bureau.

Seine Road was situated only a short distance from the Central Police Administration. The detectives on duty arrived a few minutes later. The maître d'hôtel and the cloak room employee, who had seen two harlequin's leave, gave contradictory information. But, since the body had an address on his chest, the detectives decided to transport him there. It was about 6 a.m. when Harry Times' body arrived at his home.

A bachelor, he lived with his mother, a woman of rare merit, in a luxurious apartment building He left the management of the large household to her. Harry Times was Director of the Michigan electric trams and as such he had acquired a brilliant fortune. His mother's astonishment and sorrow were understandable, but one of the policemen interrupted her in the midst of her grief to say:

"Ma'am, this small package holds what we found in the gentleman's pockets." He added, "I must tell you that the head of the Central Bureau this morning ordered an autopsy on the gentleman's body."

Astounded, Mrs. Times stood up, asking: "Why?"

"Because we have serious reasons for believing Mr. Times was murdered.

"Murdered! Him!...My son!..."

"Yes, the circumstances surrounding the discovery of the body were significant enough to require a detailed report to the Chief of the Central Police Bureau. An attempted murder requires opening an inquest."

The supposition of murder seemed so monstrous that she refused to believe it. Not knowing the state in which the body was found, the poor woman couldn't understand the basis for the police suspicions.

She looked automatically at the little package on the bedside table. It contained a newspaper into which they had rapidly put everything from the dead man's pockets. There were small trinkets without value except as souvenirs, a small silver kit of toilette articles, a book of West End subway tickets and Harry's wallet. The billfold wasn't entirely empty; it contained an envelope on which was written in big letters:

TO BE OPENED AFTER MY DEATH.

Trembling, Mrs. Times read the letter she held.

I ASK THE MEMBERS OF MY FAMILY WHO FIND MY BODY TO SEND A TELEGRAM IMMEDIATELY TO THE INITIALS: P. K. 47694, CHELSEA

STATION. THE TELEGRAM MUST CARRY ONLY THESE WORDS: "COME WITH THE FLASK." YOU WILL GIVE $5,000 IN CASH TO THE PERSON WHO COMES. YOU WILL LET HIM LEAVE WITHOUT ASKING HIS NAME OR ADDRESS. THIS IS THE EXPRESSION OF MY LAST WILL.

Mrs. Times immediately complied with the directions. She rang for the valet and had him carry the telegram to the Broadway station. Despite her sorrow, she tried to understand this posthumous order, but her thoughts were too disorganized. She wept for the only thing that attached her to life, for her own henceforth useless life, and for the tragic end of her only child.

It was exactly 7:10 a.m.

III. The Unusual Resurrection of Harry Times

The Chief of the Central Police Bureau arrived as usual at 9 a.m. Both the officers going off duty and those coming on duty were there. Sokes was there to take orders for the day's investigations. The minor current affairs were quickly disposed of and then they took up the drama of private room No.8 in the Peters Restaurant. The detective charged with the preliminary investigation recommended an autopsy. The Chief turned the report over to Sokes, telling him to report results to him before noon. Sokes asked, and was given, permission to include Miss Boston in the investigation.

Sokes went directly to Savannah City and found the detective opening her mail. At his entrance she greeted him with: "Good Morning Mr. Sokes, any news today?"

"You guessed it. I've come about an investigation."

"Where is that?"

"In East Avenue. A gentleman was found dead last night in a private room at Peters Restaurant. But the details of that death are bizarre enough to merit your attention for a while."

"And the details, Sokes?"

The Inspector brought her up to date, ending with the fact that the man the woman left with was certainly not the one with whom she entered.

"Naturally," the detective said, "the man was stripped of valuables."

"Completely. He didn't have even a dollar on him."

"An ordinary case," Miss Boston declared sententiously. "At carnival time every year we've been called in about deaths in similar situations."

"Except for the note pinned to his chest."

"Yes, and it's exactly because of that circumstance that I agree to accompany you. Let's go, Sokes. I'm ready."

Sokes took out his watch: "Ten o'clock. We're on time. The thing can be finished by noon."

A cab passing by in Churchill Street took them to Liberty Avenue to the home of the late Mr. Times. Everything there was in disorder and disarray. The servants ran hither and yon and showed not the least emotion about their employer's death.

"You'd think all those people had completely lost their heads." Sokes observed.

Suddenly the door of a small sitting room opened and a somewhat pale man was walking across the room when he saw the two detectives.

"What do you want here?" he asked.

Miss Boston answered: "We've come to examine the cadaver."

"Well," the man said, "examine me."

"What do you mean by this joke, sir," Sokes, annoyed, asked.

"It's not a joke. It's the strict and undiluted truth. I'm the corpse."

"He's a madman!" Sokes grumbled. "He may be a relative of the dead man, driven insane by sorrow."

The man had overheard and answered: "Not at all. I'm not a relative. I'm the dead man himself. It's Mr. Harry Times standing before you."

"Come now," Miss Boston put in, "let's get this straight, sir. This morning, Central Bureau detectives brought here a cadaver found in a private room of the Peters Restaurant. I am Miss Boston and this is Chief Inspector Sokes. We're here to see the cadaver."

"I repeat, Miss, I am the cadaver, or Mr. Harry Times."

"Every mystery deserves an explanation," Miss Boston retorted, "and I'm waiting for yours."

"It's very simple. This morning at seven o'clock I was a corpse. At eight o'clock I was alive again. That's the entire explanation. If you will come into my study, I'll give you additional explanations and details that will fully satisfy you."

Harry Times, because it really was he, stood back and let the two detectives pass into a plain but elegantly furnished study. He said:

"You ask me," he said, "how I can be dead and alive at the same time. I asked myself that also. I concluded that I was just the victim of a daring swindle."

"I'm beginning to suspect that," Miss Boston replied, smiling.

"You're going to be convinced of it, Miss," Harry Times continued. "Last night I decided to go to the Empire Theater ball. I'm not married and that's a distraction permitted to a bachelor. I went there about midnight and after wandering around a bit, I met a red harlequin who seemed charming. I struck up a conversation and the lady didn't seem to dislike my attention. We had a glass of champagne together and after resistance I had no trouble overcoming, I persuaded the red harlequin to have a small supper with me at Peters. There we took off our masks and when the red harlequin took off hers, I saw an exquisite young lady, absolutely delightful."

"Dark hair? Blonde?" asked the detective, cutting short Mr. Times' enthusiasm.

"Blonde," he answered, "and with admirable green eyes."

Miss Boston was surprised, but calmly added:

"Please go on."

"So we had supper. I rose to close the door which had let in a draft of cold air. Hardly had I returned than I felt ill. I fainted and awoke an hour later. That's all I know. As for the rest, the details were given me only a few minutes ago by my mother."

Miss Boston asked him to call his mother. A few minutes later, her eyes still swollen by tears, but excited by the sudden good fortune in seeing her son alive, Mrs. Times entered the study.

IV. Miss Boston Recognizes Some Familiar Profiles

"Mama," said Harry Times, "this is Miss Boston and Inspector Sokes of the Central Police Bureau. They're here about the cadaver I was this morning and the swindled man I am now."

"Ma'am," said Miss Boston, "I would appreciate your giving me details of what happened during that pseudo-death. The affair is now in the hands of the law."

"Gladly, Miss, but my mind is still troubled by all that's happened."

"Ma'am. I'm going to ask you a series of precise and simple questions. When your son's corpse was brought home, did he still have the paper with his address pinned to his suit?"

"No, a policeman was holding it and gave it to me."

"Where is that paper?"

Miss Boston read the note. Mr. Times assured her he had never written it and then showed her the one demanding an immediate telegram to P. K. 47694 at the Chelsea Station. After reading it, Miss Boston noted:

"That's a clever ruse. It succeeded as expected, I presume?"

"Yes," the old lady confessed. "I would have done anything to save my son."

"The man with the flask came?"

"Yes, less than an hour later. He asked to see the corpse. He poured some drops from a flask into his mouth. After that, he demanded the $5,000 agreed on. I gave it to him. He left immediately and ten minutes later my son came back to life. I swear to you, I do not regret the $5,000."

"It was a swindle!" Mr. Harry Times exclaimed vehemently, pounding on the desk.

"Did you ever doubt that?" Miss Boston asked laconically.

"I don't care about the $5,000, but it's the audacity that overwhelms me! I would give another $5,000 to see the individuals who pushed criminal genius to this extraordinary point locked up!"

"That's a pleasure that probably won't cost you that much," Miss Boston answered.

"You think you can arrest these fellows?"

"Yes," the courageous young woman answered firmly.

"Then you know who they are?"

"I can guess. In any case, I know the woman with green eyes is Nelly Corms, connected to a formidable and daring gang, known as the One Hundred Thousand Arms. Nelly Corms almost fell into my hands a short time ago, but she escaped. As for the man with the flask, wasn't he a hefty, dark, muscular, strong man?"

"Exactly!" said Mrs. Times. "That description exactly fits the man who came to get the $5,000."

"In that case, I know the man. His name is Grant, part of the same gang as Nelly Corms. Those are the two principal actors in the swindle victimizing you."

The detective then knew enough to begin her investigation. She assured Mr. Times that all her efforts would be directed toward the arrest of the thieves. Leaving, she said to Sokes:

"Always that gang and that Invisible Man! He's a perpetual nightmare. I won't be able to sleep until the day I see him strapped to the Sing Sing electric chair."

"May that day come soon!" said Sokes.

"I ardently hope so, Sokes. He used an unknown product to make the body resemble a corpse. He possesses the means to bring them back to life. He swindles money from sorrowing families. He has succeeded once. How do we know he won't succeed a second time? Whatever the cost, Sokes, he has to be arrested, because up to now that man is stronger than we are!"

V. The Ghost from a Famous Escape

Leaving the Times apartment, the detectives went to the Chelsea telegraph office. Mrs. Times had sent the telegraph to the man with the flask from there. Miss Boston wanted to see if it was Grant who had picked up the telegram. A large crowd was gathered around the counter. They unexpectedly found Parker, a longtime friend and colleague of Inspector Sokes, in disguise, working as an employee of the telephone section. He signaled to the Chief Inspector, who asked:

"What are you doing here, Parker?"

"I was going to ask you the same question, sir," the agent replied, smiling. "Me, I'm here to be on the lookout for crooks swindling by telephone. And you?"

"Not exactly for the same thing. Miss Boston, here, and I have come for information on an individual who may have picked up a telegram we're interested in from this office."

"Would that by chance be telegram P. K. 47694?"

"That's exactly it. But how did you know, Parker?" the detective asked.

"Oh, it's rather simple," the agent answered. "I took up my post here at 7 a.m. when the office opened. An individual standing in front of the counter asked every 15 minutes for telegram P. K. 47694. That telegram arrived about 7:40. That wait and insistence intrigued me."

"Could you give an exact description?" asked the detective.

"Nothing easier. I had time to examine the man. He was not too tall, had a weather-beaten but strong face."

"Stocky? Tall? Muscular?"

"No, of ordinary height."

"But that's not at all Grant's description!" Inspector Stokes exclaimed.

"Yes," said Miss Boston, "but that description fits another that I had deeply engraved on my memory despite the tragic circumstances."

"And that description is of...?"

"The Invisible Man! Parker's information has great importance, Sokes. The Invisible Man has this time put his hand in the pie. He's come out of hiding and is actively mixed up in the operations. So much the better. That'll make his trail easier to follow."

Thanking Parker for his information they left the Chelsea station. They had not gone ten steps when, taking the telegram out of her pocket, Miss Boston looked closely at the address. Her face lit up; she seemed transfigured.

"What's wrong with you?" Sokes asked.

"I've found it," she announced with an expression of unspeakable satisfaction.

"What's that? May I know?"

"What for many months I've been searching for: simply the name of the Invisible Man."

"And that name?"

"It's…but first, Sokes, I must remind you of an event which you have certainly forgotten. Do you remember that business of the cadaver found on the Chicago Express?"

"Certainly, and so…?"

"That affair put us on the trail of a band of thieves commanded by a man named Tommy. The lieutenant was a thief called Plock. Tommy and Plock both were condemned to death by the New York High Court. The first, Tommy, had his just sentence carried out in the Sing Sing electric chair. The second one, Plock, a few minutes before being taken there himself, mysteriously escaped. The escape has remained absolutely inexplicable as well as unexplained. That escape put all the agents of the Central Police Bureau on every possible and imaginable trail."

"In vain, because Plock has never been found," Sokes noted.

Miss Boston reminded Sokes that the encounter with the Invisible Man in the tunnel exactly fit the description just given by Parker.

"That's incredible!" Sokes exclaimed.

"However, it's the exact truth. But there's something better. What telegram did the Invisible Man pick up? A telegram with the initials P. K.! With what number? 47694! That was the Sing Sing number of the escapee. The Invisible Man and he are one and the same. His daring goes hand in hand with his cynicism."

Astounded, Sokes remarked:

"Don't let anyone talk to me now about Sherlock Holmes' genius! We have better than that in America!"

"Now we have the best of all," Miss Boston said. "We finally have the name of the leader of the One Hundred Thousand Arms Gang and the description of the Invisible Man.

VI. The Chelsea Trail

After leaving Sokes, Miss Boston returned to her apartment in Savanna City. She relaxed, leaving her investigation until the next day. That night of rest, after so many exertions, excitement, and dangers completely restored her in mind and body. Reading her mail and newspapers the next morning, she found in the *Standard*, the following news item:

Last night on 7th avenue, Mr. Jeremy Sanfield, of the Dakota Mining Association, was found dead. It is thought he died from cardiac arrest. The body has been taken to the dead man's home on Long Island.

"Well, well," thought Miss Boston, "there's a death that would seem natural to me for some poor devil, but for a millionaire, it seems to be unusually like that of Mr. Harry Times."

It was exactly 9:40 a.m. Just as she was thinking of investigating, the telephone rang.

It was Sokes. He said:

"It's the Invisible Man again!"

"The 7th Avenue job is probably his?" asked Miss Boston.

"You mean the fake death of Jeremy Sanfield?"

"Yes."

"In that case, you're not wrong. But there's something else. I must talk with you in person. The telephone is not safe."

"Come to Savanna City, Sokes," she said.

The detective hung up and she hardly had time to read for the third time the newspaper article when he rang at her door, saying:

"The resurrection of Harry Times worked too well for it not to be repeated by Plock."

"He repeated it with Jeremy Sanfield?"

"Yes, but the body didn't have a note pinned to it. They found a sealed envelope on him saying: *Open after my death.*"

"What happened before Jeremy Sanfield's fake death?"

"I don't know right now, but I know what followed. His wife opened the envelope, sent a message to the telephone office to Chelsea PK 47694. An hour later, Grant came with the flask, brought the dead man back to life and collected $5,000. But there's more. They've picked up the Invisible Man's trail."

"Bravo, Sokes," exclaimed Miss Boston.

"Don't congratulate me too much."

"Why? Have you lost the trail?"

"No, I wasn't the one who found it. You remember Parker, the agent we met at the telegraph office? When Plock came to pick up the telegram this morning, thinking to do us a favor, he followed him."

"That was an excellent idea," said Miss Boston.

"In my opinion, it would have been better if he had arrested Plock on the spot with the telegram in his hand."

"You can't think of everything, Sokes. What did Parker find?"

Sokes told Miss Boston that Parker followed Plock on a circuitous ramble. Pock finally met and spoke to Grant, who then took the subway toward Long Island. Plock there entered a saloon, ordered a beer, spoke to no one, left and went to Naval Road, where he entered No.12. He then returned to the telegraph office and telephoned Sokes with his information.

"Perfect, Sokes," said Miss Boston. "All this information is valuable. I'm going to telephone our newly resurrected victim and ask him to meet us at the Central Police Bureau. To save time I'll interrogate him about what preceded his apparent death. From there we'll go to Naval Road to see what we have to do to arrest Plock."

Three minutes later they took a cab to the Central Police Bureau and arrived at 11:03 a.m. In the office of the Chief of the Central Police Bureau, they found Jeremy Sanfield fuming with anger over Plock's $5,000 swindle.

VII. Miss Boston in Naval Road

Mr. Jeremy Sanfield was a rather apoplectic fat man, somewhat common and lower class, but very rich. That last quality excused his other faults. Miss Boston summed him up at one glance. She knew that she could get only vague information, some totally contradictory, from a man of that type. Mr. Sanfield recounted his problems mingled with complaints, lamentations, reproaches, cursing his swindlers. Naturally, all that was useless. Coldly, calmly, careful not to interrupt, the famous woman detective heard him to the end. When he finished she said only:

"Very Good."

Mr. Jeremy Sanfield took offense.

"What do you mean, 'Very good?'" he asked vehemently. "On the contrary, Miss, it seems to me this damned business is far from being good!"

"That depends on how you look at it," Miss Boston answered. "As for me, I find everything is for the best in this affair."

Mr. Jeremy Sanfield's bellow was at its height. His stupid expression was eloquent testimony.

Miss Boston said to Sokes:

"We can go back to the investigation."

The two detectives left, leaving Mr. Jeremy Sanfield to his astonishment. Miss Boston knew what she was talking about. The swindle against Mr. Sanfield was set up and carried out by the same hand as that against Mr. Harry Times. The second attack was also prepared at a restaurant where Mr. Jeremy Sanfield had also met a woman with green eyes. In the street, on leaving, he had fainted.

The illustrious detective had to admit that the thieves had been decidedly lucky. She wasn't overly concerned. She knew perfectly well that she would eventually unmask the criminals and triumph over their audacity, cynicism and diabolical genius. But it wasn't the time for thinking and discussing. It was time for immediate action. Therefore the two detectives started toward Naval Road.

It was a short, black road swarming with questionable saloons, dingy cabarets, merchants of more or less shady commerce, in a word, a true benchmark of the low thieves and swindlers of New York. Miss Boston and Sokes agreed that they could not enter as dressed, but must use a disguise. Having no time to return to the city, they used Miss Boston's make-up, bought and donned cast off clothes, used a cab as a dressing room and took on the appearance of those who frequent low dives. Even the cleverest could not have discovered their ruse except with the greatest difficulty. They themselves had to laugh at their appearance. Sokes looked dissipated, whereas Miss Boston rivaled the vilest creatures of Chelsea. Miss Boston decided to go down Naval Road to the right, while Sokes took the left. They separated at Majestic Avenue. They were to meet again in a few minutes in front of No.12, which Parker had pointed out as the one that was probably Plock's hideout. Miss Boston arrived somewhat ahead of Sokes. Together, they cautiously entered the lair of the head of the One Hundred Thousand Arms Gang, now known as the Invisible Man.

VIII. The Mystery of the Double-Decker Launch

That house was, in fact, most miserable. A narrow, filthy, sickening corridor, ending in a rickety wooden staircase filled with garbage, separated it into two rooms.

"Before going upstairs," she said to Sokes, "let's look at the courtyard."

The courtyard stored all sorts of debris: broken boxes, dirty barrels, rubble, making entry difficult. There was no sign of construction. Four badly built walls half falling in ruins enclosed it. This looked like a false path. Just as they returned to the stairway, it started to rain violently.

The next story had only two rooms. One was empty and the other was occupied by the panhandlers who swarm over all American cities, particularly New York. Several minutes spent behind that door convinced Miss Boston that they had nothing in common with those she was searching for. Sokes stayed on guard while she entered the second floor she had thought empty. Like the rest of the house, it was a miserable lodging. In the corner there was a truly filthy, repugnant mattress. Rags hung on the walls; old clothes were strewn over the floors.

Miss Boston surveyed the pitiful jumble rapidly. Nothing there indicated Plock, Grant and Miss Corms had anything in common with this hideout. Besides, its disgusting state certainly wasn't one in which the thieves, whose daring robberies netted several thousand dollars, were accustomed to live. So, this was a false trail. Miss Boston was very annoyed. It was evident Agent Parker was mistaken. Leaving the hovel, she met Sokes, who said he had heard footsteps in the corridor. They seemed to come from the courtyard.

The rain had stopped. In the courtyard the loose dirt had changed into mud, showing distinct footprints. Following the footprints, they came to a large pile of rubble behind which they found a breach in the old, half demolished wall. The high weeds on the other side were pierced by a short path, showing it was frequently traveled. It ended in a small locked door, which Miss Boston opened with her jimmy. She was astonished to find a two-decker yacht on the other side. There were no other boats in the vicinity. What did that mystery mean?

IX. A Daring Plan which is Renounced

Miss Boston proposed to board the yacht, but Sokes warned:

"That would be madness!"

"Don't we have our revolvers, Sokes?"

"Yes, certainly, but..."

"Are you holding back, Sokes?"

"With you, never! You are free to decide whatever you like, but aren't you risking your life in this dangerous act?"

"In a word, Sokes, you want to know my plan. Well, that boat is incontestably a hideout of the gang. We're going to board it, search it from top to bottom and wait until it shoves off. It will very likely stop at some spot we need to know. There we'll do whatever circumstances warrant."

Sokes pointed out several dangers. Plock might be on board the yacht and if immediately arrested, they wouldn't know where it's headed, and they wouldn't know how long they might have to wait for the boat to lift anchor.

"And the third danger is not less serious. The boat is unknown territory for us. Consequently we would operate in the dark."

"Very well reasoned, Sokes. I agree with you. I'll look inside the yacht while you stand guard here."

She saw no gangplank to the boat. How did the robbers get in and out? She soon saw the yacht was held solidly against the current by an iron chain. The criminals needed a strong wrist to pull it to the bank. Miss Boston had no fear imitating them. In less than two minutes she was on board. There appeared to be two cabins under the main deck. She opened the wooden hatch and descended. The interior was not divided into cabins, but contained only one large room with three hammocks as beds and several chests holding a collection of the most varied disguises: wigs, false beards, everything indispensable to a gang like the

One Hundred Thousand Arms. A small chest contained three flasks filled with a colorless liquid and a box filled with small white pearls which smelled of chloroform. She put one of the flasks and some of the pearls in her small purse. For the moment she knew enough. The yacht was used by the gang as a hideout and a place to change disguises. She had only to rejoin Sokes.

At that moment she heard a revolver shot on the bank of the Hudson. She jumped to the bank and saw her comrade struggling with someone she immediately recognized. It was Nelly Corms, the main character of several thefts! The woman with green eyes! How had Sokes surprised her? That was a question for later. She grabbed her arms from behind and slapped on the handcuffs. One sharp click and that was all. Nelly Corms was paralyzed and a prisoner.

"My!" Sokes exclaimed. "She gave me a hard time!"

"Dirty cop!" The woman with green eyes shouted.

"Quick!" said the detective. "Let's get the 'lady' on the way to the Central Bureau."

X. A Bird that Escaped the Net

Sokes ran ahead and found a hansom cab near the iron bridge. Miss Boston brought the prisoner, fuming with rage. Sokes hoisted the prisoner into the cab and ordered the cab driver to reach the Central Bureau in all haste.

"Well, Sokes," the detective asked, "how did you lay hands on this charming bird?"

"How?" Sokes asked. "It was very simple. She came in by Naval Road, followed the same path as we did. Apparently my appearance inspired her with complete confidence because I didn't bother her at all. She wanted to go aboard the yacht. I stopped her; you arrived; that was all."

Questioned, Miss Nelly Corms wouldn't say a word. Miss Boston gave orders that she be watched particularly closely, fearing Plock would make a desperate effort to snatch her from the clutches of the law. Nelly Corms was locked in a cell guarded by three policemen, until further orders.

Because of the constant rain, dusk fell quickly that evening. After having delivered their prisoner, the two detectives returned to Naval Road. Had the boat given up all its secrets? Miss Boston and Sokes both thought not. Since Nelly Corms was caught trying to board the yacht, wasn't it logical to think Grant and Plock could get picked up in the same way? That's why, 20 minutes later, they were on the banks of the Hudson. The yacht was immobile, heavy, dark, silent in the choppy water. It seemed entirely abandoned, tranquil, with no suspicious movement in the area. At that moment, however, Miss Boston saw a shadow appear in the direction of the ruined wall of the courtyard.

"What is it?" the Inspector asked.

"Look! There!" the detective answered.

"Ah! I see."

In the direction of the ruined wall a dim shadow appeared, carefully looking around.

"Is it Grant or Plock?" Sokes asked.

"Certainly one or the other."

"A new bird in the net."

"Wait! Too bad. He's going to see us."

"That's true. He'll see us."

At that moment the shadow stopped midway in the path toward the boat.

"Seen! He's seen us!" Sokes groaned.

"Maybe not yet," the detective answered.

A sharp whistle broke the silence. The shadow had just given a signal. He seemed to wait for a response. On an off chance, Miss Boston whistled. The shadow responded immediately. Not knowing what to do, Miss Boston didn't immediately answer. After a minute the shadow suddenly turned on his heels and ran toward the breach in the courtyard wall.

"That does it!" Sokes said in a rage. "We've had it!"

"Quick!" shouted the detective. "Follow him! Don't let him get away!"

The game was serious. The chase continued along the Naval Road. The street lamps just coming on allowed her to see the fleeing shadow. It was Grant. She had hoped it would be Plock. Nevertheless, it would be good to make that catch. Grant wasn't one of those fellows to leave in circulation on New York sidewalks. Now prey and hunters rushed toward Sea Road. Little by little, Grant, who had been shot in the shoulder earlier by Miss Boston, was losing ground, visibly tiring. Miss Boston noticed that Grant was fleeing in the direction of the river and not back towards the city where he had a better chance to escape.

Suddenly, Sokes shouted in fury. Grant had just disappeared. There was nothing marvelous or mysterious about his disappearance. He had just dashed into a saloon in the middle of Sea Road. Miss Boston shared Sokes' anger. She was familiar with that saloon. It was kept by a certain Powers, an affiliate of several gangs. He had always operated carefully in order to avoid the attention of the police. What's more, that saloon had a second exit into an obscure impasse with as bad a reputation as the rest of lower Chelsea. Grant had gone that way to lose himself in the extraordinary labyrinths of all the little lanes and impasses of that part of the neighborhood. It would be absolutely useless to follow him. The time the detectives used to find his traces again would be used by Grant to put the greatest distance possible between him and the police.

"That was going too well, Sokes," said Miss Boston.

"That's true. We would have been too lucky to take two birds in one day."

"But the day isn't over yet, Sokes."

"Aren't you giving up chasing these crooks today?"

"Me? Absolutely not!"

"What do you intend to do?"

"Return to the boat."

"Do you think you'll find Grant there?"

"I won't say yes or no. But we must finish it. Earlier is better. This evening if possible."

And in the night falling slowly over Chelsea, the two detectives went back to the Hudson bank where the yacht was moored.

XI. The Tragic Chase on the Hudson

The bank was dark and deserted. She and Sokes would have to walk almost blindly before reaching the spot where the yacht was moored. The flickering light of a street lamp, its flame trembling in the night wind, showed they were near the ruined wall on the Hudson's bank.

"The Devil!" Sokes complained. "We can't see a thing!"

"But it was here, wasn't it?"

"Yes. Let's wait until our eyes get used to the darkness."

"And our ears to the silence."

This wasn't useless advice. They suddenly heard a chain drop into the Hudson, then vigorous rowing stirring the water. The criminals were escaping into the middle of the Hudson! After listening to hear which direction the boat had taken, the energetic detective and Sokes hurried along the bank in the direction of Brooklyn. They ran until they were out of breath, stopping occasionally to guess whether the boat had changed course. Miss Boston was convinced the thieves didn't know they were being followed and that there were at least two aboard, since it required at least four strong arms to fight the Hudson's current. After a quarter of an hour, Miss Boston stopped. They had reached a landing mooring small boats that in the day were either party boats or used to board the great transatlantic steamers waiting for their entry into port. The landing was guarded by a night watchman, asleep at that moment in a little cabin on the wharf. Explaining to him why she needed a boat would have wasted precious time. She went down the wharf stairs, used her jimmy to open the padlock attaching a small boat to the landing. Followed by Sokes, she jumped in and began to row into the middle of the river, searching in the night for the yacht that must soon arrive. Suddenly her boat began to dance about violently, waves slapping its sides, indicating the approach of the yacht. Miss Boston directed Sokes:

"Man the boat. I'm going to stand in the prow."

"In which direction?"

"Follow the yacht."

There was a moment of silence. The waves around the detective's little boat rose higher, stronger, more violent. The two boats would certainly soon collide. Little by little a black form emerged from the scattered shadows and was outlined against the dark horizon. It was the yacht. It would soon reach the bright waters of the Port of New York, lit by the dazzling torch of the Statue of

Liberty. Seeing that, Miss Boston knew that if they reached that zone, the pursuit would again be in vain and their diabolical genius would have found a way to escape. So, she silently whispered to her faithful Sokes the order:

"Board."

"You want to board the yacht? That's dangerous."

"Danger is my job, sir!"

"It's your decision!"

A moment later, the boat drew up softly beside the yacht. Grabbing the side with both hands, Miss Boston hoisted herself aboard. Revolver drawn, she went forward and fell on Grant, who turned loose of the oar.

"Damnation!" he shouted.

"Hands up!" the detective shouted.

As loud as he could, Grant yelled: "Come here, Plock!"

Miss Boston answered with: "Sokes, come on board!"

She had grabbed the criminal by the throat and was holding on tightly. Sokes was there in a minute. He hurled himself on Grant, but a sudden dull sound made him turn around. Something black and voluminous, hardly seeming human, had appeared on the yacht's bridge. The thing had just balanced on the edge of the yacht. An enormous splash of water inundated the bridge. The Hudson closed over what had just fallen in it.

"What was that?" Sokes asked.

"Plock, no doubt," said the detective

An inspection assured her that Pock had disappeared. By suicide he had escaped the vengeance of the law and the just punishment awaiting him. An hour later, Grand, in handcuffs, entered the Central Police Bureau.

XII. The Fatal Experiment

Miss Boston knew the flasks she had found aboard the yacht contained the magic elixir which had allowed the robbers to extort $5,000 from Mr. Times and from Mr. Sanfield. But in what proportions? She asked the Chief of the Central Bureau to allow her to experiment on Grant, without Grant's knowledge, of course. The Chief willingly consented. A white pearl was dropped into Grant's drink and two minutes later the thief was unconscious. The detective had him placed on a table and ordered Miss Nelly Corms brought in. She was still obstinate and silent.

"Miss Corms," the detective said, "I know you hold the secret of the magic elixir and how to use it. Your accomplice, Grant, has been put to sleep with the pearls. Here's a flask of the elixir. Please wake Grant."

A look of hatred came into Miss Nelly Corms' eyes. She took the flask held out by the detective.

"Ah! Ah!" she laughed derisively. "You want to know the secret? Well, you won't get it."

With a violent gesture she threw the flask to the floor and it broke into a thousand tiny pieces.

That evening Grant was still asleep. Medical doctors called in declared themselves, after many efforts, unable to call him back to life. Plock's secret had vanquished medical science. Grant died in the night without having regained consciousness and from that moment the woman with the green eyes became absolutely mute, even when two months later the New York high court condemned her to 30 years at hard labor for her participation in the crimes contrived and organized by the Invisible Man.

THE CAPTURE OF THE INVISIBLE MAN

I. The Philadelphia Trunk

Miss Boston was in her study organizing her files when her maid opened the door to ask:

"Are you expecting a trunk from Philadelphia, Miss Boston?"

"A trunk?"

"Yes, a big, black, long and flat trunk."

"No, I'm not expecting a trunk."

"Two men from the railway station have just brought one up and it has your name and address."

She wasn't expecting anything from Philadelphia, and certainly not a trunk. What could that mean? She immediately thought it a ruse or a trick by some criminal. But to be sure, she had at least to look at it. As the maid had reported, it was now in the front hall where two men from the railway station had just put it and left after getting their tip.

It was an ordinary trunk, rather heavy and somewhat low, with leather bands. On the top it bore the address:

Miss Ethel Boston
Savannah City
New York
From: Philadelphia:
WBZ 4438. a.g. 9.

She saw the address was typewritten and, using a knife, carefully removed it, folded it, and put it in her study. The trunk had a padlock but no key. She took a little jimmy out of her purse and the trunk was opened. She first saw a pile of straw. She pushed it aside and found a large heavy mass under her hands. She uncovered it completely and let out a startled exclamation. The trunk held a cadaver, a heavy man of middle height, dark, carefully shaven. He had a large hole in the middle of his forehead showing clots of black blood. The right eye was black and singed, interspersed with grains of powder, indicating clearly that he had been shot point blank.

Miss Boston's maid lifted her hands to heaven exclaiming:

"A dead man! A dead man in the house, Miss!"

151

"Come now, Mary. Calm down and help me carry this gentleman to a couch in the living room."

"I wouldn't dare touch him, Miss!"

The detective smiled and said:

"It's true you're not accustomed to it. There has to be a first time for everything. Your first time is today. I can't carry him by myself; you have to help me."

Making the best of a bad situation, the maid resigned herself to helping. The distance from the front hall to the living room was quickly crossed and the cadaver put on the couch.

"That's astonishing," she said. "It seems to me this dead man's face is not totally unfamiliar to me. I have certainly encountered that man somewhere, but where?"

The dead man was conventionally dressed. Miss Boston's first act was to explore the dead man's pockets. His pockets contained nothing, not the least object, not the least paper.

"Why was that cadaver sent to me? For what purpose? To what end?"

Was it an obscure threat? Was it a bet? Was it a challenge? She had only one clue. The trunk came from Philadelphia. With luck she could trace the sender using the numbers and letters WBZ 4438, a.g. 9, on the shipping ticket. For that she had to go to Philadelphia. But before doing that she must at least know who the cadaver was. Except for the address on the railway ticket, which resembled thousands from all the railways in the United States, there was no exterior mark.

"However," Miss Boston thought, "if the trunk comes from a major manufacturer it must carry some sort of mark."

She returned to the trunk and smiled. The mark was there engraved in the wood of the trunk bottom: A + X.

Back in her study she took down the AMERICAN COMMERCE AND INDUSTRY DIRECTORY, leafed to the chapter on travel articles. Thousands of diverse manufacturers' marks were aligned in numerous columns. The mark A + Z was that of Pat Strom on Market Avenue in New York. What? The Philadelphia trunk was bought in New York? Why? In what circumstance? By whom? She immediately decided to go to Pat Strom on Market Avenue. Just as she was going to the door, the doorbell rang.

II. Both the Cadaver and the Murderer Identified

It was Mr. Sokes, Chief Inspector of the Central Police Bureau, her usual companion in investigations. Miss Boston asked him to accompany her if he had no other business that morning. He asked:

"What's it about?"

She quickly opened the living room door to show the anonymous trunk cadaver. Sokes, shocked, stepped back.

"But that's a dead man…"

"Yes, right, Sokes. Do you know him by any chance?"

"Yes! Certainly! That's Stanley, one of my colleagues at the Central Bureau."

"I knew I had seen that face before," Miss Boston murmured.

"How did Agent Stanley die and, most of all, how did he wind up here at your apartment?"

"I can't answer the first part of your question. As for the second, I can satisfy you immediately."

The detective motioned the Inspector to follow her to the open trunk, still half full of straw.

"That's how the corpse arrived and that's why he's here now. As for his death, the nature of his wound indicates that he was shot at close range with a revolver."

"Where does the trunk come from?"

"From Philadelphia, but it was bought in New York. I know the merchant's name and I was just going there when you arrived."

The two detectives started on foot to Savannah City. On the way Miss Boston brought up the questions she had resolved to ask Sokes in order to clarify the preliminary circumstances of the drama. The murderer had forced her to play a role in spite of herself.

"Tell me, Sokes," she asked, "was Agent Stanley working on any special mission?"

"Yes, he was investigating the robbery of the Central Bank. Day before yesterday I received his last report which told me he had a serious lead."

"Where?"

"In Chelsea."

It was in Chelsea that they discovered the hideout of the head of the One Hundred Thousand Arms Gang, Plock, the escapee from Sing Sing.

"As for Stanley, is that all he said?"

"Yes, he was to report this morning. He didn't come. I understand why now."

Miss Boston saw some relationship between his death and their fight on the banks of the Hudson. Market Avenue is on the east side of Chelsea. He was probably killed there where the trunk was bought. He was sent to Philadelphia from New York to divert suspicion. The loading station from New York to Philadelphia was on the east side of Chelsea.

"Therefore we must look for poor Stanley's killer in Chelsea."

"Indubitably!"

While they were talking, the detectives had turned in the direction of Chelsea and Market Avenue. In the middle of the street they reached the Pat Strom travel articles store. It was a large establishment filled with a crowd of customers. Miss Boston and Sokes headed immediately toward the trunk section where they found trunks in shape, size, and color exactly like the one used to ship Agent Stanley.

"There's the sister of the one in my front hall," Miss Boston said, pointing to one of them. She called one of the salesmen and asked:

"Do you sell very many of these trunks?"

"Not many, Miss. They're not a form used very often for traveling."

"In that case, you must remember having sold one some days ago."

"Perfectly. To a blonde lady."

"To a blonde lady, you say?"

154

"Yes, but the lady was with a gentleman of middle height."

Miss Boston asked for more details. The Chief Inspector was all ears and listened to the conversation with astonishment. Miss Boston finally asked:

"Was the trunk delivered, or did the buyer take it with him?"

"It was delivered."

"Where? To what address?"

A rapid examination of the sales books, facilitated by the recent date of the purchase, showed the trunk had been delivered to Mr. Weston of Philadelphia at the Central Hotel. Now light was shed on the first part of the drama. The trail was opened. Thanking the salesman for his useful statements, followed by Sokes, she went back to Market Avenue, and called a hansom cab, giving directions to the Central Hotel in the Bowery. To Sokes she said:

"Did you understand the description which the salesman gave?"

"I'm afraid to guess."

"It's the description of Plock, the Sing Sing escapee, the head of the One Hundred Thousand Arms Gang. Only one thing surprises me."

"And that is?"

"The presence of that blonde woman. Until now she hasn't appeared in the exploits, the thefts, the crimes and misdemeanors of that terrible gang."

"Is she perhaps a new accomplice?"

"I'd be surprised. I think rather that woman plays another role in Plock's life. What? I don't know yet, but I'll find out, just as I'll find the criminal himself."

They had arrived at the Bowery.

III. WBZ 4438, a.g. 9

The Central Hotel, one of the most elegant in New York, catered to rich foreign travelers and Americans wealthy enough to afford several dollars a day for a room. Why had he registered there? Miss Boston thought she could guess. He was preparing a profitable heist which would allow him to cross the ocean and live peacefully in Europe. Her first visit was to the hotel manager, Mr. P. F. Gingers, a friendly and courteous man who asked how he could help. Miss Boston answered:

"By giving me some simple information and in return I'll give you some which will interest you and be useful for your establishment that until now has had a good reputation."

"What! Does the Central Hotel risk its perfect reputation without my knowledge? What do you need to know, Miss?"

"Do you have a gentleman named Weston from Philadelphia here?"

Using his intercom, Mr. Gingers ordered:

"Bring me last week's register."

He flipped through it and stopped suddenly at the bottom of a page. " 'Mr. Roberts Weston, banker, Philadelphia. Arrived the 28th; left the 31st.' He's no longer here, Miss Boston."

Miss Boston enlightened Mr. Gingers as to the thief's activities. However, Mr. Gingers said:

"No one has complained of a theft."

"He was probably working on another job. In case he comes back, keep him under surveillance and telephone the Central Bureau."

The detective took leave of the manager and went to find the hotel porter. Given a good tip, the porter agreed to search his memory concerning Mr. Roberts Weston of Philadelphia. Miss Boston's efficient and minute interrogation mainly covered the trunk delivered from Market Avenue. The porter remembered that because of a particular circumstance. When they had told Weston, really Plock, about its arrival, he had told them not to send it to his room, but instead had put it into a hansom cab and left.

"In what direction? What street?" Miss Boston asked.

"I don't know," the porter answered, "but the groom who went with Mr. Weston to the cab might tell you." And he called him. Miss Boston posed the same questions and was answered:

"He told the cabman to go to Mina Ban in Upper Chelsea, to 18 or 28; I don't remember which."

Five minutes later Miss Boston and Sokes were on the way to Upper Chelsea.

"This is what's called following a trail step by step," Sokes, visibly happy, said.

"Provided there's not a gap in the trail," the detective answered.

"Why could that be?"

"Because a fellow as strong and daring as Plock has more than one string to his bow. He'll take his precautions, even more so since he knows we're on his heels."

The cab had arrived at Powell Station of the Metropolitan subway, very near Upper Chelsea. The two detectives soon reached Kensington Gardens. That part of the city had one of the worst reputations in New York. It was the kingdom of the criminal aristocrats, with little, narrow crisscrossing streets in an extricable jumble. However, Miss Boston and Sokes were familiar with the area and could find their way there. Without hesitating they started toward Mina Ban, a somewhat wider street, filled with shady bars and even more dubious saloons.

They first stopped at No.18. There was no concierge there and they wasted an hour searching for information. They were convinced he certainly was not at No.18. They found No.28 to be a more imposing building. There was a concierge, a colossal brute with huge fists capable of felling a bull. He became suspicious at the detective's first questions. He got up from the stool where he was sitting, reading the morning's newspaper, and asked in a tone full of menace:

"Well! What do you want with Weston?"

"We want to see him."

"Why?"

"That's our business."

"And if it's mine by chance?"

"In that case we'd put the handcuffs on you, my friend."

"What? Me? Pat Fox in handcuffs?" the giant bellowed.

"Just so," Miss Boston said calmly.

"Where's my club? I'm going to kill you, you dirty cops..." and he turned around as if to look for it, but evidently not finding it, he just said:

"I'm going to bash your faces in..." but before he finished his sentence the detectives had trained their revolvers on him. He stepped back.

"Hold on, there!" Miss Boston commanded. "Big as you are, we're not afraid of you. Put your paws down! Any movement and I'll put a bullet in your head!"

The calm daring of the young detective terrified him. He sat back down on the stool, grumbling:

"After all, it's none of my business. Do whatever you like with Weston."

"Where is he?"

"He's not here."

Miss Boston repeated:

"Where is he if he's not here?"

"I don't know anything about it. That's his business. He doesn't tell me."

"Does he live here?"

"He has a room on the third floor—door No. 12."

"Good. Sokes will you go up there and open it with your jimmy and bring down what you find interesting?"

157

"And you?"

"I'll stay here to guard our friend, Pat Fox."

While Sokes was gone the giant never stopped looking at the detective with his eyes full of hate, as if waiting for a moment to catch the detective off guard to attack her. But the two revolvers leveled at him impressed him. He calmed down, fearing as Miss Boston had promised, a bullet in the head. Sokes soon returned with a piece of paper in his hand, a shipping receipt: WBZ 4438, a.g. 9.

"Was that all?"

"There was a pool of blood on the bedroom floor."

IV. Plock's Jokes

On the way back to the Central Bureau, the detectives exchanged their thoughts.

Miss Boston said:

"There's no doubt that Plock is the murderer and that the unfortunate Stanley was put in the trunk there and shipped to Philadelphia, to be returned later to New York. That dump is only a temporary hideout for Plock. He seems to have a number of them in New York which let him slip away easily and throw the police off the track. We've lost Plock's track at Mina Ban. We must pick it up somewhere else."

"The whole difficulty of the problem is there," Sokes agreed.

At the Central Bureau the Chief agreed with Miss Boston and Sokes that Agent Stanley's body should be taken from Savannah City to his home in Beresford, a charming little New York suburb. Sokes was to concentrate solely on the dangerous Invisible Man, Plock, with Miss Boston.

"We have to finish it," the Chief declared.

"At whatever cost?" Miss Boston asked.

"Yes, Miss Boston, at whatever cost; it's absolutely necessary."

Miss Boston, Sokes and three morgue employees went to Savannah City to collect Stanley's body. A van was waiting there to take it to Beresford, to his home. It was about 2 p.m. when the little group arrived at Miss Boston's apartment.

"You're here, Miss, said the maid. "I wasn't expecting you."

"Why not?"

"The gentlemen who came told me you wouldn't return until six o'clock."

"What gentlemen?"

"Those who came to pick up the dead man. They said you told them to."

From the answers to the questions Miss Boston asked her maid it appeared clear that two hours after her departure two men, one of whom was certainly Plock, had come to Savannah City saying they were to transport the corpse to the morgue. The maid, glad to be rid of the dead man, saw nothing strange in this.

"Plock has triumphed right down the line," Miss Boston said to Sokes.

"He's reached the height of audacity. He can't go any higher."

"You'll have to admit," Sokes said, "it takes rare daring to take from your home the cadaver sent to you."

"The reason for that seems to me bizarre."

"Couldn't it be simple bravado?"

"Maybe, but until we know, we have to ask what's become of the corpse. Before everything, we must assure poor Stanley repose which these murderers seem to refuse him. On the other hand, transporting a cadaver in the middle of New York poses more difficulties than transporting millions of valuables or jewels."

The detectives went down to the building's concierge. She had seem them enter and leave.

"They were carrying a rather heavy bundle, weren't they?" Miss Boston asked.

"Not at all, Miss. They had no bundle entering or leaving."

"That's strange. That means the cadaver is still in the house."

The detective went to the door of the building, looked up at the façade, and came back to the concierge and asked:

"Would you please lend me the keys to the tenth floor?"

"Here you are, Miss."

"And now, Sokes, please follow me."

They took the elevator to the tenth floor and Miss Boston opened the apartment on the left. She entered, opened the dining room door and saw Stanley's cadaver hanging on the French window espagnolette[10] by a black silk scarf. She approached and saw a letter between his stiff hands. She removed it and read it aloud to Sokes:

Miss Boston.
The corpse was a first warning.
That wasn't enough for you.
Here's the second.
I give you 48 hours to stop following me.
You know who I am, what I can do.
Plock

"That's plain talk," the detective said. "Unfortunately, that scum had the wrong address."

"That's the height of daring and cynicism," Sokes growled.

"He gives me 48," said Miss Boston. "That's a gift I don't accept. In 48 hours I'll have this thief or…"

---

[10] A type of window-lock. (*Note from the Translator.*)

Sokes knew the detective thought it unnecessary to swear an oath she had long before sworn to keep.

V. The Fear of Sing Sing: The Beginning of Denunciations

An inextricable problem! A situation without a solution. Plock, to escape the pursuit of the detectives, had operated with such cleverness for several months already that he had gone head to head with Miss Boston, that living terror of robbers and perpetual nightmare of criminals. That was the first time the celebrated detective had fought such a formidable opponent. But for all that, Miss Boston had gained an essential point: Plock was in New York.

By the fireplace, sunk in a deep armchair, Miss Boston mentally went over the various phases of that tragic affair. Suddenly she was snatched from her reverie by the ring of the telephone. It was Sokes, who announced a new piece of information. The giant, that brute of a concierge at Mina Ban, had just come into the Central Police Bureau, but refused to talk to anyone but her. She quickly replied:

"Then I'm on my way."

"We're waiting for you impatiently."

"While you're waiting, keep an eye on that fellow."

"He's in my office."

"I'm coming!"

Five minutes had not elapsed when the detective made a discreet and rapid entry into the Chief Inspector's office.

"Here I am, Mr. Sokes. Where's our man?"

"Over there."

"Bring me up on what's happened, quickly."

"Here's what happened. While we were in Savannah City, this Pat Fox came to the Bureau. He asked for me. As I wasn't there; he was refereed to my secretary. He declared he had some information to give about Plock. They had him wait. When I returned I wanted to interrogate him, but he declared: 'I won't talk except to the little woman who handcuffed me this morning.' I called you. You're here."

"Marvelous, Sokes. I'm curious to learn what he has to say, why he's saying it."

"It could be a ruse."

"In that case, it won't take me long to find out. Have this Fox come here, Sokes."

The giant came in. He was twisting his cap between his fingers stupidly and regarded the detective timidly. She was seated beside Sokes' desk, casually playing with a paper opener.

"Well, Mr. Fox, it seems you want to talk to me. Why will you speak only to me?"

"I'm going to tell you frankly, Miss. First of all, you nailed me in a way no one has ever tempted. Next, because I don't hold to being mixed up in dirty jobs. Me, I like my liberty, and Sing Sing's a place where I don't want to finish my days."

"I can easily understand that, Mr. Fox. What did you want to say to me?"

"It's about Weston…"

"You know him only by that name?"

"To tell the truth, Miss, he has several."

"Plock, for example."

"Yes, well, it's about Plock."

Fox seemed embarrassed to go on. He turned and twisted his cap in his fingers, searching for words. To help him, the detective said:

"It's probably about what happened in Plock's bedroom at Mina Ban that you want to tell me about?"

"That's right, Miss. You may know what happened in that bedroom."

Coldly, she asked: "Do you?"

He answered: "Me, I don't know too much, but I believe Plock argued with someone. He shot him in the head, according to what the neighbors told me."

"So, you weren't there?"

"No, that evening I was at Bell Island. I have witnesses to prove it. I came precisely here to tell you that."

"I'll take the up at the proper time. And what else?"

"The next is easy. Two days ago Plock asked me to help him take a trunk to send it to the Philadelphia station. I couldn't refuse. The trunk was heavy. I immediately knew it must hold the body of the man he killed. But after all, that wasn't my business, since the police hadn't been nosing about. So I helped him put it in a cab and take it to the Philadelphia station. I got a dollar tip. Here it is." With a rough gesture, he threw it on the table. "I'm giving back the dollar. I don't want trouble for a dollar."

"And is that all you want to tell me, Mr. Fox?" the detective asked with an ironic smile.

The man seemed to hesitate, and finally, making an effort, he admitted:

"No, Miss. That's not all."

"What more? Look, Mr. Fox, since you began speaking frankly, you have to wind up the same way."

"All right, Miss," the concierge said rapidly, "I came to point out to you the way to catch Plock."

Sokes noticed a sudden, slight tremor in the detective. But he heard her respond to Fox's proposition with:

"Thanks, sir. To draw me into a clever little trap, right?"

Fox solemnly lifted his big, heavy hand.

"I swear that what I'm suggesting is honest."

At such an unusual word, in such an unusual mouth, the detective couldn't help smiling, but she answered:

"I'll agree to do what you point out, Mr. Fox, on condition that your head answer for the success of the affair."

"In that case, here it is!" Fox exclaimed, giving his head a vigorous slap.

"Good," said the detective. "Tell me where I can find Plock, and if I succeed there's $100 in it for you."

VI. Plock Appears a Perfect Gentleman

Fox sat down comfortably in a chair in front of the desk, speaking with more assurance as he saw the detective was disposed to listen to him.

"A hundred dollars," he said, "that's a good amount to earn, to pick up. But to prove my good intentions and frankness, I don't want to take it until Plock is in handcuffs."

"Understood!" said Miss Boston.

The Mina Ban brute continued:

"Pluck suspects everybody. I think he even distrusts the people in his gang. I saw him many times come back to his room in a different disguise. He's very clever. Sometimes he's dressed as a perfect gentleman, in evening clothes and cloak. You'd never take him for the dirty toad he is."

Sokes broke out in laughter. But, very serious, Fox protested:

"I'm telling the truth. Strike me dead if I'm lying! One day a woman came to ask if Plock was there. She was a beautiful person, blonde, elegant, and she smelled very nice. Plock was there. She went up to the room and on the stairs she met Percy."

"Who's that Percy?"

"He's a walk-on actor at the Empire Theatre. Percy met her when he had a walk-on part in an opera there. He told me her name was Miss Rosie Adams. Since then I learned she's more than a friend to Plock. She passes for his wife or something like that."

Turning to Fox, the detective asked:

"Do you remember those who bought the trunk at Pat Strom?"

"Yes, it seems to me the blonde lady is the same as the one here."

"Well, that's what I was thinking. Go on, Fox."

"That's all I know. I give you my word."

"But what does that woman have to do with Plock's arrest?"

"By following that woman you could find Plock's real home."

"Then you don't know that house?"

"I only know the one he has in the house where I'm concierge. He never sleeps there. You understand, Miss, I'm only giving you all this information just to stay out of trouble."

"You won't get in trouble if all you say checks out."

With this promise, the giant took leave of the detectives. They ordered him to alert the policeman on stake-out near Mina Ban No.28 if Plock returned. They also told him to intercept any mail and turn it over to Sokes when he called for it. When he had left, Sokes asked Miss Boston:

"Well, what do you think about that?"

"This time Plock is done for."

"Do you really think so?"

"Yes, really, Sokes. This stupid boxer Fox has put us on the most interesting trail we could find."

"Do you believe everything he told you?"

"Almost."

"What does 'almost' mean?"

"His role in Plock's criminal affairs must be a little more extensive than he wants to admit. As for the rest, he's certainly telling the truth and for a very simple reason. He's just trying to get out while the going is good. If things fall apart, he doesn't want to have to pay for them. That's very simple reasoning but useful in the present circumstances."

Miss Boston decided to pick up, with Sokes, the thread of Miss Rosie Adams that same day. She planned to investigate that woman's routine to find some crack whereby they could begin their investigation. Sokes was to wait in his office until alerted.

Leaving the Central Police Bureau she went directly to the Empire Theater where she was told Miss Adams was rehearsing. She resolved to wait for her and use the boredom of a long wait by observing and committing to memory each face, each passerby. At the stage door of the Empire Theatre several cabs and private closed vehicles apparently belonged to the artists. On one of the vehicles, drawn by magnificent gray horses, she saw the initials: R. A., obviously that of Miss Rosie Adams. Less than five minutes later, a young, elegant, and very pretty woman left the theatre, got in and said to the coachman, "To the house."

Miss Boston immediately jumped into a hansom cab and followed the carriage. The trip was relatively short. Ten minutes later the two cabs stopped in front of an elegant townhouse in Work Square which the blonde woman entered. The vehicle itself went into the covered storage area in the garden. That convinced the detective Miss Rosie Adams, the Empire Theater singer, lived there. That fact filled her with questions. How was that woman linked to Plock? Did he pay for that luxury? Or was she his accomplice in carrying out his sinister exploits? If not, why had the walk-on actor encountered her on the stairs of the Mina Ban house?

Miss Boston did not waste her time. She cleverly found out Miss Adams would go out only to the Empire Theater, where she was to sing that evening. She also learned she usually ate a supper at a very fashionable restaurant afterward and that her coachman brought her home about 3 a.m. Miss Boston knew enough. She went to the police telephone at Work Avenue, spoke to Sokes, and when she left she was smiling, murmuring:

"I'll play the great final match this evening: match point!"

VII. The Central Bureau's Disguised Automobile

At 9 p.m. a cab parked in the main courtyard of the Central Police Bureau. There was something unusual about the cab. Its lights were extinguished; the wheels had unusually thick tires; and its special windows had glass which shut out the view inside the cab. A curious observer would have been surprised at other aspects of the cab. It was larger and more comfortable than can be imagined. Under the benches it held cases containing a variety of disguises. This could have been the paraphernalia of a burglar. Wasn't this how the police of a big city fought criminals on their own terrain? In addition, the interior of the cab was lit by a powerful electric globe, its light ingeniously reflected by a large mirror solidly fixed to one of the vehicle's panels. It also contained the most complete of the latest modern inventions. It was an automobile, but not one with a common gas engine. It had an electric engine which deadened sound and ran at much higher speeds. This cab was the one used by the police in dangerous situations.

It had hardly been there a few minutes when Inspector Sokes appeared in the building's hallway, his overcoat over his arm.

"Has the vehicle arrived yet?" he asked one of the men present.

"It's been here several minutes," one of the employees answered.

"Marvelous!" Sokes said, and left.

"Good evening, Sam," Sokes greeted him.

"Good evening, Mr. Sokes," Sam responded. "Where are we going with this set up?"

"To Miss Boston's at Savannah City."

Before putting the cab in motion, Sam asked:

"Any special orders, Mr. Sokes?"

"Not right now, no."

The detective jumped into the cab, closed the door, and gently, softly, without the least noise, the vehicle rolled off. It passed the Administration buildings like lightning and in perfect silence moved along the brilliantly lighted streets of New York. It went along rapidly, headed toward the east side of the city where, in a peaceful suburb, Savannah City is situated. At 9:20 p.m. it stopped in front of Miss Boston's residence.

Suddenly the front hall was filled with the rustling of silk and there appeared an elegant young woman, her head covered with a pink silk scarf. She was wrapped in a beautiful fur evening jacket. The pastel color of her lace dress contrasted with the dark tone of her jacket. It was the illustrious detective. Dressed in this fashion she could pass for—which she was in fact—one of the most elegant and charming women in New York. As she entered the cab she was greeted by Sokes with:

"You are superb!"

"I must be, this evening at least," she declared.

"Really?" Sokes asked.

"Yes, actually."

There was a moment of silence. The Chief Inspector was trying to understand the reason for Miss Boston's extreme elegance. He finally said:

"Over the telephone you asked me to have the special vehicle prepared. But that's all I know. Are there some instructions for Sam?"

"None, Sokes."

"But the direction we take?"

On the right panel of the vehicle there was a speaking tube. The detective picked it up and whispered to Sam on the outside:

"To the Empire Theatre, ten meters from the stage door."

"Well," Sokes asked, "what do you want me to do?"

Miss Boston explained what she had learned during the afternoon about Rosie Adams. The restaurant where Rosie Adams ate after the performance was La Scala, in the Bowery. Miss Boston said:

"I'll be there too. I don't exactly know right now what I'll do there. That will depend on the circumstances."

"But my role in all that? What am I to do?"

Miss Boston answered:

"Here's your role, Sokes. We can only find Plock's last hideout through Miss Rosie Adams. How? I still don't exactly know. But this is where you come in. She has a carriage driven by a man named Mac Vey. You're going to take the place of the cab driver. Once you're in the driver's seat, we'll have won half the match."

"Very good. I have no objection to that. But what if, when Miss Adams leaves the restaurant, she tells me to go to the usual place without giving me the address. What should I do?"

"In that case, I'll be there. I'll take care of everything."

VIII. Coachman No.2

The electric automobile stopped a few meters from the stage door of the Empire Theater. A cabman wrapped in a big green overcoat with a collar and gold buttons and wearing a leather cap got out. Hands in his pockets, whistling a lively tune, he went toward Empire Square behind the theater. It formed a vast parking lot for cabs and waiting automobiles, either for the audience or the actors. Sokes, dressed as a cabman, after lighting a cheap bad cigar which fouled the air, walked up and down the sidewalk. He had a pimpled, flushed face like almost all New York cabmen, who add to that profession by swigging little glasses of whisky at saloon counters and bars.

While walking nonchalantly up and down he was looking right and left at the lines of vehicles. Sokes suddenly stopped. He had just seen what he was looking for. The coachman on the seat seemed to be asleep, his arms crossed.

"Hey! Well! Taking a little nap, pard?" Sokes asked pleasantly.

Startled awake, Mac Vey straightened up.

"Oh! I thought it was the mistress!...."

"Ah! You have a mistress? Me, I just have one way fares from Broadway."

"You're one of the hired cabs?"

"Naturally. Say, pard, it's beginning to cool off this evening, isn't it?"

"Yes, but it'll be still colder in two or three hours."

"Ah! You go back so late?"

"About two or three o'clock. I take my mistress to have supper in the Bowery."

"You can make the best of it," the fake cabman insinuated.

"What do you mean?"

"I mean we could go get warm with a little glass of whiskey in the saloon over there at the corner of the square."

The cold cabman gladly accepted Sokes' offer. They ordered gin as they discussed the inconveniences of their jobs. At the end of three drinks, Sokes was on good terms with Mac Vey. At the end of an hour, Miss Adams' cabman was not too steady on his legs. With two more little glasses of whiskey Mac Vey was so drunk he couldn't stand up. Holding the staggering cabman by the arm, Sokes left the Empire Square saloon. But, instead of going back to the line of cabs, the false cabman went to the left to where, with its lanterns out, the Central Bureau's cab was waiting. Gently, continuing to talk to the drunken cabman, he led him along and in a few minutes they were at its door, which suddenly opened. Sokes shoved Mac Vey and he rolled into the cab. Nothing had disturbed the silence and no one had noticed the disappearance of the actress's cabman.

A little dizzy from his fall the man vaguely understood that he had fallen into a trap. He began to yell like a bull being slaughtered. Neither Miss Boston nor Sokes made the least attempt to stop him. The Bureau cab was sound proof.

"Even so," said Miss Boston, "it would be better to stop it."

She took a flask from a box at the front of the cab, put a few drops of its contents on a cotton pad and held it to the cabman's nostrils. He calmed down immediately and five minutes later was snoring deeply. Sokes changed his coachman's attire and, examining the man, took a pair of blond sideburns out of the vehicle's boxes and glued them to his jaws. In the half-light he could be taken for Miss Rosie Adam's coachman.

IX. A Woman's Hatred

With Sokes gone, Miss Boston was in no hurry to depart. It was a little before 11 p.m. The Empire Theater drama didn't end until midnight. She had sufficient time to reach La Scala in the Bowery before Miss Adams arrived at 12:30, at least. She rolled the sleeping Mac Vey to the floor and covered him. She then repaired the disorder to her toilette caused by all the latest incidents. After that she ordered Sam:

"To the La Scala Bar!"

Fewer than ten minutes later she stopped in front of the resplendent façade of the famous bar-restaurant. The first thing she did was to call to her table the manager, Mr. Cypers, a longtime acquaintance.

"Good evening, Miss Boston," Mr. Cypers said. "It's great good luck to see you. This doesn't happen very often."

"What do you expect?" the detective joked. "Your establishment isn't, fortunately for you, frequented by the thieves and swindlers I deal with."

"I greatly congratulate myself about that," the manager said, laughing.

"This time, however," the detective continued, "I need to appeal to your friendship. I need some information. Do you know Miss Rosie Adams?"

"Yes, of course I know her. She comes here every evening for supper."

"Alone?"

"A woman from her world never eats alone; you know that as well as I do, Miss."

"Obviously. But do you know those who come with her?"

"They are known to be reputable."

"Where does Miss Adams usually sit?"

"There, in the corner to the left. That table is reserved for her every evening."

"Then I'll sit at the neighboring table."

"You have business with her?"

"I need to watch her."

"Is she mixed up in something dirty?"

"I'm afraid so."

"Oh! Oh…"

Miss Boston got up and sat down at the table next to the one Miss Adams occupied every evening. She had a good view of those who came to and left the bar. The big clock in the large dining room showed 11:45 p.m. She had only a few minutes to wait.

When the first spectators began to leave the Empire Theater, Sokes was a little uneasy as to the outcome of the adventure he and Miss Boston had so daringly and even recklessly, entered in. But as the proverb said: *The wine was poured. It had to be drunk.*

Suddenly, an elegant form appeared at the stage door. Seeing the cab, she said:

"Ah! It's you, Mac," and opened the door.

"The Devil!" Sokes, on his seat, said: "I hope she gives me the address."

As if to answer his wish, Miss Adams said:

"To the La Scala!"

"Saved!" Sokes told himself.

In his new unexpected functions, the Chief Inspector showed himself an incomparable master. You would have sworn he'd been a coachman all his life.

At exactly 12:20 p.m. Miss Adams' cab stopped at the entrance of the La Scala. An automobile without lights was parked some meters from there. With infinite grace the actress jumped out of the vehicle and entered the restaurant.

"Up until now the first part has come off without a hitch," Sokes thought, "but look out for the second! That could turn up the heat."

He whistled twice softly. Two more whistles answered. "Sam's there!" the Chief Inspector told himself. He got down from his seat to have a friendly chat with the driver of the electric automobile who was walking back and forth in front of his automobile.

"You're back again, Mr. Sokes?" Sam asked.

"Yes, Sam, and as a cabman as you see."

"Ours is a funny job," said the chauffeur.

"It has its surprises."

"And its dangers! You know something about that!"

And like two friends who talk to kill time, Sokes and Sam continued walking up and down in front of the bar-restaurant La Scala where Miss Boston held in her hands the cards of the last game.

With a feeling of joy the detective had seen the woman she was waiting for arrive. She seemed to be the pivot to the capture of the Invisible Man. Without hesitation Miss Adams went to her usual table. Two very elegant gentlemen were already seated there. They greeted the actress with demonstrations of the greatest friendship. After the greetings, they began supper. Miss Boston didn't lose a word of their conversation. It was only banalities, nothing of any importance; gossip about the acting world made up almost all the generalities. It was never a question of Plock. Was the evening going to pass without bringing about the incident so ardently hoped for, desired and awaited? Miss Boston was on the point of doubting it. What to do? It was urgent to make a move. Her decision was made. It was a matter of putting her plan into action whatever the cost. Suddenly raising her voice, she called to Mr. Cypers.

"Sir, Mr. Plock hasn't yet come to ask for me?"

"No, Miss, not yet."

At Plock's name Miss Adams had suddenly raised her head. Miss Boston saw she had hit a nerve. Her elegant neighbor had suddenly become very pale. Without saying a word, she got up, and marched straight to Miss Boston's table. There was a strange light of jealousy, anger and hatred in her blue eyes.

"You know Mr. Plock?" she asked, gazing fixedly at the one she thought her rival.

Miss Boston pretended the greatest astonishment admirably.

"Huh? What do you want with me?"

"I asked if you knew Mr. Plock," repeated the actress, furious.

The detective decided to push the actress' patience to its end. So, with the best acted coolness she said:

"I don't know you, Miss!"

At these words, the actress' fury broke loose. She had no doubt that Plock was betraying her with that pretty woman dining alone. She poured out violent oaths, indignant exclamations.

Ah! She was betrayed! Ah! She was deceived! We'd see about that! She shouted:

"Plock will hear about this! He'll find out who I am…and how I can take revenge!…"

She left La Scala in a rage. That was all Miss Boston wanted.

X. The Game Caught in the Trap

Seeing the actress leave the restaurant so quickly, Sokes knew Miss Boston had just played her last card and that the denouement of the drama was actually approaching. He jumped in his coach seat immediately. Sam regained his seat in the electric automobile. Miss Adams had just reached her coach:

"38 Bell Road!" and she slammed the coach door.

The vehicle with coachman No.2 started up. Sokes saw Miss Boston leave the restaurant and jump in Sam's automobile, which silently followed Miss Adams' carriage. Miss Boston knew that for the last part of the drama her evening clothes were absolutely useless. She got out of them and took a simpler outfit from the chest in the electric automobile.

The consequences of that encounter could be grave. It was quite possible that the outraged and furious actress was at this moment at Plock's and that she would find the game in the trap. Plock certainly wasn't going to let himself be taken without a desperate resistance. Miss Boston wouldn't hesitate to shoot him. Better to kill him than let him escape. It was better for the security of New York to put Plock out of the way.

Sam whistled to indicate the actress' cab had stopped. Miss Boston opened her window. The street was badly lit, narrow and long. Miss Adams' cab was in front of an apparently respectable house at the end of the street. As she slid from the automobile, the detective saw the actress putting her key in the lock. In a few seconds, Miss Adams had disappeared into the corridor. In one bound the detective was beside Sokes.

"Have Sam guard the two vehicles," she quickly commanded. "It will probably take two of us."

The sound of his footsteps was muffled by the rubber soles of his shoes. He followed Miss Boston into the dark and obscure corridor. The famous detective had her electric torch in her hand and lit her path as she advanced into the mystery of that unknown house. It could hold—and who could be sure?—strange surprises.

She suddenly discovered a dark opening, a secret door cleverly hidden in the wall. That partially open door was easy to understand. In a hurry, angry, Miss Adams had simply forgotten to close the secret door behind her. That discovery was doubly precious for the detectives. It gave them access to the hideout and saved them time, costly in the circumstance. They entered. Inside was complete darkness. With her electric torch, the detective saw at an angle a wide staircase which went up some distance, ending in a landing where there was a faint light filtering under the door.

"That's the way," Miss Boston said.

Followed by Sokes, she mounted the stairs and reached the door. It wasn't locked. They entered a sparsely furnished little room. Miss Boston noticed a typewriter in a corner of the room. She went to it quickly, inserted a piece of paper and wrote two or three words. That done, she slid the piece of paper into her small purse and continued her search. Suddenly the sound of violent, furious, voices broke out from the adjoining room.

"You're a scoundrel!" a voice recognized as that of Miss Adams shouted.

"What!...What's the matter?" someone, who must surely be Plock, responded.

"What should we do?" questioned Sokes.

"Listen a minute more. We can possibly learn something interesting. We'll enter at the proper time."

Saying this, Miss Boston took out of her purse a little cylindrical box that Sokes recognized as the infinitely perfected Y ray which the detective used in some cases. The Y ray has the ability to render wood transparent. In the neighboring room the discussion continued.

"You're a despicable villain!" Miss Rosie Adams continued. Her anger seemed to have increased since she was now facing the one she considered a traitor. Plock nevertheless retorted:

"Will you explain to me, Rosie, what you mean?"

"I mean that you had a rendezvous with another woman this evening."

"Me!" Plock exclaimed with the greatest surprise.

"Yes, you, scoundrel!"

"Where was that?"

"At the La Scala!"

"Who told you that?"

"Finally you admit it!"

"Don't scream like that! I don't admit anything, because I don't have anything to admit. I didn't plan a rendezvous."

"She herself told me that!"

"What's that? What woman?"

"Yes, a woman at the La Scala."

"Oh! Oh!" Plock suddenly said. "This seems to me unusually suspicious. Tell me, Rosie, what did that woman look like?"

"You know that very well!"

"Ta! Ta! Ta! Please! No more silly talk! This is now a serious matter. I'm afraid someone used you, my poor Rosie, for a purpose I'm afraid to guess."

"How's that?"

"First describe the woman to me."

The actress gave a precise description of Miss Boston and at each sentence Plock said:

"That's right!...yes...yes..."

"What does that mean?"

"Just Miss Boston, my poor Rosie. That damned detective guessed there was something between us. She thought that shadowing you could lead to my trail. Although you're a very clever actress, you've been played by one cleverer."

At that instant the door opened and four revolvers pointed from the doorway. A sharp and strong voice said:

"In fact, Mr. Plock, I'm here. I have the advantage of finally being able to meet you."

"Damnation!" the Invisible Man swore.

"You belong to the law, Plock! Up with your hands!"

"And you to death!" the scoundrel bellowed.

He fired rapidly, but four shots answered his. He was heard stomping violently on the floor and when the smoke cleared Miss Boston saw, with a cry of surprise, that Plock had disappeared.

"Flown away!" Sokes exclaimed.

"Not very far," the detective answered.

A trap door had opened under Plock's heels and in the gaping hole the fearful criminal, chief of the One Hundred Thousand Arms Gang, had disappeared.

The courageous detective didn't waste any time in vain lamentations. She ran to the hole and leaned over. She saw a low room, the flooring covered with mattresses to deaden the shock of the fall.

Plock had gotten up from the mattresses and had run toward the door. He reached it just as Miss Boston was leaning over the trap door. She knew the thief would escape again and the game would be irretrievably lost if she didn't intervene in that absolutely desperate situation.

She took careful aim at Plock's shoulder and fired. The bullet clacked with a hard sound. A cry of both rage and pain came from the room with mattresses. Plock fell to his knees and dropped to the floor, screaming. He had a broken shoulder blade.

Miss Boston slid down the trap door opening and ran to the criminal. She had some trouble putting the handcuffs on him, but she managed. As a precaution, she put a steel chain around his ankles while Sokes took care of the actress, who made no resistance.

The search of the house was long and fruitful. It was finished toward 4:30 a.m. At 5 a.m. Plock was in jail under the special surveillance of four agents at the Central Police Bureau. They decided to release Rosie Adams for the moment.

No trial had ever attracted so many people as that of Plock, the Invisible Man finally arrested, the feared chief of the One Hundred Thousand Arms Gang discovered. He had been the terror of New York for more than a year and had held in check such a long time the perspicacious and courageous genius of Miss Boston, the strong woman detective. This monstrous trial lasted almost a year. Each day a new offence, a new crime, a new theft, was added to the already long list of those the Attorney General accused Plock of having, if not executed in person, at least of having organized and prepared. Plock, seeing he was henceforth irremediably lost, denied nothing. To all the accusations, he answered:

"That's true!"

"How did you organize that attack?"

At that he rebelled and said:

"That's for you to find out!"

Miss Boston searched and found out. In this way she confounded the scoundrel about the cadaver of Agent Stanley, sent to her address from Philadelphia. She explained:

"Having found a typewriter at Plock's after his arrest, I wrote a few lines on it. I noticed a down stroke at the letter m; that the number 8 had the upper part somewhat broken off; and that the letter W was only partially visible. These same characteristics were found on the trunk address. From that I concluded they were written on Plock's typewriter."

The investigation finally raised the veil which had always hidden Plock's mysterious and unexplained escape from Sing Sing the morning of the day he was to be executed with Tommy, his accomplice in the Express from Chicago affair.

Plock had bought off a guard, thanks to a large sum an accomplice had managed to pass to him. After his last round of inspections, the guard had purposely neglected to lock the cell door of the condemned man. That allowed Plock to escape while they were preparing Tommy for execution. He was hidden in Boston for a month, then transferred to New York, where he had organized and set up that formidable and dangerous association of the One Hundred Thousand Arms Gang. When Miss Boston tried to locate the prison guard who had facilitated Plock's escape, she found all traces of him had disappeared. Had he fled to Europe or had the gang killed him to be sure of his silence? They would never know.

Arguments in Plock's trial lasted three weeks. There were many witnesses to hear, to put on the stand. They were unanimous in accusing Plock. His arrest had truly been Miss Boston's triumph. Thus the One Hundred Thousand Arms Gang disappeared from New York. At Plock's arrest all the others were successively arrested. As for the Empire Theater actress, her guilt could never be proven. She was Plock's mistress and her only guilt was having received money from him. But because of her involvement in the scandal, she was forced to leave the Empire Theater and even America. Under another name, she became a part of His Majesty's Theatre, well known to all those who have visited the capital on the edge of the Thames.

Plock was condemned to death for a second time. Fearing another attack by the One Hundred Thousand Arms Gang, the high court specifically ordered the execution to take place the day following his sentence. Hearing that, the condemned man fainted. He was transported to Sing Sing, where he was watched by several guards who never left him. Miss Boston had sworn to conduct him to the electric chair herself. She kept her word. But she conducted only a corpse there. At dawn, when they came to prepare him for execution, he was seized by nervous trembling which made it impossible for him to stand. He had to be supported. Suddenly his eyelids closed; he was white as a sheet; his body became cold. He was dead with cardiac arrest caused by fear.

"What shall we do?" the warden asked the detective.

"What are the orders of the high court?"

"That the condemned man be executed."

"Well, the order must be carried out."

They carried the corpse to the electric chair. The current twisted him for a second. They took him down to put him in a casket. The law had prevailed. Justice had been done.

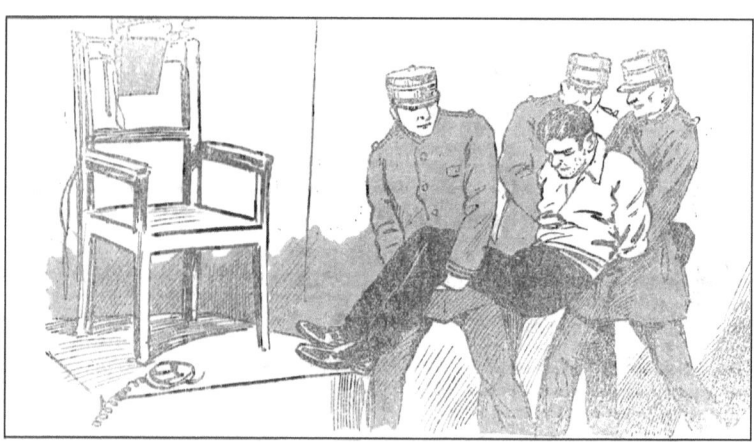

THE GROSVENOR PLACE MURDER

I. James Marmaduke's Unusual Adventure

It could have been about 2 a.m. and the snow, which hadn't stopped falling all day, continued to send flakes through the frozen atmosphere of that gloomy December night. That East New York neighborhood slept in the most profound silence. In Grosvenor Place the last saloons and bars were closing one by one. The boss of Star Bar was putting up his shutters and pushed his last client, passably drunk, outside.

"Go to bed Marmaduke," he told him, "and I'll see you tomorrow."

Marmaduke left complaining and staggering. He was a fellow about 40 years old, lazy like all those who never do anything from their earliest youth. He was rather solidly built, and worked, here and there, to earn a dollar for vague needs. That dollar was regularly passed on to the hands of Red Mull, the boss of Star Bar, in exchanged for gin and various whiskies.

James Marmaduke, still complaining, went up Grosvenor Street toward Grosvenor Place to reach 12th Avenue. His teeth chattered because the weather was extremely severe and the intense cold sobered him up little by little. He tried to stand a little more firmly on his legs because the dense and opaque darkness of the night caused him to stumble against the houses along the way. When he came to Grosvenor Place he was surrounded by an enormous snow flurry in that crossroad open to heavy wind.

Grosvenor Place forms a great circle around houses with gardens in front. Those gardens are enclosed by iron grill fences shutting off access. It was on one of those iron fences that James Marmaduke, unsteady and staggering in the snow storm, fell against. He closed his eyes to avoid the gust of snow which twisted the leafless trees in the garden. The darkened branches cracked with a gloomy and sinister sound in the darkness. Suddenly all the sound of unchained nature's tempest was dominated by a terrible cry of distress and agony. Petrified, James Marmaduke opened his eyes, still clinging to the iron fence. What he then saw made him turn loose.

A modest, two-story villa stood at the end of the garden. The ground floor was dark. But on the second floor there was light in a window which spread a great rectangle into the night. In this rectangle a form appeared. That form, rather tall, was striking with a hammer something that seemed to be stretched out on the floor. The terrible violent blows delivered by the form leaning over hit a lamp on the fireplace mantle with the hammer. The lamp fell over and the oil spreading over the floor suddenly caught fire and burst into lightening showers along the window. The dry throat of James Marmaduke, behind the iron fence of Grosvenor Place, let out a cry of terror. He had neither time to think nor to choose a course of action, because events unfolded with dizzying speed.

The bedroom was most certainly on fire since the flames now spread with violence along the walls, expanding their black fumes and invading the whole room. The form the drunk man had seen had vanished. Suddenly, he saw it reappear at the door. It was a man of middle height, wearing a black felt hat, his face masked by a piece of cloth pierced with holes for his eyes. The murderer, because it must be he, was racing across the garden toward the grill fence. James Marmaduke, struck with terror, hadn't left the spot. The man saw him. He opened the fence gate with a powerful move and jumped on the Star Bar frequent customer. It was a short fight. The assailant had all the advantages. James Marmaduke rolled into the snow while his aggressor pounded him on the head and face with formidable blows. That lasted only a minute. Marmaduke had evidently fainted. His face bloody, he was stretched out on the white ground. When the masked man saw this, he stood up, snatched off his mask and attached it to the unfortunate man's face. A few seconds later, he disappeared in the direction of 12th avenue.

The fire continued its devastation in the villa. The windows broke with a sharp sound and sinister crackles resounded from the place of the crime. Some minutes passed then a female voice cried out:

"Help!...Fire!...Help me!...Help!"

The alarm was raised. At this moment, James Marmaduke, all bloody, groaning, regained consciousness. Painfully, he sat up and rubbed his head. He had only one idea: to flee, to get away, to leave this terrible place where you saw people murdered and where you yourself risked sharing their sad fate. While getting up, he became aware that something gluey and moist was attached to his face. What did that mean? He passed his hand over his face. Was that cloth? How did that cloth get on his face? He couldn't understand it at all. Besides, his head was still confused by the quantity of small glasses of gin absorbed during the evening. What was important to him most of all, principally, was to get out as quickly as possible. However, the alarm had been sounded in Grosvenor.

It was the villa's servant who, awakened by the crackling of the fire, had raised the alarm. Some men from the police station on 12th Avenue came running. Neighbors arrived. Three minutes later, there were 30 people in the snow storm on the square. James Marmaduke fell into that group of people who saw with amazement the arrival of this masked fellow with bloody hands, haggard, confused. He seemed to be in a hurry to put as much distance as possible between him and the fire. Probably, with all that, he might have been able to disappear if, just at that moment, a policeman who had gone into the house hadn't come out shouting:

"Someone has killed the old lady! Quick! Get the firemen from Dirk Street…and the Constable."

At that word "murderer" the people assembled on Grosvenor Place understood how unusual Marmaduke's presence, thus masked, was. The same thought went through everyone's head. The murderer was there! He was the masked man, his hair tousled, his hands bloody. They rushed at him, jumped on him. With a blow of his fist on his neck a policeman stopped the poor drunk man in his flight. He staggered, stumbled, fell to his knees in the snow. Ten, twenty fists pounded him, nailed him to the ground, and certainly they would have lynched him if the policemen hadn't intervened. James Marmaduke, in a very pitiful state, was taken to the 12th street police station, followed by the boos and the cries for death by the persons who made up a shouting, furious and vociferous escort.

II. The Crime Scene

It was naturally Chief Inspector Sokes of the Central Police Bureau of New York who was assigned to investigate this drama, which at first seemed very simple despite its tragic horror. As usual, the detective went to ask the advice of Miss Boston, the only female detective in the whole world. He met her in Savannah City just before reaching her house. Sokes laid out to her the Constable's preliminary investigation.

"Oh! Oh!" Miss Boston observed, "That's a murderer who seems very stupid to me."

"That sometimes happens."

"Without a doubt, but it's somewhat rare to see murderers run around the streets with a bloody mask on their face... Has this Marmaduke been arrested?"

"He's been locked up in the 12th Street Station."

"As usual, he's been carefully searched."

"Yes."

"What did they find on him?"

"Nothing. Not a penny."

"Was there money at the victim's house?"

"Probably, since the constable found only two dollars forgotten in a drawer. Miss Worms enjoyed a certain comfortable income. It is somewhat unlikely she had only that small sum in the house."

"Certainly. And the man arrested, what does he say?"

"Some things rather odd in themselves. He claims he arrived by chance in front of the villa at Grosvenor Place, that he saw the murderer kill the victim, and afterward he himself was attacked by the robber and he fainted."

"And the mask?"

"Exactly. He doesn't explain why the mask was on his face."

"What if it was put on after he fainted?"

"Then you believe he fainted?"

"I don't believe it yet, Sokes, but I'm considering all the possibilities."

"Why would the real murderer have put the mask on his face?"

"To mislead the Police."

"In that case, he's succeeded marvelously because nobody doubts right now that Marmaduke is the real murderer."

"That remains to be seen."

Sokes and Miss Boston hail a cab to go to Grosvenor Place to examine the scene of the crime. It was particularly cold that morning. A sharp wind whistled violently. The bloody villa was guarded by two policemen who stomped up and down in front of the iron fence to get warm The fire had caused more damage than was supposed. Miss Worms' bedroom was in the worst condition; two more bedrooms had been less damaged. The two detectives began their investigations in the place of the crime. The walls were blackened and part of the ceiling had caved in. There remained only carbonized debris of the furniture, fragments impossible to identify. The cadaver of the murdered woman was stretched out under the debris. The fire had half devoured Miss Worms' body. Her clothing was in shreds around her, and the cadavers' legs were only frightful stumps. Only the upper part of the body remained intact. Miss Worms was an already old woman with white hair. Her hair was full of clots of blood, not yet dry. The top of the cranium was completely crushed, a bloody pulp. The blows must have been struck with unusual violence. The brains had spattered everywhere.

Miss Boston proceeded in silence to an examination.

"What a horrible spectacle," Sokes finally said.

"Yes, the crime was committed with unbelievable ferocity."

Suddenly she leaned over. She grabbed the cadavers' hand and opened it. Clinched in horrible agony, that hand grasped something black. The detective showed it to Sokes. It was a button, still holding a piece of brown cloth.

"That's something that may be useful for us one day," Miss Boston said, "if the murderer doesn't get rid of the clothes the button belongs to. In the heat of the fight, the old woman snatched it from him. If he notices that, he'll understand the seriousness of that clue in the hands of the police."

"Then you believe this Marmaduke is…"

"Innocent? Maybe, Sokes; in any case this button will let us find out who snatched it from his clothing."

"It may belong to the clothes of one of his accomplices."

"We'll see about that later."

The examination of the burned room gave Miss Boston another clue not less interesting. It was the weapon of the crime, a bloody hammer, covered by the ashes of a burned commode. Miss Boston found it when striking her foot against it by the greatest of accidents. A special kind of hammer, it had a sharp point, and was made of steel with a wooden handle, the kind frequently used by plumbers. Examining it, she saw it carried the letter V stamped on its handle. The detective asked Sokes to wrap it in a piece of newspaper, since she had decided to carry it with her. They left the bedroom and continued the investigation in the rest of the house. It was empty; the servant, who refused to stay there after the murder, was unavailable to answer questions.

Thinking the garden, white with snow, might show them interesting clues, Miss Boston, followed by Sokes, started down there.

III. The Address in the Snow

A wide path bordered by popular trees led from the iron gate to the door of the house. That path had been stepped on everywhere either by the firemen, the policemen or even by the simply curious come to view the fire. Miss Boston immediately knew that searching there would be useless; traces of the murderer, assuming there were any, had been irretrievably lost in the muddle. Any clues had to be looked for elsewhere. Miss Boston circled the house, reaching the back where no one had gone. Sokes noticed a smile playing on her lips. "Do you see something?" he asked.

She simply pointed to a part of the yard covered with snow like the rest of the garden.

"You see, Sokes, there is still something to find here."

She had just discovered footprints deeply sunk into the snow. If there hadn't been such a hard freeze the past night, the wind would have blown away a little of the snow which, clearly and distinctly, had kept the traces of those steps. The steps came from the back of the garden where they stopped at a low wall beside a small pathway called Pearson Street. The low height of that enclosure had allowed the murderer to get over it easily. Once over the wall, he had followed a path straight to the house. The footsteps ended there at a low door leading to the cellar of the villa. The criminal had come by Pearson Street, crawled over the wall, and gone into the cellar, where he waited for the time to commit his bloody deed. Once in the house, the remainder of his work was easy. The cadaver and the fire testified with brutal and horrible elegance to what he had done.

But those precious clues were not enough for the detective. She knelt beside the steps and measured their exact length and width dimensions. While she was doing this, she noticed something inside the prints. It was four letters stamped in the snow, forming the letters BRAD. Raising her head, she said to Sokes:

"I now know where the murderer bought his shoes. I even know the shoes were almost new."

Getting up, shaking the snow from her skirt, Miss Boston, said:

"You know American shoe manufacturers print their stamp in the shoes they make. Some of those make them inside the shoe with oily ink; others stamp them in the mold of the shoes' soles. The first marks wear off completely at the end of several hours, especially if you walk through mud or water. The second lasts longer but also gets worn away. Now, the print of these steps in the snow are clear, open and strong. Therefore the murderer's shoes are new. The stamp of these shoes is that of Brad Store in Greenwich Road. That's the explanation of the first part of the mystery."

They left the garden, returned to Grosvenor Place and walked rapidly to 12th Avenue, where James Marmaduke had been jailed at the 12th Street station. On her request, they immediately brought out the suspected murderer. The poor drunk man was in a pitiful state. His captivity had completely demoralized him. To be taken for a murderer, and risking the electric chair, wasn't a very enjoyable perspective. He never stopped lamenting and swearing his innocence to anyone who would listen. Miss Boston knew all the details of his adventure and asked him just to be silent for a moment, assuring him that if he was as innocent as he said, it would soon be recognized and he would be set free. That reassurance calmed James Marmaduke a little and he lent himself with good grace and perfect submission to what the detective required of him. She examined carefully his overcoat, his jacket and his vest. Those clothes had been torn by the rough house and his arrest, but, fortunately for him, no button with a piece of cloth attached was missing. That was the first presumption of his innocence, the truth of what he said. The second examination wasn't less conclusive. She looked at the soles of the drunken man's shoes. The shoes were old, worn, cracked. What's more they carried no stamp and did not at all correspond by their dimensions to width and length of the prints conserved in the frozen snow of the garden of the Grosvenor villa.

Decidedly, James Marmaduke was seeing luck turn in his favor.

"And none too soon," he said in a totally funny tone.

Miss Boston, however didn't smile. She didn't find the innocence of a man unjustly accused anything to smile about. She swore to make every effort to return the man the liberty of which he had been deprived. She said to Sokes:

"Are you still as persuaded of the prisoner's guilt?"

The Inspector confessed:

"A great deal less."

"I hope what follows will only confirm that impression."

"I hope so for this Marmaduke's sake. Between us he doesn't seem a person very recommendable."

"That's not a reason to find him guilty."

"I agree with you."

They came to the East station of the Metropolitan subway where Miss Boston and Sokes went down the stairway to the underground. Miss Boston hoped to find something at the Brad Shoe Department Store on Greenwich Road. She told Sokes:

"Those shoes were recently bought. The person who sold the shoes may remember his description."

At that moment a whistle announced the arrival of a train entering the station, rumbling. A minute later it departed toward the west of New York carrying the two detectives.

IV. A Masterful Investigation

At the Brad Shoe Store, Miss Boston went in with Sokes and walked toward the men's shoe department. After showing her detective's identification, she asked to see the sales books to examine them from the night before the murder. The sales books didn't carry the names of the buyers, simply shoe sizes at the date of the sales. Those were certainly very weak clues, but the exact, precise method of the famous detective was counting on solving that riddle. Three days before the murder a pair of shoes matching the dimensions of the prints in the garden at the Grosvenor villa was bought at the Brad store.

"Do you remember that buyer?" Miss Boston asked the employee.

"That's Williams' writing. He sold that pair of shoes."

"Where is this Williams? I would very much like to see him."

"Nothing is easier, Miss."

In fact, the employee, called on the spot, arrived a few seconds later.

Williams looked at the writing and tried to recall his somewhat hazy memory.

"No, really, Miss, I don't at all remember the description of that buyer."

"That's annoying."

"Obviously. If you told me, Miss, he was like this and this, dressed this way, wore his hair in a certain fashion, maybe that would refresh my memory and I could answer with more certainty. But as it is, I can't furnish any precise and exact detail."

"Well, before the end of the day, I'll give you his description."

Before they left the store Sokes said:

"You're forgetting that I still have the hammer of the crime in this bit of newspaper."

"I'm not forgetting that. The hammer is going to be the object of the second point of our research."

"I'd be curious to know how you're going to snatch its secret from that weapon."

"It doesn't remain as mute for me as you seem to think, Mr. Sokes. It tells me first the profession of its owner and then the first letter of the name of that owner."

"You...you know all that?" he asked, not trying to hide his astonishment.

"Yes, I know that, Sokes, but I'll have to admit that's all I know. The rest of the mystery is completely unknown to me."

"Can you tell me how you guessed these facts?"

"It wasn't a guess, Sokes, just simply deduction. The hammer has the sharp, flat point of hammers plumbers use. Therefore the hammer belongs to a plumber. You know how workmen mark their tools with the first letter of their name. The hammer has a V stamped on the handle. I conclude that the first letter of the killer's name is a V."

"But what if the hammer doesn't belong to him?"

"That is precisely what we're going to find out."

She returned to Greenwich Subway Station and took the train to East New York. At 12th Avenue she got off and went to the police station. She had James Marmaduke brought to her. He supposed that the hour of his liberation had come. He had to immediately change his mind. Miss Boston's interrogation had only one purpose, to obtain a description, even vague, of the man who had knocked the drunk man down in front of the iron gate of the Grosvenor villa. That interrogation convinced James Marmaduke that his innocence didn't seem hypothetical to the police.

"I didn't see the face of the man," he said, "because he was masked, but I could see his black felt hat and his height, which was average. He probably has blond hair."

That was all he knew. Miss Boston then examined the mask's material; its ties were knotted. The murderer hadn't gone to any expense for his disguise. That done, the detective couldn't keep from rubbing her hands together with signs of the liveliest satisfaction.

"I wasn't wrong," she said. She explained to Sokes.

"Sailors, carpenters, have special knots. So do plumbers. The knots of these mask ties were made by a plumber. The hammer belongs to a plumber."

Miss Boston then turned to the third point of her investigation to find out under what circumstances the murder was committed by the plumber and why it was done. She turned to the head of the Police Station on 12th Avenue who had been present at the interrogation.

"Do you know, sir, where Miss Annie Worms' servant went to?"

"Yes, the Inspector's report told me she went to stay with her sister in Clarke Street on Long Island."

"Did her interrogation reveal anything about her mistress' murder?"

"Absolutely nothing. She was in bed and was awoken by the cries of the victim. She didn't dare go down immediately and it wasn't until she heard the crackling of the fire that she decided to call for help."

"Then she didn't see the criminal?"

"No, by that time he had disappeared...That is, they had arrested James Marmaduke at Grosvenor Place."

"What's that servant's name?"

"Jane Fells."

"She wasn't asked anything else about the crime?"

"Until now, no."

"Marvelous. Then she will be valuable to hear on certain details."

Still followed by the inseparable Sokes, she immediately followed that new lead just offered to her.

V. Identification of the Murderer

The servant was a woman about 40 years old who had been in Miss Annie Worms' service for 15 years. She was still suffering from the emotional crisis caused by the tragedy. She was trembling all over when she met Miss Boston and Sokes. In a stifled voice, broken by sobs, she answered the detective's questions.

"What happened the evening of the attack?" asked the detective, who wanted to clear up the first part of the drama.

"Nothing, Miss, nothing happened."

"You didn't notice anything unusual?"

"No, nothing at all. Miss Worms ate at her usual hour. She read until ten o'clock and then went upstairs to her bedroom, as she did every evening. I locked all the doors in the house and went back to my bedroom about eleven o'clock."

"Did you say you locked all the doors?"

"Yes, Miss, just like every evening."

"Did you also lock the door to the cellar?"

"What door?"

"The door that leads to the garden behind the villa."

"I didn't lock it, Miss, because it's never used."

"But was it locked?"

"Certainly it was locked, on the inside by a bolt."

"Since when?"

"It's never been opened for years."

The detective immediately understood all the importance of that statement. It was incontestable that the servant's good faith in this affair was beyond doubt. The cellar door had always been locked. It had been opened from the inside. By whom? Two possibilities presented themselves: either the murderer had an accomplice in the house or he had already gotten in the house before the crime. How valuable was the first hypothesis? Not much, because James Marmaduke expressively maintained that there had been only one man. The examination of the crime scene demonstrated, in addition, that only the murderer had done this terrible deed. As for the second hypothesis, it was infinitely more troubling.

"Did your mistress have a lot of money in the villa?"

"A lot, no, Miss, but certainly enough."

"Explain that to me."

"I say enough because December 3rd I cashed, at the Arizona Bank, Miss Worms' $400 income. She always had me do that banking because the poor old woman no longer left the house, having pains which often condemned her to remain for weeks in the house."

"The murder having been committed December 5th, the $400 must not have been completely exhausted. Where did Miss Worms keep her money?"

"In the commode in her bedroom."

"That commode was burned," Sokes interrupted.

"Yes, but the two dollars which were found were in the kitchen."

"That was to pay for the heating wood that was to be delivered the next day," the servant explained.

"Doesn't the house have steam heat, a furnace?" asked Miss Boston who had noticed several vents in different places in the villa.

"Yes, usually," the servant answered, "but for two days plumbers have been repairing blocked up pipes. So we were using wood until the end of the repairs."

Plumbers! Miss Boston suddenly stood up. Sokes knew the trail had been found.

"Were my deductions false?" she asked him

"I hope for James Marmaduke's sake they're even more exact."

"That's what we're going to find out."

Jane Fells was not aware of the capital importance of her testimony and she continued to answer the detective's precise and clear questions.

"How long had the plumbers been working at the villa?"

"For a week, Miss."

"How many of them were there?"

"There were four at first, but the hardest of the work having been done in five days, they left only one worker to finish the work."

"What color was that worker's hair?"

"He was blond."

Miss Boston looked at the Chief Inspector.

"Do you hear that, Sokes? He was blond."

Sokes nodded.

The detective continued:

"Do you know the name of that man?"

"I know his comrade called him Vogt."

"The initial on the hammer," Sokes whispered.

"What plumbing shop did the work at the villa?" the young woman asked Jane Fells.

"It was Leander of Madison Square. They installed the system and when a repair was needed, they always sent a repairman."

"Good. One last question. Did the repairmen always work in the cellar?"

"Yes, Miss, but the day before the murder, the workman Vogt repaired the heat vent in my poor mistress' bedroom."

Miss Boston knew enough. She took leave of the servant and assured her Miss Worm's murderer would soon be in the hands of the police and would pay for his crime by capital punishment. Leaving Clarke Street the Chief Inspector exclaimed:

"Marvelous! That was a masterful investigation. The day is not yet ended and we already know the name of the killer."

"Let's hope it ends with his arrest."

"That just depends on you."

"And a little on him, I believe. If he lets himself be taken, everything is for the best. We need only his address and his house number."

"We can get it at the Leander shop on Madison Square."

On the way, Miss Boston summed up her impressions to Sokes.

"This Vogt, while working with his comrades in the Grosvenor villa cellar noticed the door leading to the garden. He immediately saw that it could be used to enter the house. He opened the bolt the day he worked alone in the house. Next, while working on the vent in the future victim's bedroom he found the money in the drawer of the commode. He then knew the way to accomplish his theft."

"But committed murder!"

"I don't believe, however, that when he entered the villa at Grosvenor Place he intended to."

"What do you base that on?"

"On two things. First of all, the hammer. It has his initial on it. He must have known that. He had it in his hand in the bedroom the moment of the crime. If he used it, it was because the old woman woke up and cried out. As for the mask, he used it to hide his features. By killing Miss Annie Worms, he didn't need to fear denunciation from her. He therefore didn't need to wear a mask. I even dare say, Sokes, that Vogt was pushed to the murder by circumstances. He became a criminal only by needing his personal security. His conduct before the drama and even the facts of the drama prove it. He came to steal and not to kill. That's my opinion and I'm persuaded the outcome of the investigation will prove its complete accuracy."

"So, then, Mr. Leander, your employee didn't come to work this morning?"

"No, Miss."

"Is that usual for him?"

"My word, yes. He's a bad worker that I only keep on because I have a lot of work. In ordinary times I'd get rid of him fast."

"Do you know where he lives?"

"He lives, I think, in Greenwich, Holyrood Ban, at No.8. But, Miss, has he done something wrong?"

"I won't know for certain, sir, until I've asked him some questions. Right now, I thank you for your information."

This dialogue was exchanged between Mr. Polly Leander and Miss Boston about five in the afternoon when she came to question him about the man named Vogt. From now on, she would walk on a sure path where she thought there would be few surprises. The essential thing was to work quickly so as not to warn Vogt. Had he already taken flight? Nevertheless, before leaving Leander's office she thought it useful to pose two more questions.

"Do you know," she asked him, "what happened last night at Grosvenor Place at your client's villa?"

"Yes, Miss, I heard about that terrible thing in the morning newspapers, the special edition of the *Standard.*"

"Is Vogt supposed to go back to Miss Worms' or is the work finished?"

"He was to have finished it today."

"In that case," the detective said, "I'll be forced to arrest your worker."

"He wouldn't be the one who...? Miss..."

"Yes, this crime is probably his work, unless he has a double and can account for his time, minute by minute last night."

"A murderer!...that Vogt!...in my shop!...in my workrooms!" Leander shuddered, desperate.

The detective, with Sokes, went back quickly to Holyrood Ban in Greenwich. Her investigation of the suspect's domicile would shed light on that still obscure part of the drama. Holyrood Ban is a little street of worker's houses. It's made up of small houses, poor and modest, without being completely poverty-stricken. No.8 was one of those houses. The concierge looked wide-eyed at the questions posed by the detective.

"Is your lodger Vogt here?"

"No, he left hardly an hour ago."

"The devil!" the detective thought. "Could he already be in flight?"

She then asked:

"What time did he return last night?"

"He didn't go out."

"What's that? He didn't go out?"

"No lodger named Vogt came in after nine o'clock in the evening."

That answer could only astonish the detective. The accumulation of proofs against Vogt was conclusive at this point. He was without doubt the killer. Therefore there had to be an explanation to this mystery.

"Let's see now. What time do you close the outside door to the house?"

"At ten in the summer; at nine in the winter."

"Good. Whoever enters after that time has to give his name?"

"Always. I'm a light sleeper. I don't let anyone in unless I've heard his name."

"I see. Which of your lodgers came in last night after nine o'clock?"

"Only one."

"Which?"

"That was Ginsby, on the fourth floor. He works for the Metropolitan Subway and comes in every evening at midnight."

"Was it really Ginsby and not someone else using his name?"

"I repeat. Only Ginsby came in after nine o'clock, and that he always comes in at midnight."

"I'm not displeased to have that assurance. Now tell me what time you open the door in the morning."

"At six o'clock."

"What do you do then?"

"I go to the corner of Circus Avenue to pick up my milk."

"How long are you gone?"

"Not more than ten minutes."

"We don't need to look any further," Miss Boston concluded. "Vogt watched when you left and went to his room while you were gone. That's the whole mystery."

"Could that be possible!" exclaimed the concierge.

The detective went up immediately to the third floor to Vogt's room. With a jimmy she opened the door and entered with Sokes. The room was in the greatest disorder. The plumber's toolbox lay open on the floor, all his work tools spread out here and there, as if they had been thrown about in feverish haste. There were pliers, tongs, screwdrivers, cold chisels. Miss Boston noticed that the hammer was missing. His clothes lay on the bed. The detective picked up a jacket of brown material which was thrown there together with an overcoat and work shirts. She turned it over. The second button with a large piece of material was missing.

"You see! Sokes! There's the witness against Vogt! We'll take that jacket to use at the killer's trial!"

"The tell-tale tear!" said Sokes.

That was all the bedroom gave up, but that was enough. In addition, the fatal button was stained with blood; no longer a doubt possible. In the street Miss

Boston asked her companion whether he saw anything interesting in the disorder of the tool box. He did not, but she did. She said:

"Vogt noted his missing hammer and he was feverishly looking for the object he had left in the bedroom of the crime."

"He wouldn't have found it."

"Naturally, but he would have gone to Grosvenor Place to look for it. We must go there immediately. If Vogt is anywhere, it's certainly there! Come on! Quickly Sokes!"

VII. The Second Fire at the Bloody Villa

Miss Boston got a shock when she arrived at Grosvenor Place.

"Sokes! Look there! Miss Worms' villa!" she exclaimed in a trembling voice.

"Oh! Oh! It's the villa of the crime that's on fire!"

But she didn't wait for the Chief Inspector. She bravely dashed toward the sinister scene of the second fire. How? Why? That double question that came to her mind would have its solution later. Right now she had to deal with the most pressing, the fire. High flames were coming out of the second-floor windows and like terrible tongues were licking the façade of the house of the crime. The window glass burst out with sharp crackling, collapsing in its frames. The ceiling rafters broke apart. The furniture spared by the preceding fire caught fire in the abandoned first floor.

The villa was guarded by two policemen walking up and down to keep warm. They dashed toward the fire station on Wilbur Street and alerted the firemen who had already been there the night before. Before they arrived, Miss Boston and Sokes had hurried to the villa garden. The heat was intense. The sharp southwest wind had scattered the sparks of flame across the leafless tree branches and on the snow on the ground. The snow itself was beginning to melt and transform the lawn into a muddy bog. Miss Boston looked at the house one last time and saw that it was lost, that the firemen could save only the calcified walls, blackened, broken and unsteady.

Realizing the second fire was so unexpected and unusual, both Sokes and Miss Boston agreed that it was certainly the work of the criminal Vogt. They wondered how and why the fire was started. At that moment the first fire trucks arrived.

"Quick! Quick!" said Miss Boston. "We must know absolutely what we're dealing with before the fire hoses start."

By way of a circular path, the famous detective went around the house into the part of the garden where she had the rare luck to find the traces of the criminal's footprints and to read the address of the Brad Shoe shop.

"Sokes," she said, "once again we're on the trail. Look over there!"

On the ground there were signs of footsteps going from the low wall to the little door of the cellar. These prints were very distinct from those previously seen and she could see that the same foot had left behind these evident signs of its passage. It was evident the killer had returned after the famous detective's visit. Why? For what purpose?

The answer to that double question now offered an obvious solution: the villa fire. Vogt had returned to the house in the afternoon that day to set it afire. That showed an unusual daring on his part. She had only to get material proof.

She led Sokes toward the house, entered the cellar and climbed the stairs. A thick, acrid smoke began to reach her. Nevertheless she went forward. Suddenly she stumbled on something and stooped to pick it up. It was a copper cylinder, twisted, dinted, battered.

"Look, Sokes."

"What is it?"

"It's a soldering lamp. He had that lamp in his work sack. That kind of lamp contains very flammable oil. He poured it on the villa stairs, set it aflame and fled, leaving this new clue behind him."

"How did it happen that the two policemen on guard outside the fence didn't notice that kind of burglary?"

"You know as well as I do, Sokes, it's not always among the members of our profession that talent and subtlety can be found."

The detectives' conversation was interrupted by a huge cascade of water which inundated and splashed the entry hall. The firemen were dealing with the fire. Miss Boston and Sokes beat a prudent retreat and returned to the garden in haste.

There they met the two policemen on duty, totally astonished, asking themselves how this mysterious fire could have broken out two steps from them, almost under their noses. Miss Boston didn't think it fit to explain it to them. She limited herself to questioning them about the individuals who came to look at the walls of the bloody villa.

The answers to her questions convinced her that Vogt had hung around the house for a while, that he had even struck up a conversation with the policemen. An ordinary conversation for them, of no interest, but not for him. In fact, Vogt had asked if a police inquiry had already taken place.

"That's the reason he set fire to the villa. When he went back to his place, he noticed he had forgotten the hammer marked with his initial, a terrible proof against him. He searched for it, and not finding it, he believed he had simply misplaced it in the house. Fearing he would be surprised by the police while searching, he preferred to finish it quickly and make the instrument of the crime disappear with the place. That's the cause of the fire. It's absolutely useless to look for it anywhere else."

VIII. Detectives Lucky to be taken for Burglars

What Miss Boston had foreseen, happened. Helped along by the lamp oil, the fire progressed with frightening speed. The stairs were rapidly consumed and while it was burning the first floor, it spread to the second floor and across the dwelling. The alarm had been given when the inside was already on fire; the firemen had arrived too late. They had to limit themselves to pouring over the inferno a torrent of water which drowned everything. An hour later it was a pitiful ruin in the middle of the little garden of Grosvenor Place, a mass of hot ashes over which the snow slowly spread its white coat and shroud. Miss Boston and Sokes didn't wait for the end of the fire to leave. Both were convinced Vogt was no longer near the premises. The important thing was to return to the criminal's trail without delay and deliver him as soon as possible into the hands of the law. In addition, wasn't James Marmaduke still locked up, anxiously counting the minutes until his freedom? A double reason to hurry.

"I think, Mr. Sokes," the detective said, "that the simplest thing is to go set up a trap in Vogt's house."

"That's also my opinion. It may be easier to bring about than we think."

"How's that?"

"If Vogt returns, we can snatch him out of the nest."

"That possibility is part of my plan, Sokes."

"Then so much the better. Everything is foreseen."

"Except Vogt's complete disappearance."

"Indeed. That would be devilishly annoying."

"If all criminals let themselves be picked up without difficulty, our honorable profession would be a dream. But up until now this business hasn't been particularly hard. The crime is atrocious and ordinary; the murderer is stupid. If, considering all that, we won't nab him in 24 hours, he decidedly had luck on his side."

"Murderers sometimes enjoy good luck, you know."

"Yes, but we finally get the best of them."

"Indeed."

"That's a consolation and an encouragement."

Approaching Holyrood Ban, they considered that the concierge might alert Vogt about their presence in his room; therefore it was absolutely essential that they got into Vogt's room without anyone's knowledge. They decided to enter the courtyard of the house through a little abandoned lane behind it containing old uninhabited huts. The detective climbed onto the roof of one of the hovels, the planks of which creaked under the sudden weight but held firm. The roof extended slightly over the courtyard and using it, Miss Boston and Sokes jumped to the roof of a little building there. At the shock of their double fall, a cry of terror rang out from a woman leaving the little shed. Not seeing the two detectives very clearly, she began to scream:

191

"Robbers!...Robbers!...Robbers!"

Miss Boston recognized the concierge of the house.

"Hopefully she'll run off before she recognizes us," she whispered to Sokes.

Very fortunately for the detective, that was what happened. The concierge didn't take the time to examine the people who had fallen from the sky, and continued to gallop to the house shouting shrill, frightened cries.

"That was all I hoped for," said Miss Boston, smiling at the turn of events favorable to her. Then she jumped down into the courtyard from the roof of the low building, and motioning to Sokes to follow her, she entered the corridor of the house, the stairs, and in a few bounds reached Vogt's room. From the street the detectives heard noise and cries; the concierge still frightened was telling the neighbors about her extraordinary adventure. The neighbors, in good will, had united in teams to give chase to the supposed burglars. Armed with clubs and pistols, they had gone into the courtyard, searching in all the corners. Cries, advice, shouts, all crossed each other, mingling in the brouhaha of the courtyard. The burglars—and for good reason—remained invisible. At the end of five minutes two policemen came, inspected the courtyard, the little shed where the concierge washed the linen, the cellar, finally everything. No trace of the burglars anywhere.

"Nevertheless, I saw them!" the concierge shouted.

They began to make fun of her. "The good woman has seen double," they said.

Finally, when calm was restored, Miss Boston said:

"And now to serious things."

Observing the time to be 4:10 p.m., Miss Boston and Sokes set up observation posts in Vogt's bedroom, Miss Boston watching from the left, Sokes carefully watching from the right.

IX. Vogt Avoids a Trap

From their position, nothing in the street could escape the two detectives. Each passerby necessarily came into their field of vision. There they were examined, scrutinized. From time to time the detectives exchanged some thoughts as to whether the murderer had already made an escape, or the question of whether he knew about the trap set for him. At 5 p.m. twilight began to fall. Suddenly a window broke. Something heavy rolled over the floor. Miss Boston exclaimed:

"He's gotten wind of it!"

What had happened? A stone had been thrown into the window behind which Sokes was hiding. Thrown with violence, the stone had lifted a thin little muslin drape and revealed Sokes' presence. Where did the stone come from? No one had crossed the visual path of the two detectives. So? What was this new mystery? Miss Boston understood it immediately. A half-finished building was being constructed across from No.8 Holyrood. The bad weather had forced the masons to temporarily abandon their work. The rock came from there. When examining the two ends of the street, the two detectives hadn't been aware of that construction. The person who threw the stone must have been in the house when the concierge stirred up the neighbors about the supposed burglars. That explained everything. Seeing a moving mass of people in the street with no reason, the scared criminal took refuge in the incomplete construction.

Had he, despite the drapes, noticed the unusual movements in the bedroom? It was very possible he had. He wanted to find out by throwing that stone and that stone accomplished his purpose very well. Miss Boston stated with scarcely dissimulated annoyance:

"That fellow is certainly a lot less stupid than I at first thought."

"He's just proven it. What are we going to do? Stay here?"

"Don't even think about it. We have to go into the house across the way. He must certainly still be there to find out who we are and what we want. We'll go down."

"But he'll see us coming and get out."

"That would be a shame, but we'll save him that trouble."

"What are you going to do?"

"We're going to leave here the same way we came in."

This time it was necessary to work with the greatest, the most extreme care. They could cross the courtyard without trouble, since the concierge was telling a group of tradespeople how she had almost been murdered by a band of fearsome robbers who, at least ten of them, had invaded the Holyrood house. In the courtyard, to climb up to the roof, walk across the neighboring hovel and jump down into the little lane, was only a game for them. The lane was fortunately deserted.

The two detectives raced to Murbach Avenue where they hoped to find a way to approach the Holyrood Ban construction without being seen. At the end of 100 meters, she saw a vacant lot at the back of which she saw the outline of a house under construction behind a fence which had to be jumped. The courageous young woman served as an example to her companion. She had long been used to the most difficult and dangerous gymnastics. This one didn't frighten her any more than the others. She therefore cleared it with competence. In a few strides they were across the vacant lot. It was rapidly becoming twilight and obscuring everything in gray cloudy light. The black and gray mass of abandoned construction could be vaguely seen. The two detectives armed their weapons and advanced in the darkness. There was profound silence. Large gusts of snow swept the floors through the unfinished windows. A sharp, violent wind howled through the chimneys. The detectives saw nothing suspicious. The construction seemed absolutely deserted. Vogt had taken flight.

"Too late," said Miss Boston.

And they left the construction for Holyrood Ban. Suddenly Sokes touched her arm.

"Over there," he said.

"Is that he, Sokes?"

"That's possible."

"Let's go see."

In the distance, in fact, in the dark and empty street, a shadow was moving away. At the end of the street, it began to run. That seemed suspicious. The two detectives didn't lose a minute and left in pursuit of the fleeing man. He turned obliquely toward Murbach Avenue. The detectives ran faster. When they came to the Avenue, the shadow had disappeared.

"Thunderation!" Sokes swore, furious.

"Calm down," the energetic young woman responded. "All is not lost yet." And she pointed to an automobile which had just started up.

X. The Fight after the Collision

It was indeed the murderer who was fleeing. The detectives had to pursue the automobile on foot until they could requisition a vehicle. The chase began immediately. The automobile had gotten ahead of the two detectives, but they gained ground quickly. Nevertheless the vehicle was going at top speed toward Kantbury. That chase, one which would have taken the breath away from others in less good shape than Sokes and Miss Boston, lasted some meters. At the corner of Moon Street, an auto lot offered clients their choice of a dozen vehicles. Miss Boston didn't waste time choosing. She jumped into first vehicle and shouted to the driver, confused by that haste:

"Five dollars for you to catch that vehicle."

The automobile was put in gear and a minute later they were flying at full speed along the trail of the vehicle in flight. Sokes took advantage of that rest to draw a deep breath. As for Miss Boston, the race didn't seem to have bothered her. At the most, she was breathing a little hard.

"Well!" she said. "I don't believe I was totally mistaken. That must certainly be Vogt in the automobile."

"Indeed, he doesn't seem to have a very clear conscience."

"Running away in an automobile proves it, Sokes."

The detective was carefully watching the progress of the chase. Their automobile was only gaining slowly on that of Vogt's. The two automobiles were literally burning up the pavement. In a populated area that chase would have lasted only a few meters. An accident would certainly have interrupted the mad flight, but this neighborhood was usually solitary, even in good weather, and positively deserted in the evening, and especially in the evening of such a snow storm.

For an hour, the two automobiles had been gradually nearing each other. A few more sudden swerves and Miss Boston would be able to reach the phantom vehicle she was pursuing. Soon there was a distance of only 15 meters between the two vehicles. Wanting to finish it, the detective leaned out of the window and shouted at the top of her voice to Vogt's driver.

"Stop! In the name of the law!"

Either he had not heard the order, or the noise of the motor had drowned out the detective's voice, or Vogt himself was relying on his stolen dollars, rather than formal orders. The driver didn't stop. On the contrary, the race went even faster. Once again, Miss Boston shouted:

"Stop!" and she added in a firm and determined tone: "I'll fire!"

Useless command. The automobile kept fleeing. A sharp and clear gunshot clacked in the night. Miss Boston had fired. It was useless. The automobile picked up speed. The detective fired a second time. That was still in vain. Four other shots sent in the same direction had no better result. On the contrary, danger seemed to whip up the driver's courage. It was now a real race to the death. The motors of the two vehicles roared and vibrated as to almost explode. Miss Boston's driver took to heart earning the five dollar tip. As hard as he could, his eyes staring straight ahead, his teeth clenched, his fists tight, he bore down on the machine's gear shifts. The decisive moment really seemed to be approaching. The road became narrower and each meter the detective's automobile gained on Vogt's. The crash was inevitable. A collision, a catastrophe, in several seconds perhaps, couldn't be avoided. Suddenly, it happened. The automobile of those doing the chase hit the automobile of those being chased. That automobile shook and turned over with an enormous noise of motor explosion. Broken windows flew out; the vehicle's hood was torn apart with a hole in it among the cries of rage and pain. Revolver in her hand, the detective jumped from the debris. Only the two drivers were hurt. Vogt, because he was in the vehicle, had no injury and like Miss Boston, he had gotten out of the automobile debris. Leaving the catastrophe there, he raced toward a wall, thus protected from any attack from the rear. Standing firm, he waited for the detective.

When she approached, revolver in hand, he made a terrible jump toward her. She staggered under the blow. She fired. But her arm, badly supported, missed. The bullet was lost in the wall and the courageous young woman felt herself thrown violently on the ground. She did not, however, lose consciousness. The criminal was strong and formidable with supple muscles, used to fatigue and hard work. He was then holding the detective by the throat and squeezing with all his strength. The cartilage could be heard cracking. Miss Boston was lost. However, she hadn't turned loose of her revolve. She held it tightly in her clinched hand. She pressed the trigger; the bullet left; and the shot was answered by a bellow of pain. Vogt had been hit in the hip. He turned loose of his victim and stood up howling. At the same moment someone jumped on his shoulders, knocked him over, and handcuffed him. Sokes had come to the celebrated detective's aid.

The Grosvenor Place murderer was caught.

Miss Boston's automobile was only slightly damaged. The one used in Vogt's escape was literally in pieces. It had to be left there on the road in ruins. The wounded driver was put on the seat. He had a broken clavicle. Vogt, in chains, was watched by Miss Boston and Sokes during the entire journey back to New York. He didn't say a word, keeping a tragic and grim silence. Miss Boston didn't say a word to him, reserving her interrogation for later. At 10 p.m. the automobile stopped in front of the canopy of the Central Police Bureau.

That same night poor James Marmaduke was given his liberty with some dollars as compensation. He danced for joy. In the morning they picked him up, dead drunk, in Grosvenor Street. He didn't have a penny. To celebrate his release, he had conscientiously drunk his "compensation" at the Star, his friend's bar. When he woke up the next day, he had a marvelous saying for a drunk man:

"For that amount," he said, "I'd gladly spend half my life in prison."

Alas, such a beautiful dream never came to pass. That was the only time James Marmaduke enjoyed in good conscience the role of innocent in spite of himself.

XI. Black Flag Time

The Investigation opened the day after the plumber's arrest. It confirmed point by point in all details, Miss Boston's deductions. Miss Worms' murder took place under exactly the condition she had specified to Sokes. Vogt, however, denied everything. During the 18 interrogations he had to undergo before his trial, he obstinately refused to recognize anything, admit anything. However, everything accused him. But the criminal faithfully followed to the letter the celebrated maxim of a famous criminal: "Never admit anything!"

The day of the trial was Miss Boston's triumph. In front of the jury she described the circumstances under which it happened, the facilities Vogt made use of, and how it was done. She called as a witness the bloody hammer and the button found in the victim's hand.

James Marmaduke had his part of success at that same hearing. But his was a success of wild laughter. To come be deposed before the judges, he had absented himself to go get a few little glasses of gin and whiskey. At his recitation of his adventure in front of the grill of the villa at Grosvenor Place, they couldn't keep from laughing despite its dramatic interest. When he had finished, James Marmaduke, very proud, returned to sit on his bench.

In spite of all that, charges, proofs, presumptions, Vogt admitted nothing. The High Court unanimously gave Vogt the death penalty.

At the time when Miss Boston dealt with that celebrated case, electrocution was not yet the system of capital punishment used in the United States. At that time the execution of the sentence was carried out by hanging in the great courtyard of the Tombs Prison. It was there, one February morning, that Vogt paid for his odious crime. A high gallows was set up in space left free by the dark building of the old prison. A ladder was set up against the gallows and the morning wind blew the hangman's rope back and forth, right and left. The condemned man was brought out by the warden and the guards. Miss Boston and Sokes were among the spectators.

They had Vogt mount seven of the ladder's steps. There they put the noose around his neck. Suddenly the hangman placed a black veil over the condemned man's head, intended to hide the convulsions of agony on the face. That done, he took away the ladder. Vogt swung in the void. Then the hangman seized the feet of the murderer in order to hasten the strangulation. At the end of three minutes the cadaver was taken down. A black flag was then raised above the door of the Tombs Prison. Fifteen minutes later, a special wagon carried the body of the hanged man to the Black Friars Cemetery.

Thus ended the affair of the Grosvenor Place murder, where, 24 hours after the crime, the murderer fell, thanks to Miss Boston, into the hands of justice.

THE SEVERED HAND

I. The Maitland Mystery

Maitland is a nice little village situated at the edge of the charming Flog, a stream which meanders capriciously to the great interior Chicago Lake.

At least two hours from New York, Maitland is the spot dreamed of by vacationers who can't go a great distance from the city and who can go there whenever they like. That village is separated into two parts in a rather strange manner. Maitland proper is on the right bank of the Flog. The village is made up of little wood or red brick houses, the way they were still constructed some years ago in America. It's not an important group; about 40 houses at most. The other part of the village, on the left side of the Flog, is scarcely more important. That one is mainly composed of cottages, or villas, or country houses. But these villas, while charming, are modest and belong to those of comfortable means rather than to the rich.

The location of that second part of Maitland, of the new village, as it's commonly called, is infinitely more pleasant and charming than the first. That one is situated at the edge if an extensive wood, at least 15 to 20 kilometers in depth. This thick wood, with powerful oaks, and bird's eye maple trees close together, forms a dream framework for the villas of New Maitland. Here the houses were built a little distance from each other, and as a consequence not connected by any regularly laid-out road. At the most, they were vaguely tied together by narrow pathways lined with hedgerows, bindweed in bloom, and young, new, and fragrant vegetation which perfumed all the countryside. All these details serve to explain the cadre in which this drama is played out and how the situation of the villa and village allowed that same drama to unfold.

Maitland, like all little townships in the United States, is administered by an official who fills, at the same time, the role of mayor, coroner, and constable. That means that through those functions he has both civil and judicial authority. At the period when Miss Boston was involved with this new adventure in her busy detective life, those official duties were exercised at Maitland by an old resident of the country, John Smith.

On the morning of 12 June, John Smith was still profoundly asleep when violent knocks on his door made him sit up in bed. He listened a moment, thinking he was perhaps mistaken. But the knocks on the door began again. Then John Smith jumped out of bed, ran to the window, opening it very wide to lean into the street. The person knocking was a young boy about 15 years old, poorly, even miserably clothed.

"Ah! It's you, Bobby. What do you mean waking me so early in the morning?"

Bobby herded sheep and goats for the inhabitants of Maitland, taking them to pasture in the countryside, sometimes spending the night out of doors. To Mr. Smith's question, the boy answered:

"I think something happened last night at Pretty Bell, Mr. Smith."

"And what is it that happened at Pretty Bell, Bobby?"

"I don't know."

"And so?"

"But I heard a cry as if somebody had been killed in the house."

The honorable John Smith frowned. There was worry in his eyes. He finally answered the young shepherd.

"Wait for me. I'll be down in a few minutes."

He dressed hurriedly, grumbling between his teeth. What could that bizarre story mean? Obviously, young Bobby wasn't lying. And if he said someone cried out at Pretty Bell, someone certainly had. There was something strange and shady there.

Pretty Bell, on the left bank of the Flog, was one of those villas located at the extreme end of New Maitland, almost at the entry of the forest.

While dressing, John Smith shook his head and putting on his straw hat, he said, between his teeth:

"I think there's something not very clear here."

Going down and opening the door, he found young Bobby sitting on the steps nibbling a piece of bread.

"Come with me," he said. "We're first going to Pol Adamson's."

He was the official who acted in some fashion as adjunct, secretary, aide, to Mr. Smith. On the way, the coroner asked the young shepherd:

"Tell me what you heard last night at Pretty Bell."

Bobby said:

"I was in the pasture at the edge of the woods. I'd made a little pen for the sheep belonging to the Wolfstam people. About eleven o'clock the dogs began to bark. That woke me and I heard a carriage roll by in the big path in the woods which leads to the Galveston Road. The dogs wouldn't shut up. That was when I heard the cries at Polly Bell. It's only 200 meters from my pasture. There was a light in the balcony windows; then the light went out."

"And that's all?" asked Mr. Smith, prodigiously interested and even intrigued by the little shepherd's information.

"Yes, the carriage again rolled back to the road. Then I didn't hear anything else. The dogs stopped barking."

"You didn't go to Pretty Bell to see what happened?"

"God keep me from that, Mr. Smith!"

"And why's that?"

"First of all, I had my goats to watch, Mr. Smith, and I don't want the Wolfstam people to say that I'm stealing the penny they give me every day."

"You're an honest boy, I see."

The little boy blushed with pleasure at the compliment, but with a certain hesitation in his trembling voice he added:

"And the...and then...Mr. Smith..., I didn't go see for another reason."

"Ah! And what was that, Bobby?"

"That was because I was a little afraid," the young shepherd confessed with embarrassment.

Mr. Smith didn't laugh at that admission.

"I understand that," he said.

While talking, they came to the Pol Adamson dwelling to the west of Maitland. It was a modest, pleasant little house, its façade covered from top to bottom with vines and ivy resembling a thick curtain of green. The house was surrounded by a thick hedge in which there was a small wooden gate which Mr. Smith pushed and entered the yard. At the sharp grate of the hinges, a man in shirtsleeves, wearing a straw hat and digging in a flowerbed raised his head. Mr. Pol Adamson was already at work.

II. The Severed Hand at Pretty Bell

"Good Morning, Mr. Adamson," Mr. Smith exclaimed as soon as he saw him.

Mr. Adamson answered the greeting of the man who was more his friend than his chief and added in a friendly fashion:

"You're up very early this morning, Mr. Smith."

"That's because serious things happened last night at Maitland."

"Alas! Adamson exclaimed, and dropped his spade in a large bed, crushing its dahlias.

He asked in a worried tone: "Something serious, you say. And what's that?"

Mr. Smith answered: "I don't know anything precise at the moment. It was Bobby here who came to alert me. Last night he was in the little woods' pasture. Some things happened at Pretty Bell that makes me think there's a tragedy. I think it's our duty, Adamson, to go there now to see if our help isn't necessary or urgent."

"I agree with you completely," he answered.

He went into the house, took down a jacket hung on a nail in the hallway and returned to Mr. Smith as he put it on.

"Let's go to Pretty Bell," he said. "I'm ready to follow you."

The two men, followed by Bobby, started down a narrow path which went down one sloping side of the stream.

Mr. Smith suddenly said: "It's strange that a thing so mysterious should happen at Pretty Bell. That's the only house in Maitland where we don't know the inhabitants."

"That's true. I believe Pretty Bell was rented by a Chicago agency to the present occupant of the house."

"That's true, Adamson, but that occupant neglected to come declare his name and his current address to me as coroner, as the law requires. He's been installed at Pretty Bell for a week and hasn't yet carried out that obligation. I dare say, Adamson, today or tomorrow I'm going to require these tardy gentlemen to carry out that obligation. Since we're going to Pretty Bell, we'll take advantage of that fact to remind him of that duty."

"We'll kill two birds with one stone."

Mr. Smith took out his watch.

"Seven ten. I think we can decently present ourselves at this hour at Pretty Bell."

The two men were walking along casually, without hurrying too much. Mr. Smith had lit his little briar pipe and blew harmonious puffs in spirals. Nevertheless, he appeared worried. During the 30 years he had lived in Maitland nothing unusual had ever broken the monotony of its peaceful, calm, and sleepy existence. His functions, which appeared to be multiple, were in fact a simple sinecure. A crime at Pretty Bell! He thought vaguely about that possibility, without daring too much yet to believe it himself. A murder! A crime! That unusual fact would bring about unusual trouble in Maitland's life. It would be better to think the cries Bobby heard came simply from an argument or a dispute. That thought reassured good Mr. Smith.

However, if, really, a crime had been committed last night at Pretty Bell, what complication would there arise from all that, from the fact that the name and the household of the renter of the villa were totally unknown. That frightening question remained for the moment unanswered and enigmatic.

They had arrived at the edge of the Flog which had to be crossed to get to the left bank where the group of villas made up New Maitland. At the bank the shore formed a tiny cove. Several boats were moored there for the inhabitants on the right to make use of when visiting their relations on the left. Adamson grabbed the oars of one of the boats and, vigorously, using all his muscles, rowed against the river current. It was crossed in ten minutes and the boat was moored at a wharf on the left bank. From there Smith, Adamson and Bobby took a steep path which wound through gardens and cottages, in the direction of the woods, at the edge of which, in a truly charming spot, Pretty Bell was located.

The walk didn't take very long and the two men and boy soon arrived in front of the cottage.

It was a delightful little house, elegantly constructed. It had two floors and a view from the balconies of the Flog as well as a view of the forest. Little white stone steps led to the entry. A vast garden including a kitchen garden and flower beds planted with ornamental flowers surrounded the house. The entire place was encircled by a high hedge and wooden fences. When Smith and Adamson arrived, everything was closed. The inhabitants seemed to be still enjoying all the sweetness of sleep and rest.

Smith wasn't sure what to do.

"How are we going to get into the house," he asked. "There's no bell."

"Just open the gate."

"Yes, but might not the proprietor reproach us for entering his property a little unceremoniously?"

"That's possible, but if we want to find out anything, it won't be by mounting guard behind this gate."

"You're right, Adamson," and with that, Mr. Smith pushed on the gate which wasn't locked and opened easily.

The door to Pretty Bell was small and low. It was apparently not the one ordinarily used. That door was blocked and it was necessary to go around the house to enter. The visitors circled the house to an entry door with an overhanging balcony which gave a view of the forest. While Mr. Smith was knocking, Adamson felt something moist and sticky fall into his hand. He looked at it and let out a long, horrified scream. A large drop of blood had just fallen on him.

"Look! Look!" stammered the assistant.

Mr. Smith saw the red stain and turned pale in his turn.

"What is that?" he yelled in a hoarse voice.

At the same moment Bobby also cried out in his turn.

"Mr. Smith! Mr. Smith!"

"What! What!...What is it?"

"There!" said the little boy, his eyes filled with terror. And with a trembling hand, he pointed to the balcony. The coroner, Mr. Smith, raised his head. He took a step backwards and his face suddenly became livid. What he had just seen, attached to the Pretty Bell balcony, bleeding slowly, drop by drop, was a severed hand.

III. The Trail of the Mafia Leader

That same morning of the 12th of June at 8 a.m., at the Circus Street Station, two people took the train for Galveston. One was a young blonde woman, slim, elegant, whose movements were at the same time both gracious and full of energy. That was Miss Boston. The other, rugged, dressed conservatively, with an impassive face was the usual companion of her dangerous adventures and perilous investigations, Mr. Sokes, Chief Inspector of the New York Central Police Bureau. By a series of circumstances, the two detectives were then in Chicago and were traveling towards Galveston, a little country village where police investigations seemed unlikely. Sokes was looking forward to a restful vacation at Maitland, which he richly deserved. While the train was picking up speed along the borders of Lake Michigan, the Chief Inspector was busy arranging in the compartment filet the light baggage he was carrying. He finished and returned to sit opposite Miss Boston, who was consulting her notebook the truly hieroglyphic writing to which she alone had the secret.

"Sokes," she finally said, "I maintain that the affair of the Mafia, which we're now busy with, is, with that of the Invisible Man, the longest we've taken up."

"Indeed. It seems to me that's gone on some weeks and months already."

"For three months and two weeks exactly, sir."

"And nothing says we'll see the end of it."

"On the contrary, I think we're getting there."

"Really?"

"Yes, the trail we picked up yesterday in Chicago is one of the most creditable."

"We've already uncovered so many leads which have ended in so little, not to say in nothing!"

"Undoubtedly. But those trails have against them the serious fault of being too complicated. This one, on the contrary, has the advantage of being unusually clear, sharp, limpid, and that's why I think its result will be definitive."

"May the god of detectives hear you!" Sokes exclaimed.

"That's a service I expect from his kindness," Miss Boston said, amused at the wish. But in a tone suddenly turned serious, she added:

"I have an inner feeling, Sokes, that we're touching a solution to the affair, the knot to the enigmatic question which has preoccupied us for such a long time. It wouldn't be useless, perhaps, to glance back over our efforts since last March to discover the truth."

Miss Boston collected her thoughts for a moment as she mentally assembled all the scattered memories of her last difficult and complicated research.

"How were we put on the trail of the affair? By the Italian police. The Mafia is originally a secret Italian society which is under surveillance by that country's police. They were the ones who warned us that several members had set sail for America."

"Unfortunately," Sokes observed, "the warning was very badly done, since several of these fellows were able to disembark without being recognized."

"I suspect they wore a disguise," the detective answered. "Naturally, their arrest on arrival would have avoided the four crimes they've committed in fewer than three weeks. However, the Italian police's warning wasn't useless, since it told us what kind of criminal we're dealing with. Our trail could have wandered after common thieves while, thanks to that, we knew right away who the authors of the attacks were."

"The vengeance, rather,"

"If you prefer, Sokes. Obviously the four victims, former members of the Mafia, traitors to their oaths and their commitments, paid for their betrayal by the emigrants' knives. Up until then the thing, however punishable, showed only the political side of the crime. What raises these crimes to the level of the common criminal realm is the theft that followed. To assassinate in the name of an ideal is, if not excusable, at least comprehensible; to steal in the name of that same ideal has something low and despicable about it which should be severely punished by law."

"That's something our fellows aren't very worried about."

"That's understandable, Sokes. But to come back to the business itself. At first it seemed simple. There were four victims: Tagliafico, a banker on 18th Avenue; Pedretti, a broker on Burk Street; Gugliemno, a bondsman at No.298 Hudson Wharf, and Bartholomeo Fratelli, Director of the Chicago Immigration Agency. All the victims were Italian and the trails of their assassins were all the same. That fact was important. What happened? The four trails ended by forming only one and that one trail ended at the real estate rental agency for the Wolfstam, Galveston and Maitland villas."

"So you believe that this Crespo, who rented a villa at Maitland, the Pretty Bell Villa, will put you on the trail of the other members of the Mafia?"

"Yes, Sokes, because I've learned that he commanded these fellows and that the execution orders which were so promptly and terribly carried out came only from him and not from anyone else."

"Then it's this Crespo who's the head of the Mafia."

"Yes, and the others are only the arms."

"And the head cut off, the arms naturally will be dead."

"You guess what I have in mind."

"And what is your plan in these circumstances?"

"It's to watch Crespo, to shadow him closely. Following his trail, we'll certainly find that of the other Italians."

"It's only when you've found his trail that you'll go into action?"

"Yes. Our wait will permit you to enjoy the pleasures and beauties of the countryside for a few days."

"All Right!" Sokes exclaimed. "That suits me!" And anticipating their enjoyment, the Chief Inspector lit an excellent cigar.

IV. Miss Boston Arrives at the Psychological Moment

Because of the insignificance of Maitland, the North Railway Company did not have a station there. To reach the little community on the banks of the Flog, travelers had to get off at Galveston, and from there, either on foot or by car, travel the two hours which separated the small city from the village. Miss Boston and Sokes got off at Galveston and inquired about renting a carriage. They were lucky to find one, an excellent cabriolet which led them at a trot toward the hideout where the detectives counted on finding the chief of the Mafia, Crespo.

Sokes took evident pleasure in rolling along, agreeably lulled, in excellent weather, across an exquisite and charming countryside bathed in the light of a summer sun. But at the end of an hour he had to be disenchanted.

"We're going to get out here," Miss Boston suddenly said.

"What? Already?" protested the inspector, who was enjoying the ride.

"Prudence demands it, sir. It's necessary, even absolutely necessary, that our arrival go unnoticed at Pretty Bell or the vicinity."

"Indeed. I understand."

"We're going to make the rest of the way on foot."

"As you wish."

From the cabman, the two detectives found out the road to Pretty Bell. In addition they had the exterior of the house described to them. Armed with these precious details, they started on their way. They were at the moment on a road cutting straight through a dense forest it. They were walking carefully for fear of unexpectedly meeting someone suspicious. Nothing, fortunately, halted their walk and they reached the edge of the forest without encountering a living soul. They were soon in sight of Pretty Bell.

"Is that really Pretty Bell there?"

"Certainly. The house looks exactly like the description given by the Galveston cabman."

"Shall we go see?"

"Let's wait a minute."

"There seem to be people gathered in front of the door."

The detectives got out from hiding behind the branches where they had taken refuge and walked toward the house.

In fact, about a dozen people were assembled in front of the door looking at a severed hand on the balcony gently bleeding little slow and heavy drops on the ground. The detectives were aghast. The most ardent of those holding forth were Smith and Adamson. They were explaining to the Maitland citizens, who had come running at their shouts, how they had discovered that macabre and mysterious remnant. However, they hadn't yet dared to go into the house.

Miss Boston immediately guessed who Smith was, drew him to one side and informed him of the goal of her visit and that of Sokes, and required him to maintain the most absolute and complete silence. Next, she ordered him to use his authority to have the curious leave the Petty Bell garden so that she would not be hampered in searching the house. These orders were carried out instantly and when the loiterers had left the garden, she walked up to the entry door. She gave the three knocks required by law and getting no answer, with the aid of her jimmy, she opened the door. Followed by Sokes, Smith, and Adamson she entered the tragically silent villa. Bobby was put in charge of guarding the door, to keep the curious from entering. And so the search began with unusual care.

Miss Boston didn't notice anything on the first floor except in a small sitting room. That room was painted a raw and violent lime white. In a corner of the ceiling a large red stain, like blood, was spreading. Sokes was the first to notice it. He said:

"Look! What's that? Especially at that place and that height?"

"A visit to the upper floor will likely tell us."

They went up as a group a few instants later. There were three rooms on that floor; two were bedrooms. Only one seemed to have been used. The bed sheets, the bolsters, the pillows and the covers were on the floor in the greatest disorder. There had certainly been a fight but there were nowhere any traces of blood. The third room was used as an office. There was a desk in the middle of the room. The papers had been examined and searched because they were scattered right and left on the floor.

"We certainly won't find anything in there," Miss Boston said in a low voice. "The Mafia people have been through here."

Everything told her the feared secret society had some part in the drama played in Pretty Bell, an unusual drama because up to the present no victim had been discovered in the silent villa. Where did that large bloodstain on the little sitting room ceiling come from? And most of all, where did the severed hand come from? A double question for which Miss Boston searched in vain for an answer. Suddenly she walked toward a corner of the room and pressed a button hidden in the wallpaper. A door opened showing a hidden wall cupboard holding a cadaver. A hand of the victim was severed. With the help of Smith and Adamson she pulled the man from the nook and in the movement something fell out. It was a Corsican stiletto. The victim had been struck between his shoulders and the blood from the wound had flowed onto the floor, wetting the planks, and the ceiling below had been moistened. That was the explanation of the purple stain on the ceiling of the small sitting room.

Miss Boston searched the victim's pockets. They contained only some pennies and a torn envelope. Putting the pieces back together the celebrated detective could read the address:

Il signor Crespo
Vittoria, via Milano
Italia, Napoli

Showing the envelope to Sokes, she said: "There's the name of the cadaver."

"The head of the Mafia!" The Chief Inspector murmured.

"Himself!" Miss Boston answered.

And in a tone showing the firm will to lead her investigation to a successful conclusion, she added:

"The mystery begins again. Still too bad! But I'm here!"

V. Trail of a Cabriolet

The search of the crime scene obviously finished, there remained only to remove the bloody trophy hung up by the murderers and to proceed to the burial of the cadaver of the mysterious Italian.

"But," Sokes asked, "what was the purpose of that severed hand being placed in that spot? On the balcony most of all?"

"For an American assassin it would be simple bravado," the detective explained, "but it's something different for Mafia members."

"Would it be, in some way, their trademark?"

"You've guessed it, Sokes. But the severed hand here certainly fills still another purpose.'

"Do you think so?"

"Yes. Before continuing, let's take the cadaver away from here. We'll see later what part we're to play in the present circumstances."

To this end Miss Boston gave the honorable John Smith some instructions. He agreed with the detective to have Crespo's body picked up that same morning, make out the warrant, and order the burial in the little Maitland cemetery. On the other hand, he was told to keep the most absolute silence about that dark event. That so many people had seen the severed hand on the balcony was already too much. Miss Boston went to place seals on the Pretty Ball door. When all was settled with Smith and Adamson, she got busy putting together the first elements of her investigation. The only testimony it was possible to get was that of Bobby, the young shepherd. Neither Smith nor Adamson knew anything about the tragedy before being told by Bobby. As for him, what had he seen? Nothing. But what had he heard? There his testimony became interesting. Thanks to him, they knew that a cabriolet, a light carriage, had come the night of the crime to Pretty Bell, and that this cabriolet had left some little time afterward in the direction of Galveston. That was a valuable clue. If Miss Boston could manage to discover in Galveston the trace of the nocturnal visitors, she had a serious chance of following them from trail to trail right to their hideout. That was the first major, urgent, point to investigate. She wasn't leaving without some clue from the house of the murder. She knew where the murderers came from, how they came, and almost guessed something about them.

Miss Boston therefore took leave of Smith and Adamson. The detective promised to return to Maitland as soon as she had acquired some facts about the criminals. Leaving Pretty Bell, she hurried to get back to the road that went straight through the woods toward Galveston. "Strike while the anvil is hot," was the proverb the illustrious young woman always followed. While walking she was looking attentively at the ground in front of her. That attention paid off at the end of some minutes by the discovery of two parallel grooves on the left side of the road.

"That's proof of the cabriolet's passing here last night," she said to Sokes.

"Right," he answered. "Those are the grooves hollowed out by the wheels."

"Look at the horseshoe prints, Sokes. We just have to follow the path traced by the members of that dangerous Mafia."

The two policemen had at least a two hours' walk ahead of them. They had all the necessary time to turn over and over the tragic problem which law and justice had handed over to them.

"Didn't you say the severed hand had been tied to the balcony for two reasons?"

"Certainly, in addition to wanting to alert passersby of their crime, to speed up the burial of their victim, they certainly wanted that severed hand to show they had carried out an act of justice."

"But no one would have thought of guessing that."

"So it wasn't for the casual passerby and just anybody that the hand was tied there, but just in case another member of the Mafia came to Pretty Bell to see Crespo."

The first houses of Galveston appeared in the distance. The two detectives hadn't for an instant lost sight of the path made by the cabriolet's wheels. Miss Boston had hopes of seeing it stop right at the door of the person who rented the cabriolet, unless the murderers had come in their own transportation. The signs of the cabriolet turned sharply to the right and merged into a shallow road. After a 15 minute walk, Miss Boston came out in front of a rustic cabaret where the cabriolet prints became confused with the pell-mell of other footsteps or wheels and disappeared. There was no doubt the murderers' carriage had stopped here. The owner of the cabaret gave Miss Boston all the information she asked for. He remembered perfectly having rented, the evening before, a bad cabriolet—it was there in the coach house—to two individuals who seemed strangers to the area.

He gave a rather precise, valuable, description. The first one was tall, thin, fashionable, with a dark complexion; the second, on the contrary, was stocky, muscular, bearded, with a sly look in his eye. They arrived at the cabaret about 7 p.m., had dined à la carte and rented the cabriolet for a drive to Maitland, where they had, it seems, a friend expecting them. In addition, he complained, not that he hadn't been paid, but that the horse had been returned in the middle of the night, foundered, as if they had galloped him at breakneck speed.

"I will never again rent my carriage under such circumstances!" he swore.

"At what time was the cabriolet returned?" asked Miss Boston, who wanted as much precise information as possible for the clues she was patiently gathering.

"Oh! It was at least an hour after sunup."

"Were you there when the two travelers returned?"

"No, it was the stable boy."

"Would you call him?"

The innkeeper went as far as the coach house but remembered that the stable boy had gone on an errand to Galveston. The detective had to wait until he returned. With Sokes, she somewhat impatiently walked up and down in front of the inn. Suddenly, in front of the coach house door, she stopped.

"Well!" she said to Sokes, "why haven't we thought about looking at that famous cabriolet?"

And Sokes opened the door of the coach house.

VI. Crespo's Execution Order Found

The cabriolet was there. The owner hadn't lied in saying it wasn't worth very much. It was an old carriage with worn out springs and a reddish leather top, coming apart in some places. The varnish of the body was flaking; one of the lanterns was broken. The whole thing wasn't worth $50. Miss Boston examined it carefully. She quickly mounted the running board to look at the interior. The coach house was dark so she wasn't at first able to see the interior of the carriage very well. But with her electric torch, she explored the body of the carriage with infinite care. She stooped down, reached out her hand and picked up a crumpled piece of paper. It had been thrown in the bottom of the cabriolet. No sooner had she unfolded it when Sokes saw her pucker her lips. Her eyes were shining and in an excited voice she said:

"Sokes, we have nothing more to do here for the moment. We're going back to Chicago by the first train."

"Immediately?"

"Immediately, yes."

They arrived at the railway station 20 minutes later. It was then 11:05 a.m. The train for Chicago arrived at 11:12 a.m. She intended for them to take that one. Just as it entered the station, she was somewhat nervous and Sokes was aware that she didn't act this way without serious and important reasons. He waited patiently for Miss Boston to tell him the reasons for her behavior. He knew very well that she wouldn't speak except at the appropriate time. While waiting, he was satisfied to walk up and down the loading platform with her and to smoke an excellent Havana cigar, the curls of smoke perfuming the air around him. Nevertheless, it was with a sigh of relief that the Chief Inspector heard the whistle in the distance which announced the train's entry into the station. He followed Miss Boston into the first class compartment she chose and waited for her to speak about her find. That wasn't long in coming. The train had hardly started out when the famous detective opened her handbag and took out the crumpled paper she had picked up less than an hour before on the floorboard of the cabriolet. She unfolded it and handed it to Sokes, who read:

Antonio Calvocoressi
Ridgway-X
The tribunal at Milan has decided.
Crespo is guilty.
You know the oath and the law.
Act.
Paola will take the head.
V. 3. —S. 2.—B. 1.

Returning the paper to the detective, he said: "I understand. That's Crespo's execution order that you found in the cabriolet. That's lucky."

"Better than that, sir."

"That means?"

"I'm saying better and more than luck. It's the address of the Mafia head-quarters in Chicago."

"Then the paper is priceless."

"That's also what I think, Mr. Sokes. You remember when we began our investigation we were lead two or three times to Ridgway, but we lost the trail just as we were getting to the end. You see we weren't very far from it, since this paper sends us back to Ridgway, to number ten, the X found beside the name of the street. That's where we're going."

"Hopefully the nest isn't empty!"

"That's quite possible because the Mafia isn't yet on to us."

Miss Boston explained to Sokes the meaning of the Milan tribunal. She told him:

"That secret jurisdiction judges the society's members and condemns them when they don't keep their oaths. That was certainly the case with Crespo, who, as the letter says, was found guilty. It also says, 'You know the oath and the law. Act.' For the ordinary person that means nothing, but for us, we know what happened last night at Pretty Bell. Doubt is no longer possible. It's a matter here of simply saying that Crespo must be killed."

"And the sentence: 'Paolo will take the head,' how do you explain it?"

"Up until now Crespo was the Mafia head in Chicago. The Milan tribunal condemned him. The sentence 'Paoli will take the head,' just means that from now on the person named Paolo will become head of the Mafia in Chicago."

"And the three initials with numbers which make up the letter's signature, what do they mean?"

"I don't know what names they correspond to, but I assume they are the three judges who make up the tribunal."

The Chief Inspector took out his watch.

"Twelve ten, he said. In 20 minutes we'll be in Chicago. May I ask what we're going to do?"

"Have lunch, first of all, Sokes."

"That's an excellent idea. I have quite an appetite. And afterward?"

"We'll get on the way to the country."

"To Ridgway?"

"Yes, but we'll try to operate only in the evening. Nevertheless what we do during the day will show us the steps to follow then. The members of the Mafia are as dangerous as professional criminals. They have an enormous advantage over them in that they are more courageous. Obviously that won't make our job any easier. That's why the most extreme and rigorous care is now the order of the day."

And the train stopped in Circus Street in Chicago.

VII. In the Mafia Den

The two detectives went to lunch at a fine restaurant on Baker Street and at about 2 p.m. started on their way to Ridgway, a commercial center that takes its name from the main street that runs through it. Everything there was close together in one district: retail merchants, bondsmen, customs agents. All day long there was enormous circulation, which allowed someone who didn't want to be seen to glide unseen into that human sea that moved about, undulated and battered by the Ridgway houses. That could have been the reason the Mafia had decided to settle in that quarter; to hide itself more easily and screen itself from searches of which it might one day be the object. Miss Boston and Sokes arrived without hindrance at No.10 as indicated on the letter from Galveston.

That building was occupied by various stores well known in Chicago for a long time. They could in no way be suspected of giving a cleverly hidden hideout to the feared secret society.

To have a clear conscience, Miss Boston thought it her urgent duty to enter the house. She entered the corridor and examined carefully all the doors that opened to it. She noticed nothing suspicious.

"Could I be mistaken?" she asked herself.

She nevertheless pushed her investigation further. There was a courtyard at the end of the corridor with a little two-story building in it. This building, for diverse reasons, drew her particular attention. The ground floor was occupied by a retail merchant. The name in gold letters on a plaque above the door was Calvocoressi. The letter of execution was addressed to one Antonio Calvocoressi. That was troubling, but what was not less so was that the two upper stories were empty and were not for rent. Miss Boston rightly concluded that they served an equivocal purpose, that she had found the Mafia den. Going in at that moment couldn't even be considered. Although not appearing greatly frequented, the merchant had some clients at that moment. In that condition, a search pushed further could compromise the final result.

But Miss Boston knew enough for the time being. The information she had just gathered informed her about her base of operations. She and the Chief Inspector agreed that they should work that evening. That decision taken, they had only to wait for nightfall when the stores would close and allow them entrance to the mysterious Mafia.

It had already been night for an hour when the courageous detective, accompanied by Sokes, entered Ridgway. The silence and solitude of the area at that hour contrasted strangely with the tumult of the day. Miss Boston went forward slowly toward the building. The door was locked but she opened it with her jimmy. The two detectives slipped into the corridor.

"Should I lock the door?" Sokes asked in a whisper.

"No," answered the detective. "We may need to find it open to get out."

They proceeded to the courtyard where Miss Boston had noticed the mysterious little building. At that hour it was completely dark. Had they come too soon? To find out they had only to enter the retail merchant's office. That is what Miss Boston did.

She first gave Sokes instructions. He was going to stay hidden in the courtyard to observe anyone coming or going. She told him to note the descriptions of anyone he saw. As for the rest, he was not to interfere or go into the mysterious little building unless Miss Boston fired a revolver shot.

Sokes hid in a corner of the courtyard blocked by cases and his shadow blended into the night. Miss Boston went to the store that had seemed suspicious in so many ways and turned the door handle. Something strange! The door was open. The young woman bravely entered. It was completely dark, but a dim light appeared at the back of the store at an elevator cage. The light was coming from a lamp hung at the height of the second floor. Like a shadow she glided into the hall where the elevator opened. Several doors which were hermetically sealed opened onto this hallway.

Suddenly the sound of muffled voices reached Miss Boston. She stopped, and as a precaution, loaded her revolver. Then she listened closely and made out the conversations, snatches of which had come confusedly through the thickness of the partitions and doors. "It's important to give that warning," one voice was saying.

But another voice answered:

"I think we should stay quiet. How do we know the police suspect us?"

"What's certain is that Miss Boston came to Pretty Bell just this morning!"

"The devil!" thought the detective. "Could they have gotten on to me already?"

The conversation continued.

"So she came to Pretty Bell this morning. What does that prove?"

"That she's on Crespo's trail."

"Why?"

One of the persons burst out laughing.

"Go ask him about it, Antonio!"

"Then you don't know anything about it?"

"No more than you!"

"So that proves that nothing is less certain than that Miss Boston is on our trail. Crespo! He's not all the Mafia! The police might be looking for him personally for some other job we don't know about! After all those he pulled off since he came to America!"

"So, I come back to what I was saying before. I think we should warn the detective in a way so that she understands that the wisest thing for her to do is to leave the Mafia alone."

"Agreed! But who will do that?"

"Antonio and Paoli. They already know the place."

"Me, I'm willing. When do we leave?" Paoli said.

"The sooner the better."

"Immediately, then?"

"That would be perfect."

"Well, in that case, I'm ready," Antonio said.

There was the sound of chairs moving about, as if the men were getting ready to leave the room. Miss Boston looked for a hiding place. She found none! No place, not a corner to hide in! If they saw her, she was lost! Run away? She still had time, but she didn't want to leave. What she had heard was enough to tell her some new criminal outrage was being plotted. She wanted to be there to know what it was about. Just as all these thoughts were running through her head, the stairs creaked. Someone was climbing up quickly, running.

VIII. A Fall can sometimes Save a Victim

The man climbing the stairs obviously seemed in a hurry. About all the detective could make out about him was that he was wearing a soft felt hat. He crossed the corridor with wide strides. He was in so much of a hurry he brushed by the detective without seeing her. He went to the end of the corridor and broke in rather than opened the door of the badly lit room. That door, thus opened, showed the watching detective a large room where three individuals were seated at a round table. That was only a fast glimpse. The door was immediately closed again.

Once again the illustrious detective could have run from the danger threatening her. But whoever would have believed her capable of that really wouldn't have known her very well. She remained courageously at the dangerous post she had assigned herself and awaited the outcome of events. It wasn't long in coming. The man in a hurry who had just entered the room was greeted with a cry of joy.

"Well! Here's Luigi!"

"Brothers and friends," the man answered, "do you know what's happened?"

"What!"

"Something dangerous?"

"The police?"

"All that," Luigi answered, "and more."

"Speak! What is it?"

"The police are in the house."

That was like a thunder clap. The Mafia members let out a triple cry of rage. One of them gave the table such a blow with his fist that it made the windows rattle.

"Betrayed! We're betrayed!" they shouted, but Antonio added:

"By whom?"

215

There was a moment of silence that Luigi interrupted, saying:
"This isn't the time for discussion. We must act."
"Luigi's right."
"But what are we to do?"
"Arm ourselves and go to the house. The police are here."
"How do you know?"
"I found the entry door to the house open."
"That's not possible! The door, open?"
"We're in danger!"

The detective was aware that this time the denouement was approaching. She was going to try to reach the stairs, stay at the bottom to pick up the criminals as they came down. But she had time only to lean against a door next to the stairs to parry any attack from the rear. At that moment the four criminals burst into the hallway. The moment was tragic. There was suddenly complete darkness followed by the noise of broken glass. What was happening? The detective had just kicked over the lamp which lit the stairs. That was evidently a prudent action because the criminals didn't yet know who they were dealing with. A bellow of fury answered the detective's ruse. The criminals ran into each other in the darkness, swearing. That jostling threw Luigi against Miss Boson and the blow was so violent that the detective felt the panel of the door she was leaning against split behind her.

"I've got one of them!" Luigi cried. And he grabbed Miss Boston.

But the detective was prepared for the attack. She dealt the criminal a blow on the head that made him stagger. But at the same time the door behind her gave way under her weight. Miss Boston lost her equilibrium and fell. She rolled from step to step down a dark staircase, without, however, losing consciousness. With remarkable presence of mind she had kept her revolver and her handbag containing her improved kit. She didn't therefore find herself at the bottom of the stairs disarmed and powerless. She was a little bruised by the blow, but courageous and determined not to abandon the dangerous work beginning for her. Where had she fallen? Where was she? She had no idea and didn't have time to find out. Taking her electric torch out of her handbag she directed the light in front of her and saw a door. Through it she entered a corridor at the end of which there was a faint light. Miss Boston ran toward it. She then saw, with some surprise, that she was in Ridgway. Miraculously, in her fall she had by chance landed near a secret entrance to the house. At the same moment she saw four shadows in the night turning the corner in flight. It seemed to be the Mafia members getting away. Miss Boston went back through the corridor and reached the courtyard where she found Sokes, still cleverly hidden, at the spot he had chosen. He had seen four figures pass by but he had not intervened since his instructions were to wait until he heard a revolver shot. No shot had been fired. Miss Boston explained who the figures were. Sokes asked:

"Then those were members of the Mafia?"

"Yes, and among them were those called Antonio Calvocoressi and Paoli who are no other than Crespo's killers."

"And they've gotten away!"

"That doesn't bother me, Sokes. I'll pick them up again."

"So you know where they've gone?"

"At least two of them."

"And where's that?"

"To Maitland."

"Why?"

"It seems it's to give me a warning. They know I searched the house of the crime this morning. They want me to know it's dangerous to go after them."

"Yes, but how are they going to warn you?"

"I don't yet know and that's what we're going to try to find out, tonight if possible, Sokes."

"Do you have a plan?"

"To return to Maitland immediately. We may be able to put our hands on Antonio and Paoli."

"And the others?"

"Let's take these first. We'll see about the others later."

However, before returning to the Circus Street Station, Miss Boston made a rapid search of the building of the Calvocoressi pseudo-retail merchants. It was absolutely useless. The Mafia had taken its precautions and there was nothing compromising in the building. Nothing indicated that the building served as a hideout for the feared secret society. The detectives wasted almost half an hour searching for clues which had been carefully erased or taken away. They had now to go as rapidly as possible to the railway that would put them down in Galveston in the middle of the night.

"But what will we do there?" Sokes asked.

"We'll go pick up the cabriolet to take us to Maitland."

"He may refuse to rent it."

"In that case we'll take it. That is to say, we'll borrow it for two or three hours without his knowledge and pay him later."

IX. The Cabriolet in the Forest

It was 1 a.m. when the Arizona Rapid put the detectives down at the Galveston station. The information they got from an employee who took up tickets proved that the trail they were following wasn't wrong. In fact, two persons, their descriptions corresponding exactly to those of Antonio and Paoli, had arrived by the 11:50 p.m. midnight express. They were a little more than an hour ahead of the detectives. The detectives knew that Maitland was the end of their night trip. Therefore they must get to Maitland. For that, Miss Boston must, as she had said to Sokes, borrow the same cabriolet that had been used the night before by the Pretty Bell murderers. The night was stormy, filled with lightning flashes announcing the approaching rain and that coolness which makes summer nights so pleasant. Miss Boston and Sokes started walking toward the cabriolet. A surprise was in store for them. A stable boy, smoking a pipe, was sitting on a bench in front of the house. There was a lantern on a bench beside him. Seeing the detectives come forward frightened him.

"Be calm," Miss Boston said to him. "We don't mean you any harm."

"Then," said the boy, "What do you want at this hour? The cabaret is closed. We don't serve drinks now."

"It isn't a drink we want," the detective interrupted.

"What do you want then?"

"We would like to rent the cabriolet from the boss."

"The cabriolet isn't here anymore."

"What does that mean?"

"Two gentlemen came an hour ago and gave me a dollar to take a drive to Maitland."

"The devil!" Sokes swore, furious.

But Miss Boston immediately asked:

"Weren't these the same two gentlemen as the ones who rented the cabriolet last night?"

"Yes, Miss."

"But didn't the boss say he didn't want to rent the carriage anymore?"

"Yes, he said that. But last night the gentlemen gave only $5 and this evening they offered $50. Then the boss didn't refuse anymore."

"You don't have any other carriages here?"

"No, Miss, the boss has only this old cabriolet."

"On foot!" Sokes groaned. "We'll have to go on foot!"

"Those are the little inconveniences of the job, Sokes," responded the detective. "We have nothing more to do here."

The detectives again took the road they had already walked during the day. In the unusually dark night they could hardly see the road which ran across fields toward the middle of the forest in the direction of Maitland and Pretty Bell. Rising wind already announced an approaching storm.

"Hopefully we won't get caught in a downpour on the road," Sokes said.

"Bah!" retorted the detective. "We'll go dry off at Mr. John Smith's house. This business must keep him from sleeping."

"For good reason! This is the first crime in Maitland's existence that's been committed there."

"Let's hope it's the last."

"I wonder," Sokes continued, "what our fellows want at Maitland. Could they have gone to pick up compromising papers at Pretty Bell?"

"We'll find out, Sokes, when we see if the seals on the house are intact. But in my opinion, that's not what it's about."

"Then why?"

"First of all because they could very easily have been taken last night, and because the fellows left precisely intending to give me a warning."

"What warning? All this is very unusual."

"Arriving in Galveston, the Mafia members had an hour head start on us. Thanks to the cabriolet, they have at least two. Those two hours would certainly have allowed them to do what they planned. It's possible we'll meet them on the return trip."

As if to prove the illustrious detective's words, there was the sound of a galloping horse in the distance in the forest.

"Listen, Sokes," she said. With assurance Miss Boston confirmed: "That's our cabriolet."

"They're coming back already?"

"I believe so. As soon as the cabriolet is on us, Sokes, you jump to the horse's head and try to stop it. Me, I'll jump on the running board, with my revolver ready, and the rest is up to me."

As soon as that decision was made, there was nothing more to do but wait for the cabriolet and carry out Miss Boston's dangerous but decisive plan. Every minute brought the carriage closer, added to the sound of the galloping horse that seemed to be coming at full speed down the road where the two detectives were stationed on either side. Holding their revolvers, they waited, calm, determined. Three minutes more…then two…then one, and the cabriolet appeared in front of them.

Sokes jumped to the horse's head. Its mouth was white with foam. Miss Boston hoisted herself to the running board. The horse reared, causing the carriage to shake and turn over, bringing the detective down with its fall. Sokes, still clinging to the horse's head, found himself carried down with the horse and rolled into the ditch bordering the road. With bellows of rage and anger, two men had jumped from the carriage and fled into the forest, abandoning horse and carriage. They made off at a sprint through the trees and a minute later had disappeared in the night.

As the height of misfortune, just at that moment the storm broke. The tempest raged, shaking the forest trees and sweeping the road with its gusts, flooding everything. Both Miss Boston and Sokes had gotten up.

"We missed them," she said, with a slight show of anger and annoyance, "but all is not lost."

She helped Sokes put the horse back on its feet, rearrange and lash the beast's harness, and, with the Inspector, got back in the carriage. It was still raining violently. The wind broke tree branches around them, and flashes of lightning lit up the night. In spite of all that, Miss Boston put the cabriolet back on the road and a quarter of an hour later, it stopped at the Galveston station. She set up a trap there in case the cabriolet travelers tried to take the train. And while waiting for them, she asked herself, without being able to solve it, the enigmatic question: "What had they gone to do at Maitland or Pretty Bell?"

X. The Resurrection of the Severed Hand

The trap at the Galveston Station produced no result. Miss Boston had set it up because she didn't neglect anything that might lead her investigations to their desired end. An abundance of precautions were not always useless because they sometimes led to the desired result. The next day she was only half surprised to note the uselessness of the Galveston trap.

The Mafia members' ruse was infinitely simple. Instead of going to the Galveston station, they had certainly pushed on through the night to a neighboring station, knowing that Galveston would be the object of a special and rigorous search.

"We'll find them somewhere else," the detective said to her companion.

"God knows where."

"I don't despair about luck, Sokes. It's miraculously helped us many times already."

"That's true, but for the moment it seems to be playing a bad trick on us. What are we going to do?"

"We're going back to Maitland."

"It's true we may find the purpose of Antonio and Paoli's trip there. And the cabriolet?"

"We're going to return it to its owner."

"He won't understand anything about that strange substitution of clients."

"I don't have time to explain it to him, Sokes. He'll be content with what we tell him."

And that's how it was. The cabriolet owner was astonished when he saw Miss Boston and Sokes come back with the cabriolet, but his astonishment grew with the reasons the detective gave him. She left him to his astonishment and with the Inspector again started on the road to Maitland. The sun was already drying the large puddles of water left by the storm of the evening before.

At the place where the cabriolet attack had taken place, Miss Boston found a rain-soaked hat. She examined the inside and showed Sokes the two letters stamped on the headband: A. C.

That hat, with Antonio Calvocoressi's initials was all that Miss Boston found, but it was enough. She continued to drive through the forest and a little before noon reached the little pathway which went down through the flowering hedgerows of perfumed hawthorn bushes toward Pretty Bell.

The first thing Miss Boston examined were the seals posted by the honorable John Smith on the doors and windows of the crime scene. The seals were perfectly intact.

"You see, Sokes," she said, "our two escapees were certainly not going to Pretty Bell."

"Well, then I was mistaken," Sokes exclaimed.

The detective remained thoughtful. The purpose of Antonio and Paoli's trip seemed more and more mysterious. The reason totally escaped her. Once again they were plunged into an unfathomable as well as insoluble enigma. But the evidence had to be considered: the house of the crime hadn't been broken into; and the reason for the Mafia members' visit had to be found elsewhere. Where? They were definitely turning in a vicious circle.

Miss Boston decided to see Mr. Smith before everything else. He might have some new information to give her. A charming walk across the sunlit countryside rested the two detectives after their sleepless night. They went across the Flog to the coroner's house. They found him having lunch under an ivy bower in his garden. He greeted his visitors with evident satisfaction.

"I am delighted to see you, Miss, and so much more so as I've just received something for you."

Miss Boston couldn't hide her astonishment.

"For me? And what's that!"

"A telegram," said Mr. Smith.

He ran into the house to get it and handed it to the detective. There was only one line:

Come. Presence indispensable at Central Bureau.

She handed it to Sokes. "Read," she said laconically.

He glanced at it; handed it back and said:

"From the Chief? What do you think?"

"I think it's just a trap."

"My intuition told me so. Who do you think sent it?"

"The Mafia, naturally."

"And you've decided."

"To stay here, me, at least."

"And me?"

"Here's what you're going to do, Sokes. Right now you're going to leave for New York and begin a discreet inquiry. You'll go to my house in Savannah City and to the Central Bureau. If there's something urgent, send me a telegram. If not, come back, tonight if possible. The remainder of the investigation will really depend on what you tell me."

At 2:05 p.m. a little old man, neat and tottering, shaking, took the train destined for New York at the Galveston station.

The day Sokes spent in New York, Miss Boston busied herself with inspecting Pretty Bell from top to bottom. The thorough examination left no inch of the house unexplored. The detective found nothing. That result convinced her that clearly the members of the Mafia had taken away from Pretty Bell all the papers that could denounce them. The truth must be looked for somewhere else. That examination took the detective until the evening. Sokes had not sent her a telegram; he was probably going to come back that night. She therefore gladly accepted Mr. Smith's dinner invitation. He was eager to hear all about her dangerous adventures as a detective. Her story was suddenly interrupted by a knock at the door. It was Sokes. He was carrying a little package and seemed worried.

"Well, Sokes, what's new?" asked the detective.

"You were right; the telegram was fake. It came from the Mafia."

"What did you find?"

"This."

So saying, Sokes opened the package he was carrying. Mr. Smith recoiled in horror. The package contained a severed hand.

"Where did you find that, Sokes?"

"In New York."

"Tell me what happened."

"Nothing extraordinary. As soon as I arrived I went to the Central Bureau; I had myself taken to the Chief, to whom I showed the telegram. He confirmed our belief it was false. I went to the office from which it was sent and the description I got there fit that of Paoli."

"Was he alone?"

"Yes."

"Good. Then I know where to find Antonio, but go on Sokes."

"The telegram was sent from the Strand Street office. From Strand Street I went to your apartment in Savannah City. When I arrived at your door, I was struck with amazement. A severed hand was attached to the door handle."

"Now I understand the kind of warning the Mafia wanted to give me," the detective said. "That's the explanation of Paoli and Antonio's trip to Maitland."

"Then you believe they went there for that?"

"Sokes," the detective said gravely, "I ask until tomorrow to prove it to you."

XI. A Macabre Theft

At 8 a.m., Miss Boston got off in Chicago, went to the Central Police Headquarters and asked to speak to the Chief, who received her immediately. As a result of the interview, the illustrious detective, 20 minutes later, was headed toward Ridgway with ten plainclothes policemen.

In the blink of an eye the false retail merchant, Antonio Calvocoressi, was raided. He was the only one present. The rest of the house was empty. Antonio took an offended attitude.

"What do you want with me," he demanded in an indignant tone.

"We'll tell you that in Maitland," the detective said.

"Maitland? What's that? I don't know any Maitland."

"That's what we'll find out when we get there," Miss Boston said, ordering the policemen to handcuff Antonio. And despite all his protests, the handcuffed criminal was taken to the Circus Street station. From that point he maintained a silence Miss Boston didn't try to break right up until the train arrived in Galveston at 11:20 a.m. It continued like that until they came in sight of Pretty Bell. Antonio probably thought it was a question of going over the crime scene, but when he saw the detective continue toward old Maitland, he started to turn pale and tremble. He was beginning to understand what Miss Boston wanted with him. She went straight toward the cemetery where, two days earlier, they had buried Crespo's body. The gravediggers, called by Smith, were waiting for the detective.

When the policemen with their prisoner stopped at the edge of the grave of the Mafia's leader, Miss Boston looked Antonio straight in the eyes and asked him:

"Why did you come into this cemetery last night with your accomplice Paoli? Why did Paoli go to New York? Why did Paoli go to Savannah City?"

Antonio's knees began to buckle, but the Italian still kept silent.

"All right," said the detective, "I'll tell you why you've come here."

Turning toward the gravediggers, she simply said: "Go ahead!"

They removed the stone covering Crespo's casket and hoisted it to the edge of the grave. They snapped off the casket top and the spectators saw the body of the murdered man. In the casket the severed hand was missing.

"That's what you came here to steal!" said the detective, pointing to the bled out stump of the cadaver.

A moan answered her. Antonio had fainted.

The false retail merchant of Ridgway was the only member of the Mafia who was arrested. All the others disappeared from America and gave no more sign of life. Antonio, however, escaped the supreme punishment awaiting him. He mysteriously poisoned himself in Sing Sing prison where they had transferred him. With him disappeared the last actor of a mysterious drama on which light was never completely shed.

THE ARIZONA RAPID TRAIN

I. The Seventh Arizona Rapid Train Raid

Miss Boston took the card the maid had just handed to her. She read:
HERBERT FOLKESTONE
Burke Street
New York
"Should I have him come in, Miss?" the maid asked.

"In a minute, Mary."

The famous detective rose and took down a volume from her bookshelf. She leafed rapidly through the first pages. That took only a minute, after which she said to her maid:

"Have the gentleman come in."

He was a man in full manhood, solid, muscular, close- shaven like all good Americans, with a frank and open expression showing the strength of a loyal character. He came forward, holding his hat in his hand.

"Do I have the honor and the good fortune to address Miss Boston?"

"Herself, sir."

"All Right! I'm really pleased, Miss."

"You are Mr. Herbert Folkestone, the President of the Arizona Mining Company?"

"Then you know me, Miss?" he asked.

"It's somewhat my job to know everything." And she added in a friendly tone:

"Please sit down and tell me to what I owe the honor of seeing you."

"It's a simple matter, Miss. As you know, I am President of the Arizona Mining Company which has headquarters in New York. The Arizona land we mine furnishes not only coal but also precious metals. We've discovered traces of platinum and silver. A stream that passes through our property has river gold. All that has given our company immediate prosperity, but exposed us to covetousness. We've been victims of that several times, and day before yesterday, once again."

"How did that happen, sir?"

"A band of thieves took the quarterly shipment of precious metals sent by way of the Arizona Rapid Train from our mines at Greenbar to our headquarters in New York."

"Now would you give me some details about the usual shipment of precious metals?"

"As I told you, Miss, these shipments are made every three months. Here's why. There are some months when the amount of precious metals mined is insignificant. That's why, as the Board of Directors, we decided to group three months together. That allows us to send the strongbox on the Arizona Rapid Train guarded by several employees, as faithful as devoted."

"The safe was taken off during the trip?"

"Yes, Miss."

"How many times already?"

"For the seventh time before yesterday."

"For how long?"

"For a year."

"Oh! That must have been a serious loss for your company."

"At least a million and a half dollars, Miss."

"The robbers, you say, come in a group?"

"Yes. They seem always to be the same ones."

"Who do you suspect?"

"A band of cowboys who operate in the savannas and prairies in the east of Arizona."

"How is the Arizona Rapid usually attacked?"

"I don't know exactly, Miss. All the guards have been able to confirm is that the bandits jump on the moving train, make their way to the boxcar, get inside and beat or kill the guards. They throw the strongbox out on to the railroad siding and immediately disappear. And that is the seventh time that daring raid has succeeded."

"What defensive measures has the company taken up to the present time?"

"First of all, Miss, we took the precaution of adding to the number of guards, but that measure only added to the number of the victims. In the place of four deaths, we had eight. As for the second precaution, that was to suspend all precious metal shipments until further notice and come to see you to ask you to take the matter in hand. We'll pay you your fees in advance."

"We'll talk about it afterwards," the famous detective said, interrupting with a brief gesture.

"Then you accept, Miss?"

"Yes."

"We'll owe you eternal gratitude."

"For the moment I ask you only some additional necessary clarification."

"I'm at your service, Miss."

"How many victims have there been in the Arizona attacks up until now?"

227

"Twenty-eight."

"All deaths?"

"No, 17 deaths."

"And the 17 others?"

"Only wounded, but rather seriously. Six of them are back on their feet; the five others are still in the hospital in Greenwich."

"Was the train always attacked during the day?"

"Sometimes in the day, sometimes at night also."

"The strongboxes aren't always put on the train at the same hour?"

"No, to throw the bandits off the track we sometimes changed the hour. But in spite of that, they've let the train where there was nothing pass by and taken the shipment from the one carrying the strongboxes. You seem surprised at that, Miss."

"Indeed, sir, and I'll tell you why later when our investigation is a little further advanced. Right now I'd ask you to please accompany me to the hospital at Greenwich where I'll ask for some information from the wounded."

At that moment the maid came to announce Mr. Sokes, the Chief Inspector of the Central Police Bureau. She introduced him to Mr. Folkestone, her visitor, saying:

"Sokes, you've come in time. Mr. Folkestone has just asked me to take charge of the Arizona Rapid Train affair; I've accepted and I was going to ask your assistance."

The Inspector said, with charming simplicity:

"I'm here. How are we to begin our operations?"

"By going to the Greenwich hospital right now."

"I'll go with you," Mr. Folkestone said.

II. The Wounded at Greenwich Hospital

The white stone buildings of Greenwich Hospital were situated in a beautiful, open and pleasant park outside of New York. The sick were taking walks in the spring sunshine along the garden paths. Despite the sun, the light and the clear air, the spot still inspired melancholy. There were only pale and wan faces, trembling hands, hesitating steps, which told of all the pains suffered. Miss Boston was truly moved, but her duty as a detective required, in the presence of that distressing spectacle, that she remain unmoved and cold. That was why, with an apparently impassive eye, she walked through the pathways full of the convalescent and sick. Followed by Sokes and Mr. Folkestone, she made her way toward the central pavilion of the hospital and was received by Mr. Bryan Brummel, the Hospital Director. She had had many occasions to see him about the wounded of the Central Police Bureau.

"How can I help you, Miss?" he asked.

"I would like to question the various wounded of the Arizona Rapid. Is that possible?"

The Director glanced at a stack of cards on his desk and removed one, holding it out to the detective, saying:

"These are the persons you want to see, aren't they?"

The young woman read the names written on the little card:

Fred Redders, 38

J.P.H. Stam, 41

Tom Modders, 26

Harry Byval, 36

"There are only four names here," Miss Boston noted, "and Mr. Folkestone spoke of five wounded in the Arizona Rapid affair."

"Indeed, Miss, yesterday there were five wounded, but one of them, the one named Reading, died in the night from his wounds. He had been shot in the lungs."

"Where are the four wounded men?"

"In room 12, Miss."

"May we go there?"

"Certainly, please follow me."

After a few minutes' walk, they reached Room 12 where the wounded were stretched out on clean, white, narrow iron cots which formed a striking contrast with the pallor of their faces all covered with bandages. Miss Boston began her interrogations by questioning Fred Redders. He had been struck in the head with the butt of a carbine. He had multiple contusions on the forehead and the rest of the cranium which required bandages on the upper part of the head. He had fainted from the violence of the blows. The assailants had probably taken him for dead. That had saved him. His days were not at present in danger.

"Well, my friend," the detective asked him, "how do you feel now that you're out of danger?"

"Better, a little better, Miss."

"Are you well enough to give me some information about what happened in the Arizona Rapid day before yesterday?"

"I'll try, Miss."

"How many assailants were there?"

"At least ten, but I don't know exactly. As I was the closest to the door, I was the first one attacked."

"At what part of the line did the attack occur?"

"At the Church Hill curve, a little before, a little after; I don't know very well. I don't remember anymore, Miss."

The few words had visibly exhausted the man. Miss Boston didn't insist and passed on to Stam, who was suffering a great deal from a bullet that had gone through his shoulder. Like his colleague Redders, he also estimated the number of assailants at ten.

"Were they masked?"

"In no way. Their faces were visible. I think they were cowboys. They had leather trousers and hats with wide brims."

"Did you notice where they set up their ambush?"

"Always the same place, Miss, at the curve of Church Hill."

After Stam, it was Modder's turn to be interrogated. Modders had shot the six bullets in his pistol at the cowboys, but a bullet in the hip had brought him down.

He didn't faint and had seen the bandits go directly to the strongboxes as soon as the guards were down. They had thrown the safe onto the railway siding and had jumped off the train some meters further on.

"Where was that?" the detective asked.

"At the Town Hill curve."

"They were on horseback, weren't they, at the Church Hill curve?"

"Yes, exactly, Miss."

Only Harry Byval remained to be heard. He was the most seriously wounded. In the fight with the cowboys he had received very violent blows on the temple.

He couldn't answer the precise questions asked by the detective except with movements of his head. He confirmed the information given by the other wounded.

Miss Boston remained thoughtful for some instants. She wished the four wounded men a speedy recovery and with Sokes and Mr. Folkestone she took leave of the Director, Bryan Brummel.

"Sir," she said to the President of the Company, I would like to leave you to continue my investigation on another terrain, but before leaving you, I'd like to ask you a capital question. Did the six previous attacks on the Arizona Rapid take place exactly between the Church Hill curve and that of Town Hill?"

"Yes, absolutely," answered Mr. Folkestone. "I can tell you that according to the declarations already given by our other wounded guards; it's always between these two curves of the line that the attacks occurred."

"Well, sir, it's important for me to know that."

"When will I hear from you, Miss, about all this?"

"As soon as possible. I'll work with all diligence to bring my investigation to a successful end quickly."

"I thank you in advance, Miss. But for now, Miss, where do you want the automobile to drop you?"

"At Savannah City, at my apartment."

The travelers were silent, pensive, thinking of the lack of information surrounding the drama where too many brave people had already been victims. The detective seemed particularly thoughtful and the two men respected a silence they knew must be devoted to studying the tragic problem.

III. The Problem of the Curve

"Well, what do you think," Chief Inspector Sokes asked.

"I think that this is a very suspicious business."

Sokes was silent, but, from the look on his face, the detective easily knew that the Chief Inspector, from what he knew, was wondering how the Arizona Rapid robberies seemed questionable to the great detective. As Sokes must share the troubles, the fatigue, the dangers of the investigation with her, she thought it useful and proper to explain her thoughts more completely to him.

"Among the many reasons that make me think this affair is suspicious, there is one, Sokes, whose importance certainly can't escape you. The cowboys are taking possession of precious metals that they can get rid of only with difficulty."

"But it seems to me that gold can be easily sold."

"As coins, yes; not in gold slug, not as raw material. That's why they're sent from Green Bar to the Company in New York. That gold in bulk must undergo very costly, very difficult preparation before being put into beaten and prepared ingots. It has value only in that second form at the precious metals exchange. There's something else. Gold in bulk isn't accepted at that exchange and whoever owns it has to put it through multiple processes to make it an object for commerce or speculation. Now you know, Sokes, that the Cowboys who live in the wild savanna, in the vast prairie desert, are hardly prepared for this sort of work, which is made totally impossible for them by the conditions in which they live."

"But who says that they don't have an intermediary, a fence who takes charge of selling the fruits of their pillage for them."

"That's what I was waiting for, Sokes, for you to put your finger on what's truly suspicious about this business. This intermediary is really marvelously informed about the hours the Arizona Rapid transports the valuables. Notice, sir, that the cowboys have never attacked any other train but the Arizona line. What's the conclusion of that? It seems that band of pillagers have special designs on robbing only one and always the same Arizona Rapid Train. Don't you yourself find that suspicious?"

"I confess that your reasoning couldn't be more logical."

"And another thing. You certainly see New York thieves, those who skim off capital, who have intermediaries, since they are in some way under their hand and it's very natural. But it's a lot less so for cowboys, half savage fellows who live 15 leagues from New York. Besides they wouldn't set foot there without being immediately pointed out to the Central Police Bureau."

"Then an intermediary in this case becomes a clear and absolute certainty."

"It'll be a certainty, Sokes, when we've put our hands on the person."

"Evidently. Unless he takes to the wide open spaces."

"If we don't take our precautions, yes."

"What do you intend to do?"

"To leave today."

"For Green Bar?"

"Not exactly that far. I'll stop in Osborn."

"Why Osborn?"

"Because that's the last station before reaching the track curves to Town Hill and Church Hill."

"Ah! Yes! Those famous curves the wounded men spoke of."

"Like me, Sokes, you certainly must have noticed in the questioning of the wounded men the role that the Church Hill Curve played in the robbery."

"Yes and the similarities of their answers even somewhat surprised me, I must admit."

"That struck me also. I wondered why the robberies always took place at Church Hill and not at any other spot along the way."

"Are you going to look for that explanation at Osborn?"

"Yes. You're free, it seems?"

"At your entire disposition today and tomorrow."

"In that case, we'll go together, if you agree."

The young woman called her maid and told her to immediately prepare a small valise with everything necessary for a few days absence. And she said to Sokes:

"And we'll take along something as disguises in case we need them. You never know what will come up."

"You're right. Let's hope we don't have too much need to act the harlequin on the way."

Miss Boston smiled, but got immediately busy making her last preparations for departure. She slid a pair of revolvers into her handbag and asked her companion if he had his. Sokes patted the pocket of his jacket, bulging with the butt of his familiar bull dog. And she took out of her bureau drawer her complete kit containing the marvelous steel instrument which gave her such admirable service.

The courageous young woman did all that with a calm and tranquil energy as if preparing for a little pleasure trip near New York or on the edge of the Hudson. But it was a matter of something very different! In fact, Miss Boston was going to immerse herself 15 leagues into the savage far west, into those lands still badly understood, covered with grass a meter high and thick forests, where there were still scarcely civilized Sioux Indians roaming and fierce and bloodthirsty cowboys a thousand times more to be feared than the Redskins living in the same region. And why? To locate a vague, unknown trail, certain to bring her into the greatest dangers and the most fearful perils. Nevertheless, she was not for an instant frightened by that perspective. She had accepted the task given by the President of the Arizona Mining Company and she would go right to the end. With her daring and a pair of revolvers, she didn't fear anything.

Sokes gallantly took charge of carrying the valise and the detective was ready to leave after having carefully locked her study.

Before picking up her tickets at Princess Place train station, the detective went to the telegraph office and sent the following telegraph:

Mr. Herbert Folkestone
Arizona Mining Company
Burke Street
New York
I'm leaving for Greenbar. The strictest silence and secrecy about my mission. B.

Four minutes later, the train carried the two detectives toward the savannas and prairies of Arizona.

IV. The Church Hill Trail

It was only the next day that Miss Boston arrived in Osborne, Arizona. That state of the Union is bordered by New Mexico, California, Lower California, and Utah. The capitol is Prescott, situated at the bottom of a vast chain of mountains that cross obliquely from California to Mexico. However, anyone who had seen the two detectives depart from New York and disembark at Osborn would have been strangely surprised at their dress and would hardly have recognized them under their new getup. In fact, Sokes had the perfect look of a trail rider: leather trousers, embroidered jacket, and a large sombrero already dirty. As for Miss Boston, she was dressed almost exactly the same, as an amazon of the prairies, her complexion a little bronzed. No one could have doubted that she was the wife of the cowboy walking beside her with an arrogant and commanding expression.

During the trip the detectives had discussed the ways not to stand out, and a stronger reason, not to be recognized. Miss Boston had thought up this disguise which would make them pass unnoticed in a country where cowboys abound. In ordinary dress they would have been recognized and denounced. Those are places where gentlemen in false collars and ladies with trailing skirts and tailored suits aren't usually seen on the streets. Miss Boston's idea was excellent and they dressed on the train. And that's why a cowboy and his wife got off the Arizona Rapid in Osborn.

There were only two ways to reach Church Hill, to walk or go on horseback. Walking would risk useless fatigue. The wisest way was to cross the eight leagues which separated Osborn and Church Hill by horseback. They asked an urchin to direct them to a livery stable. He did so and asked 50 cents for his help. The livery stable owner suggested two excellent horses which he guaranteed. Miss Boston bought them for $210. She wasn't robbed. Five minutes after the horses' purchase, the two cowboys were galloping at breakneck speed on the road to Church Hill. It was a charming ride, so much so as the mounts were really excellent and frisky. Under fast hooves they galloped over the high grass, leaving it crushed behind them.

Beyond Osborn, the country spread out in savage majesty, an uncultivated magnificence. As far as you could see, there was nothing but grassy plains swept by the wind, lifting their high, thick plants. Here and there in the distance could still be seen savage, galloping buffalos which disappeared behind little hills surmounted by thick woods.

"A trail through there is like a needle in a haystack," Sokes observed ironically.

"There's a proverb we've sometimes proved wrong," responded the detective.

"Let's hope it's that way this time."

"Wait Sokes, we're just at our beginning."

However, the journey begun in the morning was soon to end. The two detectives were gradually approaching the railway line and were now following it, while staying away a certain distance. From astride their mounts they could see the winding track in the distant green land. At the end of a 15-minute ride, the curve of the track appeared clearly. The curve was rather pronounced. A clump of thick trees rose in the loop it formed. It was probably this natural hideout that the cowboys used to get ready for their daring robbery and wait for the passage of the Arizona Rapid.

The leafy tree branches had provided a wonderful hiding place. From that shelter they had jumped onto the moving train. To jump aboard in those conditions was evidently a perilous exercise. There was a risk of inevitably breaking a shoulder. But for cowboys used to the violent life of the savanna, that was only an easily executable game. They had proved that in attacking precious metal convoys seven times.

The detectives halted their horses at the clump of trees in the loop of the Church Hill curve. Miss Boston rapidly glanced around to be sure no one was hidden there. To make sure there was no living soul in the area, Sokes climbed up into one of the trees and from the tallest branches carefully searched the horizon. Nothing suspicious appeared.

"Nothing, Sokes?" Miss Boston asked when he came down.

"Nothing."

"Then, to work!"

The horses were tied to the trees in a way so as to leave them free to graze the grass growing under their hooves, and the two detectives went toward the railroad tracks. The grass surrounding the loop was stamped down, showing that many steps had been walked there. That was the first confirmation of what the wounded at Greenwich Hospital had said. There was nothing more to do now but find the place where the strongboxes had been thrown from the train's baggage car. They went along the tracks going down in the direction of the Town Hill curve. That curve was situated 400 meters further on and had been formed so as to go around a ravine which in the past had been the bed of a small stream, now dry. There Miss Boston saw the evident proof of the strongboxes' fall. The place they fell had kept a clear and distinct imprint. All the grass on the right hand side of the track was crushed, stamped down. But there was something still better. A large, particularly flat path incontestably showed the direction in which the strongboxes had been dragged.

Miss Boston pointed out the trail to her companion, smiling jeeringly.

"You see, Sokes," she said.

"The Devil!" said the Chief Inspector. "Luck is with us."

"One would say so. You see the haystack doesn't always hide its needle maliciously."

"I perceive so. Are we going to follow that path?"

235

"Immediately, Sokes. But since I don't know how far it will lead us, I think the simplest thing is to go get our horses. That will spare us the fatigue of a long trip."

"Then you think it will go a long way, that path?"

"I fear so for two reasons. First of all, cowboys aren't afraid of long distances; secondly, they have their hideout in a place somewhat far from here."

The two detectives went back rapidly to the clump of trees at the Church Hill loop, and without stopping went toward the Town Hill loop where luck had miraculously and admirably helped them. There they picked up the direction of the trail. It led toward the west in a straight line as if toward a precise goal, always the same. The hoof prints of the horses were marvelously clear. That ride lasted a little less than an hour. Miss Boston and Sokes finally reached the edge of the dry ravine. There the trail suddenly stopped, as if abruptly chopped off.

"How's that!" Sokes said, and looked at Miss Boston with surprise.

V. The Seven Strongboxes in the Cave

The detective didn't share her companion's astonishment.

"That had to happen," she said. "The trail must finish here. Do you think the cowboys were going to travel two leagues with the stolen strongboxes? So we shouldn't be surprised to see the trail end at the edge of the ravine in front of us."

"Would they have gone across it?"

"That's what we're going to see right now."

Sokes shook his head like a man who is only half reassured. But as always, after having made his observation, he came over to the detective's opinion, because she was determined to follow her investigation to the end, whatever the difficulties.

"But the horses?" the Chief Inspector asked. "What about our horses?"

236

The detective had certainly foreseen that objection. For several minutes she had been examining the sides of the ravine which sloped gently down toward the former river bed without being too sheer. Some meters from there Miss Boston saw a narrow path descending gently at an oblique incline toward the bottom of the ravine.

"There's our way, Sokes."

And as if to show the way to the false cowboy, her companion, the detective nudged her horse toward the path. The beast was sure-footed and descended the side of the ravine in less than ten minutes and the detectives reached the dry bed of the former stream without incident. The bed was made up of little polished round stones with wild plants between them. The number of large rocks increased as the detectives went toward the east.

Miss Boston advanced with an assurance that surprised Sokes. What was she using as a guide to follow the direction taken when they entered the ravine? Looking about carefully, Sokes finally understood. Displaced stones clearly indicated a troop of horses had passed that way. The least disturbance in the soil, the least crushed plant, all showed the detective the value of the path followed and helped recognize the passage of the robbers. Little by little, however, the trail became narrower. The sides seemed to come together and gradually raise the two sides of the fissure. In addition, the nature of the ground became more dangerous. The detectives were now going through a veritable procession of rocks. From time to time there were rocks overhanging the path, digging out caverns in the sides of the deformed and broken ravine.

Certain clues told Miss Boston that the cowboys must have stopped at that location. She soon was absolutely certain. The signs stopped. Sokes drew a sigh of satisfaction. That devil of a pathway in the middle of large stones was beginning to tire the horses. Miss Boston had jumped down from hers to approach the side of the ravine. She scaled and reached the top of a rock whose colossal size seemed ready to crush whatever adventurer dared to climb it. She suddenly let out a cry of surprise and satisfaction, which made the Chief Inspector of the Central Police Bureau look upward.

"Is there something new?"

With her head the courageous young woman answered yes and with a gesture she invited him to come up. Sokes tied the reins of the horses around a block of stone fallen into the ravine bed and, in his turn, scaled the rock. Surprise made him speechless. He found himself faced with a circular hole into which a roughly formed ladder had been placed. Thus it was easy to descend into the excavation a little less than three meters in circumference and depth. The darkness inside the hole was total. The light of day made it possible to discern a sort of ledge sticking out in the circular pit.

"That's why we're going down, sir."

The detective listened for several minutes to any sounds that might come from the excavation, and finding there was complete silence, placed her foot on the first rung, her revolver in her hand. Before going further, she remained immobile. She got her bearings and mentally judged the distances.

"This seems uninhabited," she whispered to Sokes.

"Shall we slide onto that ledge, over there?"

"Yes."

"Then I'll go ahead of you."

"No. I'll go first."

"If there's danger, I wish to be there."

"Pardon, sir. I'm the one leading the investigation," said the daring girl.

The tone of Miss Boston's voice told Sokes there was nothing more to be said. He stopped talking and followed the detective, who started onto the subterranean ledge which was lit by a diffuse light, apparently from a fissure in the rocks. Daylight came through but with difficulty, enough, however, to see where they were walking. The ledge had been hollowed out of the rock by the flow of water, which, long ago, poured into the ravine. There was still a humid freshness there which told of the origin of the ledge. It suddenly turned at a right angle and the two detectives found themselves in a cavern. The rock ceiling was pierced with holes which let in dim, diffused light. Had it not been for their extreme prudence, Miss Boston and Sokes would have let out a mutual cry of amazement. Open, empty, on the ground in front of them laid the seven strongboxes stolen by the cowboys from the Arizona Rapid boxcars. Miss Boston's smile seemed really to say: "We haven't wasted our time, Mr. Sokes!"

She examined what remained of the strongboxes which had carried the precious metals from the mining company. They were cases of iron, overlaid with steel, provided with secret locks, like true safes. For the trip they had been surrounded with straw and the straw along the sides of the crates had been wrapped with strong packing canvas stitched together. The strongboxes resembled enormous, heavy packages. They must have been carried that way into the cavern, because the straw and the packaging canvas were ripped open and scattered on the ground.

"These are really rough fellows," Sokes said. "The fact that they carried the strongboxes here shows they have uncommon strength. That was a real *tour de force.*"

"We have another one to accomplish, Sokes."

"That of finding the cowboys?"

"Yes. This makes you know in advance that we're dealing with determined fellows who won't let themselves be easily taken and will know how to keep us on our toes."

Looking around her, the detective noticed the entry to a new tunnel dug into the earth going underground toward the west. It was narrower than the one through which Miss Boston and Sokes had entered the cavern.

"That's the way we continue," the detective said.

Sokes started toward the tunnel.

"Not yet, Sokes!" cried the young woman.

"Do we have something else to do here?"

"Yes, we have to examine the strongboxes here."

VI. Strange Discoveries

"Examine the strongboxes," he said. "That seems to me superfluous. It's easy to see they've been opened. It seems to me..."

Miss Boston stared at him and in a voice, the metallic timber of which strangely surprised Sokes, she said:

"Opened, yes, but how?"

"But...like all strongboxes are opened when they're burglarized, with a jimmy, I imagine."

With a cutting tone the detective coldly answered:

"That's where you're mistaken. Yes and no. They have been burglarized, yes, if you consider that they've been opened by someone other than their legitimate owner. They haven't been burglarized if you mean by that instruments ordinarily used by burglars were not used."

She quickly stepped over to the strongboxes and one after the other examined the locks. All of them were intact without traces of force.

"I don't understand; I don't understand anything at all."

"But it's easy to understand," the detective said. "The strongboxes were opened by someone who had the keys. That's the only explanation I can give at the moment."

"Bizarre! Bizarre!" the Inspector groaned in a very dissatisfied tone. "Then the cowboys fabricated a key."

"Don't you find it strange, first of all, that cowboys, used to brutal and violent things, made a false key? Isn't it more logical and a great deal more natural to believe that they would just have broken open the strongboxes in the prairie instead of putting themselves through the dangerous exercise of hauling them into this cavern, a league from Church Hill? Beside that double unlikelihood there is another one which adds to what that entire affair has that's mysterious and shady. It was not only one key, but seven keys they must have made. There must be an unusually clever person at the head of these cowboys and we may be very astonished to find him there when we lay our hands on him."

"Who do you suspect?"

"Nobody and everybody. In an affair as serious and as troubling as this, one can't take too many precautions, and that's what I'm doing. Let's move this investigation forward slowly. That's the wisest thing in any case."

"For the moment, where do we stop?"

"We're not stopping, Sokes; we're going on."

"Straight ahead then, through the tunnel?"

"Yes."

The detectives started walking again in silence, each of them preoccupied with the strange evidence that had just been found in the cave. What other unusual evidence was going to show up? That was the question their restless minds were asking, but satisfied at the same time with the turn of events. The ledge they had reached was narrow and low. Miss Boston rapidly shined the light of her electric torch along the wall. She recognized that this passage had been hollowed out naturally by the infiltration of water in the period when Arizona was still a great lake, a kind of interior sea, to which the terrain owed its fertility and luxuriant vegetation.

As Miss Boston and Sokes advanced, the air became thicker, rarer and heavier. It seemed the ledge was sinking deeper into the ground or that the fissures in the rock letting air in must be blocked or obstructed.

"What direction are we walking in now?" Sokes asked.

"Toward the west. Doesn't that direction tell you anything?"

"No, nothing in particular. And you, what does it tell you?"

"I notice that west is the direction of Church Hill."

"Yes, but we've been walking more than an hour. Certainly the ledge must have gone past Church Hill."

"That's what my estimation says also. But west is also the direction in which the Greenbar mines are located."

"And you think we're walking toward the Greenbar mines right now?"

"We'll know an hour from now. Isn't it an hour from Church Hill to Greenbar?"

"Just about."

"Then I'm right: in an hour."

They could no longer walk except with a great deal of discomfort. The subterranean heat was suffocating and Miss Boston as well as Sokes sweated great drops. Nevertheless, with tenacious courage the two detectives continued their painful walk, exchanging only at long intervals a few words and brief encouragements. The darkness made the time seem longer to them. But suddenly, Miss Boston, who was walking ahead, touched the rock. The subterranean passage had stopped. She turned on her electric torch and saw she had come to the end of the ledge. She turned slightly, and in the angle thus formed there was a little ladder. The most absolute silence reigned around them. Thanks to her torch, the detective could see iron beams above her holding up a floor. The little ladder led to a trap door in the floor. She immediately climbed up and applied her microphone against the trap door. She could hear some remnants of conversation.

"Yes," said one voice. "Percy is slow smelting that."

"He said the work in bulk takes a lot longer," another voice said.

"He went faster at the beginning."

"That's true, but since we can't do without him, we have to put up with his delays, no matter how."

"When I think that the patina of the fifth strongbox isn't ready yet today, I begin to think that Percy's holding out on us."

"I'll tell him you said so."

"That won't bother me."

A door slammed. Silence again.

"Revolvers!" the detective whispered to Sokes. "Silence!"

The Inspector obeyed and got ready to follow Miss Boston up the little ladder. She still waited several seconds, almost holding her breath. Suddenly she made up her mind. She applied a vigorous and firm push on the trap door, which opened above her noiselessly.

VII. Following Sokes' Amazement

Miss Boston entered the room where she had just discovered the secret entrance. It was a comfortably furnished office, which seemed to be that of a factory director. The desk was encumbered with papers and boxes were overflowing with documents. Maps and plans for excavations of land were hanging on the walls. Light came into the office through a large bay window, but it was halfway closed by thick curtains which shut out the view from the outside. In the distance could be seen high chimneys vomiting out thick black fumes.

The trapdoor that the detective had let close behind her on entering the office was cleverly hidden by the thick carpet on the floor. However, that examination lasted only a minute. The detective went to the desk and rapidly leafed through the stack of open letters spread out there. She didn't read any of them, only the addresses. The addresses were all the same:

WALTER SOMERS
Director of Greenbar Mine Exploration

"Marvelous," she said, half aloud.

"Where are we?" asked Sokes, who had silently followed the detective's inspection.

"Prepare yourself for a surprise."

"I'm prepared for everything."

"Well, we're in the office of the Director of the Greenbar mines."

"That's not possible! But what role does he play in the theft of the strong-boxes?"

"Not an infinitely honest role for him, I'm afraid. In any case, now that we're here, we're not going to be slow in finding out."

"Are we going back in the tunnel?"

"No, because there's no other way out but this room or two hours from here through the grotto in the ravine. We have to leave here to go explore the area."

Sokes hoisted himself up to the top of the curtain which half covered the bay window and looked outside. He saw a paved courtyard onto which the mine workrooms opened. The road passed by some steps from there, to the left. They had only to reach it and that's what the detectives did. They nonchalantly walked along the road, continuing to chat about that new discovery.

"The one we heard talk about a certain Percy, the one who smelts metals, must be this Walt Somers," said Miss Boston. "The other one must be an accomplice."

"In your opinion, this Walt Somers has something to do with the attacks on the Arizona Rapid Train?"

"The more I think about it, Sokes, the more his role seems clear to me."

"As innocent?"

"No, as guilty. Up until now, Sokes, we've established three points:

1. That the robberies always take place at Church Hill Curve;

2. That the strongboxes weren't opened by the cowboys, but by someone who had the keys;

3. That an intermediary must serve for the selling of the stolen metals smelted and converted into ingots.

"All that is established, but established isn't explained, especially in the present case."

"You're getting ahead of my thinking, Sokes, but here's the explanation, at least as I can give it with the elements of the investigation at my disposal. Why do the robberies always take place at the curve of Church Hill? Because at that very sharp curve, the Arizona Rapid is forced to slow its speed that it only picks back up at the Town Hill curve. That's what lets the cowboys jump on the train while it's in motion. That's one reason. There's another. The cavern where we found the seven empty strongboxes is in the proximity of that curve."

"Marvelously reasoned. But the second point?"

"That's the opening of the strongboxes. We know what condition they were opened in; we saw it with our own eyes. Did the cowboys have the keys to the strongboxes?" It's useless to discuss that impossibility. In that case, who had them? The Director of the Greenbar mining development, incontestably. He orders precious metal mining shipments. He's the one who locks them in the strongboxes with a lock to which he only has the key, at least at Greenbar. A key is also in New York, since Mr. Hebert Folkestone, as Director of the Company, opens the strongboxes. Therefore we are locked in this dilemma: two men have the keys and the secret of the strongboxes. Which of these two men has taken advantage of it? For me, to ask the question is to resolve it."

"That means the man in question is no other than Otto Walter Somers?"

"Without a doubt, Sokes, and the third point is derived logically from the fact that he isn't an intermediary but a beneficiary of the stolen metals. Who, if not the director, respected and well known, could carry on this traffic without danger? Who would dare suspect him? No one."

"Pardon, but we suspect him, that's a lot."

"Yes, Sokes, we're detectives. In addition, we can do more and better than suspect him: we can even openly accuse him."

"But with what proof?"

"With the conversations heard when we were in the underground passage."

"That's true, but who is that Percy he talked about?"

"A smelter, naturally, but on this point I don't know any more than you do, Sokes, and I'm waiting on our investigation of other details about this person."

"And the cowboys? Up until now, we haven't seen any of them in this business. They've miraculously vanished, disappeared, even vaporized."

"There's nothing strange in that, Sokes. Here's what I think in that regard. That troop of pillagers operate under Walter Somers' orders and he pays them.

When there's a shipment to rob, the band is alerted, it comes to Church Hill, attacks the train, throws the strongboxes on the railroad siding, drags them to the cavern and gets paid. The rest is up to Walter Somers. It's he and the head of the cowboys who must be captured. The rest are only underlings."

"Captured, so be it! But how?"

"I think I've found out how, Sokes. By organizing an eighth and ninth attack."

"Oh! Two attacks?"

"Yes, the first to capture the leader of the cowboys, the first one to jump on the train."

"And the second to take Walter Somers?"

"You have it."

"But he himself doesn't jump on the train."

"So, I won't be on the train to capture him."

"Where will you be, then?"

"I'll tell you at the proper moment, Sokes. For now, we're going to the Greenbar telegraph office to send an explanatory telegraph to Mr. Folkestone. He's the one to make the task easier for us."

"How's that?"

Miss Boston didn't answer Sokes' question until, in the Greenbar telegraph office, she composed her telegram. Only then did she hold it out to Sokes saying:

"Here's how."

And the Chief Inspector read:

Mister Herbert Folkestone
Burke Street, New York

Sir, As soon as you receive this, please send a telegram to your Director at Greenbar. The urgency of the request needs the telegram to say: 'Send a shipment of metal tomorrow Tuesday, and another shipment Wednesday; urgent request at the Bourse.' The result will be telegraphed to you Thursday. M. B.

"And now" said the detective, let's wait for Mr. Folkestone's telegram."

VIII. Preparations for the Eighth Attack

The two policemen immediately took up their observation posts. Sokes set himself up permanently at the telegraph office, checking out all the telegrams. As for Miss Boston, she was near the office of the thieving Director, watching for a moment to get inside. Part of her plan was to be present when Mr. Herbert Folkestone's telegram arrived. She had already been waiting for an hour when she saw the office door open and a person about 40 years old go down the steps toward the courtyard.

That man was of middle height, clean shaven, dressed conservatively, but his face carried signs of all the vices. His expression had something undefined:

sly, underhanded, cowardly, and animal-like at the same time. It was Mr. Otto Walter Somers, the Director of the Greenbar mining operation. He looked around him suspiciously and started toward the factory offices situated in one wing of the building while the machines for electricity and steam were installed in the other. He did not see the detective, who was cleverly hidden by the transportation vehicles. As soon as he was out of sight, Miss Boston dashed toward the office and entered without any problem. It was empty. She didn't stop to look for clues, very likely improbable to find, but lifted the trap door to the underground passage and slid in. Standing there on the little ladder, her microphone in her hand, she waited for the outcome of events. They weren't long in coming. Miss Boston had calculated that it would take at least four hours from the time her telegram left Greenbar until the arrival of that from New York, assuming Mr. Folkestone answered immediately. The four hours were almost up now and the denouement drew near with each minute.

The door of Walter Somers' office suddenly opened, and the microphone indicated through the sound of footsteps that two persons had entered.

"Close the door, Matt," said a voice that had to be that of Walter Somers.

"What's the matter?" asked the one who had been called Matt.

"What is it? I've just received a telegram."

"From New York?"

"Yes."

"Are they on to us?" Matt asked with worry in his voice.

"There you are, trembling already," Walter Somers answered, laughing derisively, "but relax, there's nothing dangerous. Very much to the contrary."

"How's that?"

"A new shipment to be sent tomorrow and the day after tomorrow. It's Folkestone who informed me. It seems the price of precious metals on the Stock Exchange has risen."

"In any case the Stock Exchange will do without ours!" joked Matt, who had regained all his confidence at that news.

"Red Boy has to be alerted," Walter Somers interrupted. "Where is he right now?"

"He's with his men beside Bello Horizonte."

"That's going to make you have a hard ride tonight, my poor Matt."

"What do you expect? You have to stay on the job. That will be for the four o'clock Rapid as always, right?"

"Yes, have Red Boy there with his men at three o'clock at the Church Hill clump of trees. The strongbox will be stamped 0 2 B on the packaging."

"Good. I'll tell him that. But, tell me, why put the metals in? It takes us a day to transport each robbery. We could just leave the strongbox in the cavern and on the packing list to New York you could put down whatever quantity of metal you like. They can't verify it, since the strongbox will be in the hole of the ravine."

"That's an excellent idea, Matt, but…but…what if by some mischance the shipment gets to its destination? It's opened, nothing is inside, and my packing slip gives the game away! No, No! It's better to fill the strongbox as if it's supposed to arrive in New York. It's better to take the trouble to bring the metal back here than to risk being found out by the company, or, what's worse, by the detectives!"

"Speaking of detectives, what I find strange is that there've been seven robberies and not one of them has come sticking their nose in the matter. Don't you find that bizarre, old brother?"

"No. You know the reports I send to Folkestone. Like me, he thinks the police can't do anything, absolutely nothing about the prairie scum that until now they attribute the Rapid attacks to."

"Well, if that's your opinion, Walter, I don't see anything to go over, but as for me, I find the police not stepping in unusual and I predict that one day or another they'll get busy finding out about our friend Red Boy."

"Let's hope that's as late as possible, old Matt!"

"You're right. I'm going to give orders to have my horse saddled for tonight. I'll leave after dinner and I'll be at Bello Horizonte at midnight. I'll be back at Greenbar at 4 a.m."

"Good. During that time, I'll take care of the strongbox for tomorrow and the day after tomorrow."

"Agreed. Until tomorrow morning."

"I'm going with you a short way down the road."

The sound of the steps grew faint. The office door closed and Miss Boston knew the two robbers had left. Now she had the key to the affair. She hurried to leave the underground passage to rejoin Sokes at the rendezvous agreed on before they separated. From there they went to the Greenbar Station. On the way the detective brought her companion up to date about the valuable clues she had gathered. The telegram trick to New York had succeeded marvelously. Walter Somers and Matt were getting ready to answer it…and also to fall into the daring trap so ingeniously set by the only female detective in the whole world.

At the station, the two detectives confirmed the train's timetable. The Arizona Rapid left at 4:08 p.m. for Osborn, where it arrived about 11:22 p.m. At Osborn, another train left again in the direction of Greenbar at 1:22 a.m. Miss Boston intended to come back by this train if her plan had succeeded in the way she thought it would.

Having introduced herself to the Station Master she asked to examine the convoy of cars that would make up the next day's Arizona Rapid, which was waiting on a track in the garage.

"In what boxcar do they usually put the valuable shipments from the mining company to New York?"

"In the last boxcar, Miss."

246

"Why not put it in the first boxcar, as is usually done for shipments of a certain importance?"

"I don't know. Mr. Walter Somers asked me to do it that way and I didn't see anything inconvenient."

Miss Boston smiled slightly. Leaving the station, she said to Sokes:

"This gentleman will be one of my witnesses at the trial of the band of cowboys."

"Why is that?"

"Because Walter Somers gave him an order that would make theft of the strongboxes easier. That's proof and testimony against him, while we wait for those we're going to get tomorrow and the day after tomorrow."

But what the detective hadn't yet told Sokes was that she had gathered information valuable in a different way, from her point of view. That information confirmed that the strongboxes were loaded onto the Rapid at least an hour before the train's departure and that during that hour the strongboxes remained absolutely without surveillance. The employees of the mining company in charge of escorting the shipments took their posts only ten minutes before the departure of the Rapid. This information was going to play an important role in what happened next in the admirable investigation directed with so much daring by the young detective.

IX. The Capture of Red Boy

There are usually few travelers for Osborn and New York on the fast 4 p.m. train which leaves Greenbar Station. However, this Tuesday, two elegant travelers waiting for the train's departure were walking up and down in front of a first class car placed in the convoy before a boxcar full of merchandise. Those two travelers were Miss Boston and Sokes. While seeming to walk about with no set purpose, they never stopped watching an enormous packet wrapped in packaging material marked 0 2 B which had just been loaded into the boxcar with great difficulty. That was the strongbox of precious metals from the Arizona Mining Company.

Miss Boston in particular seemed to size up the proportions and the dimensions. That evaluation seemed favorable, because a slight smile spread over her pretty lips.

"Ah! Ah!" said Sokes "There's the eighth prey for our friends, the Cowboys."

"Yes, but the last."

"The strongbox for tomorrow?"

"How do you know they'll take what's inside?" the great detective ironically asked the Chief Inspector.

Sokes didn't take notice of that observation of the courageous young woman and suddenly said:

"There are the five guards come to take up their post."

Five guards, in fact, had just climbed into the boxcar. They pushed the strongbox into a corner and, chatting, lit their pipes. As they passed by, the detective heard snatches of conversation.

"They say the last convoy was again attacked at Church Hill. Is that true, Bob?"

"I think so. Wasn't Reading on the convoy?"

"Yes, and there's no news of him."

"Who were the others?"

"Fred Redders, Tom Modders, and Stam."

"But Byval?"

"He was there too."

"And to say these damned cowboys will never be caught, these red boys!"

"They're red cowboys?"

"That's what Humsley, who escaped the third attack, said. He never wanted to accompany another convoy."

"He was right."

"If I had known!"

"Are you already afraid, Rob?"

"I'd rather have stayed at Greenbar."

"Come on now! You're nothing but a weakling."

"Me, I value my skin, pard!"

"And so do I! Just let the cowboys come and I'll put a few bullets in their head."

"Easier said than done!"

Suddenly there was a strident whistle from the front of the train. The doors slammed shut. They were on their way. Miss Boston and Sokes hurried to reach their compartment as the Arizona Rapid slowly picked up steam and left the glass hall of the Greenbar station.

"You'd say the Company guards don't seem as reassured as all that," said Sokes, lighting a cigar.

"That's easy to understand after the seven bloody dramas that have taken place in the Rapid. There's even one thing that surprises me."

"What's that?"

"That after all that there are still some employees willing to risk this dangerous adventure."

The train was now reaching the savanna. In the distance the waves of high grass were beginning to come into sight. Sokes took out his watch and said:

"In an hour and a half we'll be at the Church Hill curve. What are we going to do?"

"We're going to place ourselves on each side of the compartment. A cowboy is certainly going to pass by on the railing that runs the length of the train. The important thing is to take him and for that we have to use a revolver. The rest is a matter of strength. We have to grab the fellow, hold tight to him and drag him into the compartment. That's my plan."

"Daring and dangerous."

"I'm aware of that. But it's the only thing practical and realizable. Too bad if it fails. We'll see how to recover."

The train was picking up speed. The clump of trees in the loop of the Church Hill curve, still imperceptible in the distance, appeared like a small black dot. A half hour passed. They were drawing close. Miss Boston spread out handcuffs and a revolver on the bench in front of her. She had the other revolver in her hand. Sokes did the same thing and thus armed the two detectives waited for the Rapid to arrive at the Church Hill curve.

The train was slowing down for the curve. Looking out the window, Miss Boston distinctly saw a small group of ten cowboys lying in the grass, waiting for the moment to jump on the convoy. Their horses were tied to the trees. The attack suddenly took place. The bandits jumped on the side ramp of the train, some in front of the boxcar, others into the boxcar itself.

"Quick!" a voice shouted.

It was that of a big fellow who seemed to command the gang of robbers. He was clinging to the compartment ahead of Miss Boston's, and holding on to the metal ramp, he intended to reach the boxcar that way. He was going to, he had to, pass in front of the train door where the detective was waiting for him. He arrived. A revolver shot rang out. Letting out a cry, the man turned loose of the metal ramp. He was going to fall into the void. But the detective's hand, delicate and strong, elegant and sturdy, white and rugged, reached out and seized the cowboy by the collar and kept him from falling off the footboard. The Rapid, however, was still moving.

Sokes, leaning out at the door, had seen the cowboys enter the boxcar; he had, despite the thunder of the Rapid, heard the cries, the clamor of the fight, and two minutes later he had seen the strongbox, thrown onto the track siding, roll into the prairie grass. That time the attack had succeeded.

It had succeeded no less for Miss Boston. The courageous detective had not turned loose of her wounded prisoner. He was, nevertheless, fighting frenetically on the car's side ramp, but the iron hand of the detective kept her hold. With a sudden movement, Miss Boston made the cowboy tilt. He lost balance and at that moment with a movement as rash as perilous, the detective lifted him, pulled him through the train door and threw him onto the bench.

The man was so astonished he didn't have time to protest. The detective had handcuffed him. Then turning toward Sokes, she said, with a smile:

"There's bird number one."

"Compliments! You have some wrist!" said Sokes.

The cowboy was moaning. The pain from his wound contracted his face muscles. Miss Boston examined his wound, which wasn't mortal and took first aide materials out of her handbag to dress the wound and calm his suffering.

"And now," she said to him, "let's talk a little, my boy. First of all, what's your name?"

"Red Boy," the prisoner groaned.

"Good. You are obviously the chief of the fellows who've just robbed the Rapid?"

"The chief, yes."

"It seems you work on behalf of Mr. Walter Somers?"

"I don't know if he's called Walter or Somers; all I know is that he's from Greenbar."

"He's the one who pays you?"

"Yes, $100 for each robbery, for me and my men."

"This makes the eighth robbery?"

"Yes, but the first two were done by Blue Boy, who was before me. He was killed by a guard's bullet at the second robbery of the Rapid, last year."

"And naturally carrying the strongboxes into the cavern in the ravine is included in the $100 you get?"

"What!" he said, "You…you…know about the cavern…down there?"

"Yes and I even know the seven empty strongboxes are there and that tomorrow I'll find the eighth one there."

"Then…then...you're a detective?" stammered Red Boy with an expression of unspeakable terror.

"You've guessed it," said Miss Boston, laughing.

That same night Red Boy was locked up in the prison at Osborn and a few hours later Miss Boston and Sokes took the Greenbar Rapid where they arrived in the morning at sunup.

X. The Surprise Strongbox

The next day, Wednesday, five employees of the mining company came at 4 p.m. to take over the surveillance of the strongbox 0 3 B to be put onto the boxcar of the Arizona Rapid. A station employee, who, despite his little red mustache, extraordinarily resembled Sokes—it was he—watched the strongbox with jealous care. No sign of Miss Boston anywhere. Where was the famous woman detective? The little employee with the red mustache didn't seem at all worried about it. About 3:30 he had gone to the mining company office to deposit a sack which seemed rather heavy and since then he hadn't taken his eyes off the mining company shipment.

The train left at its usual hour. As the night before, a group of cowboys were waiting in the grass at the Church Hill curve. When the Rapid slowed its speed, they savagely jumped on the foot rail, shouting at the top of their lungs.

"Let's avenge our chief!"

"Let's avenge Red Boy!"

In the boxcar, there was a short but savage fight. Shots rang out. Guards were knocked down. A tragic but short moment. Three cowboys had rushed toward the strongbox and had thrown it out through the large boxcar door onto the railroad siding. So, the combat over, the assailants jumped to the prairie while the Rapid continued its course toward Town Hill.

The cowboys tied two solid ropes around the strongbox, mounted their horses, and dragged the stolen package toward the ravine. Less than an hour afterward they reached the cavern where less than 48 hours before, Miss Boston and Sokes had entered. A man was standing at the entrance of the grotto waiting for them. It was Walter Somers.

"Well," he shouted, "and Red Boy, what's happened to him?"

"Red Boy disappeared," the oldest of the group said.

"What do you mean, he disappeared?"

"Yes, we don't know what happened at yesterday's robbery. He was hanging on to a compartment door and the Rapid carried him away."

Walter Somers paled visibly hearing that news.

"The devil!" he said, thinking.

He raised his voice and asked: "His body wasn't found?"

"No, we searched right up to Town Hill and didn't find anything."

"Listen, my boys," the criminal director said, "for the two jobs, you have a right to $200, but I'll give you $300 if from now until this evening you manage to find this poor Red Boy's body."

"We'll do whatever's possible," said the one who seemed to have taken over command of the group.

While that conversation was being exchanged in the ravine, the cowboys had hauled the strongbox to the entry of the cavern and had slid it into the interior with the help of the ropes around it. Shortly afterward, led by their new chief, they remounted to begin a search for the body of Red Boy. Going back into the cavern, Walter Somers had a thoughtful and worried look.

"What could that disappearance really mean?" he grumbled. "Was Matt right to fear detectives in this?"

He went up to the strongbox just brought in. He opened a sack that was set there to hold the metal he was going to take out of the strongbox. Then, with a knife he slit open the packing material, pushed aside the straw and took his keys out of his pocket to open the steel lid. But at the same instant that lid snapped open in his face. The director dropped his keys. A svelte form came surging out of the strongbox. That form was brandishing a revolver in the face of the criminal. It was Miss Boston. Walter Somers quickly recovered from his astonishment. He jumped backward and dashed onto the ledge which in the distance ended in his director's office at Greenbar. But Miss Boston dashed after him. Making headway in that narrow ledge was infinitely difficult. At each step you bumped into the wall or you almost broke your head against the extremely low ceiling. Despair gave the robber strength. But suddenly he stumbled, cried out in terrible pain, and collapsed on the dirt of the subterranean passage.

Was it a ruse? Miss Boston raised her revolver. But nothing budged. Walter Somers was stretched unmoving on the dirt. So the detective decided to approach and shed light there with her electric torch. What she had foreseen had happened. In his losing flight, the miserable man had hit his forehead against a fragment of rock on the ceiling. The blow had been terrible. He lay there, his head literally split in two. His heart had stopped. Only then did Miss Boston notice that the director's brain had splashed in every direction along the wall of the dark tunnel.

Her job ended here. Fate had punished the criminal.

To understand Miss Boston's presence in the cavern when the strongbox was opened by Walter Somers, a few words of explanation are necessary.

She had examined the package loaded in the boxcar the evening before and that examination let her to verify that the strongbox could serve as a hiding place. It was an idea as ingenious as it was risky and dangerous. Only Miss Boston could have conceived it. Coming back from Osborn, after the capture of Red Boy she had laid out her idea to the Chief Inspector. "But that's madness!" he retorted. "That's asking for death!"

"I do that every day."

"But this time…"

"I'm not afraid."

"You've never done anything as daring!"

"One more reason to attempt it! I'll at least have the merit of having tried."

Sokes saw the detective was absolutely determined to carry out her plan whatever the cost. The next day they were at the station just as they were loading the ninth shipment from the Greenbar Mining Company into the Arizona Rapid boxcar. That shipment had no surveillance until the guards came to take up their posts. That was what Miss Boston was counting on. Her hope and her wait were not deceived. As soon as the strongbox was left alone, she gently detached the cover, and thanks to her perfected jimmy she opened the lock. All the contents of the strongbox were put into the sack and that was the sack Sokes had placed temporarily in the Station Master's office. Sokes rearranged the straw, and reattached the packing materials. When the five guards arrived at 4 p.m., all of them were far from suspecting that the most famous detective in the world was hidden in the strongbox they were to guard.

The arrest of Red Boy, followed soon by that of Matt, and the death of Walter Somers put an end to the considerable thefts which the Arizona Mining Company had been a victim of for more than a year. The trial of the two surviving criminals was taken up by the High Court of Osborn and both were condemned to be hanged. The bandits had made themselves so feared in the countryside that the news was greeted with great joy. There were no more robberies on the Arizona Rapid line.

That affair brought Sokes $500 and $1000 to Miss Boston. When she talks about it, she usually says, smiling:

"That was the time I was a cowboy!"

THE CHICAGO EMBALMED HEADS

I. The Somerset Decapitated Head

The High Court of Chicago had just adjourned. The crowd flowed across the great rooms and large vestibules of the monumental building. Everyone was talking about the judgment the jury had just rendered in a sensational trial that had for many months passionately involved the capital of Michigan. That criminal case had brought a well-known great banker before the Court. As Miss Boston and Sokes had taken charge of the part of the investigation that concerned New York, they came to be deposed at the time of the Chicago trial. They themselves were on their way to the exit of the High Court Building from the gallery reserved for witnesses.

Sokes walked rapidly, completely delighted to have finally ended a burden not at all pleasant for him. He was also happy to have several days of freedom before returning to the Central Police Bureau in New York where new cases and other investigations most certainly awaited him.

"Well. Miss Boston," he exclaimed, "what would you say to a little stroll around Chicago. The weather's beautiful; the city's pretty…"

"I gladly accept, Sokes, so much more willingly because this is the tenth time I've been to Chicago and I've never had occasion to visit the city as a simple tourist. I've rushed through it, gone across it, explored it as a detective. The seedy parts, the dives, the questionable saloons, the shady bars, that's all I know of Chicago up until now. However, I would like to see something else of it."

"This is the time to seize the opportunity. We don't take the train to New York until tomorrow morning at nine o'clock. It's one o'clock now. We have all afternoon and the evening to ourselves."

"You're leading me astray, Sokes!"

"What! Don't people have to have some distraction sometime?"

"Agreed. I consent. Let's go."

First they went to an elegant restaurant. About 2 p.m. they left, cheered by the beautiful weather and the prospect of a few hours' restful walk. They visited all the west of Chicago, going slowly down to the banks of Lake Michigan where the great prosperous city of Illinois is built. It was then 4 p.m.

The detectives went along the great interior lake, around a little tourist hamlet of summer villas called Somerset.

"How calm the lake is," Sokes was saying. "It's strange there aren't more boats out in this beautiful weather."

"In any case, there's one over there, in the distance," observed Miss Boston.

"He'll have a beautiful beach to land on," Sokes answered, pointing out the charming spot on the bank where they were standing.

"Indeed," the famous detective said. "There's a nice little cove. I'm no longer surprised that the borders of Michigan are so frequented during the summer season."

While talking, the two detectives continued their walk toward the top of Somerset. At a bend in the path they lost sight of the boat in the middle of the lake. Dusk was approaching. The detective was the first to point out that it was perhaps time to go back to Chicago. With Sokes, she turned around on the path, retracing her steps. A light gray mist spread over the lake, the twilight of a beautiful day.

The two policemen had gradually drawn near the pretty, fine sandy beach Sokes had noticed some time before. Now it was not completely deserted. A group of people had stopped there, excitedly discussing and looking at something black on the sand at their feet. Their loud and excited voices reached the detectives, who found this gathering somewhat strange, especially in such a place. What was happening there? Why that assembly? And what was that black shape stretched out on the wet beach sand?

"Doesn't that look like a corpse?" Sokes asked the detective, pointing to the stretched out form.

"That could be, but it's not possible to see exactly what it is because of the shadows."

"We must see that."

"Just a moment. Let's not get in a hurry yet."

"Why not?"

"Let's first look at these people from a distance. If there's something shady there, our examination won't be entirely useless, I think."

"But what if it's someone drowned?"

"In that case, he is incontestably dead, since no one is trying to bring him back to life."

Miss Boston watched carefully what was happening in the group on the beach. Now snatches of conversation and parts of sentences told her, little by little, the nature and the importance of the assemblage.

"Yes," said one voice, "He must have been brought in by the tide."

"No," answered another. "That's not possible."

"What do you mean, it's not possible. I know what I'm talking about, don't I?"

"But don't you see the body and the clothes, Gold?"

"Yes, I see them, but what's so unusual about them?"

"They aren't wet!"

"But what does that prove?"

Then the one named Gold retorted in a grumbling and quasi-triumphant voice:

"Then will you please tell me if the cadaver fell from the sky, or how he got here?"

"He could have been carried here!"

"And nobody would have seen him? Nobody would have met someone on the way carrying such a burden? Come now!"

"But he could have been thrown out of a boat on the lake."

"You're mad," Gold replied. "Your suppositions are out of a Sir Conon Doyle novel. The truth is a lot simpler: the cadaver was thrown in the water somewhere and the tide left it on the beach. That's all. You don't need to look any further."

Miss Boston thought the proper time had come to step in. She had heard enough. The situation was clear. What's more, the statement that the coroner was to be called was enough to press her even more. By personal experience she knew that these judicial magistrates who carry respect for the formalities of the law right to mania if not to the ridiculous, as soon as they become involved in a case, muddle the possible leads to the truth and to the arrest of the guilty parties. It was important for her to act, and to act without delay.

"Come on, Sokes," she said. "Now's the time!"

A few people had broken away from the group, probably to carry news of the tragic discovery on the beach back to the hamlet. As the detective came closer, she recognized the shape seen from a distance. It was that of a man. Coming even closer, she retreated a few steps. She had just seen the cadaver. The cadaver had been decapitated.

II. The Detective Struggles in the Shadows

Sokes himself let out a slight cry of amazement.

"Oh! Oh!" he said. And in that double interjection he put all his astonishment and all his indignation.

Then calmly, more coldly, Miss Boston considered the situation, examining the cadaver stretched before her with keen insight. The neck of the decapitated cadaver had been unusually cleanly and straightforwardly severed. The carotid arteries had been divided with a terrible blow. Nevertheless, despite the absence of the head, thanks to the cadaver's body build, it was easy to recognize that it was a full grown man. He was conventionally dressed in a dark blue suit, but the false collar and the top of the shirt were covered with blood, soaked with the wet, sticky, liquid. That easily convinced Miss Boston that the head had been severed while the man was clothed.

She immediately examined the mutilated cadaver's pockets and found to her astonishment that they contained the victim's watch, his billfold with nine dollars in it, and a railway ticket. That was all. But that discovery let the detective ascertain something new, it too something important: to know the victim had not been murdered with theft as an object. That was a valuable clue.

Then why had the crime been committed? And a problem, a dreadful and troubling problem, was posed: where was the cadaver's head? The enigma was doubly agonizing. Miss Boston couldn't help saying to Sokes to one side:

"I can't explain that mutilation to myself in any way. If someone wanted to do away with that man there, why did they need to use a method as cruelly barbaric as it was perfectly useless. There are a hundred ways a lot simpler to kill a man."

The detective shook her head thoughtfully. She said:

"I fear, Sokes, that we won't take the train to New York so soon."

"Then you want to get involved in this case?"

"Yes, Sokes, and for two reasons."

"Really?"

"The first is because I'm a detective and as such all crimes require my attention and have a claim to my professional expertise. The second is that this crime is particularly mysterious and troubling. You certainly are not unaware that I always have a mania to want to explain mysteries. That why I'm relying on your help."

"Do you doubt that a single instant?"

"No, Sokes, I know you too well for that."

During this interval the coroner from Somerset arrived. This magistrate wasn't at all like his honorable colleagues, so often disagreeable and grating. Mr. Carnegie was friendly, courteous, polite, and what's more—and that doesn't hurt anything—intelligent. Miss Boston, who believed in first impressions guessed that immediately. She introduced herself to Mr. Carnegie, who showed the greatest pleasure.

"This is real good luck and an honor for me, Miss, to have you for a collaborator in such a mysterious affair. Without you, I'm afraid, alas! It would always remain an enigma for me."

They postponed the inquest. Night had fallen and made gathering evidence on the beach impossible at such a late hour.

"Do you see any reason I can't have the victim removed, Miss?" the coroner asked. "We'll have it placed at the Somerset City Hall for the night and I'll let the administration of the Chicago morgue know so it can be taken there tomorrow."

"That's certainly the wisest thing to do," the detective answered.

The coroner asked Miss Boston and Sokes to dine with him that evening and they accepted. Naturally, during the meal they talked only of the sad thing found in the evening and a thousand guesses were made as to the tragedy which the anonymous cadaver might have been involved in. Miss Boston, always careful about logic, which was her strong point, didn't hazard any hypothesis. But to answer the coroner's questions, she summed up the known facts to that point.

"When my friend, Sokes, and I arrived at the beach, we saw a group of people standing around the bloody discovery excitedly arguing. By professional habit, we listened in on their conversation. One of them, named James, I believe, was reasoning very logically. He claimed the waves hadn't washed in the cadaver, and that was accurate. The decapitated man's clothes weren't wet. That proves he was carried to that spot."

"Couldn't he have been murdered on the beach itself?" the coroner asked.

"It could have been on the beach; that's possible," said Miss Boston, "but it's not probable. It certainly wasn't done at the spot he was found."

"Why is that?"

"Because the sand would have absorbed the blood from the severed arteries. I noticed that not the least drop of blood was seen on the beach. That's certain proof."

"But then how did he get there?"

"That James, that I've just spoken about, suggested the possibility that a boat could have brought in the cadaver. That's not at all bad reasoning. Do you remember, Sokes, the boat we noticed this afternoon in the middle of the lake?"

"Perfectly."

"That boat didn't seem to try to approach shore. We attributed that to the pleasure of the water outing. Ah! If I had foreseen! I believe that boat played a role in this criminal affair. I'll go even further. I say it's almost certain that the cadaver was in the bottom of the boat and that the man was only waiting to see the beach completely deserted to bring it ashore."

"That would explain everything," the coroner told her. "It would be necessary, even indispensable, to find that boat."

"Alas!" said Sokes, "that boat is like every other boat and I can easily presume that there are hundreds of boats that sail on Lake Michigan."

"That's precisely the complication," replied Miss Boston. "If the boat had had a sail, we could have noticed the number on the sail. Nothing of that. Like the cadaver, the boat is anonymous."

"We have only to count on luck to discover it, in your opinion?"

"A great deal on luck, sir, and also a little on the investigation we're going to start tomorrow morning. But that's not the only problem. In addition to the boat we have diverse other points to look into."

"What are they?"

"First of all, the name of the victim; next, the place of the crime; and, as a consequence, the murderer, the reason for the murder and also the missing head. Let me get an answer to one of those and I'll answer for the others."

III. Why Miss Boston Stayed on the Borders of Lake Michigan

Miss Boston and Sokes had already arrived at the beach as the Sun slowly rose over the calm waters of Lake Michigan. They had walked in a large circle which gradually brought them near the spot where, the evening before, the cadaver had been discovered. In this circle not an inch of land had been left unexplored. Nothing had been found. Now the detectives found themselves again at the tragic place. The sand had been trampled in every direction, but the directions corresponded to the circle around the cadaver and the direction of Somerset. None of those had gone toward the water. So the trail was not muddled in that direction, if that trail had ever existed. The courageous detective soon found out. Her shout of joy made Sokes come running.

"Look!" she said to him.

On the wet sand were deep footprints clearly embedded. That was an indication that the one who had left his passage thus marked behind him must have been carrying a heavy burden. Miss Boston immediately made an experiment, conclusive in every point. She had Sokes walk on the same terrain and then measured exactly the depth of his footprints. That depth was about half the depth of the other footprints. But Miss Boston made the demonstration even more complete.

"Will you pick me up, Sokes, and walk a few steps with my weight over the same terrain?"

The Chief Inspector picked up the young lady and carried her about 200 meters. They then measured the depth of the prints and confirmed that they were almost exactly the same as those they had just discovered.

"That's the obvious proof," Miss Boston said, "that the cadaver was brought in by a boat and it was most likely that boat we saw yesterday."

"That confirms what we saw," remarked Sokes, "but we're still far from the smallest lead. What we're finding here leads us straight to the lake, into the water, and from the lake to the boat. And water doesn't show a trail."

"I didn't know that," the detective said ironically.

And she fell into a reverie that kept her immobile at the edge of the beach, as if she wanted to snatch from the sand the secret the caressing wave was coming in to erase, little by little. Suddenly, she turned around. There was the sound of footsteps on the road from Somerset leading to beach. It was the coroner, Mr. Carnegie, in a hurry. He held the blue sheet of a telegram that he crumpled nervously in his hand as he ran. He arrived a little out of breath.

"Miss...Miss.." he said.

"Well, sir, is there something new?"

"Yes," the coroner, a little calmer, finally puffed. "An astonishing thing has just happened! This morning they've just discovered a new cadaver, Miss."

"A new cadaver decapitated?"

"Yes, like the one yesterday."

"Where was that? In the vicinity of Somerset?"

"No, an hour from here, near New London. My colleague, the Honorable Fred Edwards, the New London coroner, has just told me about it."

"Does he know I'm here?"

"No, at least I didn't tell him so."

"Good. Then I'm going to go to New London. It's probable that the de-capitated cadaver they've just discovered is a victim of a crime similar to the one here."

"Then you didn't find anything this morning?"

"Little, sir; so little that it's almost nothing. In any case, if my investigation has brought me confirmation, it's far from bringing me proof or the beginning of an interesting lead."

"When are you leaving, Miss?"

"Right now, sir. If I have something interesting or urgent to communicate to you, I'll get back to you quickly and inform you immediately. I'm not leaving the area."

"I hope to see you this evening, Miss!"

"That's also my earnest wish, Mr. Carnegie!"

The detectives had come to the paved road running alongside the beach and began the walk to New London.

It wasn't yet 10 a.m. when Miss Boston and Sokes reached the little quay, at the bottom of which there stretched a long sandy beach of the pretty city of New London. An enormous crowd was assembled in a circle around the cadaver.

Miss Boston, having made her way through the groups, saw the spot was empty. Out of curiosity common to crowds, the people were looking at the place where the victim had lain. Here also, the detective confirmed that not a drop of blood had been absorbed into the sand. She learned that the corpse had been found at 6 a.m. by a walker, and that the coroner when he was informed had had it taken up and transported to his office to get it away from the crowd's avid curiosity. It was easy to conclude that the tragic event had occurred at New London exactly the same way as at Somerset. To make sure, she walked to one side of the crowd and approached the water. There also she found traces of footprints deeply sunk in the sand. She didn't need anything more. The connection between the facts was clear. There remained only to see the cadaver. For this purpose Miss Boston and Sokes went to the house of the Honorable Fred Edwards.

He differed completely from his colleague at Somerset. Just as Mr. Carnegie was courteous and friendly, so Mr. Edwards was insolent and ill-mannered. The Somerset coroner was intelligent, wise, and informed; that of New London was vain and self-sufficient. The name and authority of the famous detective didn't impress him.

"I know my job," he declared peremptorily.

With irony, the celebrated detective answered:

"I would be very careful not to come to teach it to you. I simply want to know some details about the victim."

"Me, I know those details," retorted Mr. Edwards. "I know who the victim is and where he comes from."

"If there were papers on him, that would scarcely have been hard to guess," Miss Boston retorted. "But I would like to see those papers and look them over, as my function gives me the right and as the law obliges me to do."

With bad grace, the coroner let the detective see, as she had legally asked, what had been found in the decapitated cadaver's pockets. There, too, the dead man carried his money on him, $30 or so, his expensive watch, and his rings. As for papers, they proved that his name was William Fisher, that he lived at No.9, Blue Back, in Chicago, and that he was an engineer by profession.

Satisfied, Miss Boston said to Sokes:

"Finally, here's a trail. We're going to follow it immediately. The first cadaver was anonymous; this one gives us his identity. That's already something."

To finish, she examined the body. The head had been severed in the same way. Two minutes later the detective drily took leave of the insupportable coroner and started toward Chicago.

IV. The Second Trail Landmark

An electric tram runs from New London to Chicago and makes the trip in less than ten minutes. Thanks to this tram, Miss Boston and Sokes reached there more quickly than by cab. The two detectives were in Chicago when it was not yet 11 a.m.

"Well," Sokes said while the tram was rolling at full speed, "this is what's called not wasting your time. I've always liked cases where you can move ahead."

"When circumstances allow it," Miss Boston observed.

"Of course, but it seems to me that this time…"

"Wait, Sokes, how can you guess what's in store for us in Chicago?"

"That's true, but the address of the cadaver is of major importance."

"Yes, of course, if the trail goes on. What good does the address do us if that's all there is? If the address doesn't provide a continuation of the trail, it would have been of no use for us."

"Let's hope for the contrary."

"Of course. But tell me, Sokes, doesn't that address found on the decapitated man tell you anything?"

"It seemed to me rather bizarre."

"It's better than a clue. It's a moral clue, if I dare say so."

"From what point of view?"

"From the point of view of the circumstances of the crime."

"And that impression is what?"

"The crime isn't the work of a professional killer."

"Undoubtedly. And there are two reasons for that."

"I can guess them, Sokes. You mean the manner in which the crime was committed. Severed, mutilated heads aren't usually done to their victims by ordinary killers. Next, money, watches, rings found on the cadavers, valuable things which just any kind of murderer is always in a hurry to empty out of the dead man's pockets."

"Certainly. That's the basis of my deduction that the crime is one of vengeance."

"Hum! Hum!" the detective said in a tone indicating well enough her doubt.

That made the Chief Inspector look at her in surprise.

"What? You doubt that? You don't think it was vengeance?"

"Frankly, I don't think that. I think it was something else. I still don't know anything, at least to the present."

"Then what do you believe?"

"I don't believe anything. I'm thinking; I prove; and I deduct. Now here's the evident proof for the moment. The cadavers were found with everything they had in their pockets at the time of their death. If it had been vengeance, the murderer would have emptied the pockets and the address would have been done away with. Because the absent head made any identification impossible, the address took the place of the head and that's certainly not what the murderer wanted. There is one of two things: either the finding and recognition of the victim meant little to him or, on the contrary, he wanted to prevent recognition. In that case he had no need to sever the heads. It was easier to douse the face of the victim with a powerful corrosive which would have disfigured it forever. These are indisputable facts, Sokes."

This reasoning reduced to nothing the laborious deduction Sokes had established from the first facts.

Therefore, no theft.

Therefore, no vengeance.

Sokes' thoughts were interrupted by the tramway's arrival at the Back Plough terminus. There the detectives were not very far from Blue Back, the address of William Fisher found on the decapitated cadaver at New London. Number 9, an upper middle class house of nice appearance, indicated the comfortable situation of the victim. The building's concierge had not yet heard of the death. Miss Boston interrogated her rapidly and concisely.

Mr. Fisher had gone out the evening before about 4 p.m. and had not returned. Nobody found that surprising, because the engineer was very often absent for one or two days, working, and consequently didn't return to his Blue Back house. He lived in a beautiful bachelor apartment on the fifth floor and had an old housekeeper. In addition, he enjoyed an excellent reputation in the neighborhood.

Miss Boston went to the fifth floor apartment to interrogate the old housekeeper. The dead man's servant opened the door. The detective informed the poor woman about the terrible tragedy. For ten minutes there were lamentations, moans, and tears in the antechamber, because the old domestic loved the engineer. When the first expressions of sorrow were passed, Miss Boston proceeded to a detailed interrogation of the old servant. Given the formal assurance by the detective that her employer's murderer would be found and punished to the full extent of the law, the old woman agreed to answer, point by point, the interrogation.

"When did your employer go out yesterday?"

"At four o'clock, Miss."

"Do you know where he went? Did he have an appointment?"

"I know absolutely nothing about that, Miss. My master doesn't tell his business to a poor servant like me."

"Was there anything wrong with him? Did he seem worried, nervous, happy?"

"He was the same as every day, Miss. He complained a little of a toothache, as he often did. He even said to me: 'I must go to the dentist.' "

"Who was his usual dentist?"

"I don't know, Miss."

"Did he have any visitors during the day?"

"Yes, three people came to see him in the morning."

"Who? Their names?"

"I don't know their names. They left their calling cards."

Without transition, the detective asked: "Where is Mr. Fisher' study?"

"Here, Miss."

The servant opened a door on the left. The room was large and full of light. There was a large desk in the middle of the study. Miss Boston immediately walked toward it. She bent over and pulled the paper basket toward her. She emptied it on the floor, spread out the papers, and found six calling cards from the morning visitors. The first card said:

H. B. S. Hutchkiss
Solicitor
18 Bellys Road
The second:
Jeffries and Wattyn, esq.
Liberty Place
As for the third, it indicated:
Wooster & Sons
Aluminums of Texas
New York and Baltimore
Chicago, Piccadilly.
The detective slid all three into her purse and said to Sokes:

"These are identities to be verified."

She didn't leave the murdered man's study without glancing over the mail he had received the last nine days. The letters were methodically filed. Miss Boston learned nothing from reading them. They were simply business letters and none of them indicated plausibly why the engineer Fisher had left at 4 p.m. nor where he had gone.

V. The Trail Stops

The detective left Blue Back thoughtful. Sokes noted the deep frown which creased the young woman's forehead.

"Well," he asked, "what do you think about that? It doesn't seem to be going according to your wishes."

"I'm afraid that the trail found at New London has simply and unfortunately stopped here at Blue Back."

"But the three visiting cards?"

"I have very little confidence in the results our investigations will give us. Someone who thinks of committing a crime or comes to set it up at the domicile of his victim doesn't leave his visiting card behind him. In the present case, we certainly are not dealing with a murderer so stupid, foolish, or... shortsighted."

"But then, the investigations into Hutchkiss, Jeffries and Wattyn and Wooster Sons seem to me passably useless."

"Who knows, Sokes? Sometimes a word starts us on a serious lead. Don't you remember how many obscure, mysterious, and complicated cases where something insignificant has sent us after criminals, where an almost imperceptible glimmer managed to shed light on the thickest, the most compact shadows?"

Sokes shook his head. Decidedly the case of the mutilated cadavers was proving to be more difficult than he had at first thought. Miss Boston conducted a rapid and serious investigation of the people whose visiting cards she had found. Mr. Hutchkiss was a lawyer for Parquet in Chicago. He gladly explained, and provided proofs, that he had come to see the engineer about a lawsuit pending between him and Aluminums of Texas. That clue took Miss Boston immediately to Piccadilly, to Woosters & Sons. They represented the Aluminums of Texas Company. The conduct of Woosters & Sons was very far from being at all suspicious. It was Mr. Fisher himself who had asked them in—and they, in fact, showed his letter—to consult with them on an arrangement that would end the lawsuit then in progress.

That second investigation reduced to nothing any kind of criminal activity. That left the third calling card, that of Jeffries and Wattyn. They were the engineer's lawyers, but also his friends. They had taken care of his legal affairs for many years, and that relationship had made them true friends. They had been at his home the evening before to take up the business of the lawsuit with Aluminums of Texas Company.

"But what a horrible misfortune!" exclaimed Jeffries after having been given explanations. "To perish in that way! What a miserable death! And no clue as to the murderers has been found, Miss?"

The detective had to confess that nothing had helped her in the investigations begun.

"What I must find out, at any cost," she said, "is why Mr. Fisher left yesterday at four o'clock, the place he was going, and at least where he intended to go."

Wattyn thought a moment.

"It really seems to me that our unfortunate friend wanted to leave to go to his dentist. He was suffering rather violently with a toothache."

"His dentist?" Miss Boston said.

And at the same instant she remembered that a similar statement was given to her a little before by the engineer's old servant.

Where was this dentist? Did he go there?

"Sir," the detective asked Wattyn, "do you know this dentist?"

"Oh, my! No!" the lawyer answered. "Fisher mentioned it incidentally in the course of the conversation, because I saw he was nervous and in pain. I had no further interest in that detail and I didn't ask him for an address that I wouldn't have known what to do with."

"I can easily understand that," Miss Boston said. "But you can easily understand that this is the second time this dentist has come up in my investigation, and as a consequence I need to know if Mr. Fisher went to his office and at what time. That would be a valuable step in my investigation."

"Unfortunately," the lawyer answered, "I can in no fashion give you information on this point. Nevertheless, be reassured, Miss Boston that we are entirely at your disposal for everything concerning our unfortunate friend in this bloody business."

"I thank you in advance. If you have any information to communicate to me, you can give it in confidence to the Chicago Central Police Bureau. I'm going to bring the Chief of Police up to date on my investigations."

When leaving Liberty Place, the detective's bad humor was this time evident. She had lost the trail.

"This dentist," she said, "is destined to give us a valuable and truly important clue. Now it's precisely he that we haven't managed to find."

"He's not hiding, however."

"Obviously, and that's what is the most vexing in this affair."

"There could be a way of finding him, however. To take down the names and addresses of all the dentists in the city from the Chicago Telephone Book."

"And to investigate them? I have certainly already thought about that, Mr. Sokes, but I have also thought about the precious time that would make us lose. There are at least 300 dentists in Chicago. By sharing the work, it would take at least a week, and a week is something! No, we have to look for and find something else. Let's put our hope in chance, in that luck that has so often, so miraculously helped us."

"But what if it's too late?"

"Then we could always investigate the 300 dentists as a last resort. But from now until then, something new may come up."

"Let's wait for it," Sokes said philosophically.

And with Miss Boston he started toward the Chicago Central Police Bureau to inform the Chief of Police of the results of their laborious and somewhat futile investigation.

VI. No.3 and No.4

Miss Boston found Percy Jones, the Chicago Chief of Police, very moved and annoyed by the unusual turn the events had taken. Certainly, murders in a large city such as Chicago weren't anything rare, but having to record two murders as odious as that of Somerset and New London, evidently committed by the same hand, was more than significant. Mr. Percy Jones was an admirer of Miss Boston, with whom he had already worked at the time of the capture of the Mafia members.

"It's obvious, Miss," he told her, "that if you aren't finding anything, I won't. What could I do better than you? Nothing, I imagine. That's why I ask you to take charge of the case as you think right, and as for the rest, I give you carte blanche."

For several minutes more the conversation continued in the same vein, but the detective was visibly preoccupied. The Chief Inspector had no trouble understanding that. The detective didn't like to remain powerless, or simply inactive, when faced by a mystery. She interrupted Mr. Jones to ask him:

"Haven't you had any missing persons complaints?"

"No, Miss, why?"

"Because we seem to have forgotten the anonymous cadaver of Somerset. Up until now, we've concentrated almost exclusively on that of New London, but that of Somerset must, it seems to me, also hold our attention. That's why I asked you if any disappearance has been reported. You answered no, and..."

The Chief of Police's door opened. The clerk entered and passed a note to the Chief of Police, who glanced at it and asked:

"What does that lady want, John?"

"It's about a missing person."

The Chief glanced at the detective. Was luck going to get mixed up favorably in that nebulous affair?

"Have her come in," the Chief said.

A lady entered, her eyes red with tears eloquently testified to her sorrow. She fell rather than sat in the chair which a gesture of the Chief had pointed out.

"You wanted to see me, ma'am?"

With a nod of her head, she said yes.

"For what reason?" the Chief added.

Then she burst into sobs and in hesitating words told of the disappearance of her husband. He had not returned that night, and such a thing had never happened before. She didn't know what to think. He might have been murdered. Had he been mugged?

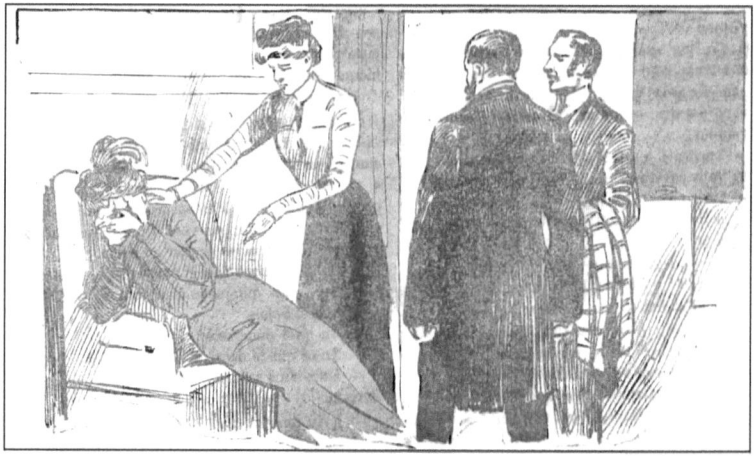

Miss Boston gently posed several well directed questions and managed to learn that the missing man was named Elias Weston and was office head of the Michigan Leather Society. His wife knew nothing about the rest, could furnish no information. Having asked several questions relating to the clothing the missing man was wearing, she was convinced that the cadaver on the Somerset beach was that of Elias Weston, and that his wife was now a widow. The cadaver was identified. The mask of anonymity had fallen away.

Mrs. Weston left, having received assurances that they were going to do whatever was necessary to find her husband. When she had left the Chief's office, the detective told him:

"Sir, this Weston is found. He's the Somerset cadaver."

"Not possible."

"Oh, yes it is. I recognize it by the description of his clothes. That's who it is and no one else."

"Terrible news for that poor woman!"

"Tell her carefully and as late as possible."

"The blow won't be any the less cruel. What are you going to do now?"

"Take myself over to the Michigan Leather Factory. I'll certainly get some information there."

"Very good. A telephone call in case of emergency, right, Miss? I can count on that?"

"Understood, sir."

Twenty minutes later Sokes and Miss Boston arrived at the headquarters of the Company where Mr. Weston had been employed. Miss Boston was immediately introduced to the Director to whom she set out the reason and motive for her visit. The director himself knew nothing personally but having called in the employees over whom Weston was head, the detective learned that Weston had left the office at noon for lunch and had not returned to the Michigan Leather Society. However, another employee had met him about 2 p.m. in Ontario Street in the direction of the lake. That was all they knew.

The two detectives immediately started toward Ontario Street. A minute and rigorous investigation was made, but Mr. Weston, unknown in the area, had not been seen. There again the trail of the investigation abruptly stopped. At 4 p.m. the detective found herself as little advanced as two hours before. Up until that time, she had followed dead ends.

With Sokes she went back toward Chicago. Coming to the top of Stated Road, the two detectives were immediately enveloped in a whirlwind of newspaper boys who, at the top of their lungs, were hawking the evening newspaper, the special edition of *The Rapid,* by means of a unified cry:

"Read about the Potbrod crimes!...Two decapitated heads...Read the evening edition!"

"What!" Sokes, stunned, exclaimed.

Miss Boston held out a penny to a newspaper vendor. She read on the front page:

A DOUBLE CRIME AT POTBROD
TWO CADAVERS TWO DECAPITATED HEADS
What is this mystery?
What is the Central Police Bureau Doing?
The Police Mocked by the Murderers!

By the special edition published at noon in *THE RAPID*, our readers learned of two decapitated cadavers on the beaches of Somerset and New London on the shores of Michigan. This double, bloody tragedy has just had a follow-up. We are entering a red era. Here are the facts:

Two new cadavers were found this morning at Potbrod. That sad discovery was made by strollers who noticed two inert masses on the sand. Having approached, they recognized cadavers which—macabre fact—were each missing a head. The Potbrod coroner was informed and immediately opened an investigation of this mystery. In these circumstances it can be asked what the Chicago police, that they claim are without a rival, are doing. Why is it that the Somerset and New London murderers aren't yet arrested? Decidedly these criminals have good reason to mock the police that are powerless to find them. When will this scandal be over? The peaceful citizens of Chicago and Illinois have the right to know.

This violent article was followed by some additional lines which drew Miss Boston's particular attention:

Our Potbrod reporter tells us just as we're going to press that the two cadavers from this morning have been recognized and identified, thanks to papers found on them. They are: 1. Max Goodby, retired, 52 years old, 180 Roseberry Street, Chicago. 2. P. F. S. Atkinson, 30 years old, stockbroker, 12 Fry Road, Chicago. The victim's families have been notified.

TO OUR READERS:

THE RAPID, always concerned with the interests of the Illinois population among whom it counts millions of readers, promises and offers $5,000 to whoever discovers the murderers of Mr. Goodby and Mr. Atkinson. Since the Chicago police are not doing their duty, THE RAPID will do its job.

Miss Boston read with apparent calm and limited herself to grumbling between her teeth:

"In fact, these journalists are right. The police haven't yet found anything."

She handed the newspaper to Sokes and pointed to the article with a nervous touch of her thumb.

"Read that," she said. "The series of cadavers continues. There are numbers 3 and 4. Will there be others added to that bloody list?"

VII. The Dreadful Series Continues

"That newspaper," she said to the Chief Inspector, "has this of value: it keeps us from going to Potbrod."

"You're going to stay in Chicago?"

"Yes, Sokes, and right now we're going to Roseberry Street."

"To the house of Goodby, one of the Potbrod dead men?"

"Just that. We're going to work with diligence."

A little before 5 p.m. they arrived at the dead man's apartment. There they found the family in tears, trying to console the wife of the murdered man. Miss Boston immediately realized the difficulty of trying to get useful information in such sad circumstances. She limited herself to asking some brief questions which furnished facts which were not to be discounted. Finally she asked the question so often asked already and unanswered.

"Why did Mr. Goodby go out?"

"He went out to take a walk as he did every day. After that he went to the dentist for an examination of a tooth he'd been suffering with for two or three days."

"A dentist!"

Again that dentist! But Miss Boston didn't react.

"And this dentist," she asked her, "where does he live?"

"I don't know exactly, but it's probably in the Baywater neighborhood."

With that valuable clue, the detective, with Sokes, went back up Roseberry Street in the direction of Fry Road.

"Well, think of that! That's extraordinary!" the Chief Inspector exclaimed. "The story of that dentist, you don't find it strange that all the dead men had a toothache?"

"After all, Sokes, that's perhaps only a simple coincidence."

"Hum! Hum! Coincidence!...very strange!" Sokes muttered and continued to walk faster. It was that way until the corner of Bedlam Avenue. There, Sokes suddenly asked the detective:

"Are you having second thoughts?"

"And about what, really, Sokes?"

"About that dentist?"

"Yes, Sokes, you've guessed right. I'm having second thoughts."

"I knew it," the Inspector exclaimed in a triumphant tone. And he added: "He's the murderer, isn't he?"

"Oh! Oh!" Miss Boston smiled, "you're rushing the job a little, sir. The Devil! You don't accuse someone you haven't even yet seen of murder in this way. My idea is simpler. A dentist has turned up twice in the trail of two similar crimes. This dentist has to be found. If he has seen the victims, it's up to us to look for what could have happened to them when they left his office. If, on the contrary, he hasn't seen them, we have to find out what happened to them on the way there. But up to now we have only the base, Sokes. This dentist has not yet been found."

"But we know he's in the Baywater area!"

"Obviously, but he isn't the only dentist in that part of Chicago. We've been told that Mr. Goodby went there. That's the only solid fact. It's the same thing with the engineer Fisher. He also went to his dentist. But which one? Mystery. And the other Potbrod decapitated cadaver, Atkinson, where did that one go? As for Elias Weston, the head of the Leather Society of Michigan, nobody was able to tell us where he had gone. In that last case, I noticed only one thing: Weston had been seen for the last time in Ontario Street."

"What deduction do you draw from that?"

"None. I simply observe that Ontario Street is in the Baywater district."

The detective had said that in a perfectly calm tone, but the Chief Inspector wasn't at all deceived. He guessed that the illustrious detective attached major importance to that similarity of neighborhood, and in an affirmative tone he said:

"Our dentist certainly lives in Ontario Street."

The detective smiled. "We'll see if you're mistaken, Sokes."

However, they had arrived at the top of Fry Road. They went down to No.12, to the establishment of Mr. P. F. S. Atkinson, the important stockbroker.

It was impossible for the detective to see Mrs. Atkinson. She had left an hour before for Potbrod to bring back to Chicago her husband's horribly mutilated body. Miss Boston could, therefore, gather no direct information, no precise clue. She was forced to proceed with interrogating the servants. One detail, given by Mr. Atkinson's valet, seemed important to her. The detective had naturally, cleverly, inserted the question of the dentist. She thereby learned that Mr. Atkinson was subject to toothaches and that the same morning as his disappearance, he had had some irritability. Therefore it was not impossible that in the course of the day he had gone to a dentist. It was once again the same trail presenting itself and the circle of the detective's investigations tightened around this enigmatic dentist. Where was he? In Baywater? She must immediately find out.

Walking up and down in front of the stock exchange in Fry Road, Sokes was waiting for Miss Boston. The detective saw him reading a newspaper the street vendors were hawking toward the end of the street. She touched the Inspector on the arm.

"Well, Sokes?"

"Look," he said. He held out the newspaper to the detective, who saw the headlines in huge letters:

A FIFTH DECAPITATED CADAVER
THE MEG STRAND BEACH MYSTERY
SEARCH FOR THE SEVERED HEAD.

VIII. The Ontario Street Dentist

"You see, the tragic series continues. We're now at our fifth decapitated cadaver. What do you think of that?"

"That we have to end it as soon as possible."

"I was thinking the same. Where are we going?"

"To Ridgway. We'll take a hansom cab."

Ten minutes later the carriage was carrying the detectives toward Ridgway. Miss Boston summed up the situation:

"It can't be doubted that this fifth crime, as well as those which preceded it, is the work of one individual. It's the same method of procedure. This man, Villars, who was found decapitated at Meg Strand, also had his papers and his money in his pockets. I'm beginning to wonder, Sokes, if we're not dealing with a monomaniac or, more simply, a sort of sadistic, dangerous, irresponsible person. That would explain everything and the only thing remaining would be to know the cause of that madness."

"That's a matter for the doctors."

"It isn't forbidden for us to know it, or at least to try to understand it," replied the detective.

"Assuredly."

At the same instant, the hansom cab driver shouted:

"What number should I stop at?"

"At the top of the street," Miss Boston shouted.

Ontario Street, in the Ridgway area, is a middle class neighborhood with very few commercial establishments. It goes down to the shores of Lake Michigan, almost touching them. Many of the gardens of the houses end right at the beach. But the sun was already going down and the evening shadows were certainly going to complicate the delicate and dangerous task of the two detectives. In the hundred or so houses on Ontario Street, it was a matter most of all to begin the search with a house that could be occupied by a dentist. Undoubtedly it was easy to knock on the first door they came to, pretend to be mistaken, and ask for the address in question. But such a ruse could be dangerous for two reasons. First of all, warning could be given to the murderer. Next, the information might not be obtained at the first effort.

Nevertheless, the dentist Miss Boston was searching for must, like all American dentists, have a plaque on the door. That removed all difficulties and would make it clear from the first moment. The search for the plaque began. Miss Boston took the left side of the street, and Sokes took the right. She went up the street and he went down. At the end of five minutes they met and exchanged a brief question.

"Well, Sokes?"

"Nothing. And you?"

"Nothing."

"Then?"

"Nevertheless, it was in Ontario Street that Elias Weston was seen for the last time. Why this mystery? Did you look carefully, Sokes?"

"Yes, I didn't pass any door without examining it."

The detective remained thoughtful. Suddenly she said:

"Sokes, go into a saloon, get the Chicago business telephone book, and look at the addresses on Ontario Street."

"Understood."

The Inspector disappeared and went down to Charing Place, where a saloon was filled with drinkers. Sokes ordered a glass of liquor and picked up the business telephone book. He leafed rapidly through the pages to the letter O. He found what he was looking for. The residents of Ontario Street took up two columns. He read them one by one. Suddenly his finger stopped under one of the names. He had just read:

Weld, dentist, 7 Ontario Str.

That was the dentist they were looking for! Back on the trail, finally!

274

He hurried to rejoin Miss Boston. The detective had at that moment stopped in front of an iron gate before a garden. In the shadows, they could see a two story house with a light in two windows.

"It's number seven, isn't it?" the detective asked when she saw her companion returning.

"Yes, but you already knew that?"

"No, I just discovered it while you were gone. The house is there, behind the iron fence."

"What are we going to do?"

"You're going down Ontario Street a few steps. I'm going to ring. As soon as I enter the house, you open the iron gate with the jimmy and go in with your gun drawn. Try to get into the house, if possible."

"Should I intervene?"

"That will depend on the circumstances. You'll judge for yourself. Only the danger will tell you what has to be done in case of an emergency."

"Good. The usual tactic, then."

"Perfect. I'm ringing, Sokes."

The muffled ring of the bell sounded in the distance somewhere in the house. There were some moments of silence. Was the house empty? Was someone going to open the door? The detective nervously asked herself that double question. Finally a door creaked. Miss Boston breathed with joy. Someone was coming to open.

IX. The Silent House Mystery

A stooped shadow went across the garden and came to the iron fence. As it advanced, Miss Boston managed to make it out more clearly. It was that of a rather old man wearing a little velvet skull cap and gold spectacles, behind which there shone little malicious and piercing, lively eyes. They held a kind of cold light, diabolical and enigmatic at the same time. With little measured steps, wrapped in a huge frock coat that the light evening wind made float around him, he approached the fence and carefully considered the visitor who was holding a handkerchief to her jaw.

"What do you want?" he asked in a brusque tone.

"Do I have the honor of addressing Dr. Wald?"

"Yes, what do you want with him?"

"I have a tooth that's making me suffer horribly, and…"

"It's too late to do anything."

"But I'm suffering considerably."

"I can't do anything."

"But Doctor…"

"Besides, I'm a dentist for men and not for women. Good evening."

And the little old bald man turned insolently on his heels and retraced his steps across the dark garden. Miss Boston saw him go up the steps, go into the house, and close the door behind him. Then there was silence again in Ontario Street. What did that conduct mean? Was the fellow suspicious? Or, rather, weren't they dealing with a gentle maniac? What was the meaning of that, a dentist who would treat only men? But that response was a gleam of light for the intelligent detective. Men! The five cadavers found were only masculine cadavers! Wasn't that point disturbing? All these thoughts had flashed through the detective's head like lightning. Now she no longer doubted that she was near a solution. She rapidly rejoined Sokes posted some steps from there in an obscure doorway.

"Back already?"

"I didn't go in."

"Why not?"

"This Weld, who, between parentheses, seems to me a questionable gentleman, claims he treats only men. He left me standing there, very uncivilly, in front of the fence."

"Then we must enter in spite of him?"

"That's what I came to tell you. Do you have on your security stockings?"

"No," Sokes said, "but I'm going to put them on."

He took from the inside pocket of his jacket a sort of flat leather case from which he took two rubber stockings. He attached them to his shoes with double fasteners. They stifled all sounds of footsteps. Thanks to that ingenious system, he could pass by like a shadow. Miss Boston had done the same and they both came silently up to the fence of Weld's house. With a flask taken from his kit, the Inspector let a few drops of oil fall on the hinges of the gate that he then opened with his jimmy. They were now in the garden. Slipping along the walls, they reached the house. The shutters of the ground floor were closed. The simplest thing for the detectives to do was go through the door and proceed with the housebreaking silently. That was the method Miss Boston adopted.

The door opened silently on its hinges and the detectives found themselves in a dark corridor. Miss Boston's electric torch helped her identify the location. The corridor was long and somewhat wide, with a tile floor of old fashioned blue and red tiles. At the end of the corridor there were wooden stair steps. There was no sound; a silence of death reigned in the house which seemed empty and abandoned.

"Where do we begin?" Sokes asked. "Do we go upstairs first, or investigate the lower floor first of all?"

"Downstairs first, Sokes."

The first door on the right Miss Boston pushed opened without difficulty. She found herself in a tidy and gloomy sitting room. It had old fashioned furniture and wasn't distinguished by anything in particular. Another door, probably leading to the operating room of this strange dentist for men only, was located at the back. That door, however, was locked. Just a pinch of Miss Boston's jimmy opened it. She wasn't mistaken. It was Wild's operating room. Aligned on a marble shelf were forceps and Weld's steel dental instruments.

"Hum!" Sokes said softly. "What's that unusual odor floating around here?"

An odor, acrid and sickly at the same time, filled the office. It wasn't the odor of a pharmacy but something to which the detective immediately gave Sokes the key.

"Nothing strange here. It's just the odor of blood."

The detective looked closely at the rug which was current colored, but in spite of that deep tone there were from place to place some stains of an even deeper color brought out here and there. Without saying a word, she went to a corner of the room and picked up the edge of the rug. Shining her electric torch on that part of the floor thus uncovered, she said to the Chief Inspector:

"Look at that!"

The floor planks were stained with big red coagulated pools which had sunk deeply into the wood.

"We're here," the detective observed. "We now know where the five cadavers came from."

"Then the five severed heads will very likely be found here," Sokes remarked.

"That remains to be seen, sir."

Miss Boston was glancing around the room as if searching for something.

Sokes noticed it and when he pointed that out to the detective, she replied:

"I wonder where the instrument of the crime is and how the heads could have been severed with that extraordinary cleanness. While we're waiting, Sokes, let's see how the cadavers could have been removed from the house."

Saying this, the detective tried to open a little low door that she had just discovered hidden by a curtain in a corner of the operating room. But it was firmly locked. Once again she was forced to use the jimmy. A whiff of cold, wet air hit her in the face. The electric torch showed her a subterranean passage into which worn stone stairs descended. Followed by Sokes, she started down them. At each step she slid in a coagulated pool of blood which indicated that this must have been the way the decapitated victims had been removed.

The detectives now found themselves in a cold, damp cellar, but that cellar was longer than it was wide. It contained all sorts of debris: boxes, barrels no longer used. Miss Boston, hoping to find either the severed heads or some other clue, examined them rapidly. She discovered nothing in them. The earth had deep impressions of tracks, showing the cadavers had been dragged through it. Following these tracks, Miss Boston reached another stairway where the traces of blood were much less apparent. Apparently, in the journey from the dental office to the cellar, the greater part of the cadavers' blood had finally drained out.

The detective climbed the stairs, opened the door, and saw sparkling before her a stretch of softly waving water bathed with the pale silver rays of the rising moon. A boat was attached to a post.

"What is that?" asked Sokes, surprised.

"That?" said the detective, "that's Lake Michigan and the boat there was used to transport the decapitated cadavers to Somerset, New London, Potbrod and Meg Strand."

And approaching the boat, she pointed out to the Chief Inspector the large reddish drops staining the bottom.

X. The Room of the Embalmed Heads

"We know enough for the present," Miss Boston observed. "Let's go back to the house. We may still have some interesting discoveries to make."

The two detectives re-entered the cellar and came out finally in the operating room through the little hidden door. Suddenly the detective stopped.

"Someone is walking above us," she said.

Sokes listened. Miss Boston was right. The sounds of steps, slow and measured, resonated on the floor of the upper room.

"That's very likely our lowlife of a dentist!" the Chief Inspector observed.

"Without a doubt," said the detective, "and that brings us back to the reality of things."

"Indeed. It's time to get to Weld, it seems to me."

"So let's go now to the upper floor," Miss Boson pronounced calmly.

"Good." Sokes answered. "I like jobs where you get to work immediately."

Their rubber soles let them reach the landing without the least creak of the steps revealing their presence in the silent house. Only one door opened from the landing. Miss Boston flashed her electric torch on the lock and saw that it was a padlock and the door was iron.

"An unusual and shady precaution," she murmured.

Opening that door without knowing what was behind it was certainly not to be considered for a single instant. So Miss Boston took the precaution of using her microphone which, applied against the iron door, told her there was only one person in the room. He was walking up and down muttering unintelligible words. Suddenly, she seized Sokes by the wrist and drew him after her down the stairs. She jumped down it with one leap rather than walked down. And opening the first door she came to in the corridor, she threw herself inside. It was just in time. The steps creaked under heavy steps. Someone was coming heavily down the stairs. Miss Boston had marvelously guessed that Weld was coming down, thanks to her microphone, and she wasn't mistaken. It was the old man coming down. He went directly to the door of the house, opened it, went to the garden, and opened the gate into Ontario Street. Like a shadow, Miss Boston followed him, step by step. When she saw him go down toward Texas Place, she re-entered the house and said to Sokes:

"We have at least a quarter of an hour ahead of us to search; quick, let's hurry."

She rapidly went back up to the second floor. The iron door was locked. With difficulty, and even fearing to break her steel jimmy, the detective managed to open it. With Sokes she went into the room where she had just breached its enigmatic and fearful secret. A lamp was burning on a round table and lit the vast room with a dim, gloomy and sepulchral glow. There were shelves along all the walls. On one there were stacked, in enormous disorder, dusty old books; on others there were arranged big glass jars, in which there was anatomical debris floating in alcohol: extraordinary specimens' of animal abnormality. Three skeletons with a brass ring in their head and suspended in this way by a hook, grimacing and laughing horribly with wide-open, toothless mouths, were in an obscure corner of the fantastic room.

"Brrr!" said Sokes. "Not much gaiety here, eh?"

"You can't always be laughing," retorted the detective.

She examined everything with a knowledgeable glance. She found no trace anywhere of the five heads missing from the cadavers. Where, then, were they? She drew near the table where the lamp was placed and examined the papers spread out in disorder, covered with febrile and labored writing. After glancing at it, the detective said to Sokes:

"That's just what I thought. This Weld is a terrible criminal, but not responsible. He has to be put quickly out of the way of doing any harm. This will be done tomorrow when we have found out how he decapitated the unfortunate men who fell under his hand."

"But the heads, where can they be?" demanded the Chief Inspector.

"I'm looking for them," Miss Boston answered.

Then she noticed some dirty material, undoubtedly hiding a door at the back of the room. She pushed it aside and saw she had guessed rightly. She opened the door but she drew back. Sokes, himself, couldn't hold back a cry of horror. The five severed heads were there!

Miss Boston examined this wreckage from the mysterious series of dark crimes. Symmetrically arranged on a cheap wooden table, the five severed heads were there, intact, rosy, fresh, as if they had been just cut off. What was this new mystery? One was smiling, the next impassive; this one had features in repose, tranquil and calm; that one had a face full of sadness; the last seemed to be sleeping a deep and natural sleep. They were all there, lined up by order of death:

1. Fisher;
2. Weston;
3. Goodby;

279

4. Atkinson;
5. Villars.

With a finger that didn't tremble, the courageous detective touched them. They were cold, glacial. The flesh wasn't at all collapsed and purple, as sometimes happens with cadavers. Here the flesh was firm with all the color of life and health. Only then did Miss Boston understand that the murderer had rediscovered the marvelous secret of the ancient people, the Egyptians, the secret of the conservation of the dead, the embalming of cadavers, a secret lost for at least 1000 years. But that discovery had cost the life of five men, whose heads were there on the wooden table, admirably embalmed.

Three minutes later the two detectives had decided to remain the rest of the night in the tragic house of the dentist, so as to be ready the next day for any eventuality. It was certainly easy to arrest Weld on the spot the moment he returned to the house. But one element was missing in the investigation so admirably directed by the illustrious detective. That element was valuable: the method by which the criminal carried out his miraculous and bloody decapitations.

XI. The Circular Guillotine

Nothing was less agreeable and enviable than the position of the detectives both cleverly and prudently hidden behind the sitting room armchairs. Listening to sounds in the house and street, they could verify that Weld returned about midnight. At least they guessed it by the creak of the iron fence gate that he opened abruptly. He closed the door of the house behind him and climbed immediately up to his strange laboratory on the second floor where they heard the heavy iron door close behind him. Miss Boston and Sokes heard him walking above their heads a part of the night, but at about 4 a.m. the nervous pacing ceased.

The two detectives then exchanged their impressions in a low voice.

"Decidedly," Sokes concluded, "this old fool is a scum of genius."

"That's too bad," the illustrious detective answered. "That man has discovered a beautiful and great thing. The heads he prepared with his chemical solution can remain in that state for hundreds of years. If that discovery is of little interest strictly from the point of view of cadavers, it is more so from the point of view of scientific studies. It's in that way that Weld's discovery has its value."

"But the scientific world risks losing it!"

"Why is that, Sokes?"

"Because first of all, we're going to be forced to arrest the criminal dentist."

"Yes, and so?"

"Next, he's insane."

"Those aren't sufficient reasons, Sokes. What if he left his discovery written down?"

"That would be different, but I don't very much believe that."

"On that point I share your opinion, but it won't be definite until after the examination of our man's papers."

"You admit that this is one of the most astonishing cases we've had to shed light on."

"Indeed, it's one of the strangest."

"It will be set down in the annals of our criminal investigations."

"I really think so, Sokes. And it gives me the opportunity to verify that almost all my deductions have largely been justified. I see that I hadn't guessed wrong in supposing that the dentist we couldn't find played a role in the crimes."

"Oh, with you, I knew we'd finally discover the truth."

Miss Boston cut short these compliments by taking out her watch and saying:

"Five o'clock, Sokes."

"Is that all?"

"Yes."

"The devil!"

"We have at least five more hours to wait."

"If it isn't more!"

"After our good luck tonight, that would really be bad luck, don't you think so?"

And silence fell on the sitting room where the two detectives were on stakeout.

At approximately 10 a.m., the entry doorbell rang. A step rapidly came down the stairs, and Miss Boston, having quickly gone to the sitting room window, saw that Weld was going to open the iron gate to a conservatively dressed gentleman. His face muscles, tight with pain, showed he was suffering.

She had only time to slip behind an armchair. The sitting room door had open to let Wald and his patient pass through.

"So," the dentist said in a high pitched, staccato voice, "are you in a great deal of pain?"

"A great deal, a lot, almost too much to bear it," the visitor answered.

"Good! Good! We're going to fix that, sir, radically, completely."

"I will be very indebted to you."

"Please come through here."

Weld opened his operating room door and with a gesture invited his patient to enter. The door closed. Miss Boston and Sokes with a bound came out of hiding.

"Be careful," said the detective. "It's a matter of not losing sight of the mad man."

With a little gimlet taken from her handbag, she pierced two imperceptible holes in the operating room door. Sokes looked through one, Miss Boston through the other. Walt had made his patient sit down in the mechanical chair used for dental work. Miss Boston noticed that a thumbscrew with a hook was placed level with the patient's shoulder. The patient sat down. Weld had him take off his false collar and thus uncover his neck. The visitor was in too much pain to notice how bizarre and strange this procedure was. He let himself be guided meekly. A diabolical smile passed over the Machiavellian dentist's lips.

He walked behind the patient and Miss Boston saw him take a circular knife out of the inside pocket of his frock coat. He placed the knife in the thumbscrew and the hook fixed to the chair. Then the detective understood the insane man's ingenious and terrible system. Attached at a fixed point, the knife sliced radically forward as soon as it was pulled backward. That's what explained the extraordinarily clean cut Miss Boston had noticed on all the cadavers.

But they had to act. The knife was already attached. The mad man was going to commit another crime. With a strong blow of her shoulder, the detective broke down the door and rushed toward the chair. She had moved like lightning. Alas! She wasn't fast enough. The mad man understood that an end to his bloody exploits had come. With a terrible gesture, he drew back the knife.

An enormous wave of blood gushed out, splashing Sokes, and a head came rolling to Miss Boston's feet, while Weld broke out in demented, savage, harsh laughter. A sixth victim had just been added to the list of Ontario Street decapitated heads.

Weld let himself be arrested without resistance, muttering meaningless words. An hour afterward, they locked him in the cell especially reserved for the insane at the Chicago Central Police Bureau. A special edition of *The Rapid* announced to the public that the famous and courageous detective had earned the $5,000 reward offered by the newspaper.

The mad man was locked up in an asylum where he remained. His confiscated papers were submitted to a scientific commission trying to find the secret genius of his diabolical invention. They have never yet found it. Will they ever?

THE ASSOCIATION OF RIFLERS

I. The Durham House Cadaver

The Chief Inspector of the Central Police Bureau had already been in his office an hour when a clerk told him the Chief wanted him immediately.

"What does he want?" he asked the office clerk. "A new case, probably," and he added, becoming truly in a bad mood: "As if I didn't already have enough investigations to carry on and finish!"

"I don't know exactly. I believe the Chief got a telephone call from 12th Avenue."

Arriving at the Chief's outer office, he went rapidly through it, knocked on the door and entered the Chief's office. The Honorable Mac Higgins was signing an enormous stack of papers spread out in front of him. With a vigorous scratch of the pen he was crossing out paragraphs from the sheets of paper.

He looked up at the Inspector's entry.

"Ah! It's you Sokes," he said.

"I'm here as you asked, sir."

"New case, Sokes."

"Where's that?"

"Around 12th Avenue at Durham House."

"All right, Chief. Should I go there?"

"Immediately, Sokes. They've just telephoned me. Get in touch with the 12th Avenue Police Chief. He's the one who telephoned."

"All right. Do you want to see the report, Chief?"

"Yes, if there's something in the case that seems complicated. If it's ordinary, no. Give it over to the coroner on duty."

"Understood."

The Inspector got his hat and coat and was immediately on his way by automobile. He arrived at 12th Avenue 11 a.m. He was glad to see his colleague already on the scene.

"I see they work fast at the Central Police Bureau."

"Oh! We're always in a hurry there. But what's it all about?"

"A murder at Durham house."

"Simple? Complicated?"

"Both at the same time. Come on. We're going to Durham House and you can see what it's all about."

A fine, freezing rain had been falling since dawn and made that part of New York perfectly gloomy. There were very few commercial establishments; mainly residences of retired, peaceful people from the tumult of the business world.

While walking, Sokes was told about how the crime was discovered.

"The building concierge told me," the 12th Avenue Commissioner said, "that the victim hadn't been seen in a week. Naturally people were worried, and, as usual, they came to inform me. I went to Durham House and had a locksmith open the door. The apartment was in rather bad shape. I found the victim in a room at the back with a rope around his neck and a bullet in his skull. That's the situation."

"That's all simple," Sokes observed, "but where's the complication?"

"In the fact that the gentleman had a bullet in his skull."

"But..."

"I understand you, sir. A bullet in the head is nothing extraordinary in an ordinary crime. Agreed. But here the cadaver had a bullet in the top of the skull."

"What?"

"That bullet was fired at him perpendicularly."

"I'd be very curious to see that," Sokes muttered.

"Nothing easier. We're coming to Durham House."

They turned to the left and were at the entrance of Durham House. Some curious neighbors were chatting and looking at the windows of the apartment where something had happened. Sokes and the Commissioner slipped into the house unnoticed and rapidly climbed the three floors where the unusually mysterious crime had been committed. Nothing there had been touched or moved in the initial investigation. The first room was scantily furnished with a cheap buffet, a round table, and three rush chairs. It seemed to be there the victim— Hop—ate his meals. In the wall to the left a little door opened onto a room transformed into a study. In the middle stood, still open, an American desk with papers scattered over it. To one side, stretched out full length on the bare, badly waxed floor, lay Hop's cadaver.

Sokes immediately examined it. It was the body of an old, thin and dried out fellow completely shaved, and whose eyebrow arches, deeply sunken, were bristling with a heavy tuff of white hair. His head was bald and in the middle a little black circular hole was hollowed out and there seemed to be powder burns around it. In addition a slender, solid rope was tight around his neck.

"So, what do you think?" the Commissioner asked Sokes.

The Chief Inspector simply said: "Hum!"

He walked around the room, examined each piece of furniture with the careful eyes of an experienced policeman. But he shook his head. Nothing revealed what he had so carefully looked for. He returned to the cadaver and tried again, even more minutely to see if he couldn't find any visible wounds on the victim.

"I understand the rope," the Commissioner said, "but what I don't understand very well is the bullet wound."

"Why is that?" Sokes asked.

"Because it's in a place where it's not very usual to find one in these sorts of cases."

"Indeed. Your remark is quite accurate. Hop was certainly surprised at his desk, because the chair turned over, not to one side, but backward, showing that the rope was thrown around his neck like a lasso. He then turned over. That was when the bullet hit him in the head."

"In that case," the Commissioner observed, "chance helped the criminal prodigiously."

"How's that?"

"Because the bullet hit the head full on and at that moment the head was far from immobile so as to allow the shooter to take aim with such accuracy. The wound was made in that spot by the greatest of luck."

"With no doubt," Sokes answered, "but what I can't explain is why they thought it necessary in that case to use the rope. The revolver was sufficient. That's an enigma. There's only one person capable of solving it."

"I can guess, sir," the Commissioner said. "You're talking about Miss Boston, aren't you? But would she look into the case?"

"We just have to ask her and that's what I'm going to do right now. What I have seen here will let me give her the first facts necessary as a basis of the investigation. If she accepts, we'll pass by to pick you up at the 12th Avenue Bureau. I think I'll be able to give you a firm answer after lunch."

The two policemen left the apartment and separated at the corner of Buffalo square, one going toward 12th Avenue, the other toward Savannah City, the domicile of the famous and unique female detective.

II. Some Strange Angles of the Case

"Sokes," Miss Boston exclaimed at the entrance of the Chief Inspector. "I'm delighted to see you. Did you come to invite me to lunch?"

"If you accept. I'd be glad to eat lunch with you,"

"I was going to invite you, sir."

"But there's something else."

"A criminal case, I'll bet."

"You've won your wager. Yes, it's a criminal case."

"Good. And you've come to ask me to go out on a case in such abominable weather as we're having? You know very well, Sokes, that I won't refuse. All right. Agreed. I'll do it. But first of all I must know what it's about. While we're waiting for Mary to say that lunch is ready, let's go into my study; you can bring me up on the case."

Sokes shook hands affectionately with the detective and followed her into the famous, simple study where all the daring and ingenious plans for criminal cases were worked out.

Comfortably installed in a deep, soft armchair, the detective fixed her cold, blue stare on the Chief Inspector and said simply:

"Well?"

"Here's what it's about. A man named Hop lived in Durham House."

"What profession?"

"I don't know but an examination of his papers showed us that his methods of existence weren't very clear, apparently. This Hop was murdered a week ago."

"How was that determined?"

"The concierge of the building hadn't seen him during that time. This morning she reported that to the 12th Avenue Police Station. The Commissioner opened the apartment and found Hop's cadaver in a kind of office. Having been given the case to investigate, I went to Durham House to look over the premises."

"And what did you find, Sokes?"

"Both a little and a lot."

"That means there's something in the case that escapes you."

"It's this: Hop was strangled and killed with a bullet to the top of the head."

"One of those two things is too much."

"That's what I thought also. The rope was enough without the revolver and vice-versa. There's exaggeration in the crime."

"In your opinion, Sokes, how was the victim killed?"

"He must have been surprised at his work desk, pulled backward by the rope thrown around his neck, and while he was being pulled backward, he was shot with a bullet to the cranium. That's how I think the murderer did it."

"Or the murderers," the detective corrected.

"Then you think there were several of them?"

"I presume that for a very simple reason."

"What reason?"

"That which prevents a man throwing a lasso from shooting a revolver at the same time. Therefore, Sokes, that's the only unusual thing in that case, at least according to what you've told me now. We'll see if there is still something else when we go Durham House this afternoon."

At that moment the maid opened the door of the study to announce that lunch was served. During an excellent meal, they discussed the Durham House crime, setting up probabilities without Miss Boston's having the opportunity to draw the least deduction from facts she herself had learned. At coffee, when Sokes had lit up a very good Havana cigar, she rose and said gaily:

"And now to work, sir."

Mindful of the terrible weather, she put on a raincoat and picking up her detective's kit, she took a cab with Sokes to the 12th Avenue police station. The Commissioner went with them to Durham House.

The first thing the detective did was interrogate the concierge. Nothing had let that woman suspect that a tragedy was taking place in the building. No noise, no outcry had disturbed the silence. As for that Hop, she gave Miss Boston some details that convinced the detective that the victim must have had a shady, or at least suspicious, life. Hop went out only in the evening and often was visited by people of dubious appearance, unusual acquaintances, since he claimed to be a businessman. All that didn't give the detective any precise clue concerning the tragedy itself. She still had to visit and carefully examine Hop's apartment. She went up with Sokes and the Commissioner.

The detective first examined the dark little antechamber.

"You had to have the door opened by a locksmith?"

The Commissioner confirmed the information. Miss Boston immediately pointed out a key on the inside which remained on a second lock placed a little higher than the one broken by the locksmith.

"Look," she said. "That proves that the door was locked from the inside and consequently there was one of two things: either Hop killed himself or the murderers left by another door."

But the detective began immediately to perform a practical demonstration. She took a little steel gimlet out of her kit and drilled into the wood of the door on the inside of the antechamber. Suddenly the gimlet stopped and hit something making a shrill sound. She didn't continue, but went to the other side of the door and began the same operation again on the wood panel and once again the gimlet was stopped.

"Oh! Oh!" Sokes said. "What does that mean?"

"It's an iron door masked by two wooden panels, that's all. And that proves that Hop was very interested in staying locked in his apartment. Hop was, without a doubt, murdered. After the murder, the killers had to leave the apartment. How? By the door? No, because the door was locked. By the windows? No, because the windows were locked. We then find ourselves faced with another problem. Its solution must be here. We're going to look for it immediately."

III. Obscurity for Sokes; Clarity for Miss Boston

She opened the door of Hop's workroom and entered cautiously. The cadaver was still stretched out in the same position, his shoulders on the floor, his arms crossed with the rope drawn tightly around his neck, marked with a violet circle. Miss Boston leaned over him and examined him with the same particular care that she brought even to the most insignificant investigations. That lasted a few minutes. She then looked at the wound in the cranium and shook her head with a look of profound doubt. When this was done, she went on to the slender rope. She took it from around the cadaver's neck and pulling on it with all her strength, tried its resistance. The rope didn't move.

"What do you say about that rope, gentlemen?" Miss Boston asked the two policemen accompanying her.

"Nothing," Sokes said, "except it was thrown around Hop's neck with a great deal of ability."

"Exactly," said the detective.

"What do you mean?"

"That the rope was thrown with too much ability for two reasons: first of all, Hop must have heard his murderers coming."

"All right, but the second?"

"The rope is very long."

The tone in which the illustrious detective said these last words convinced the two questioning her that she had found something unusually shady and equivocal. What did that mean? Was the young woman about to discover clues that had escaped them, men first of all, detectives next? But Miss Boston continued her careful investigation.

"It's not only the rope that seems strange to me," she said. "The location of Hop's wound does also."

"That struck me too. And I even made that observation this morning at my first visit," Sokes said.

"And what did you suppose?"

"I supposed that the revolver was fired at Hop just as the rope was pulling him backward."

"Doubly impossible!" the detective cut him short.

"Agreed," retorted Sokes, "but what else is there?"

Without saying a word, the detective righted the chair turned over beside the desk. Hop was sitting on that chair at the time of the criminal attack. In her turn, Miss Boston sat down, leaned over as if writing and suddenly, in a sharp and deliberate movement, she lifted her head. She stared at the ceiling and there were some moments of silence, during which Sokes renewed his question:

"So, what was it?"

She slowly lifted her finger and pointed at the decorative plaster rose in the middle of the ceiling.

"It was there," she said in a tone full of certainty.

Sokes and the Commissioner raised their heads, not without some surprise. Without saying a word, the detective got up.

"Don't you see," she finally said, in a voice where there was both irony and impatience. "Get on the chair and look."

The Chief Inspector took the chair and stood on it. For a moment he shrugged his shoulders, trying to see the invisible thing the detective was pointing out to him.

"Do you see?" she asked.

"I don't see very much," said Sokes. "It's a plaster rose, that's all."

"No point in insisting," answered the young woman, not without some bad humor. "Get down."

"You didn't see anything unusual there," she continued, "and nevertheless that's the key to the problem, the solution to the enigma. And to show you more clearly, I'm going to demonstrate to you how Hop was murdered."

Miss Boston leaned over the cadaver and detached the cord which had been used to strangle him. She rolled it up and walked to the door.

"What do you want me to do?" the Chief Inspector asked.

"Nothing, Sokes. You're going to sit down in front of the desk and write it doesn't matter what, whatever you like, whatever comes into your head. I ask you to take that seriously and not raise your head whatever happens."

She opened the door and left.

The Chief Inspector sat down at the desk, took a piece of paper, and after having dipped his pen in the little lead ink well, began to write:

REPORT DRAWN UP BY CHIEF INSPECTOR SOKES
On the police investigation of the Durham House crime.

Following the orders received from the Chief of the Central Police Bureau, Inspector Sokes went today at 11 a.m. to the building having the number 12 Durham House...

Suddenly, something passed in front of the policeman's eyes; the pen fell from his hands; he felt something tighten around his throat and he was lifted off the floor. While struggling, his foot struck the chair, which turned over. He let out a stifled cry, brought his hands to his neck, but at the same instant, the pressure ceased. Sokes, a little short of breath but not less bewildered, was back on his feet. He looked up and suddenly, amazed, stepped back. From the plaster rose in the ceiling a rope had been let down and that rope with a rather large loop had been wrapped around his neck above the work table. A hole had been drilled through one of the folds of the plaster and through that hole the rope had been let down over Hop's neck. He had been lifted off the ground and hauled up toward the ceiling while he was fighting with furious energy. When it reached the ceiling, the body had been stopped near the hole in the rosacea. A shot had been fired through this hole, putting a bullet in the cranium. That's what explained the powder burns around the bullet hole.

Sokes hadn't yet gotten over his amazement when Miss Boston came back into the apartment of the crime. Her charming face was then lit by a slight smile.

"Well, Mr. Sokes, do you now understand?"

"And how!" The Chief Inspector exclaimed. "I thought I was strangled for real. Where were you?"

"In the apartment above. What I wanted to make you especially notice in the plastic rose was the hole that was drilled with rare ability, since not a grain of plaster fell here on the floor. I immediately understood that hole must play a role in the enigma of the tragedy we're investigating here. Since the murderers didn't come into the apartment to commit their crime, they then had to remain outside. That's naïve reasoning, but the only possible one in the present circumstances. On the other hand, we found unusual wounds. The hole in the plaster rose could explain all that."

"I understood that when I was knocked out of my chair. But tell me, what did you find upstairs?"

"Nothing. An empty apartment and a hole in the floor."

"That's not much."

"That's what I think. So let's go look for something to satisfy our investigation. We're faced with a bizarre crime, carried out in unusual circumstances. We have a duty to solve one or the other. Let's go, Sokes. To work."

IV. Forgotten Papers about Hop and his Clients

The famous detective began the investigation with the desk of the murdered man. She took out all the papers that had been carefully and methodically arranged. There was a rather large quantity of letters, then sheets of calculations. The detective finally got to a little bundle of nine slips of paper concisely labeled.

1. Share of Bobby..$8,000
2. Share of Winter... $400
3. Share of Pad..Nothing
4. Share of 22X8..$4,780
5. Share of Fred...$3,279
6. Share of Allans..$4,009
7. Share of Comyn..$208
8. Share of Fif..$18
9. Share of Boy...$407

Reading that made her search further. From time to time she put a paper aside or slid it into her handbag. Sokes followed her work. He knew the detective had put her hand on sufficiently interesting clues to hold his total attention, so he was very careful not to disturb her. That lasted about an hour. Finally all the papers were examined and classified. Miss Boston stood up, thought a moment, and went to the entry door. She examined the door, scrutinized the lock and after several minutes came back into the work room. She sat down comfortably at the desk and spoke with a voice having assurance in every word. Sokes was sure she had acquired proofs of all she was to put forward.

"Gentlemen, please give me your attention for a moment. In a few words I'll tell you what happened here in this room a week ago, the circumstances of the tragedy, its causes and its origins. The man here was called Hop by the concierge. His real name is Butler and it was under that name that he was condemned to ten years at hard labor in St. Louis. He paid for those ten years of imprisonment for theft and armed robbery. When he left prison he took the name

Hop, the name under which we know him. In prison he met someone named Bobby."

"Dangerous fellow, that Bobby!" the Chief Inspector observed.

"Indeed," Miss Boston continued, "we know something about that, Mr. Sokes, because we had to deal with this fellow several years ago in the State of Wisconsin. At the time of his arrest, Bobby was head of a gang from New Orleans called the Association of Riflers."

"Amusing name!"

"A symbolic name mostly, since these fellows operated with special guns called rifles. But that's not what interested me in Hop's letters and documents. He and Bobby were released from hard labor at almost the same time. They had probably found mutual interests, because they weren't long in putting the Association of Riflers back together. Bobby was strong, daring, but a real brute, in a word, but without any formal education. Hop, on the contrary, with a weaker constitution, and older, was cunning and ingenious. They got together. One set up the jobs that the other carried out. Little by little the Association of Riflers regained its former importance and began regularly to strike merchants, bankers, everyone who was a prey, if not easy, at least lucrative. That was how Hop became bookkeeper of the group, in charge of doling out to each one his exact share of the plunder from the jobs. Four years ago the band emigrated from St. Louis to New York and that's where they've been operating ever since."

"Curious, very curious, that."

"There's more, Sokes."

"What? About the crime?"

"Exactly. Why was Hop murdered? That's what I can't say exactly. But I assume he was the victim of one or two members if the Association of Riflers who thought their share too small and they wanted to avoid in the future this disagreement so prejudicial to their financial interests. But however that may be, it's possible to reconstitute the diverse phases of the tragedy which was played out here. A week ago, those thinking of getting rid of Hop at first tried to break through the entry door of the apartment. When I say they tried to break in through the door, I'm not making a supposition. On the contrary, I'm stating a fact. The reason for that is very simple. That's because I found in the door traces of the wrench and the crowbar they used."

"In that case," said Sokes, "that explains everything."

"I'm continuing. They saw Hop had taken his precautions and that their tools broke like glass on the iron door so ingeniously hidden. They gave up, at least from that direction. That's when the idea of working in another way germinated in their heads. The apartment above Hop's was empty. They got into it; they broke a hole in the floor so as to come out at the plaster rose and there they patiently bided their time. When they saw Hop sitting at his desk, they let down their noose; they tightened it, and pulled it up to the ceiling. There, they shot him in the head. The drama has no other explanation."

"Marvelous! We should have thought about it more."

"But that's not all. We still have to put our hands on the Association of Riflers. Unfortunately the trail ends there. I know absolutely nothing about where that gang holes up."

"Then what's to be done?"

"Set up a trap, Sokes."

"Where?"

"Here."

"In the house itself?"

"Exactly."

"I can't understand the reason."

"If, as I have good reasons to suppose, Hop was killed without the knowledge of the Association of Riflers, it's certain that the chief, Bobby, will be concerned about his bookkeeper. He'll send to Durham House for news or he'll come himself."

"So much the better. We'll catch him in the act."

"Before everything else, it's a matter of setting up the trap prudently, so that nothing can make it fall apart."

"Obviously. But how?"

"You're going to stay here in the apartment behind the door. If someone knocks, I'll leave it to your good judgment and your knowledge of the situation to know what to decide. I'll go down into the street. I'll watch the entry of the house and the surroundings."

The Commissioner from the 12th Avenue precinct interrupted.

"And me," he asked, "what role are you giving me in all this?"

"None, sir."

"What's that? None?"

"Yes, you'll wait to hear from us at your office. For an investigation of this kind, one detective is enough, two are adequate, but three are too many."

"In that case, I'll leave you, Miss. And good luck! Try to catch those fellows!"

"We'll do what we can," the courageous young woman said gaily.

V. The Female Detective's Suppositions are Vindicated

When he had left, Miss Boston said to Sokes:

"You understand, sir, the delicate and dangerous ground we're walking on. So I don't need to insist. It's almost dark and the time seems right for the cautious visits we're expecting. If, for whatever reason you don't open the door when someone knocks, begin shadowing the visitor immediately. On my side, I'll catch him in the street. I'm going to take advantage of my forced stay there to transform myself somewhat. You understand that I can't take my post in the street dressed as I am."

293

The detective took various make-up articles out of her handbag. In the clink of an eye she had transformed herself into an old woman, dressed in a cheap waterproof overcoat. She had deep wrinkles and was unrecognizable. Sokes, for his part, had been busy and when she returned she found herself facing one of those loiterers in the street who have a lewd expression, a cap pulled down on his head, smoking a little wooden pipe, held cynically in the corner of his mouth. He looked as if he was used to little glasses of gin and whisky from saloons and bars.

"You are perfectly filthy, Mr. Sokes," she told him, laughing.

And he in the same tone answered:

"You couldn't give me a more touching compliment. Besides, in your case, you're marvelously disguised."

The job was done. After new and last suggestions to Sokes, the courageous young woman slipped out of the apartment in silence, and cleverly hiding, went down the building stairs. She came without difficulty to the street. It was still getting dark. The rain hadn't stopped and filled the deserted street. In the distance rare passersby appeared like silhouettes hardly visible in the mist.

The detective took up her position in the corner of a door facing the house of the crime. She crouched against the door shutter, blending in, almost disappearing into the half light of the corridor. In that place she was exposed to the wind and rain, but what did that matter?

The essential thing at that moment for Miss Boston was to have a good observation post, and she had one. Nothing else was important.

She looked at the time. It was almost 5 p.m. The lamps were already being illuminated in the windows of the neighboring houses. Evening silence enveloped the street. An hour passed. From time to time, busy passersby hurried past the house, cabs went down either in the direction of East River or that of Trafalgar Station. The detective's eyes, on the lookout, pierced the darkness, probed the least shadows. She suddenly saw two dark bent-over forms turn the corner of Terlington Street. The forms were walking rapidly, but what made them particularly suspicious to Miss Boston was the care they took to look around the area.

"Could those be my fellows?" she wondered.

She was soon convinced. The two men went down the sidewalk of the crime building. At the entry door, with a sudden and rapid movement they disappeared inside.

"I wasn't mistaken," Miss Boston told herself. It was evident they had certainly not come without some relationship to Hop and the Association of Riflers. What? That's what Sokes might learn up there and also what shadowing them after they left might find out. Miss Boston had only to wait until they came out, and patiently she waited. During that time the two suspicious men went up to Hop's apartment. In front of the door they stopped and listened.

"Is he at home, Bobby?" one of them asked his companion.

And Bobby answered: "There's no sound inside, Pad."

"Hum! That's unusual. Knock then, Bobby."

Bobby hit the door and then he gave three other soft knocks slightly spaced. That was probably a signal agreed on between the Chief of the Association of Riflers and his bookkeeper. That knock had no answer.

"Knock again, Bobby," said Pad.

The signal was given a second time, but with no more result.

"What could have happened?" asked Bobby. "Could Hop be dead?"

"We'll find out," said Pad.

"But what if he's left?"

"Left? Where to? Why?"

"With our cash!"

"No danger," said Bobby in an affirmative voice. "Hop's an honest boy."

Sokes, who was listening attentively behind the door to that conversation, couldn't keep from smiling at that character reference to a thief by his accomplice.

"I think we should go in," said Pad. "At least that way we'll know what we're dealing with."

"You're right. Do you have the little tools with you?"

"Here's the lock pick."

"Good. Go ahead then. I'll stand watch at the stairs."

Sokes heard the thief slide the lock pick into the door lock and operate the pick. The door suddenly creaked, but the lock didn't move. Pad continued to work but obviously the unusual resistance of the door tired him and intrigued him at the same time.

"Bobby," he suddenly said, "we can't get in. The door is locked on the inside."

"In that case, that means Hop is in the apartment. Why doesn't he answer?"

"Do you want to tell him to?"

Bobby leaned over the lock and through the opening yelled:

"Hop, open up. It's me, Bobby."

Still silence. Seeing all his efforts were useless, Bobby said:

"We'd better get back to the barn. We'll consult with the Rifles' members as to what to do. Has Hop skipped out on us? Or have the detectives gotten involved?"

Sokes heard the stairs creak under the thieves' footsteps. When the sound was far enough away for him to be sure they had gone down at least one floor, he gently opened the apartment door and slipped out himself into the stairway. He saw the two thieves slipping out ahead of him. He shadowed them. A moment later he was in the street, looking for Miss Boston. A few steps from him he saw an old woman walking along painfully, her shoulders stooped under the rain. That old woman was Miss Boston who was shadowing them. Sokes hurried to join her and in a few words informed her of the conversation at Hop's door.

The detective smiled:

"Then I was right," she said to the Chief Inspector. "The Association of Riflers' members are totally ignorant of the bookkeeper's death. Bobby's visit tells us that. As for the rest, we knew that from examining Hop's papers. We've learned only one thing. The band is holed up in a barn."

"Yes," said Sokes, "but where?"

"We'll find out by following them."

VI. The Milpont Barn

Bobby and Pad were some distance in front of the two detectives. They were talking excitedly in a low voice, but the distance made hearing them impossible. The important thing at the moment was not to lose sight of them. At the end of Terlington Street they turned into President Lincoln Ban and stopped at the West New York electric tramway station. Miss Boston thought it useful to separate from Sokes, who would reach the office by the left, while she would get there by the right. Sokes arrived at the tramway station two minutes later, at almost the same time as, others would think, an old woman.

Miss Boston was delighted to see her plan carried out with such precision. The trail seemed to lead directly to the hideout of the Association of Riflers. The tramway was one of those electric lines which leave from the center of New York and go toward the outskirts. The detective now understood why the robbers had taken that line. The barn they spoke of wasn't fictitious. It must be located in the outskirts at the tramway terminal. Hearing Bobby buy two tickets for Milpont, the detectives did the same. The two thieves were sitting in a corner continuing their conversation begun at Durham House.

The trip seemed short to Miss Boston. She and Sokes were the last to get off the tramway. They found themselves in a desolate area of the deserted countryside. Here and there, could be seen some cottages without lights, leafless trees bent over by the wind, while the slow, monotonous rain continued.

As soon as they got off the tramway, Bobby and Pad immediately started down the road known as Dirk Ban, leading to the open country. Their shoulders bent under the heavy rain, they walked rapidly. This time they must have felt themselves absolutely secure, since they didn't turn around once during the walk. The detectives slid behind the trees planted along the road. Fortunately the darkness was profound, allowing them to hide. Caution was essential.

The journey was rather long. At the end of a quarter of an hour, the two thieves left Dirk Ban to enter a little road going across the countryside. The narrow and muddy path was lined with dark hedgerows. The detectives continued their shadowing behind that shelter. They left it to go down a little road running alongside a stream that they crossed on a wooden bridge. Finally they arrived in the middle of a field. There in the darkness stood the black framework of a big barn where there were no lights. The thieves went toward it, circled it and disappeared. Shadowing had ended. The prey was in the trap.

"Finally," Sokes said, "we've got them. Not without some trouble; I'm drenched."

"And so am I!"

They stopped behind a small clump of stunted trees, as much waiting for events as drawing up plans of execution. It was then near 8 p.m.

"What are we going to do," Sokes asked, "enter the barn?"

"I would be very tempted," responded the courageous young woman, "but…"

"But what?"

"I wonder if all the members of the criminal association are really there in the barn at this hour."

"If they aren't would that be an obstacle? What are you afraid of?"

"That we would be surprised by the arrival of some unexpected member we didn't see coming. If that fellow raised the alarm, the whole band would take flight."

"That's true."

"We can't in any fashion operate just the two of us alone. They have a large number and in case of resistance on their part, we would be outnumbered. It would be disastrous. In this circumstance we have to operate differently."

"Do you have a plan?"

"Yes, we're going to wait here a little while longer. When it's late enough we're going to examine the hideout of the Association of Riflers. What we do later will depend on that examination. What do you say?"

"We couldn't act more reasonably."

"In that case, Sokes, let's wait."

At that moment, and as if to prove the illustrious detective right, they heard the dull, soft sound of footsteps in the distance. Sokes listened and looked carefully, but could distinguish absolutely nothing in the darkness.

Miss Boston said:

"That's someone coming across the wooden bridge of the stream."

A shadow was now approaching with rapid footsteps, moving in a straight line toward the silent barn. That alert was renewed three times, bringing seven visitors to the mysterious hideout of the criminal association. When the last one had passed by, Miss Boston said:

"I think the band must be complete this time and we can begin our operation."

"I await your orders," the Chief Inspector said.

And they slipped through the shadows.

VII. Worries of the Association of Riflers

The barn formed a large quadrangle and in the left side of the clay and straw wall there was a wide two-door opening for wagons. That door was broken into pieces and the wood debris lay on the threshold. Sokes was at first somewhat surprised. Why was the access to the barn not better defended? Why leave it open in this way to the wind and to the curiosity of the first passerby tempted to enter? Did the Association of Riflers then have nothing to hide? Miss Boston, on the contrary, immediately understood the ingenious ruse of the thieves. By leaving that door in ruins, didn't they remove all suspicion of the barn? Who would ever think that shanty without a door, beaten by the wind and rain, abandoned in the middle of the countryside, would be used as shelter for criminals. Nobody, certainly. Therefore it was well thought out.

The detectives slipped into the barn. The floor was made of hard dirt. But in certain places, rain coming in between the spaces of the boards in the walls, had transformed the soil into a muddy marsh. All the downstairs of the barn was empty. On the walls there were rotting cribs for the animals that had been kept there in the past. Here and there lay stacks of straw transformed into true dung. No trace of the smallest trap door. Where, then, did the criminals meet? Miss Boston examined with the greatest care all the recesses of the barn and she was forced to admit that the retreat had been very cleverly hidden. It had to be found, but how?

The detective suddenly pulled Sokes by the arm and made him crouch flat on his stomach behind a stack of fetid straw. A shadow had just entered the barn. It was a very tall man, shaking off the water which had drenched him. He went to a corner of the barn and whistled in an unusual way. There was immediately a square of light in the ceiling of the old ruin. A trap door slid back and a face leaned over the edge. A voice asked:

"Rifler?"

"Yes," answered the man who had just whistled.

"Who is it?" asked the voice from the ceiling.

"Comyn."

At this name, the man leaning over the trap door answered:

"All right. Come up."

A rope ladder was thrown out of the trap door. Comyn grabbed it and rapidly ascended the steps.

"We were searching on the ground," the detective said to her companion, "and our birds' nest was in the air."

"What are we going to do now?"

"Just find out what's happening up above. Do you see that rafter? Thanks to gymnastics and your help, I'm going to climb to it and stay suspended there to find out what's happening in the loft."

"That's a position that's going to tire you out."

"Oh! I've known lots of others in dangerous moments, Sokes."

The detective did as she had said. She stood on Sokes' shoulders and thanks to using her arms in a way that would certainly have made her the envy of a professional acrobat, she climbed to the central rafter of the barn. She now could touch the ceiling of the first floor of the barn and could hear perfectly all that went on above her head. The sound, however, came to her muffled, because the upper floor of the barn must have been covered with wool cloth or a rug. The robbers had taken every precaution. There must have been a number of them because the sound of their voices crisscrossed in dull confusion. The detective gathered that the mysterious absence of Hop, the murder victim of Durham House, was the subject of all the conversations. Finally, Bobby's voice dominated all the others and he said:

"I must tell the Association what I learned today relative to the disappearance of our bookkeeper."

"Where is he?"

"What's happened to him?"

"Let the Chief talk!"

"Speak Bobby."

All the interruptions stopped at the same time in every corner of the loft. When there was quiet, Bobby continued where he had left off.

"I went to Durham House today," he said. "I knocked several times. I called and Hop didn't answer."

A voice said: "He might not have been home."

Bobby answered: "Hop was certainly at home because the interior lock on the door was set."

"Then he's dead!" another member exclaimed.

Again there was uproar of cries and exclamations. Bobby had trouble establishing silence. When he had done so, he said:

"It's because the circumstances of Hop's disappearance are so unusual, I thought I should warn the Association. Because Hop has our interests in his hand, I ask the Association what should be done in these circumstances."

"We must get into the apartment."

"I tried," Bobby said. "It can't be done because of the lock on the inside."

There was silence. The thieves saw that they had reached an impasse without seeing the possibility of a way out. There was confused discussion. Miss Boston was listening with great attention when suddenly the trap door in the ceiling opened. A face leaned out and that face saw Miss Boston. There was an immediate alarm. Without losing a moment, the detective let herself drop down to the floor and cried out to Sokes.

"Get out!"

They both made a dash toward the barn door and ran into the night. They ran at breakneck speed through the rain and the mud in the direction of the river bridge. Behind them the rope ladder had been lowered and five or six thieves, revolvers in their hands, had rushed down. They ran after the detectives and several shots were fired. But it was in vain. In that darkness, pursuit was impossible. Besides, Miss Boston and Sokes had several minutes head start on them. Those several minutes put them out of danger. But the warning given to the Association of Riflers was a more serious thing for them.

VIII. The Two Fake Telegrams

Without stopping, the two detectives had run straight to the tramway station that had taken them to Milpont. At exactly that moment, a tram was leaving for New York. Miss Boston and Sokes hurried to jump on it and didn't breathe easy until the tram was moving at full speed toward Percy Avenue.

"We just barely escaped," Sokes said.

"Fortunately for us, unfortunately for our investigation," said the famous detective. "I don't know how we're going to repair all that."

"Don't you intend to do anything tonight against the Association of Riflers?"

"I think it would be useless. The band must have taken flight after the alert."

"Do you think we were recognized?"

"I know absolutely nothing about that, Sokes, and I hope not, with all my heart. But even if we weren't recognized, the group has easily guessed that their hideout is in peril. As for the rest, I think we would be very wise to put the case off until tomorrow. I have an idea that the Association will try something around Durham House, to work out the enigma of Hop's disappearance."

The rest of the tramway trip passed in silence. The two detectives were evaluating, each in their own way, the different chances there were now to put their hands again on the Association of Rifles. To tell the truth, the chances now

301

appeared to Sokes to be smaller and smaller. He no longer had confidence except in the genius of the illustrious detective and in luck. On her side, Miss Boston was mentally constructing the scaffolding of a plan that would end in the capture en masse of the group.

At the MacKinley Station, they separated. Miss Boston told Sokes to wait to hear from her before doing anything whatsoever. The detective had her plan, and she intended to put it into effect to the end.

All the following day, Miss Boston traced the Association from clue to clue. With admirable deduction which wasn't once wrong during all her laborious research, she was able, almost step by step, to follow across Chelsea, the trace of four of the criminals, those named Fif, Boy, Fred, and Allans. The others escaped her. Her investigation showed them to her in certain places but they disappeared in others so that their trail necessarily remained incomplete.

It was thus that, little by little, but surely and inflexibly, the circle of the detective's deduction closed around a shady cabaret in Tree Point Street, in lower Chelsea, in the area of the Hudson River, the usual rendezvous of the most unmitigated bandits in the Union. It was there she must set up a raid. She telephoned the Central Police Bureau to tell them to have a squad of 15 policemen ready to raid, in the middle of the night, the Tree Point Street saloon. That done, Miss Boston intended to go by to see Sokes, have dinner with him, and to wait there until time for the raid. Nevertheless she first went by her apartment in Savannah City to get her necessary disguises and a spare revolver.

"A telegram for you, Miss," said the concierge as she passed by her lodge.

The detective opened it. It contained only one line:

Come urgently to Milpont barn

"What can that mean?" The young woman wondered.

She turned over the telegram, examined it. That seemed seriously suspicious and shady to her. How could Sokes have sent a telegram? They had agreed that he would wait for the detective's instructions. And that agreed on, how could he have set a meeting for the barn at Milpont, where he had nothing to do? Decidedly, the thing was so dubious it jumped out at her. Miss Boston checked the telegram's point of departure. It was sent from Milpont. This time, she was no longer in doubt. The telegram was false and a trap was being set for her.

The detective went up to her apartment hurriedly, picked up what she needed and came back down. She took a hansom cab, which in a few minutes set her down in the center of New York, at the porch in front of the white marble Central Police Bureau. She went directly to Sokes' office.

The clerk on duty asked:

"Are you looking for the Chief Inspector, Miss?"

"Certainly, but why do you ask, John"

"But, he left a half hour ago—after getting a telegram from you."

The detective frowned. It now appeared clear to her that the Association of Riflers had used the same stratagem on Sokes they had tried to use on the detective. Unfortunately Sokes seemed to have let himself be caught in that criminal ruse.

"Do you know," the detective asked the office clerk, "where the telegram Mr. Sokes received set the rendezvous?"

"Then it wasn't you who sent it?"

"No, I can bet right now that's a plot. But answer me, where was the meeting?"

"I don't know, Miss, but it seems to me Mr. Sokes left the telegram on the desk in his office."

In his office, she went immediately to his desk. The clerk had told the truth. The telegram was there. She read:

Sokes Central Police Bureau, New York
Come urgently, Milpont barn.
Miss Boston

Now there was no doubt possible. The same hand had drawn up the two telegrams. The place of the rendezvous clearly showed that the Association of Riflers had laid a trap which Sokes had fallen into. The danger was pressing. Immediate action was needed to keep the Chief Inspector from falling into the trap laid for him. Miss Boston went immediately to the Bureau Chief, told him the situation quickly in a few words, and got permission to take the squad of 15 policemen with her to Milpont. Five minutes later she left with the men piled into two automobiles, speeding toward the suburbs.

Twilight had fallen and enveloped the countryside with its gray fog. That obscurity wasn't against Miss Boston's plans. She preferred to arrive unseen by the men in the barn at Milpont. That weather at the end of a gloomy day suited her marvelously.

The trip ended without incident. The automobiles stopped on the road some hundred meters from the barn. Three policemen stayed to guard the automobiles. The dozen others, silently, single-file, from tree to tree, from bush to bush, slipped behind Miss Boston, who, courageous and daring, as always, had taken the head of the police column when they stopped.

The heavy shape of the barn, without lights, could be seen in the distance. Not the slightest noise, There was complete silence. Nothing. Wind. Rain. Night. They had not seen the least trace of Inspector Sokes. What had happened to him? Had he already arrived? A double enigmatic and mysterious question.

The head of the police squad asked Miss Boston for instructions.

"How do we go in, Miss? By force?"

"No, sir, cautiously at first."

"That means we're going to surround the barn?"

"Exactly!"

"And then?"

"I'll go in first alone. At the first gunshot, come in, weapons drawn, shoot everything that can be brought down. We'll see after that."

In a low voice, the squad leader communicated his orders to the men, and still in the most profound silence they deployed in a half circle to surround the barn. Miss Boston, herself, alone, slipped ahead. Softly, almost creeping, she reached the barn. Something strange. The door, that same door she had seen demolished, in pieces, was upright now, firm and solid. That put her on guard. She examined it and heard vague movements on the inside, sounds of muffled voices, footsteps on the dirt floor. There was no question of opening the door. The alarm would have been immediately raised. Before going into action, Miss Boston wanted to know exactly what was happening inside the barn. The barn walls were made of straw and plaster. Miss Boston took a knife from her handbag and, dug out a piece of plaster with the point. A glimmer of light came through the opening. Miss Boston looked inside. What she saw made her draw back in horror. A tragic spectacle met her sight.

Sokes had fallen into the trap set by the Association. How did that happen? It was not until later, in the course of the investigation of the case, that the illustrious detective found out. The criminals had seized him, gagged him and tied him up with a strong rope. Thus, totally immobilized, the unfortunate Inspector had been hung, head downward, from the central rafter on the ground floor of the barn. The criminal band surrounded him, laughing. In the first row, a revolver in each hand, was Bobby.

Miss Boston knew she had to act. She ordered the agents to break through the door and she herself would be the first to enter. But, alas, the door was solid. The detectives redoubled their efforts. But the noise of the attack had alerted the Association of the police's arrival.

Bobby yelled: "Those are the cops! Let's save our skins, but first let's get rid of this damned Inspector."

"Kill him! Kill him!" screamed the band.

"Hurry! Hurry!" cried the detective to the policemen.

The door was cracking under the strong battering of the policemen. At the same time a formidable salvo of shots rang out. All the Association had just fired into Sokes' suspended body.

"Alas! Too late," cried out the great detective.

The policemen redoubled their efforts. A new salvo of shots rang out among mad, savage shouts. The door split open, demolished, flying into pieces. The policemen rushed into the barn. One of the criminals turned out the lamp lighting the tragic scene and the terrible battle, the ferocious fight, took place in the shadows. Shots were fired from right and left, followed by cries of pain.

"Get some light! Get some light!" cried out the great detective.

There was suddenly a spark of flames. A clump of straw had just caught fire in a corner of the barn. The flame lit up the field of carnage and showed that the policemen were masters of the terrain. A stray shot had cut the rope suspending Sokes from the central rafter. He had tumbled to the ground, head first. Their attentions to him were useless. The Inspector's skull had been fractured in the fall and a dozen bullets had hit his body. Sokes was dead.

The policemen examined the criminals. Four of them were stretched out on the ground, wounded or dead. The others had disappeared, taking advantage of the darkness and the tumult. There were pools of blood everywhere, stiff and convulsed bodies. In addition, five policemen had fallen, victims of their duty.

Sokes was placed in one of the automobiles left on the road; the other victims were placed in the second. The sad cortege returned to New York, arriving at the Central Police Bureau in the middle of the night.

As for the members of the Association, the head of the police squad drew up this list:

Bobby: dead
Winter: dead
Pad: wounded, two bullets in the head and shoulder
Fred: disappeared
Allans: shot in the thigh
Comyn: disappeared
Fif: disappeared
Boy: disappeared

There were solemn funeral rites for Sokes and the agents killed in that murderous case. No cortege more impressive had ever made its way across New York. At its head walked Miss Boston, whose mourning was immense, and the Chief of the Central Police Bureau, profoundly affected by the loss of an agent so often valuable to the police of the Union.

A funeral eulogy was pronounced at West Point, where the burial took place. At the end of the ceremony, the detective took leave of the Chief of the Police Bureau. Shaking his hand, she said:

"Don't worry, sir, I will take charge of avenging poor Sokes."

And, in fact, she kept her word. Within a week she had arrested the Association members who had escaped from the expedition to the barn. Only one escaped: Fif. He had really disappeared from America. The police never heard of him again.

The investigation and the interrogations led by Miss Boston in person showed her how the band had operated. Sokes and she had been recognized at the barn at their first visit. Not having succeeded in stopping them in their escape, the Association had immediately set up the trap Sokes fell into. The two false telegrams might not have succeeded. They were running that risk. It had half succeeded, however, since Boston had escaped it.

The investigation was closed in less than a month and the members who remained appeared before a High Court of New York jury. They were tried in a week and all were sentenced to the electric chair. Sokes' death had been avenged and formidable criminals had been forever removed from action.

IX. Why the Memoires of the Famous Detective Stop Here

Sokes' death had greatly affected Miss Boston. He had been her constant friend and companion in every danger. He had shared all the perils with her, and now he was no more. She felt herself henceforth sadly alone in life. Little by little, that isolation made her distrust a profession to which she owed her fame. What was she to do alone? She must begin life over. She felt she didn't have the courage. She retired to her small country house. There she drew up the memoirs we have given to the French public which set out the highlights of her dazzling career. And it's because of this bereavement that the illustrious detective, the only one in the world a woman, ends with this last and tragic adventure which the public has welcomed with favor and for which the publishers want to thank her.

THE END OF THE ADVENTURES AND MEMOIRS OF MISS BOSTON

SF & FANTASY

Henri Allorge. *The Great Cataclysm*
Guy d'Armen. *Doc Ardan: The City of Gold and Lepers*
G.-J. Arnaud. *The Ice Company*
Charles Asselineau. *The Double Life*
Cyprien Bérard. *The Vampire Lord Ruthwen*
Aloysius Bertrand. *Gaspard de la Nuit*
Richard Bessière. *The Gardens of the Apocalypse*
Albert Bleunard. *Ever Smaller*
Félix Bodin. *The Novel of the Future*
Alphonse Brown. *City of Glass*
André Caroff. *The Terror of Madame Atomos; Miss Atomos; The Return of Madame Atomos; The Mistake of Madame Atomos; The Monsters of Madame Atomos*
Félicien Champsaur. *The Human Arrow*
Didier de Chousy. *Ignis*
Captain Danrit. *Undersea Odyssey*
C. I. Defontenay. *Star (Psi Cassiopeia)*
Charles Derennes. *The People of the Pole*
Georges Dodds (anthologist). *The Missing Link*
Harry Dickson. *The Heir of Dracula*
Jules Dornay. *Lord Ruthven Begins*
Alfred Driou. *The Adventures of a Parisian Aeronaut*
Sâr Dubnotal *vs. Jack the Ripper*
Alexandre Dumas. *The Return of Lord Ruthven*
Renée Dunan. *Baal*
J.-C. Dunyach. *The Night Orchid; The Thieves of Silence*
Henri Duvernois. *The Man Who Found Himself*
Achille Eyraud. *Voyage to Venus*
Henri Falk. *The Age of Lead*
Paul Féval. *Anne of the Isles; Knightshade; Revenants; Vampire City; The Vampire Countess; The Wandering Jew's Daughter*
Paul Féval, *fils. Felifax, the Tiger-Man*
Charles de Fieux. *Lamékis*
Arnould Galopin. *Doctor Omega; Doctor Omega & The Shadowmen*
G.L. Gick. *Harry Dickson and the Werewolf of Rutherford Grange*
Edmond Haraucourt. *Illusions of Immortality*
Nathalie Henneberg. *The Green Gods*
V. Hugo, P. Foucher & P. Meurice. *The Hunchback of Notre-Dame*
Michel Jeury. *Chronolysis*
Gustave Kahn. *The Tale of Gold and Silence*
Gérard Klein. *The Mote in Time's Eye*
Jean de La Hire. *Enter the Nyctalope; The Nyctalope on Mars; The Nyctalope vs. Lucifer; The Nyctalope Steps In; Night of the Nyctalope*
Etienne-Léon de Lamothe-Langon. *The Virgin Vampire*
André Laurie. *Spiridon*
Gabriel de Lautrec. *The Vengeance of the Oval Portrait*

\

Georges Le Faure & Henri de Graffigny. *The Extraordinary Adventures of a Russian Scientist Across the Solar System* (2 vols.)

Gustave Le Rouge. *The Vampires of Mars The Dominion of the World* (w/Gustave Guitton) (4 vols.)

Jules Lermina. *Mysteryville; Panic in Paris; To-Ho and the Gold Destroyers; The Secret of Zippelius*

Jean-Marc & Randy Lofficier. *Edgar Allan Poe on Mars; The Katrina Protocol; Pacifica; Robonocchio; Tales of the Shadowmen 1-8*

Xavier Mauméjean. *The League of Heroes*

Joseph Méry. *The Tower of Destiny*

Hippolyte Mettais. *The Year 5865*

José Moselli. *Illa's End*

John-Antoine Nau. *Enemy Force*

Marie Nizet. *Captain Vampire*

C. Nodier, A. Beraud & Toussaint-Merle. *Frankenstein*

Henri de Parville. *An Inhabitant of the Planet Mars*

Gaston de Pawlowski. *Journey to the Land of the 4th Dimension*

Georges Pellerin. *The World in 2000 Years*

Pierre Pelot. *The Child Who Walked on the Sky*

J. Polidori, C. Nodier, E. Scribe. *Lord Ruthven the Vampire*

P.-A. Ponson du Terrail. *The Vampire and the Devil's Son*

Henri de Régnier. *A Surfeit of Mirrors*

Maurice Renard. *The Blue Peril; Doctor Lerne; The Doctored Man; A Man Among the Microbes; The Master of Light*

Jean Richepin. *The Wing*

Albert Robida. *The Adventures of Saturnin Farandoul; The Clock of the Centuries; Chalet in the Sky*

J.-H. Rosny Aîné. *Helgvor of the Blue River; The Givreuse Enigma; The Mysterious Force; The Navigators of Space; Vamireh; The World of the Variants; The Young Vampire*

Marcel Rouff. *Journey to the Inverted World*

Han Ryner. *The Superhumans*

Brian Stableford. *The New Faust at the Tragicomique;The Empire of the Necromancers (The Shadow of Frankenstein; Frankenstein and the Vampire Countess; Frankenstein in London); Sherlock Holmes & The Vampires of Eternity; The Stones of Camelot; The Wayward Muse.* (anthologist) *The Germans on Venus; News from the Moon; The Supreme Progress; The World Above the World; Nemoville; Investigations of the Future*

Jacques Spitz. *The Eye of Purgatory*

Kurt Steiner. *Ortog*

Eugène Thébault. *Radio-Terror*

C.-F. Tiphaigne de La Roche. *Amilec*

Théo Varlet. *The Xenobiotic Invasion; Timeslip Troopers* (w/André Blandin); *The Martian Epic* (w/Octave Joncquel)

Paul Vibert. *The Mysterious Fluid*

Villiers de l'Isle-Adam. *The Scaffold; The Vampire Soul*

Philippe Ward. *Artahe*

Philippe Ward & Sylvie Miller. *The Song of Montségur*

MYSTERIES & THRILLERS

M. Allain & P. Souvestre. *The Daughter of Fantômas*
A. Anicet-Bourgeois, Lucien Dabril. *Rocambole*
A. Bernède. *Judex* (w/Louis Feuillade)
A. Bisson & G. Livet. *Nick Carter vs. Fantômas*
V. Darlay & H. de Gorsse. *Lupin vs. Holmes: The Stage Play*
Paul Féval. *Gentlemen of the Night; John Devil; The Black Coats ('Salem Street; The Invisible Weapon; The Parisian Jungle; The Companions of the Treasure; Heart of Steel; The Cadet Gang; The Sword-Swallower)*
Emile Gaboriau. *Monsieur Lecoq*
Steve Leadley. *Sherlock Holmes: The Circle of Blood*
Maurice Leblanc. *Arsène Lupin vs. Countess Cagliostro; Lupin vs. Holmes (The Blonde Phantom; The Hollow Needle); The Many Faces of Arsène Lupin*
Gaston Leroux. *Chéri-Bibi; The Phantom of the Opera; Rouletabille & the Mystery of the Yellow Room*
Richard Marsh. *The Complete Adventures of Judith Lee*
William Patrick Maynard. *The Terror of Fu Manchu; The Destiny of Fu Manchu*
Frank J. Morlock. *Sherlock Holmes: The Grand Horizontals; Sherlock Holmes vs Jack the Ripper*
Antonin Reschal. *The Adventures of Miss Boston*
P. de Wattyne & Y. Walter. *Sherlock Holmes vs. Fantômas*
David White. *Fantômas in America*

SCREENPLAYS

Mike Baron. *The Iron Triangle*
Emma Bull & Will Shetterly. *Nightspeeder; War for the Oaks*
Gerry Conway & Roy Thomas. *Doc Dynamo*
Steve Englehart. *Majorca*
James Hudnall. *The Devastator*
Jean-Marc & Randy Lofficier. *Royal Flush*
J.-M. & R. Lofficier & Marc Agapit. *Despair*
J.-M. & R. Lofficier & Joël Houssin. *City*
Andrew Paquette. *Peripheral Vision*
R. Thomas, J. Hendler & L. Sprague de Camp. *Rivers of Time*

NON-FICTION

Stephen R. Bissette. *Blur 1-5. Green Mountain Cinema 1; Teen Angels*
Win Scott Eckert. *Crossovers* (2 vols.)
Jean-Marc & Randy Lofficier. *Shadowmen* (2 vols.)
Randy Lofficier. *Over Here*

HEXAGON COMICS

Franco Frescura & Luciano Bernasconi. *Wampus*
Franco Frescura & Giorgio Trevisan. *CLASH*

L. Bernasconi, J.-M. Lofficier & Juan Roncagliolo Berger. *Phenix*
Claude Legrand, J.-M. Lofficier & L. Bernasconi. *Kabur*
Franco Oneta. *Zembla*
L. Buffolente, Lofficier & J.-J. Dzialowski. *Strangers: Homicron*
Danilo Grossi. *Strangers: Jaydee*
Claude Legrand & Luciano Bernasconi. *Strangers: Starlock*

ART BOOKS

Jean-Pierre Normand. *Science Fiction Illustrations*
Raven Okeefe. *Raven's L'il Critters*
Randy Lofficier & Raven OKeefe. *If Your Possum Go Daylight...*
Daniele Serra. *Illusions*